Murder at Willow Slough

Murder at Willow Slough

Josh Thomas

Writers Club Press
New York Lincoln Shanghai

Murder at Willow Slough

Writers Club Press
an imprint of iUniverse, Inc.

For information address:
iUniverse
2021 Pine Lake Road, Suite 100
Lincoln, NE 68512
www.iuniverse.com

ISBN: 0-595-15686-X

Printed in the United States of America

To my late mother
Betty Rees Moore,
B.S. Pharm., Purdue University, 1961
Hail, Hail

slough \ 'slü \ *n* (1): a large wet or marshy place; SWAMP (2): a small marshy place lying in a local depression (as on a prairie) (3): a state of moral degradation or spiritual dejection into which one sinks or from which one cannot free oneself

Webster's Third New International Dictionary

Acknowledgments

Writing is a solitary crime, but its perpetrators must have accomplices or we'll be locked up. Jack Dawson was a great partner who helped create my venue. The maddeningly wonderful Bruce Tone made many helpful suggestions. Dick, Steve and Evie Moore believed in their kid Bro. Cincinnati's remarkable Weyands—Bob, Peggy, Michael and Martha, the Condom Queen—took me into their family, which I'll always cherish. Dave Kessler gave me a tip, from which I built a career. Dr. Steve and Kim Egger shared their expertise in the study of multiple murder. Homicide investigators in many departments and disciplines opened their cases to me and won my deepest respect. May they all find loving traces of themselves in this book.

There are three kinds of writers. Reporters are legal, as long as they stick to the facts. But a certain percentage, thankfully small, go bad and start committing columns, inflicting their opinions on people. The most dangerous of all become novelists. They're power-mad, they want to control everything that happens in their depraved little worlds. Not only that, they make you pay for it.

Welcome, suckah, to my criminal world…

1

News

"Schmidgall's dead." Jamie leaned into his editor's cubicle. "Press conference tomorrow in Chicago. Lawyer's releasing the victim list. Can I go?"

"Sure. Clear the budget with Louie. AIDS?"

"He's been bad, I knew it was coming."

"How'd you hear?"

"Her paralegal just called me."

"How do you feel?"

It took Jamie awhile to tune into his body. "Bad for Anna, that she has to go through it. Bad for Cznynowski's sister, she always cries. The Gregorys will be overjoyed. Bad for the Weinsteins, but that's just because they're Jewish and middle class. I should feel the same way for everyone else, and I don't, there are too many of them. So guilty, too, somewhere. Glad this phase is over.

"As for him, I know it's wrong, but I almost liked him. What's her phrase, 'superficially charming'? So slightly sad. You don't want anyone to die that way." He snorted. "Unless it's him. Especially him. Maybe the Red-Haired Boy will finally get his name back."

"What's the hook?"

"For the dailies, the list, 'Schmidgall Speaks from the Grave.' For us, for her, the message to the horse doctor."

"Those phone lines'll be burning up between Eastwood and Indianapolis."

"Hope so. More phone records."

"You want me to monitor TV, the Chicago station?"

"Tape it. They won't have anything I don't, but I'd like to see how they play it, after I write it up and get back home. I bet they give the victims five seconds total. We've got to do better than that, Case."

"We will." Casey double-clicked his Schmidgall folder to see what file photos he had.

"Would you call Rick while I'm gone? Just see how he's doing."

"Sure. Don't worry." Jamie left to inform the publisher. Casey already had a victims' photo stack, laid out and ready to drop in on a page. But what he thought about was how scared Jamie was to leave his lover for 24 hours, even to chase the story of his career.

* * *

The news spread quickly, and people's reactions, just like the victims, were all over the map. Sgt. Barry Hickman heard about it from his partner Bulldog Sauer in an empty school gym.

"Schmidgall's dead," Bulldog panted, dribbling, trying to drive past him.

Hickman threw his hip. "Good. Couldn'ta happened to a more deserving fella."

"Anna's gonna announce 21 names, have a big news conference tomorrow. You think we oughta go up there?" Bulldog darted past, if it could be called that, slow as he was. But compared to Hickman, he darted. Went in for a layup. Missed.

Hickman rebounded, headed back to the foul line. "For what? It's a long drive. We know the names. That son of a bitch, what would we get out of it?"

Bulldog rubbed his shoulder. It had ached since he tackled that prisoner trying to escape at the courthouse. Maybe he was getting too old for this stuff. Hickman started down the lane, so Bulldog put his arms up. "See if she's come up with any more evidence on Dr. Crum."

Hickman pulled up, a six-foot jumper, good. "There's gonna be a mob at that press conference. She ain't gonna want to talk to nobody. You think Jamie's going?"

Bulldog chuckled, clutched the ball to his chest. "Maybe he'll drive over from Columbus and we can all ride up together."

"Just what I need, that fag in the car for five hours. You gonna play or stand there?"

Bulldog spun, twisted, got past. "I'll tell him you said that." Swish!

"Okay, I'll go. As long as it's just you and me. You keep your trap shut with him." Hickman took the ball out, tried a three-point airball.

Bulldog retrieved it. "I might give him a call, just to let him know. If he doesn't already. Nice shot, keep it up."

Hickman heaved for breath, got back on defense. "He knows, Bulldog, don't waste your dime. Call the lawyer instead. She'll need somebody to take her to lunch afterwards. Maybe we can talk to her then."

Bulldog headed for the baseline, Hickman followed. A bank shot rattled off the rim. "I'm gonna call Jamie anyway. You never know when we might need him. It won't hurt to stay on his good side."

Hickman tipped the ball off the glass and in. "I didn't mean what I said. I just don't wanna listen to him talk all that time. Yap yap yap, he never shuts up on that Gay rights crap."

It wasn't true, Hickman knew it wasn't; but before Jamie, he'd never heard anybody yap for any length on that Gay rights crap—and four cold, Gay murder cases made him listen.

They weren't Schmidgall victims; they were strangled, not stabbed, and they turned up after he was already in jail. But they were just as Gay and just as dead, and they didn't deserve to wind up in Quincy County, Ohio.

Schmidgall had a partner; maybe more than one. But Bulldog and Hickman, try as they might, couldn't prove it. No one could.

Those four cold queers ate Hickman alive. He tried another three-pointer and cried, "Downtown!"

He didn't need a hot queer like Jamie feeding on him too.

* * *

"Schmidgall's dead," Richard Gregory said, cradling the phone. "That was Anna. She wants to know if we'll go up there. She's having a news conference tomorrow, would we like to represent the families?"

"He's dead?" Betty Gregory put down her watering can, made the sign of the cross. "He's really dead?"

Her surviving son came, put his arm around her. "Late last night."

She stared at her shelf of African violets, fluffed one to encourage it. *Billy always liked my violets. He loved purple.*

"What should I tell her? You want to go? Are you up to it?"

"I wouldn't miss this for the world. Those poor other boys. Their poor families. Finally. I can't believe it." She resumed pouring. "Did he suffer, did she say?"

"He had AIDS, Mom. That's what got him."

"Did he have a fever? Was he out of his mind? Was he in terrible pain?"

"She didn't say any of that, now."

"I hope he was so sick he begged God to let him die."

"Mom, take it easy. Please?"

"Six months ago. I hope he begged God six months ago."

* * *

"From Chicago, word that mass murderer Roger Schmidgall is dead at 41. That story, after this." Sergeant Kent Kessler, Indiana State Police, turned up the radio in his cruiser.

* * *

"Roger's dead." She reached for the handkerchief she always kept in her pocket.

Her husband put down his newspaper, frowned. "I'm sorry. That's too bad."

He stood, came to her next to the dining room table. She leaned on it for support. He took her in his arms. "I just hope he didn't suffer, that's all. My poor son."

"Well, it's over now. It's all over. There, there, let it out, dear."

She did, but only for a few seconds. "He had good in him, I know he did!"

Then it was time to get lunch on the table. She went off to the kitchen, dispassionate again, dead still.

* * *

"Roger's dead," Randy said over the pay phone.

"Shit."

"I'm sorry, Tom."

"Well, that ought to make things easier on you, huh?" *Asshole.*

He thought about it. "Maybe. Still, it's sad."

"Tell me. You weren't his lover for five years. His best friend for twenty."

"You going to his funeral?"

"Are you out of your mind? It'll be crawling with cops. Who else'd go? Cops and reporters, just what I need. Jamie Foster'll lead the fucking delegation."

"Roger's mom and step-dad will be there, I guess. His sister."

"No way I'm going."

"Me neither. Well, I thought you'd want to know. I'm sorry, Tommy."

"Yeah, I'll call you later, Doc."

"Don't call from home, though." He hung up, glanced around him, got back in his sports car. Decided to head for the ice cream store, buy the biggest sundae they had.

Schmidgall's dead. Heh heh heh.

2

Mail

The next afternoon near quitting time, Casey Jordan hit Save on his front-page design and checked his e-mail. It was probably too early to expect anything, but he knew his chief correspondent would be pumped, exhilarated. That boy was addicted to his own adrenaline.

He keyed in his password, hit Enter; a sound effect in his computer said, "You've got mail!" like it was all happy. He double-clicked, his screen blinked, and Casey read the first draft of his cover story.

[P. 1] "I Know Who You Are"
[P. 3] Schmidgall Dead, Lawyer Says He Killed 21
Records Sought from Alleged Accomplice

By James R. Foster
The Ohio Gay Times

CHICAGO, March 8—It was, his lawyer said, the only decent thing the man ever did. Even that was only because he no longer had anything to lose.

Roger Schmidgall, Death Row murderer, openly Gay, died of AIDS in prison Sunday night, knowing that terrible things would be said about him today, sorry that he wouldn't be around for his last 15 seconds of fame.

His attorney Anna Moulter obliged him this morning, releasing the names of 21 teenaged boys and young men Schmidgall told her he murdered during a four-year rampage through the Midwest. See Sidebar [next file], "Victims: Not Statistics, but Men."

Schmidgall's targets were students, hustlers, petty thieves, normal guys—young men he could sweet-talk into his pickup, dangling booze, drugs, money, sex, whatever pushed their buttons.

Of those who got in, only one ever got out alive. And even he dropped charges in exchange for a measly $700 in hush money.

But the most shocking death of all is the one Schmidgall denied to the end, the murder that landed him on Death Row. He claimed someone else killed Chuckie Pont, a 15-year-old Chicago hustler and police informant. He claimed someone stabbed him in Schmidgall's apartment while he was gone.

When he returned to find a dead body and blood everywhere, he had to get rid of the corpse. So he hacked Chuckie to bits, stuffing body parts in garbage bags, leaving them to rot in the dumpster outside his apartment—where a maintenance man saw something, smelled something.

Anna Moulter reluctantly believed her client. It's why she stayed with him when she knew he was scum: there was someone else in that apartment the day the Pont boy was murdered.

Nagging Questions

Moulter, court-appointed—Schmidgall's third attorney—looked at the evidence and decided it didn't add up. She listened to the client she terms "disgusting" and "manipulative," and tried to figure out what part of his story wasn't contaminated by lies and deceit. Almost none of what he said was the whole truth.

But she became convinced someone even more dangerous and deceitful stabbed the Pont boy over and over for the fun of it, then left Schmidgall to dispose of the evidence or take the rap.

Schmidgall died before his lawyer could win a new trial. So Anna Moulter came to the Cook County Hall of Justice today to do the only thing she could, to close the book for the survivors and reclaim her own humanity: admit publicly what those families, friends and police officers had always known, without fully knowing; that Roger Schmidgall killed their loved ones. He didn't admit it out of the goodness of his heart; she talked him into it—as revenge for being set up.

But she had her own purpose today, the same one that kept her going through three years of fruitless appeals in the Pont case. She wanted to send a message to the man she suspects is the real killer: "I know who you are."

Suddenly

Other people think they know who he is, too: police, prosecutors, journalists who have followed Schmidgall's bloody trail through Indiana, Illinois and Wisconsin for fifteen years.

If Schmidgall told the truth, her suspect is allegedly Dr. Randolph Scott Crum, 59, a veterinarian in Eastwood, Indiana—Schmidgall's former sugar daddy.

Schmidgall and his then-lover Tommy lived in Crum's farmhouse, drove his car, ate his food. Schmidgall claimed he used his once-youthful attractions to pick up victims for the older man.

The plot seems straight out of Tennessee Williams's *Suddenly, Last Summer.* But Schmidgall was no Liz Taylor and Crum is no Montgomery Clift. The horror remains; the crime wasn't sodomy, it was murder.

Schmidgall never said publicly that Crum killed the Pont boy; the lawyer didn't mention Crum's name today. But he paid for Schmidgall's apartment where Chuckie was killed; he was present in the apartment that day; and he paid Schmidgall's original lawyer, facts hidden or glossed over during the trial.

Years earlier, Crum even paid off the first, surviving victim, whom Schmidgall drugged, stabbed and let go when the victim begged for mercy.

If you were a sugar daddy and your boy tried to kill someone, would you pay hush money, rent apartments, buy lawyers? What power could he wield over you to make you pay?

Blackmail might work.

Acquitted

The one time Crum was put on trial—in the murder of Sammy Barlow of Crab Orchard, Indiana, which Schmidgall belatedly confessed to participating in years ago, claiming Crum "directed the scene" like a filmmaker—the veterinarian's powerhouse defense team won an acquittal.

"Who do you believe?" Crum's lawyers asked the jury. "A man like Roger Schmidgall, a known liar, a notorious person? Or a respected professional in the community, a doctor who takes care of sick animals?" The panel took less than an hour.

Billy Gregory's mother, brother and sister-in-law were here to witness Moulter's announcement. They know who Crum is, too. They looked him in the eye every day during the Barlow trial.

He never looked back.

Knowing, Not Knowing

Betty Gregory gasped when Moulter read her son's name this morning. No part of her was surprised, but she was still shocked to have Schmidgall take responsibility for her son's death, even in such a roundabout, selfish way.

"It will always eat at me," she told reporters. "I'll always have that pain. But now we can go on.

"Do you understand what it's like to lose a child?" she cried, supported by her only surviving son. "To have your baby ripped from your arms, and not know for sure what happened?"

Closure; she needed it desperately. So did Ron Cznynowsky's sister, and Fermin Rodriguez's ex-lover, also present. They declined to talk to reporters.

Roger Schmidgall had no compassion in life. But once he was dead and couldn't use his silence as a bargaining chip anymore, he had nothing to lose by allowing his lawyer to read the names.

Besides, he'd be famous again. The cops would look stupid again. Anyone who ever did him wrong would feel guilty again—he hoped.

So Anna Moulter read the names, all 21 of them, slowly and respectfully.

Four will always be anonymous. Schmidgall couldn't remember who they were—maybe never bothered to ask. He forgot them like faceless, five-minute tricks.

Police officers were grim, sad, but didn't feel stupid. Even if they put Schmidgall away for the wrong crime, they put him away.

"Half a loaf is better than none," shrugged retired Chicago Police Detective Ben Schwartz, one of the first on the scene when Chuckie Pont's body parts were pulled out of the garbage.

Ongoing Appeal

Though the case appears moot, Moulter says she intends to pursue Schmidgall's appeal posthumously. It's her way of keeping the pressure on her alleged suspect—her way of pursuing justice for the victims, of making sense of her client's senseless acts.

She claims her investigation of Pont's death revealed numerous pieces of evidence that were never brought up during the trial. They all point to another killer. So she sent her message: "I know who you are."

She intends to take her evidence to prosecutors. But with Schmidgall's deathbed confession, further police investigation of the murders is unlikely. Some of her alleged evidence suggests Chicago police misconduct; she'll get no help from them. "Why did they allow a 15-year-old hustler to ply his trade on the streets? Because he was a useful informant. Why didn't they protect him from Roger Schmidgall?"

The cases were effectively closed today by her decision to reveal the names. Who else has any stake in vindicating a 21-time killer? If there were a dripping knife she'd have found it by now. She hasn't.

But she suspects who has it; "I know who you are."

Compulsions

She has no illusions that the other killer, if he exists, will step forward. If anything, she expects him to try to foil investigators with even more vigor and intelligence than Schmidgall did—and he won 20 of 21 rounds.

If she can't nail the suspect, she hopes to persuade him to leave evidence behind when he dies, to repeat Schmidgall's tiny act of contrition. "Society has a right to those records," she told The Ohio Gay Times. "Even after the alleged perpetrator is deceased, I want those records."

The accomplice is a compulsive man, she says, a man who keeps computer documents, photos, videotapes of his crimes hidden away somewhere. She wants that evidence someday so Betty Gregory and her children can sleep at night.

Silent Witness

Beyond today's spectacle, the sensational news story, Schmidgall's last burst of fame, the attorney's haunted search, the families' tears, the alleged accomplice's glee—beyond them all is a final question: how much did Schmidgall's ex-lover Tommy know?

Was Schmidgall pure vanilla back in Eastwood, when they lived together at Crum's farm?

What did the lover do when Schmidgall overpowered his first victim and stabbed him? What did the lover do when Crum paid that victim off?

What did Tommy do when Sammy Barlow was strung up and hacked to death at an abandoned farmhouse a few miles from home?

Did Tommy sever all ties and run away, try to forget it like a bad dream, start a new life? Did he keep his mouth shut, hoping against hope it wasn't true? Or did he help his lover from a distance, a more silent accomplice, stealthier, more clever even than Schmidgall himself?

"I know who you are," Anna Moulter said today.

-30-

"Sweet Jesus," Casey shuddered.

Schmidgall the Stabber wasn't originally an Ohio Gay Times story, no local connection—but police suspected his friend Tommy might be the Quincy County Strangler, whose murders were the biggest scoop of Jamie's career. The Strangler violated Gay Ohio, Jamie's territory, and no one did that without paying a price. What started out as four Indianapolis men dumped across the state line in rural Ohio mushroomed to twelve victims in nine jurisdictions, once Jamie went looking for them.

What would the Strangler think, as he stared at giant headlines, "I Know Who You Are"? Casey forwarded the file to his libel lawyer, proud as punch and scared as hell.

3

Louie

Publisher Louie Mascaro was outraged. "What do you mean you refuse?"

"What's not to understand?" Jamie shrugged.

"A national Gay magazine wants to do a cover story on you and you won't do it?"

"Reporters don't make news, we report it."

"But this is national."

"Louie, don't be naive. There's no guarantee it will run on the cover, that it will be favorable or even about me. Those Clarion boys will slum their way in from L.A., spend as little time here as possible, write their 2500-word quota and print whatever they want. Out-of-town reporters will promise anything to get a story. Local reporters have to live with the consequences of our work, but those guys will have long since skipped town."

"But what about the publicity? It'll be good PR for us."

"I appreciate that. But Louie, we can't let the killer think I'm getting more publicity than he is."

"But surely you want your reporting to go national."

"They constantly rewrite my stuff without crediting us—which tells you everything you need to know about this so-called interview. It's probably just a cheap shortcut to the Strangler story."

"Maybe they heard how famous you're getting to be."

"Fame is the last thing California concedes to Flyover Land."

"I'd think you'd like the professional recognition."

"If you think The Clarion compares to being a Pulitzer finalist, your girdle's too tight."

He used Employee Ploy #1, invoking Louie's former drag career; but Jamie's series on the Quincy County Strangler was the first Pulitzer finalist from a Gay publication. "I can order you, you know. I can even talk to them myself. I'll tell them all about your insubordinate behind."

"Yak your head off, but check my contract. You can't order me to say hello."

"Then I'll make Casey order you."

"If he did I'd quit. He won't do it, he agrees with me."

"We'll see about that." Louie headed next door to Casey's cubicle.

"Don't even start, Louie," Casey said, refusing to look up from his computer. "If he doesn't want the interview, he's not doing it."

"But why? How could they not put him on the cover? With that face, their sales would jump through the roof. Think of how our readers would feel, Jordan. Jamie goes national. A reporter who looks like a Falcon exclusive."

Jamie teased, "Except smarter and much better hung."

"Puny-dicked and too smart to know what's good for you," Louie shot back. "My God, don't they have any common sense at Harvard or Yale or wherever it was?"

"Columbia, Louie. Graduate school at Columbia, now I'm working in Columbus. Connect the dots."

Casey said, "He's just trying to get your goat, Jamie."

"The only goat around here's our employer. Baa-aa, a nanny goat at that."

Louie couldn't believe it. "The cover, Jamie. They'd have to say who you work for."

"Louie, have you seen their covers in the last five years? They used to have newsmakers; now they have starlets. Their message is that queers can feel good about themselves because some fourth-string actress on a sitcom you never heard of reveals she's got actual Gay friends. The Clarion is about show biz. I don't do show biz."

Casey said, "Forget it, Louie, there is nothing so effective in this business as no comment. Thank God more people don't know that."

"Please, Foster?" Louie said unctuously. When the oil pan started dripping, the boys knew the engine was about to conk out. "Think of the exposure."

"If you want exposure, go wave at the Today show."

Casey said, "Jamie got plenty of exposure last fall doing election analysis on Channel 9. There isn't another Gay paper in the country that got an opportunity like that."

Jamie added, "Plus I do the Andy Fredericks Show every time he asks."

"Public radio," Louie sniffed. "Nobody listens to it."

"Andy's #4 in afternoon drivetime, which is damn good. He's got an affluent, intelligent audience of opinion leaders, exactly who we want to be exposed to."

"Why does somebody in the media not want to be in the media? Tell me that, Foster."

"I do news, Louie, I am not a featurette."

"He makes The Times more valuable that way," Casey said. "Be glad you have somebody who isn't a whore. Well, except for moonlighting at the escort service…"

Jamie chuckled over the cubicle wall, "Fuck you."

Casey called back, "Anytime."

"What about Rick?" Louie pleaded. "Wouldn't Rick be proud of his coverboy?"

It was a much better attack than Jamie expected. "Not when I tell him I'd feel ashamed. End of discussion, Louie. I don't do celebrity profiles."

"You heard it, Lou," Casey declared. "How could he have gone under-cover for the 'Homeless & Gay' story if his mug was grinning on some magazine?"

"You queers have no common sense," Louie scolded, giving up, slink-ing past the newsroom up Writers' Alley, trying not to notice Jamie's and Casey's awards on the wall. Three of them were for the 'Homeless & Gay' story.

He went into Bookkeeping and plopped in his sister-in-law's guest chair. "Looking a gift horse in the mouth. I'll never forgive them—much less understand them."

"Maybe this will cheer you up," Doreen said. She handed him a printout.

"What's this?" He stared dully at the graphics.

"The bar chart is profit and loss from our founding to the present, marking Casey's first issue, the day he changed the name, and the first issue after he hired Jamie. Notice the slope, Lou, up and up. The pie charts show profit as a percentage of sales. You can't argue with those boys' numbers."

"All I ever wanted was a bar rag," he muttered. "To advertise my drag shows and strippers, sell a few ads on the side. What's so tough about that?"

But the customers had changed since the old days. They'd been through Stonewall and clones, Pride marches and AIDS, Generation X, Y and Z. Now they wouldn't pick up the paper unless he gave them something to read. So he hired Casey, a journalism major, fresh out of Ohio State, good grades, Black too. Louie thought he was doing a good thing.

Then Casey changed the name from Gay Times to The Ohio Gay Times, hard news from a Gay point of view; the paper started to take off, and he stole Jamie from the mainstream daily. Circulation zoomed, and all of a sudden they were Murder Central.

Casey hired Jamie the day they met, told Louie after the fact, breaking Cardinal Rule #1: **You** Don't Spend **My** Money. Doreen did it up in needlepoint, with a feather boa for a border, and hung it in the office—a reminder to Casey not to do it again, and a reminder to Louie that he got away with it.

At first Jamie seemed like an ideal choice, scary even. His face alone sold newspapers. He'd interview some smalltown activist, snap a few photos, and a week later there was a thousand dollars in new subscriptions from Coshocton, because Jamie Foster spent an hour there.

His bright blond hair was eye-catching, but what shocked humanity senseless was his face. When Louie first met him he cried, "My God, look at that!" It was embarrassing, a completely wrong thing for an employer to say, but he couldn't help it. Casey nicknamed Jamie "STG," short for Stop-Traffic Gorgeous.

James R. Foster could make trains derail. At 25, he had amazing presence; giant, intelligent green eyes, a patented swoop of thick shiny hair. Flawless, translucent skin. A little on the short side, which only set off his muscles; a college athlete with the chest and abs and arm-bulges to prove it. The tiniest waist led to an amazing bubble butt. He was built for action, made to slam a guy down for love.

Sharp dresser, too, the latest fashions, a perfect little package to cuddle with. No wonder Coschocton drooled; an aggressive reporter and butch to boot.

Louie wadded up the printout and threw it in the trash. "Good job, you made your point. But don't ever show them that. Don't even print it out again."

He pushed up and crossed the hall to his own plush office. Livvie from Circulation dropped the new issue on his desk. The headline was big enough to be read in a dark Gay bar, if not from a dance floor half a block away. The sixty tabloid pages were meticulously researched, stirring, at times even eloquent; with a news staff of five, Casey set the tone and Jamie the content.

Page One had photos: the lawyer at the press conference, a file shot of Schmidgall in prison garb. Louie turned to Page 3, read his latest thousand-dollar opus. *Plane tickets, hotel rooms, computers, the Internet; why don't I get to see money like that?*

When he finished, he glanced at the center spread and the back page, his house ads; tossed the paper onto a chair and wondered how they ever got into this.

At least Schmidgall was dead. Louie knew he'd never have any peace until the Quincy County Strangler was, too.

The clock on the wall read 5:00; all its numbers were fives. Louie turned out his lights, lumbered out for his other business and a big, tall drink.

He drove toward the Capitol and cocktails. Suppose he did give The Clarion an interview, tell them the real inside story? He picked up his cell phone and dialed, imagining the look on Foster's face when he found out.

The interviewer said, "I hear he's quite handsome."

"In the bar business he could make a mint, be a porn star, tour the nation. But no, he's a 'journalist,' he's above all that. Employees got brains, they want to run things. They got ethics, you can't get away with squat. Don't try to change the world, try to make money off it. I'm paying the handsomest man I've ever seen, and I can't exploit him for a single goddamn dime."

"What makes him so handsome? Anyone can be blond and bland."

"His intelligence, his eyes, the structure of his face. This ain't some prettyboy. He's distinctive, charismatic, mysterious even. He makes you stop and stare."

"Is he sexy or just cute?"

"He constantly projects sex appeal, and then turns out to be monogamous! Have you ever heard of such a crime? The world needs all the tops it can get! But after his lover's had eight amputations, Jamie's right there with him, committed, when he could have any guy he wants. Faithfulness only adds to his mystique. Every man in town wants that little cocktease, women chase him down the street. He's gorgeous and I can't make money off him? What?"

"I heard he tools around in a Jaguar."

"I wouldn't call it tooling around, he's restricted to 3000 miles a year for insurance reasons."

"Still, he lives in the most expensive suburb, in a townhouse full of artworks."

"He spent all of five figures on that condo. He's decorated it very nicely, well within his means."

"He wears designer clothes, too."

"So do I. So do you."

"Listen, I heard he's being kept by a very big designer."

Louie laughed. "In Columbus, Ohio? Then what's he doing with a cripple like Rick Lawson?"

"There isn't another Gay reporter in the world who drives a Jaguar. Where'd he get the money?"

"A man's money is his own business," Louie snapped. "If this is a hatchet job, I'm hanging up."

"That's not my intent, sir." So they discussed Jamie's approach to the news. By assuming that the justice of Gay rights was obvious, he applied journalistic principles in new ways. Like a World War II correspondent, he seldom interviewed Nazis, he found contrasts in his own community instead; and it all had to be on the record, verifiable by any reader. He reported on troop movements, battles, victories and losses, and how things were going on the home front. He profiled GIs and generals, criminals and profiteers. He scoured the Statehouse, the courthouse, city halls and police stations, criss-crossing the state for hard news.

Then there were the sick wards. He visited caregivers and fallen soldiers, reported the action those men and women had seen, the valor they'd shown.

Scoops came easily to him; queers were the civil rights flashpoint of the decade and the Straight dailies never looked for a Gay pulse; they learned to rely on him for that. He had great news judgment, so his stories often went mainstream, and suddenly the mayor withdrew her latest homophobic appointment. From first word to last, Jamie grabbed readers' attention, he made them care.

The nuances were lost on Louie. "So why not run Foster's famous photo with his stories? Seems like a no-brainer to me, but Jordan utterly refuses. Other papers do it all the time, with ugly people. I begged almost. But no, some crap about 'that's only for opinion pieces.' Next thing I know they're both wailing at me, like the readers even know the difference. Don't overestimate the public. But Jordan won't work without a contract that specifies all his little editorial prerogatives, and Foster is twenty times worse. College boys. What for? 'Hire the smartest people you can find,' what business school bullshit. It doesn't apply in the gay community.

"Oh, sorry, 'we have to capitalize Gay too.' And Black and White because *Ebony* magazine does, and there is a theory and—spare me. Don't they know there's only one thing that matters to faggots? Dick! Nothing else. You want to make money, give 'em dick. Better yet, make 'em **think** you're giving them dick. The old strip tease, right? I didn't invent this stuff. Maybe Jamie did."

Louie stopped at a traffic light outside the #2 bar. "Not too many cars here. How nice. Business at my own bar is up 500% now that I have Casey and Jamie. It's called advertising. Then hire young bartenders for a little tits and ass. It's real simple, fellas."

"Don't handsome, principled young journalists add to your paper's cachet?"

No way Louie would admit that. "I've never forgiven Jamie for calling me a profiteer, even though the article was fair overall. I paid to be pilloried in my own paper! It established once and for all that The Times is editorially independent, but it cut me like an incision. I should have fired their asses for insubordination—but they did tell the truth, that the bar makes a very tidy profit."

Only later did he realize the article boosted his status; he was a successful entrepreneur. That's when he started running more fundraisers, like the shitheads wanted all along. It was even good for business, but Jamie was too damn smart.

Louie went on, "It's admirable, I suppose, that Foster and Jordan are always trying to make Gay rights some big political thing. They're right, not that I ever let on. Here lately I even vote the way they want me to, for every high-tax Democrat that comes down the pike. Standing in line with my Times Voters' Guide like every other fag and dyke in Columbus. There are whole precincts here now—Clintonville, German Village, the Short North—where half the voters are clutching their handy guide out of The Times. It makes voting fun, a town meeting of the Queer Society. Guys whooping it up in church basements while elderly precinct committeewomen try to act like nothing's happening, 'Do you still live on Whittier Street?'

"And a whole chorus screaming, 'When he's not on his knees in the park!'

"At least we've got something to show for it. The judges are getting better, and that's important in the bar business. You never know when some customer—or employee—is going to show up with a tale about being entrapped, abused, beaten up, robbed, hit over the head with a baseball bat. With a real newspaper now, with the hotshots' precious credibility, we can pressure the cops, tell everyone what happened, warn people even. Go after the bashers, attend their trials, publish their pictures, wave bye-bye as they shuffle off in leg chains.

"That's something I don't mind paying for. Anti-Gay crime is no longer tolerated in Columbus, Ohio. Foster goes after the bashers like a junkyard dog. The Strangler thing was just another anti-Gay crime at first. But that was so long ago, so many dead guys ago, I can't even remember when it was."

"It's a publisher's job to be a cheapskate."

"Foster's even got an expense account! If I didn't think so much of them I'd fire them. Now we just threaten each other with it once a week. Foster will have a tantrum, or Jordan will yank out his contract, and soon I'm talked out of another thousand bucks. God, they can make a racket. Then five minutes later, smooch smooch and we're back to normal. Just like kids—they always cost money too."

His youngest daughter got accepted at Princeton last week. He clutched, so proud of her. But the tuition bills would kill him. He wondered if the customers would tolerate a 10¢ price increase on a Bud.

He eyed a skyscraper. It wasn't tall enough to contain his pride.

"The cops are getting better, too, it helps to have a little clout. It's fun to have candidates for mayor traipse through my office every four years, looking for that endorsement and its automatic 40,000 votes. They have to sit in my office, even if they think they're there to talk to Foster and Jordan. You come to me, baby! Plus I get to throw in a few business-related questions, which the hotshots never think about. Of course they always outvote me on the endorsements. They don't know I just vote for whoever they don't want. Keep 'Em Honest, it's another of Mascaro's Rules.

"And every December for the last several years, we get three big Christmas cards: The White House, Washington. Know why? The Ohio primary was very competitive last time. We're circulated statewide, our endorsement matters. We influence every Gay and Lesbian voter in the swing state of Ohio.

"Not too shabby for an immigrant's son who never went to college, eh? Even if I do like dick. The entire world likes dick, why should I be any different?"

"Excuse me, except Lesbians."

"I have Gay women on the payroll, they're hard workers. The only problem with Lesbians is that there aren't enough of them, and they don't spend anything like the guys do. The women have two bars, the men have ten. The men's bars advertise, only one of the ladies' can afford to. Demographics, I didn't invent this stuff. But jeez, next time, hire stupid people and tell them what to do. No more 'journalists.' Hire fags so stupid they'll make bartenders look like scholars. And change the name back to Gay Times. That's what started this whole thing."

"The Times is one of the few Gay papers built on the classic model, with a successful businessperson running the money, but having no influence on the editorial content. What does being the publisher mean to you?"

"People look at me with new respect. I'm not just a bar owner anymore, some old drag queen, keeper of a sleazy tavern; I'm giving something back. The Gay community associates me with The Times and my Gay and Lesbian bookstore as much as the bar now. So do the media. Every reporter in town subscribes to us to read Jamie. He's a star, advertisers fly out of the woodwork. He adds excitement to Columbus, sophistication, sparkle. We helped the city make up its mind about Gay rights. A few years ago John Preston even named Columbus the best Gay city in America—not New York, not San Francisco—and here I am, right in the thick of it."

In a rare flash of modesty Louie added, "But it's not just me. The whole Gay and Lesbian community here is looked on with more respect."

Besides Stonewall Union and the all-important activists, it was Casey's and Jamie's doing, but he'd never let them know that, it broke a rule. *Don't tell 'em you love 'em, they'll want more money.*

"If he's that goodlooking and talented, how long can you keep him?"

"That's the real question. At contract renewal the non-Gay weekly made me shell out an extra five grand for his services. The Pinnacle has three times our circulation and Jamie loves the power of big numbers. But he also needs the freedom Casey gives him."

It was unspoken, but Louie knew why. *If anything happens to Rick, I'm toast.* Jamie didn't change jobs for fear he'd be stuck on assignment when Rick needed him.

"What's he like privately? Help me get inside his head so I know what to ask him."

"I have to admit, he's kind and thoughtful. But so hurt inside, so aloof. He won't set foot in bars unless there's genuine news, and I'm not talking Mr. Ohio Leather.

"But I know human nature, his self-control won't last forever. Maybe he's really a vampire. You know he's going to kill you, but he's so beautiful you can't resist. Go ahead and bite me, so I can feel alive!"

Jeez, fantasizing over an employee. Louie swore off reading any more Anne Rice books.

"What else? Last call, Mr. Barman."

"When I hired Casey, I basically left him alone. When he hired Jamie, we turned into a real newspaper. I started going into the office every day, business really picked up. We bitch at each other constantly, it's fun. I like him, and I know he respects me. He's very sensitive and caring sometimes, when he's not being a spoiled brat."

Having softened his subject up, the Clarion reporter went for the kill. "He's very well-known in New York. You admit he has the looks of a supermodel. Multiple sources indicate he was, or is, Calvin's lover."

"Then your sources are full of it! I can name the exact day Jamie lost his virginity and with whom—Rick Lawson. Jamie came swaggering in the next day like he'd just invented sex. As for New York, he went to journalism school at Columbia, where he learned to be a Pulitzer Prize finalist, not some gossip-mongering queer in La-La Land." Louie punched off, click!

He fumed. It was a hatchet job, all right, the guy didn't even ask about the Strangler. Once again Jamie was right.

But Calvin's lover? Not even Jamie could pull that off. Louie laughed all the way to the bar.

He parked his new black Cadillac. What's the use of owning the #1 Gay bar if you can't have your own spot next to the door? "Make it a double, Miss Thang," he called, hoisting himself onto his stool with the Don't Even Think About Sitting Here sign.

The boy behind the bar with his tits hanging out scurried. *Like an employee, for once.* If Louie wasn't careful, he'd even break out in a smile. But he was careful enough to notice that everyone in the place had his nose buried in the latest issue of The Ohio Gay Times, where they couldn't help but be exposed to ads for the #1 bar in town. Damn smile broke out anyway. Nippleboy brought his drink, "What are you so happy about?"

Louie growled, "I'm raising the price of beer ten cents."

* * *

His passions were beer prices and porn stars; Casey had other things to worry about—a reporter's sexual magnetism versus a killer's sexual violence. *Dear Christ, why did we print something so inflammatory?* But the libel lawyer vetted the piece, and Casey fought hard for Jamie's incendiaries.

A week later an unsigned note arrived from Indianapolis. It said, "I know who you are, too."

4

Counties

A year and a half of scoops passed, eighteen months of pain and death; a time of increasing accomplishment, though Jamie didn't catch the Strangler and neither did anyone else.

Labor Day weekend, via I-70, Jamie headed west for Indiana and his mother's house. He was fine until he hit the Quincy County line. Then the green highway sign reached inside the Acura and slapped him.

Since Schmidgall died, he hadn't had to think about it so much; no new victims. Now he could think of nothing else: "ENTERING QUINCY COUNTY."

He drove on, stunned at first, then angry. He found himself glaring at a lush cornfield. Beyond, scrubby oaks marked a ditch separating the field from a pasture, where a dozen lazy Angus grazed. *Damn cattle, why didn't they tell the cops what they saw?*

Through Dayton he'd enjoyed Sheryl Crow on the CD player, but now he couldn't stand her cynical ennui. He hit Stop so hard his finger burned.

The A/C suddenly wasn't putting out enough. He cranked it up a notch, then another. Cool air rushed his face to make amends.

Ahead of him an old lady in a K-car full of pre-schoolers poked along. He slammed down his turn signal, lurched into the passing lane. Kids squealed out the windows like a farrow at its first trough of slop.

The strangulations started when Jamie was in junior high, so the Strangler's 15-year run wasn't his fault. Still, he and Casey bore a singular guilt, which they could not absolve with a Pulitzer nomination. They failed to follow up on a tip a year earlier; two men died as a result.

There is power in journalism, power to uplift or to destroy. Jamie and Casey learned their lesson the hardest way. Once they finally broke the story, they pounded it fiercely, diligently, long after everyone else gave up. But what looked like heroic enterprise was really a shameful game of catchup.

In three years since, no fresh kills. Was The Times at all responsible for that? In their deepest hearts they hoped so, but it was hubris even to ask.

Jamie looked left, saw an image of Aaron Haney form on a white-painted barn, smiling in an out-of-focus Polaroid at his last birthday party. That was in Year 10. Around Labor Day in Year 11 someone found him strangled and dumped a few miles south of here in Tenmile Creek, a Gay child of poverty who made himself a nurse. Haney was the one who convinced them that the murders could be serial. Kenny Dyson, their closeted Dayton stringer, tried to tell them a year earlier, when Christopher Carnes turned up in a creek outside New Lisbon, the third young Indianapolis man to wind up in Quincy County with the life wrung out of his neck.

Kenny remembered Buddy Trueblood in Year 6, then Brian Greene in Year 7—a space of three years, then Carnes, all single young men from Indianapolis dumped in the same Ohio county. Kenny argued that Carnes showed the murders could be connected. But Kenny had no documentation, so Casey didn't buy it. In Year 11 Haney paid full price instead.

As Bulldog told Jamie after the scoop, "Two is a coincidence, three's a pattern. We knew exactly what we had as soon as we found out Carnes was from Indy."

Two smalltown cops knew what they had, but they didn't notify the media, they didn't warn the Gay community; they didn't ask for help. Bulldog and Hickman were competent investigators, but it was like Barney Fife and Goober going after the Unabomber.

When Kenny relayed the Haney news, Jamie got confirmation from the sheriff and broke the story. The Straight media ran with it. Then, two weeks later, the Strangler dropped Bobby Hanger in an abandoned railroad bed one county north of here in Stillwater, as if to say, "Your move, Mr. Queer Reporter."

For three days the murders and The Ohio Gay Times were front-page in the Dayton market, with big play statewide. Bulldog's boss called a press conference, admitted 10% of what was happening and down-played the rest like mad. Jamie himself was the lead on all three Dayton TV stations that night, and front-page the following Sunday ("Tiny Tabloid, Big Story") in the Dayton Tribune.

Then there were new fires for the dailies to chase, new celebs to hype, and the Dayton blow-drieds stopped talking about those five young men from Indiana strangled and dumped across the state line.

Later, when Bulldog trusted him more, he told Jamie that Indiana had six more cases that fit the pattern, "victims with ties to the Gay community in Indianapolis." On his own Jamie found another in northern Ohio, despite the sheriff's repeated denials.

And then there was the topper: the alleged connection between the Quincy County Strangler and Schmidgall the Stabber. Jamie couldn't report it, though he wanted to desperately. He closed his eyes briefly, wondered why he was alive.

Haney was the link, Jamie the publicist, Hanger the exclamation point. All within ten miles of this goddamn interstate. Why had Casey killed the story after Carnes? Why hadn't he made Kenny call the sheriff, ask around, dig a little deeper?

Then Jamie remembered, Kenny was just a sharp tipster; he couldn't call the sheriff without revealing his own Gayness. Meanwhile Casey was battling Louie because the workhorse computer was crashing every day, not enough RAM, not enough staff; Rick was getting sick and no one knew why, and...

"Because we were scared to death. Stupid and naive and terrified," Jamie said aloud. Sadness and shame tingled quietly down his spine.

He passed an exit. The killer had turned left instead of right off the interstate, north to Stillwater County and the spot he'd picked out for Bobby Hanger. The killer sure knew great places to dump bodies. Sometimes it took months before someone discovered them, then even longer to figure out who they were. Police can't solve a murder when the victim's name is Doe.

Did the Strangler's success at concealing bodies mean he was from around here? Some people, locals, thought so; they didn't take into account that he'd been equally successful in five other counties. To Jamie it meant that the guy spent his spare time scouting out dumping grounds, like Schmidgall and his sugar daddy had, taking poor Sammy Barlow to the abandoned farmhouse and hacking him to death. Jamie made a fist and pounded repeatedly on the steering wheel.

This was getting him nowhere. He punched the Accel button on his cruise control, and the Acura sucked in fuel and air. He didn't let up till the dial hit 80.

If he got busted for speeding here, he'd just hand over Bulldog's business card: "Prosecutor's Investigator, Quincy County, Ohio." He might get a ticket anyway, but none of the cops would fuck with him. They'd all heard about that Gay reporter and them thar homicides.

Today of all days, he wanted out of here.

The sun was in his eyes now. He reached for neon yellow shades and put them on. In his rearview mirror he saw a blue Miata convertible gaining on him. Grimacing, he mashed Accel another 10 mph. The blue car didn't compete, not that this gave him much satisfaction.

He didn't slow down till he reached the Indiana line. Over the eastbound lanes, Ohio had a big steel arch advertising the governor's name at taxpayers' expense. Indiana had got rid of that nonsense; its modest westbound sign read merely, "The People of Indiana Welcome You." No politicians. As a native Hoosier, he took a little pride in that.

The change of venue calmed him a little, but the highway turned bumpier. He eased the cruise control down to 65. The Miata soon whizzed by.

He switched on the radio, country music out of Richmond, Indiana. He couldn't stand country music; it had nothing to do with where he was from. He jammed the seek button, finally landed on WOWO out of Fort Wayne. Stopped there and didn't know why.

A DJ and a newswoman were talking about festivals, restaurants, a nearby lake, outings for the holiday weekend. It was a real conversation, not the usual radiobabble between commercials. Jamie didn't recognize any of the places they were talking about. It was hopelessly smalltown.

He liked it.

He turned the sound down and pictured his mother. Thelma was going into the hospital for an aneurysm operation and Jamie volunteered to be the Hallmark card. His older brother Stone lived in southern Indiana, but no one thought of him to stay with their mother. Stone hadn't spoken to Jamie in twelve years, since Jamie came out as Gay. Big Bro Danny had long ago fled to Denver; he was more than willing to fly back east, but Jamie could drive to West Lafayette in four hours.

Besides, he was good at cheering the sick. Experienced too. On the tenth it would be six months since Rick died. He didn't let himself follow that thought, trying to prevent an anxiety attack.

The land turned hilly; he wasn't sure why. But the valleys made a nice contrast to the prairie. He drove on, past the turnoff to New Castle and the Indiana Basketball Hall of Fame. Its billboard had a giant pair of black hi-tops in 3-D. A smile cracked his lips. What other state has a monument to high school hoops?

College practice would start next month; how would Purdue do this year? He remembered Coach Reed's postgame interview on the radio after the ten-point loss at home to North Carolina, what, four years ago already? He said bluntly, "We've got to recruit us some guys who can play." Then he went out and got himself a big dog.

Ah, Carolina and the freezing rain at Christmastime. After the game and a forty-degree temperature drop, Jamie chased through unexpected sleet to get the car for Rick so he wouldn't have to brave the ice in his wheelchair. Rick whispered, "Thanks, pops," as Jamie helped him into their brand-new Acura, Thelma climbing into the back seat while Jamie, ice in his eyelashes, stashed the chair in the trunk.

It took him 20 minutes of violent shivering to get warm, with the car heater blasting. Rick and Thelma, above all others, knew how Jamie hated to be cold.

Funny how a basketball game could figure into one of his proudest moments. He could remember a thousand other scenes of minor sacrifice during Rick's illness, but when Jamie put his own body on the line, they'd known love was real.

His eyes misted, but no tears came; instead a never-forgotten word from French 101, *tendresse.*

Next was a billboard for the fleabag motel he'd stayed in, the afternoon after his failed conference with the cops in Indianapolis two years ago, Jamie trying to set up a multi-agency task force himself, since the cops hadn't done it; the police couldn't even figure out who should organize it if one was needed. *If one was needed!*

Reporters, the renowned forensic pathologist, the sociology professor who'd been on the Schmidgall task force, the Indianapolis P.D. detective, all were no-shows after giving their word they'd be there. Jamie was humiliated—and he cost Louie a ton of money; three hundred dollars anyway, and to Louie that was a ton. Jamie heard about it for months.

The only attendees were Dr. Steve Helmreich, an ex-street cop turned serial murder expert from the University of Illinois, and the team from Quincy. Someone put the word out that Jamie's conference was too hot. Those who attended went ahead and discussed what they could, as the hotel caterers wondered what to do with all the extra turkey croissants. Finally Jamie resorted to an emotional appeal: "The cases need more publicity. The mainstream media don't care about long-dead faggots, but we can make them care." Bulldog and Hickman looked doubtful, but they seemed to go along.

Jamie got drunk that night, crashed at a hotel, and was still shaky the next day. As he drove back home he suffered his first anxiety attack, terrified he'd plunge himself into a bridge. He didn't know what was wrong with him, he only knew he had to get off the highway. The town was called New Castle. He got a motel room and called Rick. "I'm sick, I have to go to bed. I didn't mean to stay overnight and leave you without a car. I should have taken the Jag." The Acura had Rick's hand controls. "I fucked this whole weekend up, I'm sorry." Then Jamie called a priest, that was how much of an emergency he was in. The priest brought a Charles Kuralt book, and Jamie read till he calmed down and went to sleep.

Looking back, he realized he was emotionally exhausted that time, with serial killers and a seriously ill lover. He'd learned more about anxiety attacks once he'd had a few; they were a physical mental illness, and he had some control over them since he made decisions about his physical health. He seldom got drunk, and should never have done it that night. The fact that he did showed how distraught he was over that failed conference. What was "too hot" about assembling some homicide experts? Who stood to lose face?

Not Bulldog and Hickman. Therefore it was the other departments, more concerned about their face than their citizens.

He was glad to make it past New Castle today.

Next was Hancock County. Seat: Greenfield, home of James Whitcomb Riley, the Hoosier Poet, "When the frost is on the punkin'." No one read him anymore, probably not even here. But Jamie remembered when high school kids came to his grade school to recite Riley.

Victim: Riley Jones...

Jamie's eyes sunk into their sockets. "Fuck!" he said, thumping the steering wheel again. "That bastard! How could I have missed that?" He scowled, grinding his teeth unconsciously till his dentist told him to stop it.

...who disappeared over the Indy 500 weekend in Year 3, to be found near the Big Blue River. The deputy had talked to Jamie a good long time after all those years, but later Bulldog told him other officers considered the dude lazy for one, a bigot for another.

Not that "bigot" was how Bulldog put it, but Jamie knew what he meant. How many other victims were shrugged off by homophobic cops?

South of here was Shelby County. Victim: Mike Cardinal, Year 8. Dumped near Flynnville, a town so small Casey could only approximate it on their push-pin map on the newsroom wall. For months, the Shelby deputy delayed the FBI conference Jamie'd been pushing after the earlier failure, before the cop finally broke down and admitted he'd lost his crime scene photos. It was the lowest blow of the entire sordid mess. A man was murdered and the cops couldn't figure out a file folder.

Indianapolis P.D. later made new prints for Shelby, and the FBI conference finally went on in Greenfield, a year late and without Jamie. Didn't accomplish a thing, as nearly as he could make out. Not a single headline in any point size, though there was a serial killer profile circulated. Jamie had never gotten his hands on it. It was the FBI's own report, but the FBI told him that releasing it was up to the locals, then Bulldog wouldn't release it, it might piss off other cops; and the other cops wouldn't release it, it might piss off Quincy.

Nobody worried about pissing off Jamie. That was a mistake. He was the one with the power to tell the world about the missing file folder, and tell the world he did.

Indianapolis suburbs were next. The speed limit went down to 55, marked by red flags, Speedway-style. I-465 would intersect in two miles. Lt. Phil Blaney of Indianapolis homicide reopened the cases four years ago on his own initiative, and was working with Quincy County. He showed Jamie some of his photos and interview notes, and Jamie wrote it up big, trying to reassure Indianapolis Gays that IPD did care, wasn't to be feared, at least not entirely, so please if you know anything just call... The story didn't coax out a clue, not even a single phone call.

He turned north onto I-465, past Fort Benjamin Harrison, where Arnie bought discount groceries and cigarettes for Thelma in his retirement. South of Connor Prairie, a restored pioneer farm village and tourist trap, the interstate cut through Hamilton County, with the first three victims: Wayne Allen Wilson, Year 1, a 15-year-old high school hustler. Nobody knew nothin'. *Poor kid. Cute, too. A lot of them were.*

Hustling at 15 years old. What was he thinking?

He wasn't thinking. He knew he could have mowed yards, detassled corn. He didn't want to do that.

Dead at 15.

Also John-Mark Barnett, Year 3, in Weasel Creek, who went unidentified for eight months because his mom, the only one who ever missed him, was in the nuthouse when he checked out; and Kelvin Farmer the same year. Three cases, two different jurisdictions; the state police got to Barnett first, so they owned him, couldn't do a thing with him. The county mounties had the others, with the same result.

But Kelvin was different, everyone agreed about that. Different enough was the question.

In the opposite lane, a tractor-trailer barreled past, for a chain of local appliance stores. Jamie swore, "Not here, you son of a bitch! Not here!"

He could never forget the photos of Kelvin's body. Smooth, naked, 14-year-old Blackboy skin gleaming in the sun by the side of the road, sleeping in the weeds. Easy to spot, quickly recovered and ID'd. The only African-American, the youngest of the bunch. Hyoid bone crushed in his tender teenaged neck, a sign of particular violence, the killer probably male.

There'd been a suspect: middle-aged, unmarried son of a wealthy appliance dealer. He got off with bigtime lawyers, thanks to an incompetent prosecutor who got a conviction only for prostitution with Kelvin in a hotel room the day of the murder. Even that took a Supreme Court case.

Some cops said Kelvin didn't belong on the list. Maybe he was a copycat case; no one supected Maytag Man in the other murders. But Jamie kept Kelvin on his list anyway till someone could prove otherwise. Kelvin ranked with Aaron Haney in Jamie's mental hierarchy, and the cops had been wrong before about their list—witness the Doe in Defiance, Ohio. For three years Doe went unidentified, while the sheriff insisted to Jamie that Doe wasn't part of the chain. Jamie always included Doe in his reporting, and when Defiance finally came up with his name last year—Barry Lynn Turner of guess where, Indianapolis—he went from "possible" to "police have confirmed" in The Ohio Gay Times.

How many other Does were out there? That was the hardest thought of all.

It took forever for him to get around the city to the I-65/Chicago turnoff. Traffic instantly thinned out, urban to rural. This was the road home.

He passed the WIBC tower, tuned in the station for news, but quickly shut off the box and its homophobia-for-ratings squawkers. From here on would be Mom's time.

In a few miles, he felt safer. Thought about what he would cook for her this weekend, some last good meals before she went into the hospital. He spent that last hour making himself cheerful. Then his face lit up as he saw the giant billboard. He tooted at it, WELCOME TO TIPPECANOE COUNTY, HOME OF PURDUE UNIVERSITY.

Soon he crossed the Wabash, exited on River Road and pulled into her driveway in the little subdivision outside West Lafayette. He was ready for fun; so was she. They hugged and chattered happily.

Later, he baked a big pan of lasagna so there would be leftovers to freeze for her. Lasagna was a family liturgy. Good-Bro Danny had brought home the recipe back in the '80s while he was on leave from the Air Force. The family had never eaten Eye-talian before—*God, we were such rubes*—and Danny's version was scrumptious. Now lasagna was a way to have Danny back there when they needed him.

The next afternoon, Jamie drove Thelma to Hoosier Hospital, stayed and gabbed for an hour and a half until he'd exhausted every topic he could think of. His mother smiled and told him to go home.

The minute he left the building he felt lonely. Its being a Sunday, the town's only Gay bar was closed.

5

Breathing

They finally let him see her, after he'd chased from intensive care to recovery and back again, frustrated with a hospital that lost track of its patients.

He entered ICU and started at how awful she looked. Her pretty face, tanned all summer from golf, had no color; her cheekbones looked crushed from the inside. He couldn't show his fear. But how had an operation in her gut ravaged her face?

Her eyelids fluttered open. "Don't leave me," she gasped, trying feebly to brush aside a clot of plastic tubing on her neck.

"I won't, Mom," he said with all the steadiness he could muster. He got the plastic away from her neck. Behind her, a small screen monitored vital signs and who knew what. Yellow-green squiggles purported to trace the shape of her heart. Whenever she moved, numbers jumped, blinked, threatened to screech alarm. His hand found hers. "I'm here."

He peered into her pale blue eyes with love and grounding and assurance. He smiled and held her with practiced eyes, hoping she could take in his strength.

But who could say? He held her small, cold, freckled hand, and his eyes were drawn to the red light of a sensor taped to her middle finger. "E.T.," she whispered, "call home." She smiled weakly, wiggled her magic digit up and down.

That heartened him a little. "E.T. was sick, but then he got well and went home." When Rick managed a little joke after one of his amputations, Jamie knew the worst was over.

But he couldn't think about Rick now. She blinked a time or two, then lapsed out of consciousness again.

The computer box began to beep, low but insistently. A lavender-clad nurse, peroxide and 35, swept quietly in. "My, you have beautiful hair," she told him. He gaped at her. She stood at the little screen and pushed unseen buttons on the glass. The beeps stopped. The screen changed to reveal more detail, and she pressed here and there on it, squinting as it changed again. A number dropped from 90 to 87.

She adjusted twin tubes stuck up his mother's nose. "You must have a great hairdresser." Eighty-five percent now. Eighty-two percent. She frowned.

"I'm your patient's son." *Think we could worry about her, not my hair?*

"I'm not surprised. You two look a lot alike. She's a lovely lady."

"Thank you. She's a former Indiana's Junior Miss."

He released his mother's hand, laid it on her hip, stepped away to allow Peggy to work. She reached up to finger a plastic bag of clear IV fluid dripping into a tube. "Is your father blond too?"

"Um, yes, actually, he was."

Peggy adjusted another bag. Eighty-eight percent of whatever it was. Then ninety. The screen stopped blinking. "I see you're wearing a wedding ring."

The original screen reappeared, quantifying the human being imprisoned in intensive care. "It helps fend off unwanted advances."

She twisted a valve on another tube. Checking her watch, she picked up a catheter bag, measured urine output, recorded it on a chart on the pull-table. "Is your wife blonde too?"

"I don't have a wife, and he wasn't blond."

She didn't react to the news. "We're stabilizing her. She's a fighter. Try not to worry. Are you all right?"

No, bitch, I'm scared for my mother while you cruise my hair. "I'm okay. Thanks for taking care of her."

She left. He sat in a high swivel chair, quickly floated six inches lower. *Hello, gravity. The chairs are crazy too?*

He maneuvered clumsily over to the bed, found four free fingers and an E.T. one. Eyelids fluttered again; his mother breathed hard. "You're still. Here."

"Back home again, in Indiana," he softly sang. She blinked acknowledgment, then passed out.

She stayed unconscious awhile, so he decided to get some fresh air. He circled around the hospital complex, refamiliarizing himself with streets, the way people lived, how things hummed or didn't in the town. He hadn't lived there in 13 years. Finally he went back inside, checked on his mother, still sleeping. He found the chapel, plain and uninspiring, and sat there, not praying, hoping that just sitting was some kind of prayer; that there was a God on the other end to receive it.

A little later he went back to her room and heard voices. Some woman came out in street clothes, followed by his brother Stone, three years older. Jamie said, "Hi, you came! Thanks."

Stone eyed him, grabbed the woman's arm and hustled her toward the elevator.

Jamie stared at their backs, hurt, angry—then he hurried inside to do his job, to take care of his mother.

* * *

Peggy said he should go home, and at 2 a.m. he and his hair agreed. But he got outside and felt lost; he knew West Lafayette but not its larger twin Lafayette, separated by the Wabash River. West Lafayette had the big university; Lafayette had the hospitals and factories. There was an easy way to get from hospital to highway, but he couldn't remember it, so he drove through town the way he knew.

Still, his heart started pounding; maybe that was just worry and lack of sleep. He crossed the river into his side of town, past fraternity houses high on the bluff, the apartment complex they'd settled into when Thelma finally divorced his terminally blond father; past steep DeHart Street, which Jamie climbed every day of that first semester before Ronald came menacingly back; to the waterworks substation with its flowerbeds, where at 13 Jamie stole three tulips to take to his mother.

He never forgot that theft, the guilt or pleasure of it. For years he believed it was as criminal an act as a Hoosier was capable of—until the Strangler, Hoosier like he was, invaded his life.

Still, he took comfort in the old familiar sights. He climbed to the top of the hill, where Happy Hollow Road dumped out onto the fearsome Bypass.

A car sped towards him. *Christ!* He let it pass, eased out onto the highway, picked up speed. He tried not to think that every other car would crash into him. He tried to forgive stupid acts by other drivers.

He safely pulled his mother's car into the garage on Tad Lincoln Drive, cut the engine and was instantly overcome with an impulse to call Rick. *Does heaven have phones?* If so, no angel had given him the area code.

He opened the car door and swung his legs out, taking care to avoid racking his knee on the hand controls. There were no hand controls on this car, he noticed. But his body swung low and left just the same.

Rick is dead. Mom is in intensive care. When I get back home I'm going to have the hand controls taken out.

His eyes adjusted to the dark family room, found the lamp between the twin, pale blue recliners she kept for herself and Arnie. He headed into her Astroturfed kitchen. His fancy Bunn coffeemaker sat inert on the counter. It could brew a pot in fifteen seconds from its reservoir of hot water, but she decided it jacked up her electric bill too much—*what, five bucks a month?*—so she kept it unplugged. It might as well be a Mr. Coffee now. *Mothers are ridiculous.*

He flipped the kitchen light, was greeted by gruesome fluorescents, oh-so-'70s green/yellow/brown carpet, ragged remnants of which she'd placed in front of the stove and the sink; and cabinet doors she'd re-covered in yellow wallpaper to lighten the room with its northern exposure. *Do all Gay guys critique their mother's décor?*

Under the sink a Jack Daniels bottle sat next to the no-name vodka she used in her martinis. He found an amber rocks glass he remembered from Morocco, a village 75 miles north that was their original hometown. He filled the glass with half-moons of automatic ice. A cloud of freezing air shoved past him like a convict fleeing prison.

He made a weak drink and claimed one of the La-Z-Boys. He found a remote control; her 19-inch non-stereo TV bounced three times before finally settling down. He found Headline News. The familiar, nasal sound of Tonya Tilley, a former colleague from Cincinnati, greeted him as she narrated footage from Yugoslavia. He muted the words; what did they mean anymore? Just inevitably bad news of ethnic cleansing while the world let the Serbs exterminate everyone in sight.

It reminded him of Reagan, Gay men and AIDS: do nothing, let the bastards die. Jamie came out to himself at 12 in the face of it; then 20 Mule Team Borax-for-Brains finally mentioned the disease of the century six years after it was discovered. Ronald Reagan determined Jamie's politics and his sex life; genocide has a way of doing that.

He was a Midwestern boy; so he took on the task of helping to secure Gay rights as a personal responsibility. His mother went right ahead and voted for Reagan anyway. She disapproved of Gay people. It took him over a decade to argue her to the point of tolerance—and argue he did. *Why do I have to fight my own family?*

Her illness raised so many feelings in him; love, of course, and fear; but also the confusion of trying to understand a mother who was both essential to his life and maddening. He utterly respected her as a professional; she used her brain to climb from poverty to affluence. He benefitted from extra opportunities because of her; every year he had new shoes. He completely admired her judgment and values, about everything but sex, and tried to conform his life to them. But she also exposed him and his brothers to a violent, criminal father. He'd never forgive her for that; or he would, if only she'd apologize, explain herself.

He loved his mother like the Best Little Boy in the World; she was a victim too, who couldn't bring herself to acknowledge the wrongdoing, much less apologize.

But mostly he worried; Thelma looked like shit.

He took a sip of Jack-and-water. His head vibrated at the taste of poison. Gray cells thudded between his ears.

He reached for her half-used package of Light Menthol 100s, extracted a cigarette and frowned. *I don't smoke. It's not me, it's the antithesis of me. Then people around me get sick, die even, and all of a sudden smoking is me.*

A half-full ashtray, orange plastic from 1975, was stained black at its molded ridges. *What do ashtrays cost, Mom, a dollar?* He yawned, stretched, decided not to switch up the sound on the sports segment. The NBA was headed into a lockout, and he was half-glad; he loved the college game. Baseball was only now recovering from its last strike; Mark McGwire and Sammy Sosa were staging a home run derby and the Yankees were on a tear. Maybe he'd take an interest in baseball again.

He took another pull on sour mash. Cold liquid drained into his belly. Where should he sleep?

He didn't want the $150 sofabed where he'd slept the last few nights. All those pillows to remove, a three-inch mattress to sling out; no. He tried his drink again, stubbed out the smoke. Promised himself he wouldn't start drugging because Thelma was sick.

Then reminded himself that was exactly what he'd done when Rick died.

Jamie would sleep in her bed. It was the only place with both a phone and a clock. If something happened…

He stripped off his shirt, caught a glance of his chest in the mirror. As long as his abs stayed cut, he'd be all right. He decided to buy a two-week gym membership here.

Body thoughts led idly to sexual ones. He wondered what was wrong with him Sunday night, when he found himself wanting to fuck a hole—a man's, a woman's, it didn't matter; all he visualized was the hole. His cock wanted to follow its instinct and just fuck something.

That too was unlike him. He found out that he was as capable of tricking as anyone else. Maybe it was the twin pressures of Rick and his Mom. His ideals hadn't changed; he wanted monogamy, intimacy, mutual love, a sexual relationship with a lifelong best friend. He didn't base his life on a "heterosexual model"; he simply believed in commitment. He was proud that Rick was his only lover.

Now with Rick gone and Thelma sick, at a time Jamie most needed human contact, where would he find it, with whom, why? Because his cock wanted to fuck? Not good enough. Vaseline would satisfy his cock. It wouldn't satisfy his heart.

He didn't want a man who loved his looks. He wanted a man who knew and loved his heart. His brain, his work, his values; his heart.

Anything else was a cheap thrill. Rick's face was pock-marked, his body went soft after he left the Marines, and then it started getting chopped up. But inside, Rick was as beautiful as ever. Then to share sexual ecstasy, short-lived though it was, was the deepest joy imaginable.

All Jamie could hope was to find it again one day, if he could meet a man who saw beyond his body.

He got undressed and pulled aside the yellow quilt, which was cheerier than Florence Henderson, sat on rumpled Sears sheets and swung his legs up. He sank his weight onto his mother's bed and pulled Florence on top of him. Why not, she was a Hoosier too.

In bed, before sleep, his sadness and fear took center stage. *God, if that phone rings, you are not a god at all. Just like when Rick got sick and you didn't care.*

He crossed himself anyway, let the mattress support his back, and slept.

* * *

When he woke three hours later, he hadn't moved an inch.

The clock read 6:04 a.m. It was getting light outside. He rubbed his eyes and forehead. Sleep or get up? He couldn't decide. Peggy got off her 12-hour shift in ICU at 4 a.m. The relief nurse hadn't felt a need to call him. He fought off the impulse to make sure. What's more banal than a family member needing absolution?

He snoozed till 6:16. Too early to get up and too late to switch off his thoughts.

He remembered a deep-breathing technique his therapist had taught him years ago in New York, in a session which revealed that every emotion he'd ever repressed was stored in his body. All his fears in all the years of Thelma and Ronald; all the lonely pain of being called faggot and queer in grade school, because he minded the teachers and didn't pick fights—all the men and women who wanted him, whom he didn't want—came flooding back as he lay on an apartment floor on Central Park West, a dictionary on his abs, exhaling.

But abdominal breathing, using all his lung capacity and expelling the "dirty air" completely, had taught him how to sleep when he couldn't. He set the alarm for 10 a.m. He'd be up in plenty of time for the start of ICU visiting hours at noon, if the hospital didn't call.

He was a total wreck and he knew it; but he breathed.

6

Agate

Jamie gathered newspapers under his arm and drove his own car to the hospital. He made his way to the entrance, passing under shirtless hard-hats in September heat. A young brunet working on the roof was hunky, but the others were lip-curlers.

Outside the doors a knot of smokers gathered. "So I says to Alice, I says to her, Listen, if you'd gotten him looked at before this, you wouldn't be in this fix." She was a thin-lipped White woman, prematurely aging in faded jeans, a NASCAR shirt and Marlboro Lights. Jamie strode past her trying not to feel superior.

Then feeling superior, what the hell.

He moved past the volunteer shop with its guilt-free, wilt-now flowers, to the elevators. He followed signage to double doors, behind which his mother lay incarcerated. He stopped at the nurses' station, gave his mother's name and his own. "How is she?"

"It's been a tough night," a nurse named Terry said. "We're trying to stabilize her blood pressure. But she's a fighter."

They're all fighters till they're dead. He entered Room 10. There was Thelma, beautiful and wasted, with tubes in places he didn't want to look. She was asleep.

A nurse named Sandra, hair tied up in a Mennonite bun, punched up numbers on Thelma's monitor. Satisfied with her readings, she moved past Jamie without so much as a nod. He could have been a used catheter.

He found Thelma's inert right hand, the one with the red light taped to it. He stroked her hand, knowing it wouldn't do any good or any harm. She still looked devastated, but maybe her color was a bit better; or maybe that was merely what he told himself.

Today there was a big visitor's chair for him, and after a minute he sat down and picked up the local paper. Besides Yugoslavia, the front page focused on the prospects for this year's corn harvest; the weather was cooperating so far. The local section had a big spread about a gazebo in Columbian Park, and he devoured every smalltown word.

Then he spotted something in the agate.

Body Recovered in Slough

MOROCCO—A conservation officer discovered the partially-clad body of an unidentified white male in woods near a lake in the Willow Slough Fish and Game Area yesterday afternoon, state police said.

The victim, wearing only white socks and athletic shoes, appeared to have been strangled, police said, but final cause of death is pending until an autopsy can be performed. No identification was found at the scene. Police estimated that the victim had been dead up to two weeks.

The victim was between 25 and 35 years old, according to State Police Sgt. Kent Kessler of the West Lafayette post, the detective in charge of the investigation. No other details were available.

Chills started at the crown of his head, ran down to his toes and didn't let go for ten full seconds.

He made a fist, looked away. *A man's murdered and he's only worth the fine print?*

He searched the local section of the Indianapolis paper, but the Sun didn't have a report. He watched his mother's monitor for a second, then gazed out the window at nothing. *A quick phone call, when Mom no longer needs anything, might be all it takes.*

"Whatcha doing over there?" his mother croaked.

Jamie jumped up, put on his game face and strode over to lean across the bedrail. "Just wondering how much beauty sleep you need today, lady," he grinned.

She coughed, blinked, tried to clear her throat. "A lot," she murmured. But her eyes worked at smiling too.

He stayed with her for an hour, during which she fell asleep twice and asked him to mow the lawn three times. At 1 p.m. he drove back to West Lafayette, opened the garage door and pulled out the mower. It was heavy, and he had to figure out how to reattach the grass-catcher, which was full from the last time Arnie mowed.

Shapes had always puzzled Jamie; he was wired for words, not objects. He finally got the grass-catcher to hang behind the mower. He was starting to work up a sweat and he hadn't even got the mower out of the garage yet.

He went into the house, pulled off his shirt and changed into gym trunks. There was no helping his white cross-trainers; they were the only shoes he'd brought besides boots and dress shoes, and they'd just have to get grass-stained.

He had a leftover tan from Amsterdam, where he covered and played in the Gay Games with thousands of athletes, exactly his idea of a good time. He carried the banner for Team Columbus in the opening ceremonies, then spent two weeks stripped down to serious, sexy trunks, showing off his buff body for all it was worth. He'd never forget the spirit of the Games, an atmosphere of support and respect and celebration. He had a blast in Amsterdam, his first fun since Rick died.

He found sunblock. But mowing was a bear. The grass catcher filled up every five minutes, the mower weighed a ton, and the drainage ditch in the front yard was impossible. The job took him two hours, and Thelma had a little yard. By the time he was done he knew he would drive to the Slough.

* * *

The local TV news barely mentioned the murder and had no additional details. After Dan Rather, Jamie headed back to the hospital. His Mom was awake when he walked in; that was a first. "How's the grass?" Thelma asked.

"Chopped to smithereens," he said with mock exasperation. "Manicured within an inch of its life. Worthy of Augusta National, though you'd never let the public tramp through your estate. Yet they may look through the palace fence with the other commoners, once or twice a year, noblesse oblige." She smiled, waited for him to finish. "As for me, I've got a sunburned nose. How are you?"

"I've got burns too," she replied, touching her belly where the grapefruit had grown.

"It took me two hours. That mower's heavy."

"That's twice as long as it takes Arnie. The mower's self-propelled, you just hold down the lever."

"How was I to know? Do you think you might have mentioned it?"

She said meekly, "Sorry."

Oh, how cute she was when she was guilty. "Lord, she sends a Gay guy out to wrestle a machine and fails to give him the most basic instruction. Mom, the gene that makes me Gay prevents me from being mechanical, it's some kind of on-off switch in the brain!"

She laughed, "Thank you for getting it done."

He held her hand, kissed her forehead; it felt like sandpaper. Something in the drugs she was on had completely dried out the skin on her face. If he couldn't do anything for the pain in her abdomen, at least he could help her moisturize. In a cupboard he found a bottle of cream. "Time for your facial, dear," he chirped, squeezing white, cool liquid onto his palm, warming it, then using two fingers to apply the lotion to her forehead in gentle, circular strokes.

She closed her eyes. "Ooh," she breathed. "That feels **good**."

Jamie saw a picture of Lettie, Rick's mom, after her last surgery. She rallied, got off the ventilator, tasted water. Even sick, her eyes twinkled at the boys. "Water. That's the **best stuff!**"

Jamie still had that plastic tumbler with her name and room number taped to it. His mind's eye could see it on his bookshelves in Columbus. He and Rick buried her a few days later, with most of the responsibility on Jamie. Rick never could think during a crisis. Usually Rick was rock solid; in an emergency he turned into a jumble of nerves.

With more lotion, Jamie traced figure-eights on Thelma's cheekbones. Her breath seemed to come a little deeper. He smoothed and rubbed from cheekbones to jawbones and back again. Even her earlobes had dried out, but the rest of the ear seemed all right. Then back to the cheeks, first one and then the other. Her chin needed some special attention, then gently down the neck. The dry area seemed to end under her shoulder blades, at the top of her chest, a good stopping place.

When he was done she opened her eyes again. She didn't say anything, she just looked at her son. Jamie acted as if it was all in a day's work. But inside, he smiled.

On his way home he paused in the twilight, remembered the construction worker from that afternoon. Neither of his Straight brothers would have thought to notice Thelma's skin.

First thing the next morning he phoned the state police and made an appointment with Sgt. Kent Kessler.

7

Hyoid

The state police post was on River Road, next to the interstate. "Hello, my name is Jamie Foster," he smiled at the young woman behind the Plexiglass shield. "I have an appointment with Sergeant Kessler."

"Just a moment. Please have a seat," Trooper J. Campbell said. She was pretty and, like all women cops, very authoritative.

Jamie thanked God for his mother, a clinical pharmacist who had also entered a "man's profession" and helped make it everyone's. Though he seldom sat in waiting rooms, he sat down immediately at police stations so cops could keep an eye on him.

A door on the left opened, a tall officer leaned through and said, "Mr. Foster?"

"Yes," Jamie said, getting to his feet right away.

"I'm Sergeant Kessler," the officer said, stepping into the waiting room and extending a greeting. They crushed each other's hands. "Please come in. Down this hallway to conference room 1, second door on your right." Jamie entered interrogation room 1. "I'll get my file."

The room was equipped with a round oak table, four vinyl-padded chairs. In the corner a video camera was hung from the ceiling; on end tables sat soft-lit lamps, houseplants, a small audio recorder. A wall held an observation mirror. Cement block walls, painted light blue, were decorated with safety posters and a scene of the Indiana Dunes National Lakeshore. Fish swam in an aquarium. For an interrogation room it was cozy; the browbeating probably took place in interrogation room 2. Jamie sat.

Kessler walked in, all business in his uniform of navy blue shirt, light blue tie, gray trousers with side stripes, black shoes, Glock 9 millimeter on his left hip. Twin brass pins on his collar denoted a sergeant's stripes. There was nothing subtle about the uniform; the tie conveyed professionalism and the rest was naked power. "This is about the John Doe in Newton County," Jamie began. He looked up and it hit him like a neutron bomb.

His sweat popped out.

"Right. Now who is it you work for again?"

Sergeant Kent Kessler was stunningly handsome.

Jamie's abs flexed, he felt like he'd been kicked in the gut. It was painful, disorienting. He hadn't quite looked at the man before, just the uniform.

But he was trained to keep control in a stressful situation; to perform. This was no way to begin an interview. So he breathed deeply to relax, then said firmly, "The Ohio Gay Times. Chief correspondent." He wanted to see the cop react to the word Gay.

The cop looked neutral. "Does that make you Gay too?"

"They tried to hire George Will, but his wife didn't want to move to Columbus."

Kessler smiled, asked smoothly, "So what brings you to our neck of the woods?" His black hair was wavy and well-cut.

"I work in Ohio, but we circulate in Indiana and I'm originally from West Lafayette. My mother's in the hospital and I'm here to help out. Meanwhile this John Doe in Willow Slough sounds like it could be a Gay-related murder. Is it?"

"Could be, maybe not. I'm trying to get an ID first. I asked him about his sexual practices, but he just couldn't say."

"Stiffs aren't too good with answers. Questions, those they're good at."

"Tell me. What makes you think it's Gay-related?"

"The nudity."

Kessler frowned. "It's possible."

"Four years ago I broke a story about a serial killer dumping bodies of young men from Indianapolis in Ohio and Indiana. A dozen of them. This sounds similar, if the Union-Gazette reported it accurately. Why do you have the case? It's Rensselaer's territory."

Kessler's eyes narrowed. "Rensselaer just does traffic, drugs and lesser felonies. They don't do homicides."

It was a lie and Jamie knew it. Every state police post handled every type of crime. *First thing out of the guy's mouth is a lie.*

But it was such a handsome mouth. Kessler's hair framed a tanned, unlined face of deep-set brown eyes, a narrow, straight nose, tucked-in ears, a strong chin. The features by themselves weren't so remarkable, but there was something about the eyes that made the total package dazzling. They took on a look of smoldering emotion Jamie had never seen in a man, much less a cop. Jamie shook his head, tried to focus on the lie.

"I've heard Lowell does some of Rensselaer's homicides. Why do you have it? They're much closer. You're an hour south."

Kessler leaned forward, put his arm on the table. "You're asking a lot of questions, little man."

Jamie eased out a chuckle; he was not a little man. "That's what we both do for a living, sergeant, ask questions. Maybe I can help you with this. If it does turn out to be Gay-related, you need access to the Gay community. They're not always friendly to cops. If it's not Gay-related, I'm out of here. If it is, I'm your access card. You think his girlfriend overpowered him, choked him, stripped him and dumped him?"

Kessler eyed him conspicuously, then opened a red file marked JOHN DOE and the date. "No. What do you want to know?"

"I'd like to know why West Lafayette has this case and not Rensselaer or Lowell."

"Whoa, you're getting ahead of yourself," Kessler said, chopping his head down. "I don't know you're a reporter yet. Heck, I don't know you didn't kill him yourself."

The Big Challenge: but Jamie had heard it all before. He shrugged to let the guy know he wasn't fazed. Kessler said, "All I know is I've got somebody here who says he's Jamie Foster, says he works for some paper in Ohio, says he's interested in a murder in Newton County. Ain't that all I've got?" His eyes bore right through Jamie. Those eyes were thoroughly convincing at the authority game.

Jamie reached for his wallet. "Sergeant, my business card. My driver's license with social security number. My press badge is in the car, I'll be happy to get it. Here is the card of Detective Homer Sauer of the Quincy County, Ohio prosecutor's office, and one for his partner Sgt. Barry Hickman. Here is one for Lt. Phil Blaney of Indianapolis P.D., homicide investigator. I've got enough of these to play 52-card pickup. You want Jasper County, Hamilton, Hancock, Shelby? Stillwater, Defiance, Kickapoo? Give any one of them a call. Check me out."

Kessler studied Jamie's card with the color mug shot, blond hair swooped perfectly. He stood. "Please wait here," he said, scooping up Jamie's license and the cop cards.

"Or I can get my press badge from the car," Jamie thumbed toward the parking lot.

Kessler moved to the door. His teeth looked like a sales poster for orthodontists—straight, shiny white, perfect. "Sure. You show me yours, I might show you mine."

Jamie didn't watch him leave. Instead he walked out of the air-cooled building into heat and humidity. He unlocked the passenger door on the Acura. The sun was already scorching its interior. He reached into the glove compartment, poked around among roadmaps, napkins, insurance papers, shampoo samples, condoms in case he got lucky some year; found the badge on its neck chain. There was no need to lock his car at a state police post, so he lowered the windows, then looked back at the building, steeling himself. *It's the eyes. Professional but open. Masculine, intelligent, sensitive. Will you marry me?*

Jeez. Be a reporter! He strode back up the sidewalk, trying to get a grip.

He stopped at the front desk, caught Trooper Campbell's eye, showed his press badge. "Sergeant Kessler wanted to see my ID."

"Okay, you can go back in. To conference room 1 only." She buzzed him in, then stood in her doorway and made sure he went to interrogation room 1 only.

Kessler reappeared a minute later, pulled out his chair and sat down, six-feet-four and 225 pounds of muscular grace and narrow hips. Jamie forced himself to look away.

"IPD says they know you, they've worked with you on some murders, you were helpful. Very helpful, in fact." Kessler crinkled his eyes a little. "And also a pain in the butt. Thanks for the ID. You look like you're 19, not 26. Where are your corrective lenses?" He tossed the cards back to Jamie.

"Line 1 of my job description says, 'Be a pain in the butt,'" Jamie smiled. "I wear contacts in lieu of goggles. Here's my press badge."

Kessler picked it up, measured Jamie's face against it, returned it. "How long have you been lying about your height?"

Instant raw nerve. Jamie had lied about his height for so long he now believed it. "I'm five-ten."

"You're not even five-nine."

"I'm every bit of five-ten." He had to be, would never have gotten jobs without it.

"We've got a height chart in the other room. Want to stand next to it?" Jamie's eyes got big. Was this cop throwing his weight around over height? "No, didn't think so," Kessler smiled.

"I'm five-ten. It says so right on my ID."

"Uh-huh," Kessler chuckled. "Just teasing you, man. You lie a little about your height. So what do you want to know?"

Jamie pulled on his earlobe in frustration and embarrassment; he was at least five nine and three-quarters—and could always stretch tall. Besides, it had been years since he'd measured, maybe he was five-ten now. He glanced down at his notebook. *Start over, stay on the good side of this cop. I'll get nowhere if he categorizes me as a pushy faggot. I am not short, I am five feet ten!* "Let's start with the basics, shall we? White male, between the ages of 25 and 35?"

"Correct."

"Body recovered in the woods near Lake Murphey in Willow Slough, nude except for white socks and athletic shoes?"

"Right. The name of the lake wasn't in the newspaper. How come you know it?"

"I'm from there, the Slough's my old stomping grounds; I was born in Rensselaer, lived in Morocco and Kentland, moved to West Lafayette when I was 12. Do you have autopsy results back yet on a cause of death?"

Jamie knew that by admitting familiarity with the area, he'd just given Kessler another reason to suspect him.

"We have a probable cause, strangulation. Medical examiner is still waiting on drug and alcohol screens, blood work, the usual. Those take awhile."

Jamie made notes, felt his own sweat. "Is Dr. Webster the pathologist?"

Kessler hesitated, raised his head to look at Jamie. A beat. "Yes, Dr. Webster. This is getting interesting."

Thank you. Webster was internationally known, he'd been the first to connect the dots on Schmidgall, and he'd worked all the Strangler cases in Indiana. He'd also said he'd come to Jamie's cop conference fiasco and not shown up. Still, he was a great forensic pathologist, a source to cultivate. And if he had the autopsy there was a reason. "You were present for the autopsy?"

"Of course."

"Last meal?"

"Pasta salad, lots of vegetables, possibly for lunch. He was ready for another meal."

"Pasta salad," Jamie frowned. "That isn't right."

"It's what he had in him."

"Okay, but it doesn't fit. All the other victims have been poor. The poor don't eat pasta and vegetables, they eat burgers and fries."

"Good point."

"Condition of the liver?"

"Smooth, no scarring. But he'd had a couple beers."

"Who discovered the body?"

Kessler returned to the front of the paperwork. "A conservation officer at the park, Officer Suzanne Myers. She was cataloguing the early geese migration when she found something at the edge of a woodpile. It wasn't a goose."

"Height, weight, condition of the body? How long had he been there? Was it directly in the water? If so, water should have helped preserve him, though it might also wash away possible evidence."

"It's been awful hot up there lately, so we've got a combination of waterlogged and, uh, slightly cooked. Again, all we have is an estimate. We're putting it at possibly two weeks but I bet it's only a day or two, he wasn't that cooked. To the other questions, six feet, 190 pounds, some of which could be water weight if he was killed on-site."

"Two weeks. That would include Labor Day weekend." *Does this make six murders over Labor Day?*

"Right, we're calling it August 25 to September 7, but it's all preliminary."

Jamie wrote that down. "Okay, you said he was strangled. Ligature? If so, what type, and was it still on him?"

"Ligature, yes. Not found on him. Waiting results on what might have caused those marks."

"Neck? What about hands and feet?"

"Hands and feet were clear. You've done this before."

"Did you ever hear of Roger Schmidgall?"

"Schmidgall? Did you work on Schmidgall's cases?" Kessler's eyes widened, his voice went higher.

"I just caught the tail end of him, when he pleaded guilty in the Barlow case four years ago and tried to blame the veterinarian. I've visited his crime scene in Newton County, those four men on the abandoned farm next to the Kankakee River, which he confessed to through his lawyer when he died 18 months ago; and the Red-Haired Boy in Jasper County whose name he forgot."

"Ah yes, the absent-minded veterinarian. Couldn't remember slashing that guy to ribbons, could he?"

"And photographing the results," Jamie growled. "The prosecution was almost deliberately incompetent."

"Don'tcha just love politics?"

"Truth, justice and the American way." *Will you buy a commiseration ploy?* "So, about this John Doe. Above-average height, not fat. Build?"

"Slender but muscled. He either had a strenuous job or worked out regularly."

Jamie got an idea. "You're an athlete; what sport might he have played?"

Kessler thought. Finally he said, "Basketball. What a great question, it humanizes the guy. Maybe he played in a league somewhere."

"Maybe you can find out. Rectum dilated?"

"Six point two millimeters," Kessler said coldly. "No evidence of semen."

"Signs of a struggle? Contusions, lacerations, broken bones? Specifically the hyoid?"

Kessler plunked his elbow on the table, sank his chin onto his upraised fist, leaned toward his subject. "You're quite a piece of work, you know that?"

Jamie put on his trust-me face and waited, saying nothing. But he wished he'd never had to learn about human neck bones.

Kessler eyed him a little longer, then sat back in his chair. "Why should I tell you?"

Now or never. "Because I'm someone you can use.

"Sergeant, don't tell me anything that only the killer would know; but use me if I can help. Most officers have a hard time when they've got a Gay-related murder. You're overworked to start with. The victimology is harder with Gay people. Parents may not know their kids are Gay, or who their friends are. Friends won't talk half the time, all they know is 'cops' and they want zero to do with you.

"If this case isn't Gay, isn't related to the others I'm following, I'm history. But it does sound like the others a little, and one possible marker is that hyoid."

"Hyoid was crushed. How did you know about that?"

Jamie recited them from memory. "Michael Cardinal, Shelby County, 1987. Strangled, hyoid broken. Riley Jones, 1988. Strangled, hyoid crushed. Four similar in Quincy County, Ohio, 1989 to 1995. Stillwater County, Ohio, 1995. Defiance County, Ohio, 1993; identified 1996, Barry Lynn Turner. Let's see, who am I leaving out?" Jamie gazed at the video camera hanging from the ceiling. "Ah. Kelvin."

"I get the picture. No other contusions, lacerations, no signs of a struggle."

"Rats. My cases never show signs of a struggle. Yet they're all young, healthy men who could fight back if they had to. If they were able to, that is. Which makes the drug screen all the more important."

"I know."

"Make sure the lab screens for all known animal tranquilizers."

"Huh?"

If Jamie explained this he'd give out too much information. "You must screen for animal tranqs. If the victim is drugged, by something you wouldn't ordinarily test for, it may be why he never fights back. The victims don't have a chance, because the killer puts them to sleep surreptitiously. Easy to kill someone that way. Don't stop screening if you come up positive for marijuana, keep looking. Marijuana didn't put that guy out; something else did. Something fast-acting. Entice the victim with reefer, then five minutes later he's sound asleep. Look for animal tranqs."

"Gee." Kessler made a note of it. "Were any other victims found to have something in them?"

"I know of six positive for marijuana. The animal tranq's never been done, but it's logical; everyone else let their tissue samples get away. Talk to Bulldog Sauer of the Quincy County prosecutor's office. Here's his card."

Kessler had Xeroxed all the cards, so he checked off Detective Sauer. "I will. Thanks for the tip."

"Sergeant, you might have Victim Number 13."

"That's why I've got this case." Kessler looked him in the eye. "You wanted to know, I'll tell you. I'm sorry for pussyfooting around before." Jamie nodded, all ears. "We're halfway between the crime scene and Indy, if there is any possible connection with these other murders, which is a big if. If there's no connection, it goes back to Rensselaer for disposition. If there's a connection, we get in some new blood, maybe a different investigative team can come up with something. Probably not, but it's worth a shot." And then the threat. "You tell anybody else that, much less put it in the paper, I'll cut off your access to every trooper in this department."

Jamie wrote, kept eye contact. "You should go off the record before you say things I can legally use."

Kessler glared at him, ticked off, stirred up.

Jamie relaxed, got smaller. "I'm here to help, sergeant, as well as to get a story if there is one. I understand you need confidentiality, and I appreciate getting a straight answer. Do your work, I won't use the quote till you're ready. Meanwhile I've seen every one of these crime scenes, talked to every investigator on every case. Think about it; it's my readers who are getting hammered. My paper's got a stake in this. We want these cases solved, that's all. If I can help, I will. You tell me if I can help."

Kessler backed off, glanced at the mirror on the opposite wall. He knew Campbell was watching; so did Jamie. "It's very, very preliminary. No one's calling it serial yet. I want to emphasize that. We don't know nearly enough to begin to say that, and we don't need you scaring people."

"But you've already notified the FBI." It was a guess, a stab in the dark.

Kessler gaped at him. Training said he was already giving this reporter a lot of information. Why was instinct telling him to keep risking it?

Because no other reporters were asking about Doe; they didn't know how important this victim might be. "Quantico's overnighting the forms. You'd think I could download them, but the Feds want paperwork."

"Jeez, have you ever seen those forms? You'll be working overtime just on that." *Do you go for sympathy?*

"Tell me about it," Kessler wagged his head.

"Who did the crime scene? Are you satisfied with it?"

"The naturalist called Rensselaer. They came out and said, 'yeah, that's a dead body, all right,' and notified headquarters. I got a call, and they assigned Sgt. Warnecke in Lowell to assist me. He and I did it together. I'm very satisfied, we work practically the same."

"Who assigned you? Major George F. Slaughter?"

Kessler stared again. "Major Slaughter, yes. Deputy Chief for Investigations."

Jamie's heart speeded up. *George is on this. That makes Kessler his hand-picked man.* "By any chance are you or Sgt. Warnecke certified as crime scene technicians?"

"I am, last year. But my specialty is homicide. I figure by taking a case from start to finish, it helps me solve it."

"Fantastic. Certification is a rigorous program."

"Yeah, not that many troopers have completed it. We don't have a crime scene unit at our beck and call like they do on TV, this is rural Indiana. So I learned all I could about it."

"You're very dedicated." They exchanged looks. "So, what physical evidence? Tire tracks, clothing, trash, a weapon? Metal detector results? Carpet fibers? Crushed grass, the body dragged from a car? What do you have?"

"I don't have a darn thing. That's what worries me."

"Fingernail scrapings? Latent prints on the body?"

"Nothing. Zero. The killer must have worn gloves."

And a rubber. "Still, there's a needle in that haystack. Where's the haystack exactly?"

"Shallow water on the edge of the campground, next to a woodpile, directly accessible by car. They have sixty or eighty campsites, never used this time of year. The killer could have driven to the exact spot, popped the trunk and dumped out the body, then driven away with no one seeing a thing. The park rangers only work till 3 p.m. Anybody can come in, day or night. There ain't even a front gate."

"Sure makes it easy on law enforcement." *Sympathy does work with you.*

"With the rain lately, there are no tire tracks, no crushed grass, not even fibers. Just a body in the water behind a woodpile. That's the sum total of what I've got."

"Tough case," Jamie frowned.

"Listen, if you find anything, I want you to know you can come to me. Will you do that?"

The preliminary close. "Sure. These are my readers. I'm a confidential informant for seven departments. I don't work for the government, I work for my readers. All I want is the crime solved. If it's part of this pattern, I'll gladly work with anyone who will help to solve it. I'll go beyond anyone who stands in my way. Fair enough?"

Kessler's jaw set. "Fair enough. I won't stop till I've got the guy. Or guys. I don't care what the victim did with his personal life, he didn't deserve to die. It ain't no crime to be Gay. Therefore he's a citizen. I investigate the murder of citizens."

"Thank you, sergeant, very much. Gay Indiana thanks you."

"So you're the famous CI. Man, you sure work fast."

"The famous one?"

"When I got this assignment I was told there was a very interesting informant. I sure never expected you to walk into my post before I even found out your name. Jamie, it was only one inch in the newspaper."

"It's happenstance that I'm here; any Gay reader might have wondered, with a naked male victim. Now then, you've got photos?"

"I'm Mr. Kodak." Kessler pulled out eight-by-ten glossies, laid them on the table.

This was the part of the job Jamie hated the most. Looking at murder victims, Gay murder victims, made him feel vulnerable, a feeling he loathed.

When he was a rookie, the victims haunted his dreams. Now he slept okay, but still, he knew he over-empathized with them.

He hesitated a minute, steeling himself, spacing out. This part meant having Casey on his back, arguing facts and phrases, libel and space limits; and Louie too, bitching about budget. While Jamie got to examine popped-out eyes, decomposing bodies.

I know you weren't a sweet little kid, Kelvin, but you sure looked that way in the photos.

God, help me get through this. I'm stalling. Jamie picked up the stack of photos, swallowed, started to study. John Doe's skin had a slightly bluish cast—except for his neck, where he had black, even bruises an inch wide on both sides of his windpipe, an eye-burning, horrific sight.

Jamie remembered Dr. Steve Helmreich, the serial murder expert, making him look at pictures of multiple gunshot wounds, dismemberments, splayed brains, poisonings, strangulations, heads bashed in, shaken baby syndrome. *"Cops have to look at the gore to comprehend the evil that people inflict on each other, and how they did it in this case. Jurors, too. And reporters, if you're going to get good at this."*

Jamie was such a sissy about violence he couldn't even watch the Indy 500.

Mr. Doe was sprawled on his side with his eyes closed, in water and weeds, legs tilted to his left, where he fell probably. The socks and sneakers looked ratty as hell.

The biceps were large, chest and shoulders well-defined. Good abs, small of waist, thinner in the thighs and calves. *Nice tan line, bikini boy. You're Gay, all right.*

He studied Doe's face. Young, but not hustler age anymore. Mildly handsome, in a Midwest farmboy kind of way. It was hard to judge whether he was poor or prosperous; muddy, matted hair splattered every which way, the mouth closed, no evidence on dental care. The hair wasn't hustler-long, though.

In a third photograph he noticed an untanned line where a wristwatch had always been.

He searched more pictures until he got a good angle on the left hand. Another little untanned stripe, the width of a missing wedding ring.

He rubbed his forehead, wondering how much death he had to go through. He handed the pictures back. "He's Gay. I can tell you several things about him."

"You can figure out his sex life from a photo?"

"Tan line." Jamie traced it as Kessler watched. "European-cut bikini. It shows a bit of the buttocks. That's not considered proper for men in this country, it glorifies the male body too much. It's a definitive marker, because the only Americans who wear them are Gay men."

"Gee," Kessler said, staring at the photo. "I never even noticed that."

You weren't looking at his ass. "The tan line on his wrist says he always wore a watch, so he's middle-class or higher. The two facts together suggest where he may have lived. Look for an upscale home near downtown Indy: Lockerbie, Chatham Arch, those apartments on the canal; or Riley Towers, I know it's got a pool."

Kessler made more notes. "Where do you get all that?"

"He sat around the pool all summer in those little bitty trunks. Could have owned a suburban home with a pool, but downtown near other Gay people is more likely."

"What makes you think that?"

"There's no theater in suburbia."

But the cop looked blank. Jamie said, "Look for a place within walking distance of the entertainment district, the galleries and nightspots and Gay bars."

"Gee," Kessler said again.

"Either he was heterosexually married, or he had a lover he was committed to. The killer stole his wedding ring. Call Indy P.D., missing persons. The wife or lover probably filed a report. If not, the significant other probably did it."

"Man oh man, are you a certified crime scene technician?"

"Hardly," Jamie smiled. "What about comparing these ligature marks with other known victims?"

"Haven't got to that yet. The counties have the photos and I have to obtain them. What are you looking at?"

"Memory tells me they're all the same width."

"Possibly indicating the same murder weapon?"

"I was looking at an old, narrow tie in my closet the other day. And I thought, wrap a tie around the neck and yank on the ends. Instead of relying on hand strength to choke someone, the perp puts shoulders, arms and chest into it. Much more strength—hyoid crushed." Jamie showed the move. "Bizarre thing to think about as I dressed for work."

"Added strength is a reason people use ligatures. A tie might be the right width."

"Doesn't Dr. Webster have photos too? Why should you hassle with the counties?"

"Sure, he's got photos, but only from this state, not your ones in Ohio. I'll pay him another call."

"Good job. How are the victim's teeth?"

"One well-maintained filling, plus evidence of a recent root canal on a back molar."

"Terrific. Root canals are expensive. So he's certainly middle class, had a good job, health care benefits, access to money. Therefore other people knew him and you'll get an ID. Do you have a victim sketch?"

"We'll have one tomorrow, headquarters does that. You want one when I get it?"

"We can print it in our next issue, pending your confirmation that he even belongs in my paper. When you locate survivors with a photo, we'll run it, urge our readers to call you with any information. Do you have an 800 number? If he's from Indianapolis, it'll be a long-distance call to West Lafayette for your informants, whether they're in Naptown or Morocco. You have to give them an incentive to call."

Kessler handed over a card with an 800 number. "I sure appreciate all your help."

"If he is Gay, if it's related to the others, you're going to have to overcome both paranoia and denial in the Gay community. Afraid of the cops, plus some of them know there have been a lot of killings there. We'll reassure them, but it won't be easy. The last time we tried there were no results. Some people will be eager to help, but others will never have heard of the murders, they think being Gay is only what they do in the closet. And the rest will say, 'It could never happen to me, I'm always careful.' Right. Like they're so much smarter than this guy with a good job, a root canal and pasta salad for lunch."

"Gee," Kessler said, trying to picture more than one homosexual reaction.

"If you get a match, will you give me an advance quote that you won't discriminate against informants? On the record, sergeant."

"Sure. But don't even print it unless you hear from me. We don't want to imply the guy's Gay or anything till we know. We could get in big trouble for that." Jamie agreed. "You ready? The Indiana State Police actively requests the help of all citizens..."

"Slow down, please, you talk faster than I write." Jamie never used his tape recorder on the first cop interview, it scared them off.

Kessler gave a very good statement, then asked, "How was that?"

Jamie finished scribbling, folded up his notebook. "Great. But 'lifestyle' is the wrong choice of words. Sexual orientation is the right way to say it, makes you sound like you know what you're talking about."

"Huh?"

"'Lifestyle' implies a choice," Jamie recited. *Homo 101, yet again.* "How many people do you know who choose to have TV preachers call them the devil incarnate? Nor is it a 'preference,' like ketchup on your hot dog instead of mustard. 'Orientation' describes the biological causes of sexuality, which isn't a choice. Even the Catholic bishops agree, it's biological, and therefore morally neutral."

"Okay, um, sexual orientation then," the officer corrected, but with a look on his face, almost doe-eyed, Jamie couldn't figure out.

"Will you do it? Not discriminate? I don't assume you will, but three-quarters of my readers in this state will be scared to death you'll get their names, call their employers and say, 'Did you know this employee is queer?'"

The trooper shook his head. His black hair reflected little flecks of light. Jamie looked away again. "I'm sure you wouldn't, sergeant, but it's often been done. You know that. So I'm bound to let you know, not a threat or anything so please don't take me the wrong way." Jamie faced the man. "I'm simply stressing the importance of this. Only an idiot would turn in his own informants. Today's officers are so much better trained and better educated. But if you do discriminate, which is what those informants are afraid of, I'll spray your name and 'Indiana State Police' in 200-point type all over my front page. And I won't let up till they hand me your badge."

"You have the power to do all that?"

"No, sir. But I write for the public, and readers do have that power."

Kessler's face paled a shade, and doe-eyes came back. Jamie had used these words before with cops, but this time he felt guilty all of a sudden. *All cops know discrimination exists, what's with this one? Is he trying to co-opt me with a sincerity act?*

Or is he really sincere?

The moment passed, Kessler's color changed and he said firmly, "I will never in my life discriminate against anyone on the basis of their sexual orientation. Or any other basis. Not race, not color, not creed, none of it. You get me? It's not the policy of this department, period; and it's not who I am either, no matter what you think. This is murder, for heaven's sake. You think cops don't care about victims too? You think we don't go home every night and love on our families every chance we get, 'cause we know how fragile life can be?"

Jamie found himself taking a dip in dark brown, long-lashed, fiery pools. He'd hurt the guy's feelings, pissed him off if this was genuine.

That wasn't my intent, man. I know you're human. But given how much crap cops pull on us… You seemed so dispassionate. Jeez, I don't want to screw this up.

He became aware of more sweat under his arms. Broke the stare. Shook his head to clear his brain, felt like he'd just shit on the Queen of England. *Get control of yourself! What the fuck is going on here?*

He stood up to get distance, pushed away from the table. Kessler got to his feet too. Jamie, taller than both his parents, felt short all of a sudden.

"I'm sorry," he stumbled. "But I had to know you won't discriminate. My readers have to know—or you'll get nowhere. Now I can tell them to trust you. We all want you to succeed." He stuck out his hand.

Kessler looked at him for a long moment, shook his hand solemnly, firm as a state trooper. "It's all right. Guess you're just doing your job. Maybe I'd be suspicious too, if I was in your shoes."

"May I offer the slightest tip for future reference? Don't ever lie to a reporter. I'd rather hear no comment than an untruth."

"Here's a tip for you. Don't ever lie to a cop."

"I haven't."

"Said you were five-ten." Jamie started to protest, but Kessler grinned and grasped him by the shoulder. "Seriously, if you play ball with me, I'll never lie to you again."

"Batter up. But why do you tease me? You don't even know me."

"I always tease my teammates. Helps 'em play loose."

Jamie growled, "Bring on your height chart, sergeant."

"Right this way." They went into a prisoner receiving room. Most arrestees were taken directly to the county jail, but occasionally one wound up here. Jamie stood next to the chart on the wall.

Kessler looked at him skeptically. "I guess I'd say 5'10", but half of it's blond hair."

Jamie laughed, immediately stepped away. "Thank you for your dedication and skill, sergeant. Thank you for caring about the victims. Good luck in the investigation. I hope it turns out to be easy, routine and unconnected. So you can go home and love the ones you're with."

"So do I."

"May I call you in a couple of days?" *Get the agreement, then get your ass out of here, fool!*

"Please do. Call me if you come up with something. If it's important they can page me."

"I will." Jamie beelined for the exit, toward humidity and the other kind of heat.

Kessler gathered his papers. Trooper Julie Campbell leaned into the doorway. "Whatcha think, Kent? Did he have anything? I didn't get in till the middle of it." Kessler, back toward her, picked up Foster's business card, eyeballed the color mug shot and turned to answer one of his best buddies at the post.

He smiled sheepishly. "He gave me a ton of things to think about. Otherwise, that's about the toughest little banty rooster I ever met. And to think he's…" He shook his head and dropped the card into his chest pocket.

"He's a cute one, though, goodness. Handsomest man I ever laid eyes on! Can you get me a date? You know I go for good-looking blonds, and he's just about my perfect size, age, shape, looks, you name it. That body, those clothes—that face! The way his hair swoops across his forehead? Like he just stepped out of 'The Bold and the Beautiful' and wound up in my state police post. Ooh, gorgeous, come to mama!"

He laughed. Julie rubbed her palms together and grinned lasciviously. She was in perfect profile; pretty face, round but not too broad hips, firm pert breasts stretching out the pockets of her trooper's shirt. A real fantasy girl, a "Women in Uniform" photo-spread for Playboy. He half-expected to see her there someday.

"Throw that one back, Julie. He's good-looking, all right, but he's also Gay. Not exactly your catch of the day."

"Oh, no, you're kidding. He's a queer?" Her face puckered, but only for a moment. "Hey, maybe he just hasn't met the right woman. I might be the one who could show him a thing or two."

"I'll make you a deal. You fill out that FBI questionnaire for me and I'll fix you up with him."

"Ain't no man in the world worth that, sergeant. Fill out your own darn paperwork."

"Well, ya can't blame a guy for trying."

"Or a woman neither," she shot back, disappearing down the hall.

Kessler went to call Dr. Webster to ask about ligature widths, animal tranqs, tan lines, Gay neighborhoods and the sociology of pasta salad.

8

Junior Miss

Jamie drove to the hospital. He put on his cheerful mask, then tossed it away when he saw how good his mother looked. "Hey, what an improvement! Another couple of weeks and you'll be our Junior Miss again. Do you feel as good as you look?"

"A little better. Not much, but maybe a little." She accepted a kiss, smoothed blond hair over her ear.

He liked that, wanted her to take an interest in her appearance. "Shall I call Connie, ask her to come up here in a few days? You'll feel better, like a beauty shop visit."

"The beauty shop comes to me? That would be fun. You think of the nicest things."

"You should get out of that gown, too, put on those satin pajamas I bought you."

"Such a pretty maroon."

"It would help your mood just to feel them on your skin. And every day I'll spritz your jammies with perfume." She giggled. "Let's get back to normal life, honey."

"I want to."

"Did you have lunch yet? Did they have anything that appealed to you?"

"Mashed potatoes. They were out of the box, but they had gravy and I think I ate all of them. Otherwise, not much. Maybe some Jell-O. They have me on a soft diet."

"I'm glad you're eating, you have to build up your strength. But potatoes out of a box, that's ridiculous. I can make real ones at home and bring them in."

"I know." She coughed. He frowned. She was having a hard time clearing her lungs.

He said, "Homemade mashed potatoes, maybe a little hamburger gravy?" Her eyes smiled at that one. Hamburger gravy was repulsive to Jamie, but his mother grew up poor and still liked the foods of her youth. "If there's any food you want that you can't get here, just name it and I'll bring it. How does a banana split sound?"

"Yummy, but too much."

"A strawberry sundae then."

"Okay. Nice."

Behind her, the monitor started to beep again. Nurse Terry was there in ten seconds. She shushed the monitor, started fiddling with an IV line. "I think we got our tubes crossed up here, Thelma," she called out, loud enough to be heard in Peoria. Thelma was not hard of hearing, but Terry was talking, treating her like a person. Jamie liked that. "There, that's better. I see you've got your son here again today."

"Yes, he's been up every day. He's staying at my house," Thelma had to cough again, "and he mowed the yard yesterday."

"Where are you from?" Terry asked him.

"Columbus."

"Indiana?"

"Ohio. It's a big enough city, a million people, that we try not to say what state anymore." He smiled, "But we always have to."

"I have a nephew who goes to Ohio State."

"What does he study?"

"Agronomy. Ohio State's a land-grant college, isn't it?"

"The nation's largest."

"How are you doing, honey?" Terry turned to her patient. "Can I get you anything?"

"A cigarette?"

"Lord, we'd blow up the ICU," Terry chuckled. "I know you want one, but how is that patch working? Didn't the doctor give you a patch?"

"Yes, it's right here," Thelma said, pulling down the shoulder of her gown. "I think it made me sick earlier today, but I'm doing all right now."

"It's that nicotine, it can make you sick if you haven't had any for awhile. But it's the nicotine that got you in here in the first place." Terry said this without being judgmental, which Jamie appreciated.

"I know," Thelma said. Then she made a sad face at her youngest son.

"What's wrong?"

"I'm sleepy already. I don't want to sleep with you here. But I'm going to."

He smiled at her. *Such a strong woman, and here she is, reduced to such dependence.* "Tell you what. I could give you another facial, and you could shut your eyes and drift off while I massage your pretty cheekbones."

"Would you? That would be lovely."

He got the lotion. Terry smiled support at him and left the room. He bent over his mother and rubbed cream in.

It was perfectly innocent, but it reminded him of something; he'd always taken care of her. He didn't want to remember that, but he couldn't help thinking about it. Here he was again, taking care of his mother. Had she ever taken care of him?

It was a stupid thought, of course she had; but it was so long ago. He rubbed in lotion, cooed at her, said smart, funny things, to which she chuckled. When he finished he tossed his arm out and sang, "Oh, There She Is, she's our Junior Miss."

"Here I am," she grimaced and sang along, "some ideal." She coughed, but it was her best laugh yet.

When she fell asleep, he left. *Now what am I going to do about that cop?*

9

Cabin

When Kent Kessler's shift was over, he put everything out of his mind, like a baseball game after the last out; win or lose, it was tomorrow that mattered. That was his policy.

He worked out six nights a week, then he might watch TV, especially his favorite shows, "Home Improvement" reruns and "NYPD Blue," which once had the Bible-thumpers riled over nudity. To him it was just a darn good cop show, who could get excited over the occasional bun shot? But when Rick Schroeder's girlfriend showed her tits, that was definitely worth tuning in for.

Every Friday night Kent drank a beer because his bowling buddies did, but he was just as happy with diet pop. He couldn't dance, so he never went bar-hopping with the guys afterward.

He played his guitar; he volunteered at the Boys and Girls Club, since Little League was over for the summer. He loved the kids, and he hoped he was doing some good. Every Saturday night he studied for his lieutenant's exam.

On weekends he went to football games at Purdue, or in Indianapolis or Chicago, and hung out with jocks he knew. The Boilermakers were good this year, and last year's team won a bowl game. The new quarterback settled right in; if anything, he needed better receivers. The kid was confident, a nice guy who knew who Kent was, before a coach introduced them.

Kent ate supper on Wednesdays and dinner on Sundays with his Mom at the farm; he sang in the little country church choir, as he'd done since he was a kid. He liked to sing, and if the preacher didn't make much sense, so what?

After Sunday dinner Kent rode his horse. Or back at his cabin on the Tippecanoe River, he fished or went rowing, by himself or with anyone he could talk into it.

Since his first Slough visit the day the body was discovered, he'd been looking forward to hunting season. He cleaned his guns in anticipation. He came in second last year in the state police pistol accuracy contest, and headed off to the firing range, vowing not to stop practicing until he won it.

He worked at becoming a better archer, and wanted to bag a deer that way too; taking them down with a rifle was a challenge but not a sport. He donated half his venison to the FoodFinders, they always seemed happy to get it.

He loved hiking and being out in nature, watching birds, bugs, wolves. He'd been to all but three state parks, and made plans to get to the last ones this year, matching hunting seasons with his days off. Maybe he'd go hunting at Willow Slough this fall.

There was also the sandhill crane migration at Jasper-Pulaski in October, where the only shots to take were with his camera. The birds were beautiful to watch as they flocked and fed; then hundreds would take off, soar, big wings flying, legs stretched out behind them, as they led their babies south for the winter. The majestic birds made him feel like part of the life cycle, something larger than himself. He thrilled to them, never missed their flight.

He and the guys got to go water skiing on Lake Shafer for maybe the last time of the season, a glorious afternoon. Kent didn't spill once; everybody else hit the drink two or three times. He loved driving Major Slaughter's speedboat, hair flying, as much as he loved kidding his buddies about falling off the towline.

Kent and Julie sometimes went to a movie with a married couple from the post, but he never went out with her alone, because of office romance syndrome and because he just didn't want that kind of relationship with her. Thought he ought to want it, but knew he didn't. Hoped she understood. Thought she did, but then he just felt bad again. She was a great gal, and if sex was all he wanted it might have worked out; but he didn't love her and never would. She had a crudeness about her that turned him off.

He wanted a son to teach things to, like his Dad taught him. Hoped he'd meet the right girl soon, so they could get started. He wanted love; he wanted a son.

He met women all the time, he had no shortage there. But they never clicked; most of them single mothers, divorcees, and he didn't want some other man's kid, he wanted his own. He wanted a woman he could respect, a professional woman with a career and a goal. But there weren't any women like that, at least none who'd go out with a cop. His looks brought him women he didn't want; his job scared the women he did.

He wanted a family to provide for, even if he did make only 26 grand a year. He still had his baseball money, his family'd be set for life. But he never went out with anyone long enough to dream that far.

His cooking skills were limited to grilling steak or fish, and he tried some new seasonings a trooper's wife gave him. Otherwise he grabbed a lot of fast food.

Heard on the radio that Alan Jackson had a new CD out, so he had to have that. There were so many records he wanted, he had to keep himself from blowing his paycheck.

When he absolutely had to, when he felt bad about asking his mother to do his washing all the time, he went to the laundromat, stuffed jeans, tees, sweats and dress shirts in the machines, hit cold water, dropped in quarters and went for a walk. Even in the most familiar environment, there were always new things to notice.

He ran the sweeper once a month, but drew the line at dusting. He stowed the vacuum in the junk room and congratulated himself for only having four rooms to deal with.

He loved his little cabin; and thought about building a garage for his big new pickup. Bought a $10 book about garages at the hardware store, figured up how much money he'd need for lumber and supplies. Then figured how long it'd take him to save up the money, given the price of lumber these days.

Every night, having pushed his body in the ways he liked, he slept the sleep of the innocent in his BVDs. He got up every day at the crack of dawn, refreshed and optimistic, and drank orange juice out of the carton. After his morning run through the forest, he usually ate cereal for breakfast; but today he got ambitious and fried sausage, scrambled eggs. Melted cheese on the eggs, dumped the skillet onto a plate and ate standing up at the sink, watching a scrawny fawn eat hickory leaves in his yard.

Knew it would starve to death this winter. It was sad, but nature's way.

He told himself he had a full life, that he was lucky. He was healthy, he was happy, he had fun every single day. So why was his life seeming kinda empty right now?

Decided he was just in a slump here lately. Probably because of the case. No crime scene, no evidence, no witnesses? No case.

Might as well get rid of that business card; but he couldn't, it might be evidence. *It's just the case, that's all; the case. What am I thinking about the case for?*

He was off duty. Therefore he wouldn't think about it. If the same feeling hit him at the post, then he'd think about it.

At work he was always so busy he never thought about it.
Then a dream that night scared him to death.

10

Casey

Jamie called his editor. Casey asked about Thelma, heard the news and the emotional tone, sympathized. "Did that brother of yours ever show up?"

"Stone visited 20 minutes tops, the day of the surgery. He's back in Bedford now with his girlfriend-of-the-month. Didn't say a word to me."

"Homophobic pig."

"Listen, Case, there's a story here." Jamie told him about it, the condition of the body, the handsome young cop.

"Ooh baby, just my type," Casey enthused. "Tell me about his nightstick."

"Extremely straight."

"Well, most cops are. How come you get to meet all the studly guys? I'm the one who's into uniforms, and I get stuck here writing the Black Gay Dear Abby."

"And it's the best-read piece in the paper, as you never fail to remind me. But man, I need your help to maintain some professional distance with this guy. Don't be making sexual jokes about him. You get the uniform—I want him out of it."

"He's that attractive?"

"I've never had such a reaction to a man. Casey, I've been around beautiful men my whole life."

Casey said softly, "I can imagine."

"I have to remind myself, as I've done before, that this guy is off limits, to maintain a professional relationship. Then I'll have no problem. But don't tease me about him."

"I won't, then. You're smart to ask for what you need."

"So let's focus on him professionally. He's the wrong cop from the wrong place and that's very significant. But it's only preliminary, till they get an ID."

"Of course."

"Let's test my reasoning. I'll give you some facts, and when you have enough to draw a logical conclusion, say it. First, on the victim: a White guy, he had a good body and worked out regularly; he's very tanned, except for a European bikini."

"He's Gay."

Jamie smiled. "He always wore a watch, even when he sunned himself. He kept his hair fairly short. He ate pasta salad and vegetables for lunch. He had one dental filling, plus a recent root canal."

"Middle-class, business or professional. Gee, that would be different, if he's connected to the others."

"There was also a narrow tanline on his ring finger."

"Like a wedding band? No other rings are that narrow. Either he was married or he had a lover. None of the rest of them did."

"I wonder if it means they'll get a fast ID. On the police officer: he's young, not a line on his face. He's a sergeant."

"He's been promoted quickly. He's a top cop."

"He's a certified crime scene technician, which means massive FBI training and passing a tough exam. He'd qualify as an expert witness in any court in the country. Crime scene techs are usually civilians; this guy's armed. He sought the training to solve crimes."

"He's one of their best detectives."

"Even though he's 75 miles away from the scene, he was assigned to the investigation by Major Slaughter."

"Wow. That has all kinds of implications. You've lobbied Slaughter every month for the last four years. He's getting more active. He's almost assuming…"

"Say it."

"…That it's connected."

"Casey, we've dealt with these cases for so long, we may not realize how unusual they look to the police. If a woman's body is discovered naked, sad as that is, it feels common enough to them. It's rare for a man to be found naked."

"It's evidence of a sexual motive, along with the violence."

"The victim's rectum was dilated."

"Oh, jeez," Casey moaned. "I don't like to think about this."

"You don't have to look at the pictures," Jamie retorted. "Now returning to the officer: he is a serious athlete. He is overpoweringly handsome."

Casey's ears shot up. "Overpoweringly, to you?

"Stay on task. Cop's a handsome young athlete."

"Every Gay man in Indy will talk to him."

"Exactly. Slaughter assigned him to a case he knew I'd get involved in."

Casey mulled that one. "He's using the handsome cop to reel you in?"

"I wouldn't put it past him. The victim was discovered three miles from my boyhood home."

"Jesus, Jamie, be careful!"

"Illogical. Not enough data."

"But that kicker."

"We blew it, man. As in totally."

"With Bobby Hanger one county north, two weeks after you broke the story, there was no question of linkage blindness anymore. He sends you messages, Jamie."

"Remember Bulldog. Two is a coincidence. Three is a pattern. This is only two."

"It remains a distinct possibility. And don't forget that note. This is three, Jamie."

"Logical."

"I don't like it."

"I'm not thrilled either."

"Any chance Kessler could be Gay?"

"Let's examine the data. I handed him my business card with the name of the paper on it, and he wanted to know if that means I'm Gay too."

"Not likely he's Gay. Who else but Gay people work for Gay papers?"

"He called it a lifestyle. He never even noticed the bikini tanline. I had to point it out to him, tell him what it meant."

"He wasn't looking at the guy's ass! Then he has to be Straight."

"Logical. And he's completely indifferent to me."

Casey was the only person in Columbus Jamie could discuss this with. A moment of silence ensued. "No one is indifferent to you, Jamie. He didn't look once? Even Straight guys check you out, I've seen them. The air gets charged, they stand closer and closer to you, wondering what it'd be like to have your dick up their ass."

"Calm down, Casey. He didn't look once. Entirely businesslike. I wasn't always, but he was."

"Well, so much for that. I didn't know they made 'em that Straight."

"Next: Slaughter sends a young, Straight, handsome, expert investigator into the Gay community."

"Cop's mentally flexible? He can work with anybody."

"I like that, Case. I sensed it but you've made it explicit. For now I don't think he discriminates, he volunteered two anti-bias statements. But he sure plays head games. Six times he tried to intimidate me."

"Intimidate the Intimidator? Six times he lost."

"Once he won, but I'm not going to tell you over what."

Casey squealed, "Your height!"

"Fuck you."

"Anytime, Jamie. Anytime at all."

Jamie smiled, changed the subject. "There's a sketch coming, so save space for it."

"What are your next steps?"

"There's not much to do until he gets an ID and confirmation. Help me figure out how to get background on the cop without tipping off my competitors. If the local printjocks hear 'Gay homicides,' they'll ask me, 'What Gay homicides?' I want publicity for the cases, but they can either quote me or do their own damn work. They've given this victim all of three grafs in the agate."

"You're a freelance reporter interested in police/Gay community relations—are the cops getting any better?"

"Save me some space, but prepare an alternative, too. I'm not doing a 'possibly connected' story; it's either hard news or it's no news at all."

"Right. It helps Kessler—not to be macabre, but it helps him to have a fresh corpse in his state for a change."

"God, that's sick. But of course it's true. If Kessler's a hotshot, he may get an ID sooner than usual; he sure wasn't blown away by the serial connection. He knows to look at missing persons out of Indianapolis."

"Unlike the John Doe in Defiance. How much space you gonna need?"

"I doubt an initial story would run more than 500 words, all I've got is a dead guy dropped in my hometown. A dead guy, naked, who wore a European bikini."

"Your hometown? You said something about a Willow—what was it you called it?"

"S-L-O-U-G-H. Old English, this one's an 'oo.' When a snake sheds its skin, the same spelling becomes an 'uff.'"

"Someone ought to reform English before the bough breaks, though slough's enough."

"Very clever!" Jamie chuckled. "My slough's all that remains of the Grand Kankakee Marsh, which was once bigger than the Everglades. Remember Schmidgall and the Kankakee?"

"We put 'Along the Kankakee River' in the dateline. Then there was that kicker. Enough of the logic, Jamie, what if the killer's trying to send you a message? That would be scary. You know he's reading you. Lord, James, maybe he's trying to tell you something."

"Like what? We don't know it's connected yet, and until we do, I can't worry about that."

"Now listen, man: take care of yourself. This can be dangerous. And I ain't writing no more obituaries, child. I am plumb sick o' that. If I have to write 'complications of AIDS' one more time I am gonna lose it."

"Right." They both hated obituaries.

"Good luck with your mom, Jamie. Don't push yourself too hard. Take care of you, too, kid."

"Thanks, Case. I think she's going to be okay."

* * *

That night, with the help of a few drinks, Jamie thought about the friends he'd lost; an activist in Cincinnati; a composer in New York; the national political leader Steve Endean, who made Jamie his first stop in Ohio, only to discover that Casey was Black, handsome and had an apartment nearby. And Tom Stoddard, whose looks, brains and TV skills made him the Great Gay Hope, till he got sick. Jamie wondered how many people he knew at Gay Men's Health Crisis were still alive.

He thought of Kelvin, and Aaron Haney, and a young man dumped in a slough. He cried for his beloved Rick, whom he would never get over.

Then his sweet, smart, formidable Thelma, source of life, whose strength of personality created him in grandiose humility; and finally, for the longest time, he cried for himself, the hardest sobs of all, exhausting him, cutting his abs anew, cutting his heart, with a vision of spurting, ineffectual blood; saving no one.

Hours later, the prairie's dawn was objectively beautiful, but he could not be consoled by it. He went to sleep finally, angry and depressed, unable to stop anything or be done with anything.

11

Slaughter

Nighttime. He covered it up well, but Kent Kessler was in maximum disturbance.

He stood straight, in pressed khakis and a crisp blue oxford-cloth shirt his mother had ironed; he got off the elevator at the top, 11th floor. He swiped his smart card, looked into the security camera.

The door hummed, he opened it and stepped into a deserted corridor. He waited until he heard the door click shut behind him. Then he made his way past empty cubicles, a secretarial pool with screen-saving monitors, toward a light at the end right office. On the left was a door with a name plate: Office of the Superintendent, Col. Jackson R. Potts, Indiana State Police.

He rapped lightly on the door of the Deputy Superintendent for Investigations. "Come in, Kent," a bass voice boomed. Major George F. Slaughter was standing, back to his visitor, gazing out walls of windows to the left and in front of his immaculate desk. Beyond him, night lights burned at Market Square Arena, the City-County Building, the Hoosier Dome and Monument Circle. The new Conseco Fieldhouse had half a roof.

Slaughter could make out the Kennedy-King Memorial, sculptures formed from melted-down guns turned in by citizens. He coordinated ISP's role in the collection drive; the artwork gave him much satisfaction.

Who in Indianapolis could forget that night in 1968? He'd been a rookie on patrol when the news came in about Dr. King, high alert, reports of looting in other cities. And there was the slain president's brother Bobby, campaigning in Indiana for president and against the war; but screwing that, preventing a riot, being human with the people, announcing the murder, mourning with a sea of Black faces, American faces, his words lifting up hope for a better future by his own tragic, courageous example.

Only to be shot down himself in California weeks later. With a handgun.

And they shall beat their swords into ploughshares. And they shall make war no more. The sculpture made Slaughter damn proud.

A high-intensity desk lamp was the room's only illumination. Kent waited, noticing flags of the U.S. and Indiana in stands on either side of a carved etagere. On the wall were photos of the deputy chief with athletes, beauty queens, a famous native rock star, Republican and Democratic presidents.

Slaughter turned finally, held out an arm in greeting, motioned to a chair. He wore a perfectly-tailored burgundy blazer, gray slacks, pink dress shirt open at the thick neck. He was only 5'11", but his 215 pounds looked ready for a barroom brawl.

"Can I offer you something to drink?"

"Whatever you're having, chief."

Slaughter opened a door in the etagere, pulled out two glasses, a silver ice bucket, a liter of chilled water, a bottle of Glenlivet. For his sergeant, a tiny splash of brown liquid over ice, with plenty of water. For himself, two fingers of neat Scotch.

"Thank you, sir." Kent sipped gingerly.

Slaughter redirected the lamp to eliminate glare, settled into his black leather swivel chair. He reached into a drawer, withdrew an Arturo

Fuente cigar, waved it in Kent's direction. Kent shook his head. Slaughter waited until the first cloud of smoke climbed toward the ceiling. "You wanted to talk, son."

"Yes, sir."

"The strangulation case?" Kent nodded. "I thought so. Tell me about it."

"I had a visitor two days ago, chief. It shook me up a little bit."

Slaughter waited, studying his smoke.

"A young man came in, he'd made an appointment to see me. He's a reporter."

"Who is he with?"

"A Gay paper in Columbus, Ohio."

Slaughter nodded, rubbing his cigar back and forth between his thumb and two fingers.

Kent said, "I've barely gotten started, and all of a sudden Brad Pitt's quizzing me about hyoid bones."

Slaughter laughed. "Jamie Foster of The Ohio Gay Times."

"Yes, sir."

"He does get around. Go on."

"I'm not sure how to handle him, sir."

"What's the problem, Kent?"

"I'm not even sure, sir. He's very knowledgable, knows exactly what he's doing. But something doesn't feel right. I got the idea he's obsessed with these cases, very determined, very… what? Dangerous, almost." Kent chuckled slightly. "But he's just this little guy, near-sighted as a maple tree. He's pushy as all heck, but I checked him out, sir. Before I knew who my chief witness is, in walks my chief witness. But man, he's pressure. He can blow the mercury out of a barometer."

"You can handle pressure. Mr. Foster's the confidential informant I mentioned, for our friends in Ohio."

"I know, but I almost don't want to work with him. I mean, I do, but I don't. He's extremely bright and well-informed, of course I want to work with him. So why do I hesitate? I can't figure it out."

"I see." Slaughter took another pull on his cigar, carefully deposited ash in a gleaming onyx ashtray. He gazed again at the curl of smoke he was making. "Because he's Gay, I take it."

Kent looked down at his hands, folded in his lap like a schoolboy's, then back up at his mentor. "I guess so, chief." Slaughter looked him sharply in the eye. "Yes, sir. That's the reason. Because he's Gay." Kent couldn't believe his voice rose so high.

"You told me you weren't prejudiced."

"I ain't, that's the truth. I just never met nobody like him before."

"Good. I need you to stay open-minded."

"I am, sir. Up to now, anyway."

"What's wrong with him, to you? What makes him difficult to deal with?"

Kent sighed. "He ain't at all what I expected. I didn't know such a thing was possible. He's… sir, he's all guy."

"Indeed. What were you expecting, son?"

"This sounds terrible, but… a sissyboy, I guess. Not a guy, aggressive and all. First thing out of his mouth, he wanted to know why I had the case when it ain't Lafayette's jurisdiction. Right to the heart of things. I tried to put him off, but he didn't buy it for a minute. I almost lost control of my own interview."

"I've heard he's quite aggressive. Is there something else?"

Kent put his hands on his knees, looked to his left and then his right for an answer. He stood, walked over to the bank of windows where he'd found Slaughter. The chief heard him sigh three or four times. "Yes, there's something else."

"Take your time, son." Slaughter shaped his ash into a perfect cone.

"If what Blaney at Indy P.D. tells me is true, Jamie is close. He lacks a few cards, but he's holding an ace we don't have. He's got a pipeline to the killer in that paper of his. What happens if he gets too close? We're dealing with a very successful killer here."

"The young man is quite vulnerable. But he's not so naive as he once was."

"Naive? He ain't naive at all, sir. I mean, hyoid bones? Animal tranqs? In one interview he constructs a whole scenario on the victim—and I bet he's right."

"Once he was naive and obsessed. Now he is skillful and committed. So perhaps he knows how vulnerable he is." Slaughter adjusted a miniature death mask, crooked on its little pole; remembered the artist who presented it to him in Nairobi.

Kent turned around, leaned over the desk. "Exactly. He's committed. But chief, he can't know what he's in for. That body was dumped a mile from his home town. Why?"

Slaughter read the face, reached up, clasped his junior officer's shoulder briefly. "But he may lead you to your killer, son."

Kent's shoulders slumped, he looked down at the desktop. "I know. But a Gay reporter who broke this story, looking like he looks, he'd make a great target to a Gay killer who dilates his victims' rectums."

That got under even Slaughter's thick skin.

Kent sat. "Chief, I don't know if I can do it. I want to, but…"

Slaughter waited, then finished for him. "The rest of you doesn't want to be responsible."

"Right."

"Doesn't want to put him at risk."

"Right."

"Doesn't want to work closely with a Gay man. Or be seen doing so by other officers."

"That too. Jeez, I'm gonna take some ragging. That's okay, though. Let 'em rag."

"Doesn't want, in short, to take down a killer who's eluded us for fourteen years and twelve, no thirteen murders. Is that correct, sergeant?"

Kent looked up, searched Slaughter's face, which seemed disembodied now, surrounded only by blackness. A cold chill crawled down Kent's back.

The chief was challenging him; so his emotions changed. "No sir, I do want that. In the worst way. He's taken out too many people. We've got to stop him, sir. I'll catch the dude."

Slaughter leaned back out of the light. A red ember glowed in the dark. In his commanding voice, not quite matter of fact: "Then catch him, Kent. Put the son of a bitch out of commission for the rest of his miserable life. If you have to use your blond reporter to do it, then use him. Without pity and without remorse."

He let the words sink in. Then his arm reached for the Scotch on the desk, and his face, visible again, sipped for two seconds, savoring. His adam's apple rose and fell. Kent saw a slight smile of satisfaction on his face. "Foster is willing to take the risk. So should you."

Kent frowned, looked away again. "Yes, sir."

Slaughter got to his feet, came around, sat on a corner of the desk. "Listen, Kent, let's talk man to man. Not senior officer, not junior, just man to man."

Kent nodded. This was exactly what he needed.

"It is no reflection whatsoever on your masculinity to associate with this witness. In fact, it's the most macho thing you can do." Kent memorized it. "If other officers can't see that, well, they weren't appointed Task Force Commander, were they?" Slaughter paused, saw the resolute body language he was looking for. "I don't have to tell you how important this is, Kent. It's the highest priority of this office."

He jabbed Kent's shoulder. "I selected you for this job because you are young, smart, talented and flexible. You have shown me in a few short years that you can deal effectively with a wide range of people. You are a skilled investigator. You think on your feet. You stay objective. You are honest; I respect that. You are not some overfed trooper ripping off contraband from the evidence room till he can collect his pension and start double-dipping. Kent, you are the kind of investigator this department needs desperately. And you know, I don't say 'needs' lightly. I don't say 'desperately' to any son of a bitch."

Kent nodded, cheered by profane praise.

"You've never shown me that you were intimidated by anyone before."

"Intimidated, chief?" Kent sputtered. "I ain't intimidated by no killer."

"It isn't the killer who intimidates you."

Kent thought. *Who do you mean, then?*

Oh. "He's just a little squirt, though. A hundred and seventy-five pounds. He's a matchstick." He laughed, but too nervously. Slaughter bored into him. Kent had to break the contact. "You're right," he said finally. "Intimidated. Oh, man, can you believe that?"

Slaughter moved back to his chair, smoked. "Enlist him, Kent. He's both Gay and a guy. Maybe that's what these cases need. It's all right to feel some fear about the Gay thing, but don't let yourself be ruled by it. Or else the killer wins. And I won't have that, Kent. I won't have that in my department."

Kent's heart beat faster.

"Show me what you can do, son. Be cautious, but be bold."

"Yes, sir. I will, sir."

"You have to play this string out, wherever it leads. Including right smack dab into the Gay community. You promised me you could do that without judging people. That's what I've seen tonight."

"I want to, believe me. It's just… Him and me sparred a lot, but the guy's so impressive. And he could get killed. Now that I know him—I have to prevent it is all."

"It's a tough case. That's why I put you on it. Do you know how many officers I cannot assign to a Gay case?"

"Most, huh? That's what Jamie said too."

"Most, as in 99%," Slaughter spat. "Just hitch up your trousers like you do with the ladies and don't think about it. You've got to have cooperation from the Gay community, and help just walked through your door."

"I know. Man, do I need a tour guide. Jamie's great at it, though."

"Otherwise it's just police work, which you're darn good at. Don't focus on the sex. Work the homicide."

"Thank you, chief. This was just a mental toughness issue, huh?"

"Bound to happen when dealing with the unknown; you're handling it effectively. Kent, you did the right thing to call me. It took guts. I've been there, staring down the barrel, and I know. Call me again if you need to, anytime. What we say will never leave this room. I'm proud of you, son."

"Thank you for this assignment, chief. And the talking-to. I appreciate your confidence. I won't let you down." Kent rose to go.

"One other thing. Call him Foster. Use only his last name when we talk."

"Sir?"

Slaughter looked into the future, tried to empty himself. "Objectify him, sergeant; depersonalize him. He's not Brad Pitt, he's a witness, a confidential informant. A thing. We objectify CI's. When you talk about him, think about him, it's Foster. Nothing but Foster."

"Sure, chief, right. Foster."

"Befriend him, but also objectify him. He's only a means to an end. Use him; it's what he wants." Slaughter glanced at his cigar. "Otherwise his reputation is he intimidates everyone; you're not the first officer who's told me that. It's his stock in trade. He uses it to get whatever he wants. I suppose that's the mark of a good reporter, barreling in, Gay flag flying, asking about neck bones. All but daring you to make something of it. Even if he is a little squirt." Slaughter smiled slightly; Jamie was very well-built, but "squirt" was still apt.

Kent grunted. "He's something else, all right."

"Not your typical Gay man. Not that I know what one is anymore, Kent. Times are changing, that's for sure. It's a new world and we've got to change with it."

"Takes all kinds, I guess. Thank you, chief. You're fantastic. I'll bring you the killer, sir. I swear it."

"Do that, son." Slaughter's eye found his peace memorial, nodded at it slowly. "Bring me his head on a goddamn platter."

* * *

Kent was halfway back to Lafayette before he realized he hadn't told Slaughter that Jamie—*Foster*—was blond. *But heck, the chief knows everything about everybody.* He put it out of his mind.

So doom set in; massive guilt. He drove, desperate, clueless, praying hard.

The chief was right; the only solution was to get the killer's head on a plate.

* * *

Slaughter poured himself a second drink and returned to his meditation spot.

It was a high-risk strategy, putting this young sergeant on the case. To get to a Gay killer, he'd assigned an investigator so handsome he was a Gay man's dream. With him and Jamie working together, doors would swing open, they'd get access, entrée—an ideal pairing, fast, efficient, potentially lethal.

It wasn't just looks; Kent was the best he had. He could also impose police control on Jamie, who was tougher and more independent than ever. *He now criticizes his Quincy County friends in print. And he's hammered the FBI, rightly so.*

But the relationship had to work. Jamie wasn't the problem, he'd even work with ignorant rednecks, as Bulldog Sauer proved. The potential problem was Kent. If he couldn't control his feelings, all hell might break loose. Not only could it put Jamie in harm's way, a new round of killings seemed sure to follow; while the department tried to pick up the pieces at square one. Again.

Slaughter searched his mind one more time, his own devil's advocate. The key to it all was how Kent handled homosexuality, handled Jamie, handled himself.

Slaughter flashed back to the Academy five years ago: Kent a scrub-faced boy scout, eager, easy to train. Educated, smart, dedicated, competitive as hell; with physical skills the others could only marvel at. He could make his body do anything he wanted; he only had to be shown a move once. An excellent shot; by graduation almost as good with a baton as Slaughter himself, and Slaughter was a master.

The faculty had to back off to keep Kent from knowing how good he could be. Yet he was never cocky, only confident, eager to learn more. A man's man, as popular with the men as the women; which meant damn popular.

Yet a caring guy, not macho-stupid when someone hurt. Great with kids. He knew when to let his compassion come out, and when not to.

With that personality, plus some political seasoning, he could go anywhere in policing. He could take over the department one day.

But not till after I'm done with it, boy. Slaughter smiled at his Scotch.

A Little League coach; a regular church-goer, but not the rigid kind. *Hell, they say he even sings in the choir.* Slaughter shook his head, picturing his macho toughguy in a Methodist choir robe, singing angelically. He did enjoy the young man.

Twenty minutes later, his drink killed, his cigar stubbed out, he turned and noticed his desk lamp. The troops all thought he used it to convey power. That made him smile. They didn't know he used it to watch their eyes undetected, easy as pie.

He switched off the light, heard his office door lock behind him, went for a late dinner. Kessler would stay Commander for the duration.

12

foster.com

"What are you doing to keep yourself busy, son?" Thelma asked, between bites of her strawberry sundae. "I hate for you to be cooped up here all the time. I'm awfully glad you're here, I'm just feeling guilty, I guess." She muted the mini-TV set. For the first time since her surgery she had the tube on. TV was progress, normalcy.

Jamie patted her shoulder. Today was the first day she was sitting up in bed, too. "No guilt. Actually it's rather nice to be back home. I'd forgotten how scenic it is here. I did the recycling, then went down to Fort Ouiatenon and just stood on the riverbank with huge, century-old maple trees, watching the river flow by. It was such a peaceful feeling, to think of the Weas and Miamis and French fur traders. The one constant over the centuries is the river. We take it for granted, but it's why this city is here."

"Mmm, this tastes good. I'm glad you got the recycling done."

"And I keep in touch with the office. Casey and Louie send you their best. Louie always asks if you're still in intensive care. He's afraid he'll have to spring for a bouquet, and he knows they're not allowed in ICU."

"Now, James," his mother smiled. "I do hate to take you away from your work. Are you able to get anything done here? Did you bring your…" She was interrupted by a coughing spell. This wasn't her usual smoker's cough, but a deep, rattly hack and wheeze. And it didn't seem to do her any good.

When the spasm was over she sagged deeper into her pillow for a few seconds of rest. Then she opened her eyes, found Jamie and finished, "Your laptop?"

"Sure, Mom, I don't go anywhere without my equipment. Don't you remember, I put it on the kitchen table when I came in Saturday afternoon? Then we decided it should go in the computer room."

"Oh. That's right, we did. Are you getting any writing done?"

Jamie hadn't told her about the body at the Slough. But now she was asking. "Well, there is a possible story here, but I'm not doing anything on it right now. You're the story I'm here for," he smiled, filling up her ice water from the pitcher, fully aware that hospital patients with visitors have an endless supply of ice water.

"There's nothing more boring than sitting around a hospital room waiting on somebody. I want you to have fun while you're here, and I think for you, working is kind of having fun, isn't it?"

Yeah, Ma, chasing serial killers is my idea of a good time. But she was right; working for him was fun. "I don't even know if there's a story in it."

She leaned on her elbow to shift position, then looked at her youngest son. "If I weren't stuck here, what would you be doing?"

Damn, a direct question. "Just talking to some cops," he shrugged. "The usual."

She was silent for a moment, mulling this over. "Where's the body?"

Jamie didn't want to concern her with this, but she'd trapped him. "Willow Slough, believe it or not."

"It's not Pauline, is it?" she chuckled and coughed. "I used to have dreams about putting Pauline there."

He was suddenly six years old again. Pauline was the Morocco town slut; she'd had an affair with Jamie's father. When Thelma found out—in a small town one always finds out—Ronald promised to give Pauline up. But he was much better at making promises than keeping them. "My mother, the murderess." He grinned at the unlikelihood.

"In the right circumstances, anyone's capable of it."

"Anyone's capable of the fantasy. Like you, they're not capable of the crime. This is an unidentified man. We don't know whether there's any connection. Without an ID there's no way to know where he's from, and that's a major step in figuring out who killed him. So don't worry about it. There's no story yet."

"Strangled?"

"Isn't it about time for your medication or something? Aren't they going to try to get you to sit up in a chair tomorrow?"

"Yeah, they said something about it, but I don't know whether I'm up to it. I suppose they'll decide when I'm ready."

"And you won't have a thing to say about it," he predicted.

"I pay them to know when I'm ready."

She set aside her sundae, looked tired again. Jamie asked, "Do you want a nap?"

"Well, I was kinda thinking about it."

"I don't want to tire you out."

"Here I'm not doing a durn thing and you'd think I'd been working an eight-hour shift."

"You are, Mother. Recovering from surgery is a full-time job. Now it's break time."

She smiled, "This Bud's for me."

Jamie was struck for the 9000th time by the irony of illness. Rick was never more loving than after he came down with the disease. Here was Thelma, chipper and intelligent and sick. "Take your break, dear. I'll be back this evening."

"Okay." She sighed. "Jamie?" He moved to the edge of her bed. "You can go on up there if you need to. I don't have to have you here all the time. It's only an hour's drive."

He held her hand in both of his, kissed her fingers. "If and when I need to, we'll talk about it. I don't need to today, and I probably won't in the future. It's probably not connected." After a moment he said, "I love you, Mother."

"I love you too, James. You're my baby."

He had long ago given up protesting this term. "See you later." And he left his mother in intensive care.

It's been days. Shouldn't she be in med-surg by now?

He drove to the Union-Gazette office downtown, found a parking place across from St. John's, where he had been an altar boy for years, and headed into the old four-story building on Ferry Street. He tried to visualize 19th Century people, horses and wagons crossing the Wabash River by ferry.

He stopped at the front desk, gave his name and asked for Bob Schwartz. Schwartz's was the first byline he'd learned as a paperboy. In the '80s, Schwartz was the political writer, now he was executive editor. Jamie figured he must be ancient; two decades ago his columns had pictured a very large man with a very bald head.

Soon Jamie was cleared to go up. His watch read 2:05 p.m.—late enough that the afternoon edition would be on the streets already. Then he remembered the U-G was a morning paper now. Two o'clock was prime time, he couldn't take more than five minutes. He made his way through the newsroom, an open arrangement crammed with desks, strewn papers and brown-screened monitors with yellow squiggles full of tomorrow's copy. Jamie was glad The Times used Macintoshes, the elegant machines.

A harried young man walked towards him, reading without looking up. Jamie touched the reporter's shoulder and the guy looked up quizzically. "Schwartz?" The young man pointed to a glass-enclosed office, then went back to reading.

Jamie knocked. "Enter," a voice barked.

Jamie stuck his head in. "Mr. Schwartz, I'm Jamie Foster. I only need five minutes."

"Come in," the editor said, rising slightly from his desk and motioning to a chair. "What can I do for you?"

Schwartz looked just as old as Jamie pictured him, and yet no older than the photo atop his column 20 years ago. *Lost his hair early.* "We've met before, chief, but there's no reason you should remember me. I'm from West Lafayette, I used to carry this paper in grade school and junior high."

"I know you," Schwartz smiled. "We're surrounded by talent in this town, but farmboy prodigies still stand out. What are you doing now?"

Jamie was taken aback; the last time he'd been called "farmboy prodigy" was 14 years ago in the Union-Gazette. "I'm Midwest correspondent for The Clarion, the national Gay and Lesbian newsmagazine. I'm based in Chicago. I'm working on a piece on police/Gay community relations: Are they getting any better? I thought I'd look in on conditions here, specifically the state police, in a college town that just passed some slight version of a human rights ordinance."

"Right. What do you want to know?"

"I've talked to some of the officers at the post—a Sergeant Kent Kessler, an Officer Campbell, a few others. They seem young, not my picture from years ago of the middle-aged, barrel-chested trooper. Do we have a new breed of cop here? Younger, well-educated?"

"Talk to Karen Wilson on the police beat, but yeah, there's something to it." Schwartz mopped his face with a handkerchief. The air conditioning seemed fine to Jamie, but Schwartz was sweating like a Hampshire hog. "Troopers can't afford to stay in state service, the pay hasn't kept up. Worst-paid troopers in the Midwest. We've got trooper families on food stamps."

"That's shocking. I'm sure you've covered the story."

"The minute they can, they hire on as sheriff's deputies at ten grand more a year. The attrition rate is terrible, richer counties get excellent, experienced officers without having to pay for training. Meanwhile poor counties depend entirely on the state police.

"Kessler's a farmboy prodigy too. Chief detective in this post. He's from 20 miles south of town, we covered him all through high school, multi-sport athlete, three times Mr. Baseball. Made it to the Major Leagues, a brief but spectacular career with the Atlanta Braves, then knocked out of the World Series by tragic, career-ending injury."

"Indeed." Jamie joined the hog club. His sweat popped out.

"Front page, above the fold when he got hurt. Broken back, ruptured spleen. All of Indiana mourned for him. Every sports store in town still sells his jersey."

"What an accomplished man. Then to become a state trooper, how unusual."

"Talk to Elliott in sports if you want the rest. Everyone says Kessler's a great trooper. Did the lion's share of tracking a big drug case in White County a year ago, before the DEA came in and tried to steal the credit. He works the major felonies, the youngest faculty member at the state police academy. Wilson would know, but he's supposedly a crack interviewer, the 'good cop' who works on the wife or girlfriend. They say with his looks he could get a confession out of Dillinger's mother. And that old broad didn't talk to nobody."

Schwartz indulged himself with laughter, pulled a fax out of the machine, glanced at it, tossed it away.

"Kill the ladies with kindness?"

"But tough on the suspects, physical courage, plays by the rules, he's the whole package. Talk to Wilson."

"I will, chief. One other thing. Are any of the local agencies doing any kind of Gay sensitivity training? Police brutality has a long history in the Gay community. Are any of the departments doing anything to prevent it?"

Schwartz scratched his pate, looked blank for a moment. "I don't think that's been tried anywhere in the state. The Gays spent so much time and energy on these ordinances here the last few years, I don't think they had time for that. Plus the state hate crimes bill. God, they got creamed on that one. Indiana likes hating Gays."

"So I've noticed. Is Wilson in right now?"

Schwartz stood, looked out his glass box and pointed her out; a young, plain-looking brunette in a long floral dress. She couldn't have looked dowdier if she came from Lafayette, Indiana. "Thanks a lot," Jamie said, extending his hand. "You've been a big help, chief. I read the U-G every chance I get. Your Web page is great, I read Purdue sports on it constantly."

"Thanks, we work at it." Schwartz held the door open for him. "One other thing. You any good, boy genius?"

"Genius isn't potential, it's accomplishment." Jamie trotted out his modest ones: "Columbia J-School. GLMA Best Investigative Reporter in the nation, twice. AP citations, a Pulitzer finalist last year. Hold off on the genius till I win it."

"Pulitzer finalist, wow. How'd you like to move back to Lafayette?"

"Chief, that's a fate worse than death."

"No, it isn't. If you ever come back here, call me. You should go mainstream."

"Thanks, I started out mainstream in Columbus, Ohio, but the company and the product were anti-Gay, and I quit. The news industry discriminates, it doesn't have the guts to take on the bigots of the day. The L.A. Times had no Black reporters to cover the Watts riots; Martin Luther King was 'the militant Negro leader' until the day he was shot. I won't go into hiding to do my job."

"Man, you're quite forceful. Don't forget, boy wonder, the verb makes the sentence, and the lead makes the story."

"Will do, chief, thanks. I've admired you for years." Then Jamie went to shanghai Wilson on the police beat, thrilled that Schwartz would ask about mainstream. Jamie wanted good mainstream desperately. *If I could pull Casey in too, we'd make a dynamite team.*

His heroes were Woodward and Bernstein, in an era when people despised reporters.

* * *

On the sidewalk, he flipped past baseball stats to make one last Wilson entry in his notebook: *Has overwhelming hots for Kessler.* "Get in line, honey."

When he got back to his mother's, there was a message on the phone machine. "Mr. Foster? This is Sgt. Kessler. Call me when you come in, if you would, please. I'll be here until 4:30. Or leave a message. Thanks."

"All right, hotshot, but you're not going to co-opt me. You figure you'll get over because you're handsome and I'm Gay. No way, fella. To me you're just one more cop ready to beat my faggot brains in."

He found a can of diet cola and downed it in six gulps. He decided to check his mother's mail and take out the garbage, and let El Hunko stew for awhile.

Meanwhile Kessler was playing 52-card pickup. "Detective Sauer, did you ever hear of someone named Jamie Foster? Says he's a reporter in Columbus, Ohio."

"Sergeant, call me Bulldog. I'm an expert on Jamie Foster. Think of him as a rose. Looks real pretty, smells good, but watch out for the thorns or you'll get pricked."

"Is he reliable?"

"He's invaluable. But wear your garden gloves."

As they discussed animal tranquilizers, Kent tapped Jamie's—*Foster's*—social security number into his computer, found out all sorts of interesting things: make and model of vehicles (Acura and a Jag), arrest record (clean, one speeding ticket), credit rating (perfect). Everything checked out.

Kent tried ohiogaytimes.com, then Meet the Staff; blond with a swoop, same as the business card. The bio had Jamie getting a master's degree six years ago. He'd have been 20 years old. Kent whistled, "Whee-oo."

He tried jamiefoster.com and jamesrfoster.com; no match. He made one last try with foster.com—and what he saw knocked him back in his chair.

He sat there staring at pictures of Jamie. Kent hit "More Photos" a dozen times, till he realized there were endless pictures of Jamie in designer suits, clubwear, sportswear, jackets, swim trunks, underwear, workout gear, jock straps, no frontal nudity but nothing at all. The home page claimed he was one of the most downloaded men on the Internet.

His pictures were for sale, with posters, videos, calendars, the clothes themselves. There were also links to sites for other models, famous designers, home accessories, exclusive retailers, artworks, click here for Neiman-Marcus, click there for Russell Simmons. At 40, Cindy Crawford was now a "Classic Beauty." It was all a subsidiary of infashion.com, a major, publicly-traded Web e-tailer that advertised on TV.

The guy's body was big business. No wonder he drove luxury cars.

Kent went back to Jamie's home page, hit "Best Sellers." The #1 picture showed him standing teenaged and naked, drenched, head down and hair in his eyes; perfectly ripped muscularity, only a wadded-up pair of wet Calvin jeans to cover his crotch.

Several downloads were free, but the shirtless stuff cost twenty bucks. Posters went for $40, signed posters $75. Posters with his butt cost a hundred. Kent picked a random underwear ad in case it was evidence. Tapped in his credit card number and e-mail address, got the $20 download and printed it out. With just one glance he held it up to his chest so no one else could see; found a file folder, slipped it inside and carried it out to his vehicle. He couldn't risk putting it in the case file, letting another trooper stumble upon it. He'd have to keep it at home.

Bulldog wasn't the expert he thought he was. Kent's CI led a double life. No wonder Jamie knew about European bikinis. What else did he know about?

13

Advocate

"Sergeant, this is Jamie Foster, returning your call."

"Thanks. How's your mom?"

Here we go, trying to cozy up already by taking an interest. "She's fine. What's up?"

"If she's in the hospital she's not so fine. Can I ask what the problem is?"

Don't ever lie to a cop. "Aneurysm surgery."

"That's a pretty big operation, an uncle of mine had it. I bet your mom's awful glad you're here for her right now."

"Was there a reason you called, sergeant?"

Kessler changed voices. "Well, we got an ID."

"Indianapolis?"

"Yeah, I just got the fax. It's him, all right."

"Great. That's fast work for a decomposing body. Congratulations, good job."

"It's IPD's doing. I talked to your Lt. Phil Blaney there in the grand jury's office. He got right on it."

"Phil's a good man. I'm glad you're working together."

"He says I should talk to you some more, that you know more than anyone about these strangulations." Jamie could smell the butter coming. "And I could save a lot of time just talking to you. So what do you say? I know your mom's your first priority, but I'd like to get together and compare notes."

Jamie couldn't find anything wrong with the mutual-using game. "Sure. What do you want to know?"

"No, not over the phone, man. Let's get together somewhere."

Jamie stalled. *I'm not going back to that state police post.* "I've got to be at the hospital at seven, and my Mom has things she wants me to take care of here."

"I could swing by later tonight, if that's all right. What would be a good time? Let's get together this evening after the hospital. Why don't I bring a pizza? We could talk there at your house, no other ears around."

Don't let this cop buy you stuff. Don't let this cop look at your mother's things, snooping around over pizza.

But Jamie didn't have any better ideas. "Hey, you gotta eat," Kessler coaxed.

"I don't want you going to the trouble." Jamie knew as soon as he said it that it was lame.

"No trouble!" Kessler boomed. "The best pizza in town's there on Salisbury Street. Whaddya say?" He pronounced it Sal's Berry.

Jamie cast about, then knew he was licked. "Okay," he mumbled, and gave the address.

"I'll be there at 8:30 sharp." Jamie took it as a warning.

*　　　*　　　*

Thelma muted Pat and Vanna as soon as she saw him. But she didn't look well.

Jamie kissed her forehead, noticed her fever had returned. "Do you hurt?"

"Yes. I do. And they won't do anything about it."

"Tell me."

"They say," she coughed again, "they can't give me but so much pain medication, that if they give me more, my blood pressure will go way down again. Yes. I hurt."

Jamie swung into action. "Maybe I should talk to them. Sometimes it helps to have an advocate, someone who's not the patient but is on the patient's side."

She looked doubtful. She also looked afraid. "Maybe. But don't, you know...you hafta be polite."

Jamie looked grim and also light. "Oh, I'll be polite. I know how. I've done this before, remember?"

She nodded, thinking of how much Rick suffered, how strong Jamie was for him.

"They have to balance the pain meds and the blood pressure. That's what the science is all about."

"They're afraid I'll be addicted."

"They're always afraid people will be addicted. But you and I know better. You are not a drug-taker."

"I won't even take an aspirin unless I really, really need it."

"So meanwhile you don't have to be in pain. I'll talk to them." Jamie picked up her hand. "I'll be polite. I'll ask for information. I'll find out how they see the problem."

Thelma squeezed back, but it wasn't with her golf grip. "That might be a good idea."

*   *   *

At 9:20 he hit the sidewalk, walking briskly past the last smokers, the scaffolds and piles of bricks. Kessler just had to wait. Jamie'd left a message at the post, didn't feel the least bit guilty.

After an hour's gentle, in-control but very assertive harangue, he finally got Sandra the Mennonite to phone the anesthesiologist, who was in charge of post-op pain meds in this hospital instead of the surgeon, a policy Jamie had never encountered before. A pharmacist delivered a new pain shot, explaining that they'd had to compound the substance by hand. Thelma liked hearing that. Jamie waited till she was asleep before he left.

He drove out to the Bypass, turned north and sped up the hill. He was angry and filled with pride and stressed out; he had run interference with doctors and nurses and social workers and fucking hospital administrators so many times with Rick, and before that for buddies with AIDS, he knew exactly how to get what he wanted. It was a crock that people in pain had to have an advocate to make the system meet their needs. *What if I hadn't been there?*

He crossed the river. It was the loneliest stretch of Bypass at night, between the two cities. A tear spilled out as he crested the hill to the West Side. He let it roll as far as it wanted to, which was barely to the bridge of his nose.

A huge red pickup, complete with running lights across the roof, sat on the left side of Thelma's driveway. Its rear window showed a gun rack. Chrome custom wheels gleamed extravagantly. It was called a Ford F-250, and it even had some kind of cow-catcher thing on the front. *Testosterone on wheels.* Jamie checked; no Confederate flag. He was a little proud of the guy for that.

He punched the garage-door opener and eased the Acura next to Thelma's GrandAm. Kessler swung down from his truck, smiling and holding a pizza box. Jamie got out of his car, left the garage door up, said hello and headed toward the front door, not the garage entrance to the family room. "I got your message, how's your mom, is she all right?"

"She's in a lot of pain tonight. We got her a shot. She's resting." Jamie unlocked the front door and hit a light switch in the living room.

The cop was inside the house. "Table," Jamie said, pointing to the dining area. He didn't want Kessler in the private rooms; this was to be formal. "Be right back." He headed to the main bath to get himself together.

Soon he was back, through to the kitchen without turning on lights, taking two Corelle dinner plates down from the cupboard, finding forks and a sharp knife in the drawer below. He placed them on the glass cocktail table in front of the living room couch, carefully picked up his mother's porcelain birds to set them out of danger. He hadn't figured out how to bring in napkins without turning on a light in the kitchen, because he'd have to turn on a light to find them. He didn't grow up in this house, so he didn't always know where things were.

She had to sell his favorite house to pay off his father after the second divorce.

Kessler stood tensely in the middle of the living room. "Listen, I'd better go. You're upset. I have no right to put you through this when your mom's laid up."

Jamie remembered a light over the oven. "It's all right, sergeant," he called over his shoulder as he found napkins, tried to remember where the salt and pepper shakers were. He skipped them. "Let's get this over with. I'm ready to work." He retrieved the pizza box and set it in the middle of the coffee table. "Have a seat. I'll nuke Mr. Pizza. I'm very sorry if you had to wait."

Then he noticed something surprising, Kessler's taste in clothes. People dress for their peer group, to say "I'm one of us." Kessler did not dress like an off-duty Hoosier cop; his peers were top athletes. He wore expensive jeans, a short-sleeved pullover with MCI Worldcom Challenge noted tastefully on the chest; one sleeve had a small Nike swoop. He also wore tiny white socks, marketed to women as anklets and to men as joggers, just enough cloth to protect his feet. He probably sported a gold chain under the pullover—a fine athlete who quietly looked like one.

"No, Jamie, I'm sorry to trouble you. The case can wait, it'll still be there tomorrow. I wanted this to be easier for you, not harder. I'll go."

"I'm quite all right," Jamie said firmly. "We can talk. It's important."

But Kessler headed toward the door, and Jamie realized he felt relieved. He turned on the outside spots, gazed at the night before turning to face the trooper. Kessler looked down at his very white Nikes, then back at his subject. "If there's one thing I've learned in police work, it's this. Nothing should interfere with family." He stumbled, "Or, or friends."

Jamie registered the amendment in spite of himself.

The cop raised a big hand, placed it awkwardly on his host's shoulder for 1.5 seconds, said softly, "Jamie? Please call me if I can help." Jamie looked up at empathic brown eyes; then Kessler was gone. Big chrome wheels flashed away into the night.

Jamie sat motionless for an hour in a dark living room as the last pizza smells died. He didn't eat. The hospital didn't call.

14

Slough

Jamie arrived at ICU the next day. He'd left a message for Kessler, but he was out, so Jamie came in early. Thelma was finishing lunch. "Hi," she said, much more energetically than yesterday. She was even wearing her new satin pajamas.

"How are you doing, sweetie?" he asked, bending to kiss her. "You look good. Did you get some rest last night?"

She swallowed a bite of bread. "Yes. That shot really helped."

"Great." He spritzed her jammies with perfume.

She smiled and sniffed the scent. "Nice. I feel much better today."

"Wonderful. Now what's this?" he teased. "Bread, butter and sugar?"

"See how I am?" she grinned.

He hadn't seen bread, butter and sugar since, well, since he was a kid and she fed it to him. "Comfort food," he pronounced it.

"It's the only thing that tastes good," she said, sprinkling sweetness onto her Wonder bread.

"Well, then it's what you shall have, madame," he said grandly, waving his arm in a headwaiter's flourish.

"That and Jell-O. I've had more Jell-O in the last few days."

"It's good for your stomach," he opined.

"I can keep it down, anyway." She munched her bread, took two more bites and set it on her tray. "Here, will you get rid of this? I'm done, I think." He removed the tray, busied himself with straightening the room. "How is your story coming?"

What should he say to this? "Well, there may be a story, but I haven't had a chance to get the updates."

"Are you going up there? To Willow Slough?" He stopped in mid-motion, looked at her. She saw his concern. "You could go up there. I don't know if you'll find anything, but you won't know till you get there."

"I don't want another incident like last night."

"Last night was bad. I'm glad you were here, that's what got things taken care of. But I feel so much better today."

"I'm not going anywhere till you're out of here."

"Jamie, look around you. This is ICU. They provide wonderful care, they just don't know me like you do."

"Hospitals are always paranoid about drug addiction."

"And your father was a prime example of why. But I'm doing better. They had me sitting up in a chair today."

"Really? How was it? Was the transfer hard?" Transfer was a Rick word, moving a sick body from bed to chair, wheelchair to car seat.

"Yes, but I got through it. They helped me. I sat up. They're even talking about moving me to med-surg."

"Terrific. I wish I'd been here to see you sitting up."

"It was about 10:00. I only lasted 20 minutes. Then I asked if I could go back to bed. I think I fell asleep, and then it was lunchtime, and then you came."

"Who'd have thought your dance card would be so full?"

"That's what I'm saying. My calendar's full, and yours is empty. This is your story, you've worked hard on it and won all those awards. It's okay if you want to take off for an afternoon. You know where to find me when you get back."

"Maybe tomorrow."

"The weatherman said it's going to rain tomorrow. Chance of thunderstorms 80%. You don't want to be tramping around that slough muck in a thunderstorm."

"Are you trying to get rid of me?"

"Jamie, I'm trying to be proud of you."

What could he do but give her a hug?

*   *   *

Kent found he had e-mail from Foster, a canned but friendly note thanking him for his purchase, reminding him of the other great links through infashion.com, and listing his upcoming appearances—in Europe, this magazine, that fashion show, a TV interview "where I'll practice my Italian. Hope with me that when I mean to say, 'The pasta's divine and all the women well-dressed,' it doesn't come out, 'The pesto's dead and your Grandma's naked.'"

He offered an easy way to unsubscribe and a free download of a head shot. Kent printed it out and added it to the case file.

They hooked up by phone and arranged to go to the Slough together. Nothing was said about e-mail. Jamie didn't know and Kent wasn't telling.

*   *   *

Sgt. Kessler eased the patrol car away from the last stoplight in West Lafayette, and Jamie settled back for the hourlong trip. He was glad they were taking the old road and not the interstate. He stowed a small paper bag in front of him.

On their right, a woman made her way from a blue pole barn toward a white frame house. She looked up as they passed, in case she would recognize the car. But she turned away. Farming and farm culture—agriculture—began one foot outside the great college town.

The corn was tall and green; in a month it would yellow and dry. Corn and beans filled the prairie as far as the eye could see, the landscape punctuated by silos here, a stand of trees there, protecting a farmhouse, marking a stream. There were a lot of trees—it was Indiana, not Kansas—but before the White man it was all forest and prairie grasses. Then those gave way to feeding people. The land was beautiful to Jamie; it was where he was from, and he was glad to be back home again, even under the circumstances.

The college town was home, too, but not in quite the same way. There's a difference between home when you're 13 and home when you're six.

Towns whizzed by without their having to slow down. Every town had a grain elevator, even if it no longer had much else. They were all on the main highway once, before it was relocated to skirt them. Then the interstate came through with zero tolerance for towns. "Oh, look," Jamie said, pointing. "Cattails."

"A strange brown wildflower, unique to the wetlands."

"I love the tall, wavy leaves. Cattails symbolize home to me. I remember as a kid picking some to take to my grandmother. She thanked me and put them in a vase, but maybe she was thinking, Lord, what do I need with a bunch of weeds?"

Kessler smiled, "I'm from south of here. When I was a kid, if we traveled two towns away from home, we'd gone pretty far. Now we're so mobile, all these towns are pretty much the same, the distance is nothing."

A memory came back to Jamie, one of the few good ones about Ronald. "I remember a scorching summer night when we lived in Morocco. I was eight. My father got inspired and piled us all into the car to go for ice cream in Kentland. We had to go there if we wanted ice cream at night, there was no place in Morocco to buy it. So off we went—an exciting, amazing extravagance, all that way just for ice cream—a whole 15 miles down the road. It was expensive, the gasoline and all, just for a treat? My parents had nothing extra to spend. What's funny is, I had never been to Kentland before. I'd been to Chicago, he'd take us to White Sox games, but I'd never been to the county seat. And here I am, telling you about it 20 years later, it's such a clear memory. The Amazing Ice Cream Excursion. You'd have thought we were going to Saudi Arabia."

Kessler laughed. "That's how we lived then. Now it's nothing for me to zip from one end of the state to the other, then back home again by nightfall."

"And the towns do look alike. It's just that some are more prosperous than others."

"Your dad liked the White Sox?"

"And the Indians. He saw Larry Doby play."

Kessler looked at him sharply. "Is that a fact."

But Jamie was scared of discussing sports, much less baseball, with this man, so he searched for a way to broaden the topic. "I grew up watching the Cubs, I've been to Wrigley many times. It's the best ballpark I've ever been to, so easy to strike up a conversation. 'The friendly confines.' Midwesterners are friendly." If the topic stretched any broader it would collapse.

"Who do you think will win the home run derby this year, McGwire or Sosa?"

"I hope it's Slammin' Sammy, in honor of Jack Brickhouse and Harry Caray; but Sammy says Mark's the man, so I believe him. I hope they both break Maris's record, if only so his triumph can finally be honored. New York mistreated Roger Maris for the sole reason that he wasn't Babe Ruth. No city's more hometown provincial than New York."

"Who's your favorite player? One all-timer, one current."

Jamie thought. "The greatest player in history changed America itself." Kessler nodded. His grandfather proudly played against the man.

"Jackie Robinson stood for human rights and dignity. Among active players, Tim Virdon."

Kessler looked away. "A pitcher? Most people go for home run hitters."

"He's smart. He looks sensitive. He doesn't just hurl the ball, he pitches. He can win a ballgame all by himself. He's even good at the plate." Not only that, he was cute.

"Ol' Spot. Nice choices."

"I don't know much about the game," Jamie apologized, sorry that he'd ever mentioned baseball, because Tim Virdon won Cy Young Awards for the Atlanta Braves.

"What makes you a sports fan?"

"My brother Danny; plus I'm a competitor. All reporters are."

"What's a home run in journalism?"

"The exclusive, the scoop."

"You get many?"

"Yes, actually. Rather a surprising number."

"Home run hitter, man, I believe it."

"It's my job to put the issue in play."

"Issue of the paper, you mean?"

"No, the Gay and Lesbian civil rights issue."

"Oh."

So much for that. They got to Fowler and were hit by the traffic light. Jamie went to work. "Do you want to start with the background or the latest victim?"

"Both, maybe. You know the area around the Slough, so I'm hoping you'll help navigate some of those country roads; last time a trooper from Rensselaer drove me over, and it was jog and turn and zig-zag and double back, confusing."

"I need to hear about the victim, what IPD has come up with."

"I need your help. Jamie, I don't know a thing about Gay life. And I don't know that Glenn Ferguson—that was his name, Glenn Archer

Ferguson—was Gay, but it was a male roommate, Gary Tompkins, who filed the missing person on him."

Jamie dug out his notebook. "I'll find out."

"You told me he had a roommate. You told me his life story. Guess where he lived, a high-rise downtown called Riley Towers. Exactly where you predicted; it's got a pool. You asked what sport he played. I guessed hoops. Know who he worked for, as a marketing manager? The Pacers."

Jamie was quiet. Kessler said, "Man, I'm impressed. You got me the match. I was talking to your guy Lt. Blaney in Indy, told him your reasoning, and he said, Wait, a guy just disappeared from Riley Towers. He faxed me Mr. Ferguson's photo and that was it. It wasn't a computer search, Jamie, it was you knowing what to look for and Lt. Blaney staying up to date on missing persons. I want both you guys on my team."

"If I can help you I will."

"You're fantastic at what you do. I can't put it into words, but… thanks."

"Your words are kind, but most of it's simply knowing the Gay community."

"It's also knowing how to investigate a homicide. Man, can't many civilians do that."

"I wish I couldn't."

"I suppose I could ask the roommate if Mr. Ferguson was Gay, but even then it's hearsay. I'm not going up to his parents and say, 'By the way, was your murdered son homosexual?' They're already in mourning, they don't need that."

"If he had parents. If they even knew he was Gay. You don't need a witness's statement, his sexual orientation can be established by his possessions, a single Gay-related object. A magazine. A tanline."

"See? I could use your Gay expertise."

"IPD could use some openly-Gay cops. So could the state police."

Kessler frowned, a guy like that'd be hounded out in one minute flat. Jamie had to be kidding. "How would that work?"

Jamie tried to tailor message to audience. "Gay people come to the attention of police a fair amount; any group as large as we are does. Mostly we're the victims of crime, but sometimes we're the criminals. I once uncovered a drag queen credit card ring, stealing people's cards to buy their dresses and pay the rent. How do you understand them? Were they primarily drag queens—or primarily thieves?"

Kessler thought. "Thieves, huh? I get it."

"Gay and Lesbian cops would have an easier time solving that crime; familiar with drag queens, looking only for criminal activity regardless of what the perps wear. Who cares what they wear, they're criminals."

"Huh. Yeah, you're right."

"Other times we're murdered by a hustler, Gay-bashed by a football team, shot by the Ku Klux Klan. And sometimes we get a first-hand look at police brutality. Although it's always other cops who do that."

"Well, now, I thought we'd gotten through that one, kinda."

"We did, sergeant." Jamie went further. "I believe in you. You told me Gay people are citizens."

"They are." Kessler drove. "Other cops don't treat you like you are?"

"Some do, some don't. Some are lifesavers, some are thugs."

"We don't recruit in heaven, Jamie. We're stuck with human beings."

"So the issue is education and training."

"And paychecks. What's the worst you've ever seen out of cops?"

"A few years ago a Lesbian serial killer was captured down in Florida. She was born in Ohio, so I called the arresting officer, told him our interest because I was following someone killing Gay men. He said, What's wrong with that?"

Kessler's stomach turned over. "That had to hurt."

"I didn't use the quote; maybe he was slap-happy after all he'd been through. It was talk, it wasn't behavior; maybe he treats us fairly in person. Damn right it hurt."

Kessler sighed, empathized as best he could; unable to transcend his categories, wondering why they were still so darn important, when people are people.

Jamie said, "Police have a long way to go to reflect the society around them. Police abuse has happened to me personally; I've written a ton of scoops about it. The worst ended up on 'Larry King Live,' with the pictures to prove it. The guy made a vaguely disrespectful remark to a cop hassling him about jaywalking at midnight, with zero traffic. After they beat him he asked for a doctor; he was HIV-positive, so the cops cooked up a story that he tried to bite them. He ended up in the hospital with a charge of attempted murder. But you can't get AIDS from saliva and they didn't have any teeth marks. The charge fell apart in court."

"Things sure can escalate quick. All that from jaywalking? What idiots."

"Crossing the street twenty yards from the Gay bar they saw him walk out of."

"You got him off?"

"It takes public opinion to sway a judge when it's a cop's word versus the defendant's."

"Jamie, I'm absolutely opposed to police brutality. The blue wall of silence crumbles the minute I hear about it. No coverups, no excuses. It's criminal behavior, same as any other; except worse, it's police. I don't tolerate it. Don't accuse me of tolerating it."

"I don't! I admire your position tremendously. I wish more officers felt that way."

"They do, more and more of us every day. I know you didn't accuse me, sorry. Why should I put my butt on the line to protect some criminal with a badge? Get him out, convict him, fire him, before he becomes a complete menace to society. You know how most officers feel about Rodney King? Besides that King was a known lawbreaker? We'd like to do to the L.A. SO's—sheriff's officers—what they did to Mr. King. Not to hurt 'em, with foam rubber bats maybe. Then just pound the crap out of 'em. It's not just the image, it's what it means. That police officers are out of control, beating people's heads in. That ain't the way it is." Kessler looked at a dozen head of cattle trying to escape the heat. "Except sometimes it is. Then the media screams about it a million times. No wonder there's no respect for authority."

"If authority were more respectable, more people would look up to it."

"I know. I'm doing my best, man."

"I know you are. I respect you."

"Do you hate cops?"

"No! I admire good cops, like Bulldog, who tells me you've been checking up on me." They glanced at each other. "It's okay, I understand. I've done the same thing to you at the Union-Gazette."

"Nothing wrong with that, I guess."

"They speak very highly of you. They also say there isn't a police agency in the state that's undergone training in Gay and Lesbian issues."

"Well, gee, do they do that elsewhere?"

"I helped train the Cincinnati Police Division, 980 officers including the chief. They now advertise their job openings in my paper."

"I've never heard of doing that. What was your basic message?"

"It was about change; that they can't do an adequate job of law enforcement if they don't adjust to changes in society. Things have changed with Gay people. We used to be the out-group, but now we've joined the in-group. So police must redefine their constituents to gain the community's trust and support. We're citizens, just like you said. We can be cops too. Openly-Gay cops and citizens' groups help departments adjust to change. Without them, policing's what it used to be, the most homophobic occupation this side of Fundamentalist TV mouth-foamers."

"Gee. I've just been trained." They smiled. "There's no excuse for prejudice. Put me to the test, you'll see. What do you think my job is, but the enforcement of everybody's civil rights?"

"How beautifully said. Thank you, sergeant." Jamie made his own doe-eyes out the window. "Let's make this less personal. I know you've got the world's toughest job. Most officers I've met are excellent human beings."

"Thank you. You're right."

"They've impressed me with their professionalism, logic and commitment. But I've also come across incompetence, corruption and bigotry."

"So have I." *God, Jamie, I try so hard.*

"Teach me about policing, sergeant. I don't know what officers face, only what my community's experience is."

"Teach me your community, man. I don't know what it's like to be a minority."

"You're in a macho business. It has to be, but that scares us. We're very aware that some male cops can't even accept women officers. Women victims relate better to them, and women officers can be incredibly courageous; yet most departments tolerate sexism, even encourage it. There's no excuse for institutional bias in an armed force. As for racism..." Jamie shrugged in frustration. "My editor is Black, and he gets stopped all the time for driving 35 in a 35 mile an hour zone. Why should he be stigmatized? He's a brilliant man, but he's scared to buy a new car for fear he'll be labeled a drug dealer."

"DWB, Driving While Black. It happened to a friend of mine, a 15-year trooper driving home in his own suburb. He sued the local cops and got a nice little payday."

"I've heard of that story. I didn't know he was your friend."

"Profiling comes from inadequate leadership, Jamie, inadequate training. You can't escape the demographics of who commits crimes, it's basically the poor. What's rotten about America is we stick it to Blacks and Latinos so we've always got poor."

A cop who critiqued what's rotten about America made Jamie say, "Sergeant, I trust you with my civil rights."

"Thank you. I'll treat 'em right."

"Policing is so difficult. I admire people who do it well."

"It's twice as hard when you get blue-collar guys with backward attitudes taking blue-collar jobs. Who else'd trade their butt for mere health insurance?"

"How succinct. Thank you for educating me, this really helps."

"Want to cut the crime rate? Hire smarter cops—and pay 'em."

"Man, you should run for Congress."

"What a cool thing to say. But also crazed, 'cause I hate politics. Hate it, hate it."

"Proves how smart you are," Jamie grinned.

"Tell me what police work looks like from a reporter's point of view."

"It's tough to get a story right, it requires so much shading. Most reporters take what a cop says as the gospel truth—partly so cops will keep talking to them. But no source should be treated unquestioningly. With these cases I've seen great police work, and I've seen pathetic. So the right approach is one of mutual respect leavened by an ability to doubt. We're both supposed to be professional doubters, that's why we checked up on each other. We're both supposed to rely on fact."

"Man, you media guys can hurt us. One little allegation and it's off to the races."

"But a lot goes on that we never hear about. We only find 1% of police brutality, ineptitude, discrimination and corruption."

"Then the whole force gets labeled."

"That's where we're wrong; reporters have to shade things, it's not the whole force, it's just these alleged bad apples. But why should society have to wait on police to get their act together? They scream long and hard that they're the good guys. They have one of the most sophisticated public relations teams in all of society. L.A.P.D. has its own TV show, complete with sportswear and memorabilia for sale."

"L.A.'s next door to Hollywood. Of course, they never show you their screwups."

"I know it varies by individual and department. I'm glad you believe as you do. The system is the problem and the individual officer can't do much. But when will the system ever change? Only when it's forced to, by civilian outrage. That's where the media come in."

"Well, I can see that. Go on. Gay cops too? Someday?"

"Dozens of cities have them right now. If there were openly-Gay and -Lesbian cops here, you wouldn't be stuck when you have a Gay-related crime, wondering how you get such basic information as 'Was Glenn Ferguson Gay?' Everyone on the force would know who the Gay cops were, you could simply go to them for help. Instead you have to reinvent the wheel, victims of your own institutionalized homophobia."

"I don't want that, Jamie. That's why I've got you along."

"In the Quincy County cases, I actually had Bulldog come to me after I broke that story and ask me to help them find the Gay bars in Indianapolis. Which was slightly hilarious. Quincy's a rural county, what do their cops know from Gay? I don't blame them, they did the best they could. And it worked, so give them credit. I handed him a map of the bars in two seconds. We publish it in my newspaper every week.

"It was ridiculous that they had to rely on me. But there was nobody at Indy PD they could go to and say, 'We need a list of all the Gay bars in town.' An openly-Gay or -Lesbian cop could have given them a list in those same two seconds, complete with directions, descriptions, the manager's name. But the Quincy cops were afraid even to ask the question of IPD—that's the point. Crack dealers, murderers, rapists, child molesters, they could all discuss without a thought. But law-abiding Gay people, cops couldn't even bring up the subject with each other! That's wrong. It's continually impeded the investigation."

"It sure would slow things down, huh?"

"They're scared for their own heterosexual reputations. Afraid that if they are seen as comfortable talking **about** Gay people, everyone labels them as Gay themselves. Which is precisely the time your commanding officers need to impose discipline and non-discrimination. But they don't. They're just as afraid of the Big Lie as everyone else. It's mass hysteria. It's bigoted and entrenched, needless and unfair."

"What happened with Quincy?"

"There are only two investigators in the whole county, Bulldog and his partner Barry Hickman. Before they knew I existed, they wracked their brains trying to figure out how to locate the Gay bars in Indy. They asked themselves, whom do we know in Cavendish, their county seat, who might be Gay? Then how do we approach that person?

"They finally went to the town barber and said, 'We need your help, we don't know if you're Gay and believe us we don't care, we absolutely don't care; but if you are or know someone who is, we're trying to get a list of those bars over there.'" Jamie chuckled, he had the quote down perfectly. "Their approach was fine, but they had to rely on the town barber, for God's sake. What if they guessed wrong and he threw them out on their butts? To whom would they have gone next? Or would they have gone to anyone?"

"Most likely gone back with their tails between their legs."

"Trying to track a serial killer by going to the town barber! Is this efficiency or what?" Jamie chuckled bitterly. "But they lucked out, guessed right, he's Gay. He gave them a five-year old bar guide—a book that lists all the Gay businesses in the country. So they traveled to all the addresses listed for Indianapolis, but most of them were parking lots by then, bars go in and out of business all the time. They ended up finding only two open, and there are a dozen Gay bars in town. They went on a Sunday night, when Indiana has blue laws!"

They both laughed at that one. "Those poor guys. It's tough when an officer has to cross a state line. The laws change, you lose jurisdiction."

"The admirable thing was they took time away from their families and went on their day off. Nobody paid them. Yes, I poke fun at them, but I respect them too."

"That comes through, Jamie. You're very fair, the way you talk. I hear it."

"Please don't accuse me of hating cops. You guys are heroes, you're lifesavers."

"Sorry." *We're both so paranoid.*

"The two bars they found weren't the ones they wanted; one of them was Lesbian, which didn't exactly help. And they didn't know enough just to ask a bartender, 'Where else do Gay people go in this town?' Instead they drove all the way back home, having wasted their time. If it weren't for homophobia and ignorance they'd have saved themselves months. Not to mention what happened once they got to the one men's bar they did find."

"Tell me." They were approaching Kentland now, and there was another stoplight ahead. It would be the last one. Kessler eyed the turnoff to his grandmother's house.

"Hickman and Bulldog were playing good cop/bad cop; Hickman's the bad guy. He goes swaggering into this bar, 'cop' written all over him, 'Straight' written all over him, ready to smash a few heads together. Naturally everyone runs for cover. But what's really going on is **he's** afraid—afraid some guy is going to come on to him. So he's macho'd to the max, but it's so absurd. You should see Barry Hickman. He's a good investigator, a friend—but he's an ugly bumpkin who won't get propositioned in at least one thousand years. He wore Roebucks jeans to a Gay bar!"

Kessler chuckled. "Still, going to a Gay bar would make me nervous too. I wouldn't know what to expect."

"Expect the same thing you'd find in a Straight bar, sergeant—people quietly boozing it up with their friends."

That option had never occurred to him.

Jamie said, "Hickman was projecting Straight men's fantasies toward women onto Gay men. The stereotypical Straight man's attitude of 'If it moves, fuck it.' As if Gay men are that out of control." He fumed out the window. "I've never in my life put the moves on a Straight man. I never wanted to. I never will."

"Okay. That's good, I guess. No imposing yourself. I respect that."

"Journalism's just as bound up in stereotypes; look at Gays in the military. Sam Nunn tramped through bunks on a submarine talking darkly about 'close quarters,' and reporters didn't even think about challenging him, they broadcast stereotypes as if it's dangerous for Straight men to be around us. The danger is to us, not to you!"

"Gee." Kessler tried to think of whether he'd ever heard of a Gay-on-Straight assault.

"We know the harassment women go through; 95% of Gay men decided long ago never to do that to anyone else."

"Whew," Kessler said, as the turnoff to Ade and Brook passed by. The gas station that used to be on the corner was long gone. "You've thought a lot about this stuff."

"I've had to. These murders would have been solved a decade ago if they'd had a Gay cop. The last twelve victims have died for lack of a Gay cop."

Kessler stared straight ahead.

"I respect the job you do. Bulldog, Hickman, Blaney are doing their level best, and I'm terribly grateful. But overall police performance has been pathetic, ignorant, underfunded and bigoted, except for them. With them it's just been ignorant and underfunded. Which has played into the killer's hands repeatedly. No wonder he's never been caught. Police homophobia keeps him free to kill again."

Kessler's ears burned. "How else have the cops screwed up?"

"Quincy tried to go it alone. Twelve Gay victims, two cops who know nothing about Gay people, and they tried to go it alone."

"Machismo. 'I can handle it, I don't need help.'"

"Quincy's one county west of an organized, visible, sophisticated Gay community in Dayton. But did they talk to Gay leaders there? No. They talked to the town barber."

Thus did Kessler understand how deep a hole he was in.

"Small, rural counties lack the resources. When the Son of Sam killed six women in New York, 200 detectives were assigned. Here, with twice as many victims but no money or publicity, you are the sole fulltime investigator. If you don't find anything in a week or two, we'll go right back to zero."

"It ain't fair, Jamie. I feel what you're saying."

"The social status of the victims matters profoundly. If Gay people were high on the list, these cases would have been solved. As it is, we're only slightly ahead of prostitutes and migrant workers. So we have to take responsibility for changing that. It's significant that these murders happened in Indiana. If they happened in Ohio, I'd have 50,000 people marching on police headquarters."

Kessler thought. "If it's done right, a march like that could really help."

"So now you've got this case, sergeant, and you're all alone. To solve it, don't be ruled by ignorance and fear. Seize the advantage from the killer. If you've got a question about Gay life, please, just ask me. Don't beat around the bush like your macho quotient will automatically go down. Open your mouth and ask. It takes a lot to offend me. No, we don't all wear dresses. And please don't worry about your terminology. For the duration, whatever your question, I guarantee I've heard it a thousand times before. I won't put you down for it—I'll praise you for asking."

A video of Slaughter's face, cigar smoke and shadows played in Kessler's mind. "Why did you become a reporter?"

"It's what I've wanted to do all my life. It's the most important public service I can perform."

"Why a Gay paper, then? You're smart enough you could work for anyone."

"Because someone's got to organize the migrant workers and whores."

"Yeah. Good for you."

"I'm trained for mainstream journalism; I'd love to return to it. But I've learned the lesson of Ronald Reagan and AIDS: Gay media save lives. Silent, Straight media take them—including Glenn Archer Ferguson's."

"Man, you're powerful."

"I don't have nearly enough power, sergeant. Turn left on State Road 114, the next major intersection. Or as major as these intersections get. That blinking light."

Kessler eased up on his speed and said, "Jamie, if we're gonna work together, do you suppose you could call me Kent instead of sergeant all the time?"

Blood and embarassment rushed to Jamie's head; so did pleasure somewhere. Still, he didn't want to offend, officers like to be properly addressed; and he didn't want to get in too deep either, investing hope in some damn police officer. That was how Bulldog co-opted him years ago.

"Sure, Kent. Whatever you like. But I don't want to be your friend." They both started at that harshness. "I'm sorry, I'm sure you're a worthy friend. But I'm not here to be co-opted or manipulated or to make friends. I'm here to do a job. Nothing gets in the way of that. Nothing. Same for me as for you. You're the cop, I'm the CI."

"All right. If that's how you feel."

There was an old green directional sign, Willow Slough Fish and Game Area, with an arrow pointing west. The sign for Morocco was down, hit by a car and bent double. It was rusted, looked like it'd been down for years. No one in Morocco bothered to call the highway department. No one in Morocco figured it would do any good.

15

Quicksand

They came to a town of a thousand souls. "So this is Morocco. Don't look nothin' like Humphrey Bogart."

Jamie chuckled, "The town founder's trademark was his Morocco leather boots. He impressed the Hoosiers, but that joker wasn't a world traveler, he organized a town on top of a swamp. He was good at the con."

Kessler laughed. "Thieving land speculators."

"Oh, there's my grade school. I used to play on that ballfield—softball, every day during recess. I led off my first Little League game there."

"Gee. Gay guys play Little League?"

Jamie was shocked; but he'd just promised not to be. "We're raised Straight. Which shows you it's not in the raising. Gay guys play Big League."

"Not openly, they sure don't."

Jamie's eyes blazed, "Then whose fault is that?"

Kessler couldn't quite bring himself to answer.

"Oh, there's our house. Goodness, it's tiny."

"We're practically out of town already. We didn't miss a sign somewhere, did we? We're going to be in Illinois any minute. This ain't how the other trooper came."

"There's a gravel road up ahead, on the state line. My grandfather took great delight in driving up the middle of it—'half the car's in Illinois, and the other half's in Indiana.' That's entertainment in a place like this. He always drove up the middle. He'd have shared the road if someone else wanted some, but no one ever did."

Especially after a tense moment, there is something about sharing a laugh; it promotes forgiveness.

They found State Line Road, turned north. Kessler realized he was driving smack up the middle. Jamie said, "It's paved now. I'm surprised Indiana paved both lanes."

They found the entrance to the Slough. Everything was quiet, the place was deserted. Jamie couldn't see the geese yet, but he could hear them, "Aranh! Aranh! Aranh!" Kessler parked, they entered the administration building. Officer Suzanne Myers was a compact woman, maybe 36, with long brown hair tied up to fit under a ranger's hat, and generous hips that filled her pants. She was a law enforcement officer too, her uniform brown, her weapons a citation and a rifle. Her smile was immediate and friendly. "Sergeant Kessler. I see you found us all right."

Kessler removed his hat, they shook heartily. "Officer Myers, I brought me a native scout who's familiar with this here territory. Otherwise I don't think I'd have made it. This is Jamie Foster. We're partners on this case."

Jamie shook hands too. "I'm originally from Morocco, but I'm not much of a scout. I can claim to have once nearly drowned here, though." She gave him a quizzical look. "Ice skating. Thin ice. I fell through, but they got me out. Damn near froze to death." It occurred to him that maybe that was why he was so averse to cold; he was afraid of dying because of it.

"Happens every year or so," she warned. "We post signs about the ice, but some folks think they know more about it than we do."

"There didn't used to be signs—or conservation officers. Anyway, I do all my ice skating now at the mall. I don't ever want to be that cold again."

Kessler began, "Thank you for taking the time to see us today. I know you're supposed to be off at three, but this was the soonest I could make it and I really appreciate it."

She frowned, "No problem, glad to help. That poor guy, did you ever find out who he was?"

"Yes. His name was Glenn Ferguson. He was from Indianapolis."

"What was he doing up here?"

"That's what we'd like to know."

"Where do we start?"

"At the scene. Tell my partner what you saw."

She reached for her hat and grabbed a windbreaker. They headed outside, Myers locking the door behind her, and crossed a parking lot. Her vehicle, a late model black and silver pickup, sported a World Wildlife Fund sticker and a ribbon decal, pink and red, for breast cancer and AIDS. "Over here, in the camping area," she said, leading the way. "Site 16." They passed a children's fishing pond, picnic tables, in-ground cooking pits, gravel trails to the campground, a comfort station. "This way."

Jamie hadn't noticed the wind before, but a stiff breeze off the lake whistled through his ears. The air was warm, but the wind made his hair stand up. He wished he had a windbreaker and a hat.

They came to picnic table 16, and Myers stopped, pointing again. "Right there, behind the woodpile." Jamie dug out his camera, took a photo.

Behind the pile he noticed a shimmer on the ground that marked the sloughland. There was nothing between the end of the gravel trail and the stacks of tree branches. "He didn't have to drag the body. He just drove right up to it. Popped the trunk and dropped his load."

"Easy as pie," Kessler agreed.

They walked thirty more feet to the woodpile. "He was right back here," Myers said, pointing and turning away.

Jamie took another shot with the wide angle lens, then changed to the zoom. "What caused you to come back here? This isn't your busy season. Were there any campers back here?"

"No, fall's when it happens here, hunting season. We'll be busy in another two months, trying to keep the hunters from shooting each other. Summers, there are a few people boating on the lake, fishermen mostly, very few campers. The campers usually go back yonder, as far as they can get from the entrance, so's they feel like they're escaping from the world. The road that way ends in a turnaround, and there's fencing to keep people out of the woods. Course, the wetlands will stop them if they try to go further, unless they've got waders. Take one wrong step and you're in muck to your ankles just like that."

"Quicksand," Jamie said. "River muck."

"Course, it's not the dangerous kind like you see on those old TV Westerns. There's plenty of trees and vegetation you can grab a-holt of, and the soil composition is such that it doesn't suck you in very far. But it scares outsiders real quick, and they learn to steer clear of it. Didja ever see 'The Big Valley?' Miss Barbara Stanwyck got sucked into the sand once. She'd'a took one look at this stuff and thumbed her nose at it."

"Insufficient scenery to chew." Jamie and Officer Myers laughed at each other.

"I checked the records like you asked," she said to Kessler, "and we haven't had any campers here a'tall since late July—registered ones, anyways, and see, it's all voluntary—and the last ones signed into a couple of sites in the 60's, back yonder like I said. And that was over a month ago." Jamie took a photo of them conversing.

"There isn't a gate at the main entrance," he said. "So there's nothing to keep people out of here at nighttime?"

"No. There's not much population in this county, and what there is is figuring out how to move to Layfayette or Portage or Chicaga." Jamie's father had pronounced the big city that way too, when he wanted to annoy Thelma—or Jamie. "We're so isolated, we don't get any tourists to speak of. Hell, there ain't nobody driving 41 anymore except the locals. The folks that live here, the young people need jobs. The farmers that are making it, and not that many of them are anymore, they're too busy to come out here. Or they're too old. There's people in Morocca and Lake Village ain't never been here in their whole lives. And you," she smiled at Kessler, "a state trooper had to have a native scout to even find this joint."

"I coulda found it if I had to," Kessler pouted cutely.

"What brought you back here that day?" Jamie asked.

"Had a load of wood to dump, no other reason. I let down the load, Ralph—that's the other wildlife officer here—he and I were stacking it, and I noticed a lot of squirrels chattering behind us, some big old crows and a couple of Canadas squawking, so I went to see what all the chat was about." She stopped, recoiling at the memory.

Kessler said, "Lunch."

"Chowtime. Welcome to the boofay table. They hadn't started yet, but you could tell they was taking a notion."

"Have mercy," Jamie groaned.

"So I shooed them off and threw a tarp on the body, then I called Rensselaer, and you know the rest."

"A tarp," Jamie frowned. "I suppose you had to."

"Why not a tarp?"

"Disturbed the crime scene perhaps. But you had to protect him from the animals. I appreciate your honoring his humanity."

She looked away. "I never thought of that."

Kessler said, "You did the right thing. Anybody else around here see anything?" He knew the answers but wanted to see if she told her story the same way a second time.

"Who's to see? This is a pretty lonely life. Course, I like it like that, too. That's why I'm here, the woods and the geese and the deer and everything else we got. Humans, them we ain't got. I don't miss 'em."

"And no physical evidence, sergeant?"

"We figured what you said earlier. All he had to do was drive up and pop the trunk. He could have come in late at night, no one to see him, no one to stop him, no one to know."

They surveyed the scene in silence. Kessler said, "Well, shall we go back? There's nothing else here for us to see."

"One more thing," Jamie said. "Officer Myers, tell me about the sloughland here. It's been rainy this month? Is the water higher, more spread out than usual?"

Kessler clarified, "In other words, did he dump him behind the woodpile to hide him, or in the water deliberately, or both?"

"You are from here, aren't you?" she said to Jamie. "You're right, the slough is always changing. We've had moderate rain, a little bit more than usual, one and four-tenths inches since the first of the month, and it's been a relatively wet summer. The slough has been getting wider the past few weeks. Ordinarily, we keep our powder dry—keep our woodpile away from the wetlands, because we burn wood in the fireplace inside in the wintertime. Still, this is a slough, it's bound to change on us. This water has been pretty close to the edge here for a month or so. Ralph and I talked about whether we'd have to move the wood to another location, but it didn't seem that bad. It hasn't changed that much, just slowly creeping up."

The killer seemed to want water, concealment and the ease of offloading.

"Anything else?" she asked. She plainly wanted to go.

"No, no. It's good of you to show us again," Kessler said. "I know it's no fun for you, finding that poor guy. I really appreciate all your extra time, Officer." She liked being addressed that way by a state trooper.

Jamie shook her hand and whispered, "Thanks for the ribbons."

They headed back toward the parking lot. She said, "Someone bags a deer in season, no problem; it's nature's way. They want beavers, we got beavers. Squirrels, pheasants, quail? Just check your calendar. And fish year-round. But don't hunt the humans, dammit. Not in my park."

No one dared to cross Miss Stanwyck, either.

16

Picnic

They sat on a picnic table. Puffy clouds scudded above Lake Murphey as the wind made whitecaps on the water. Willow Slough was lovely in its loneliness.

"I've heard there's a suspect. But I've stayed away from that, I didn't want to fit my facts to a pre-existing theory."

"How logical your approach is. Your job isn't to find some serial specimen, but the killer of Glenn Archer Ferguson."

"Now that it does seem connected, it's time to examine all available data. Do you know anything about their suspect? Who is he?"

"I don't know much. Other people know more." Jamie fiddled with his camera bag. He wanted mug shots of the sergeant, but now wasn't the time.

"Tell me what you know, how you think about him."

This headed onto dangerous ground. *Why should I tell this cop about the phone calls?*

Half a dozen maple seeds had blown off a nearby tree. Jamie picked up a seedpod, turned it over in his fingers, tried flipping it into the water. It pooped out after three feet. "When we were kids we called these whirlybirds."

Kessler picked up a seed and with a sidewise flip, sent it spinning. It landed in the lake thirty feet away like it was supposed to. "We called them helicopters. I wonder how the wing helps the seed take root."

"It doesn't. It disperses the seed beyond the tree's canopy." If Jamie didn't share his information with this cop, he would find out about it soon enough from Bulldog or Blaney. Maybe he already had, and he would never be able to trust Jamie again.

If he did share it, and Kessler misused it somehow, Jamie might end up dead.

He looked at the cop, sailing another maple seed. The sun and breeze made whitecaps on the black waves of his head. He was dazzlingly handsome.

I won't make this decision based on that. I refuse to.

Jamie thought of Aaron Haney, of Kelvin, of Riley Jones—of Glenn Ferguson lying 200 yards away in the muck.

Jamie had no choice. It could be the break that Kelvin needed. *Young and handsome, a miniature Casey.* The trooper had shared a lot of information with him, more than most cops would; Kessler deserved to know everything if he was going to catch the Strangler. "Quincy County has had a suspect for years. Two guys, Tommy Ford and Jerry Lash. They're friends, and there's one other thing. Ford is Roger Schmidgall's ex-lover."

Kessler whistled through his teeth, "Whee-oo!" The screech was unlike any Jamie had ever heard.

"Ford and Schmidgall lived together years ago in Eastwood. One liked blood, the other one hates it. Or so Bulldog's theory goes."

"Eastwood. Sleepy farm town close to Crab Orchard, the Barlow death scene."

"And there's the place they lived together, the home of Dr. Randolph Scott Crum, Schmidgall's sugar daddy."

"Man oh man." Kessler worked on his breathing. "The three of them together?"

"Plus Lash, who didn't live there. He's a more recent Ford associate. But Bulldog suspects him."

"What's a sugar daddy?"

"Older man who pays a younger man for sex. Crum has a long history of that, even before Schmidgall."

"Jeez. This is real sick."

"It's sick because of murder, not their sexual orientation. Remember the drag queen thieves."

"You're right, Jamie, I won't forget. Keep going."

"When Crum was on trial in the Barlow case, Ford drove Crum's sports car around Indianapolis. It's an ongoing relationship."

"So the theory is, there are really three or even four killers here. But only one's ever been convicted."

"And that was probably a bad conviction. Schmidgall's lawyer's still trying to get him off posthumously. She'll never succeed, but if she did, she might take down the whole bunch."

"Donna Quixote? Who does she say did it?"

"Crum paid for Schmidgall's apartment in Chicago where Chuckie Pont was killed. Crum bought the original lawyer. But stick with the apartment. Why would a guy in rural Indiana pay for his boy's apartment in Chicago? He wasn't getting any services out of him."

"Blackmail?"

"Bigtime. Crum was Schmidgall's meal ticket."

"And meanwhile Crum goes free; and these other friends of theirs go free."

"No one's ever officially connected the two sets of murders—the stabbings, allegedly committed by Crum and Schmidgall, who liked to see blood—got off on it—and the strangulations, allegedly committed by Ford and Lash, who aren't into blood. Blood after all is messy, strangulation is more sanitary. Nothing to clean up afterward, no stains to worry about. No DNA to leave behind, no HIV to catch. Just hyoid bones to crush."

"Was there something else about photos, maybe?"

"If Schmidgall was telling the truth, and I firmly believe he was, Crum likes snuff pictures."

"Good Lord." Kessler said it quiet as a pallbearer.

"At Crum's trial, a man testified that twenty years earlier, when he was 15, Crum used to buy him things in exchange for taking nude pictures of him. They never had sex; Crum wanted the pictures. Then Crum moved to Eastwood, met Schmidgall and his lover, moved them in and took pictures of them. Schmidgall did his first stabbing, and Crum paid the victim's medical bills. Schmidgall went on to kill 21 young men and Crum got him an apartment in Chicago—in part to get rid of him, because the cops were closing in. When Schmidgall was charged with the Pont boy's dismemberment, Crum paid for his lawyer. Along the way did he lose interest in pictures of naked young men?"

"You make a compelling case. Snuff pictures. Now that's a sick man."

"He's worse than that. He's evil."

"I'm amazed you compiled all this information."

"Now let's see if we can tie it to your case. When Roger turned on his old man and accused him of directing the Barlow murder like a filmmaker, Crum went on trial and Ford, the ex-lover, was seen driving Crum's car. What's that about? Was he taking advantage of Crum? Doing him a favor? Or doing himself a favor? This other set of strangulations had started up, all the victims from Ford's home city, all discovered in rural areas out of town. The killer had to drive there to dump the bodies. He didn't transport them with Crum's sports car."

"He used his own. Which he was happy to park once he got access to Crum's. What does Ford drive?"

"An old, beat-up, brown Toyota." Geese scattered, regrouped on a nearby sandbar. Jamie shivered. The wind was cold now. "Ford knows he's a target. But his full name has never been in the papers."

"Why not?"

"Police haven't officially named him; my paper and the Straight daily in Dayton are the only ones that follow these cases, and the day I got my scoop, the Oxford murders went front-page nationwide. Four students at Ole Miss knocked us out of contention. The lower the status of the victims, the less likely the murders will get publicized. With no publicity, there's no pressure on police to commit resources.

"Serial murder investigation is hugely expensive. Bulldog's never lacked for dedication; what he lacks is budget from the county commissioners. That's why he and Hickman decided to go it alone, investigate on weekends, with no publicity. If Quincy County ran a million-dollar investigation, how many sheriff's deputies, court clerks and schoolteachers would the commissioners have to lay off?"

"Man, you're taking me to school."

"That's why Gay people have to be included in the Hate Crimes Act, it provides Federal funds so rural counties don't bankrupt themselves when a Black man's lynched in south Georgia. But Trent Lott and the Republican bigots oppose including Gay people, they're in favor of hate crimes."

"But what makes hate crimes different from any other kind of crime?"

"The number of victims. Burn a cross in front of a synagogue, you intimidate every Jew in town."

Kent felt like his brain was exploding. "Steer us back to this case, Jamie?"

"It was infuriating to watch four college kids become more important than a dozen Gay guys. Oxford was a textbook in how not to do it."

"What happened down there?"

"There were police leaks left and right. Departments competed with each other, jealous and suspicious, every one trying to show how responsive and committed it was. Then someone leaked a suspect's name. But the cops couldn't pin the murders on him at all, while the guy's life was destroyed. Two years later they got a guilty plea out of someone else. Classic. So The Ohio Gay Times learned not to publish the names of unconfirmed suspects."

"Cops and jurisdictional fights. Competing with each other instead of cooperating. Leaking stuff. We studied that in college, we go over it at the academy all the time. But it never changes, unless you've got total pros heading those departments. And most of them are political bozos."

"Bulldog's got a colorful term for it: cops in a little boys' pissing contest."

"Little boys and their wee-wees."

Jamie smiled. "But Ford knows he's a target."

"Why is that?"

"He and I have talked on the phone about it."

"What!" Kessler swung around to face him.

Jamie glanced at him, stared back at the lake. "He's called me several times. It took him three or four tries before he got up his courage the first time."

"How do you know it was him?"

"I don't know for absolute sure. But I know that the phone line that called my office was registered in his name—and this is so stupid, he calls on our 800 number. He doesn't want his long-distance records subpoenaed, so he figures he'll outsmart the cops. As if any call you make isn't traceable. So I have them traced, and the phone company gives me names, dates and times. We have Caller ID now. Several calls were made between his home number in Indianapolis and my office, including one lengthy one where the phone company's data matches the notes I took."

"What did he talk about?"

"He was strange. He called to complain about my coverage of Schmidgall's confession in the Barlow murder. How Schmidgall was innocent, what a nice guy he was, a real sweetheart. He'd just confessed! But now he's Roger the choirboy.

"Conversely, Ford also wanted to praise my coverage. I was the only one doing anything, he said. Then he talked about the strangulations, which Schmidgall had nothing to do with. He was already in jail in Illinois when the strangulations started, so why bring them up at all, if he was calling about Schmidgall?

"Thus he linked the two sets of murders himself."

A chill raced down Kessler's back. "Man, you're onto something major."

"He wasn't calling about Schmidgall, he was pumping me for information about the Strangler, to see how much I knew. So I strung him along, kept the call going as long as I could. As soon as I gave him the reassurance he wanted, he abruptly hung up."

"That he wasn't a suspect. Even though he is."

"I hate lying. I couldn't believe he fell for it."

"What else did he say?"

"He turned on this big Gay rights routine, the media don't care, the cops don't care, they're all homophobic, how terrible for the victims. Lots of anti-cop rhetoric."

"No doubt. Did you record this?"

"No, I didn't know the technology then. We knew he had been calling and we thought we were prepared, but we weren't. We only had two lines then and we were going to put it on our answering machine, but it only records on line one; when he called, line one was busy, so the call kicked over to line two. I didn't realize there was technology to allow me to record from any phone."

"Gosh. That would have been a golden opportunity."

"Right. I blew it." *Thank you, Columbia, for your useless, elitist education.* "Afterwards Bulldog supplied me with some $2 microphone you can buy at any shopping mall. Ford's called again and I've recorded it, but the conversations are nowhere near as revealing."

"Did you make notes?"

"Sure, while we were talking, then as soon as I got off the phone I wrote it up. Bulldog thinks they may not be admissible, but some courts have held that reporters are trained observers and our notes are given a certain weight. It's not the same as tape recordings and voice prints, but..."

"Who has these notes?"

"I do, and no one else. Quincy has my statement based on those notes, which I wrote immediately afterward. I don't give up the originals, so don't even ask. Both Ohio and Indiana have reporter shield laws. Journalism is not an arm of government, we practice our craft unfettered."

"I know. I enforce the First Amendment too."

"We volunteered the summary so you'd understand his state of mind. He's scared you're getting closer."

"So this guy Ford reads your paper."

"Right." Jamie watched the geese playing in the reeds.

"Jesus H. Kristofferson. Everything you write..."

Silence.

"Everything you know..."

Silence.

"Jamie, did it occur to you this might be dangerous?"

No reply.

"Who else knows about this?"

"Phil Blaney at IPD. Bulldog of course. Jo Hansen at the Dayton Tribune. My editor, Casey Jordan. My publisher, Louie Mascaro, knows only the barest outline, no details. There is no reason to put him at risk. It's dangerous enough just working for a Gay paper."

"Why is that?"

"We never know when a firebomb is coming through the front window from the Army of God."

"Lord, have mercy." Kessler put his elbows on his knees, held his chin in his hands and stared at the western sky.

At last he said, "Give me the rest."

"He knows I'm from here. I did a story once about Schmidgall's four bodies on the Kankakee River bank a few miles north, and the identifier said I'd grown up here. It was a mistake. It was a great kicker, but we should never have printed it. I revealed personal information."

Kessler waved his hand for Jamie to continue.

"Ford said something about being hounded by Schmidgall questions at his last job and having to quit. He's a social worker, he was working at the state welfare office, but he said the cops came around so often to ask him about Schmidgall that he had to quit or be fired. I interpret that to mean he decided to quit because cops were getting too close." *A social worker. And Lash runs a recreation program for kids. Plus a veterinarian. Maybe it's atonement for all the cats Crum strung up when he was ten.*

"Has he taken any other evasive actions?"

"He sold his house a few years ago, went down to St. Petersburg because of the heat up here—what little bit of heat I was able to generate. But I hear now he's back. I had a Straight reporter in Tampa, an old classmate, keep an eye out for me while Ford was down there, but they never found any young men strangled in the bay."

"Why St. Pete?"

"Crum's parents live there. Built-in support system."

"This is great, but it's all circumstantial."

"Quincy has some physical evidence. I don't know what it is, but that's why Lash is also a suspect. They also have an eyewitness that puts him near the scene."

Kessler made a mental note. "What about him?"

"He has a police record—indecent exposure in a park in Indianapolis. But that could mean anything."

"I don't get it."

"It's disgusting, but some Gay men, those who are closeted or not very out, sometimes cruise in public places looking for sex. So Lash was arrested in a public park. That's all we know. The arrest could have been a setup. Or a complete phony, just round up the faggots."

"Why do you say that word 'faggots'? Sounds nasty."

"It takes the sting out of it to use it pre-emptively. I can use it within the Gay community. If you use it, I'll put it in the paper and smash your face."

Kessler slowly chuckled. There was nothing funnier at the moment than imagining himself in a fight with a short blond toothpick.

Still, he had to respect the guy. *Tough little dude, challenging me when I've got fifty pounds on him. "Smash my face." That's cute.*

Don't laugh, though. You know he's willing to try. "I never use the word, I'm a professional. So what are you saying about Lash's arrest? Entrapment?"

"Or he could have been breaking the law so much that a Gay cop would have arrested him. Lots of serial killers have had other sex crime arrests—rape, child molestation, B&E, kidnapping. Don't forget Crum and his child porn."

"You're big on Gay cops, aren't you?"

"Yes. A Gay cop could solve this case. My problem is I don't have one."

"Let's try this: one ignorant cop plus one smart Gay reporter equals one smart Gay cop."

"Doesn't that also leave us with one ignorant Straight reporter?"

Kessler shrugged, "I wasn't gonna point that out."

They backhanded each other. It felt great to establish that first physical acceptance, in guytalk, a language they both spoke.

"But get serious again. This is very valuable, Jamie."

"A sheriff's detective in Jasper County, Jack Snyder, has photos of the whole group. You should take a look at them. Jack's only fifteen miles away."

"Good idea. Thanks, you always have good ideas."

"Schmidgall talked about Ford in court when he confessed in the Barlow murder—mentioned 'Tommy' until he realized what he was saying, then he changed it to 'this other friend who lived with us.' I heard that with my own ears, and that did make it into the paper."

"Why? I thought you tried to keep his name out of it."

"Not at all; it was said in open court. I didn't fill in his last name. But we printed it so he'd know that I knew."

Kessler was startled. "You're both playing this cat-and-mouse game. You're doing it too."

Jamie tried flipping a maple seed. This time it flew like it was supposed to. "I'm a reporter. You're goddamn right I push it as far as I can go."

"This is incredible."

"How do you think I got his attention? The story he called about was the one with his name in it. I'd never have got the phone call without that. Or therefore the evidence that he called, which I hope you'll someday be able to use in court if you need it."

They were still with their thoughts. *Not just a CI, an investigative reporter. Damn, little man.*

Jamie remembered the argument he'd had with Casey over printing Ford's name; it was the closest they'd ever come to a breach in their relationship. Then when the call came, it seemed like vindication, triumph even; maybe they'd smoked out a killer.

Kessler said, "Any other ideas?"

Jamie looked off into the distance. "Why would a killer call a newspaper? What does it say about him?"

"He wants to find out what you know."

"True, but more than that, perhaps. He's insecure, he's worried, so he took the risk, made the call, after four hangups. Try to get into his head."

"Man, without more physical evidence, the killer's head is Exhibit A."

"If you'd killed a dozen people, what would be going through your mind? You'd be scared to death of cops. Every time a cruiser passes on the street you'd be scared. 'Is this the one who's going to get me?' You could never have a burned-out taillight, never go ten miles over the speed limit. You'd be obsessed with being caught.

"And then something would happen; your emotions would shift. You'd start to get into the pleasure of all that power you have, of life and death over people. You'd get cocky, drunk with it. The emotional payoff of serial murder has to be that sense of power, the adrenaline rush of committing a heinous crime. So when are you more likely to make a mistake—and thus get caught? Not during the careful phase. During the manic phase."

"Man, you're smart. Role-play that manic phase."

Jamie climbed off the picnic table and began to pace. Then he leaned over and looked Kessler full in the face. "I'm so clever I can get away with murder. Not once, but a dozen times. I've figured out how to commit the perfect crime, over and over again. I've outsmarted cops in two states! Hell, half the time they don't know who the victim is, much less who killed him. I've outsmarted the State Police. The FBI, even! I can get away with anything. If anyone ever asks me about it, I give them my most sincere concern—they fall for it every time. Cops are stupid. But me, I'm smart, I'm something special."

"You're special, all right. You haven't got an ounce of self-esteem, you know you're scum."

"Those guys I killed? They were gullible, man. They're lucky I got to 'em first. They were accidents waiting to happen. Suppose it had been Roger who got 'em, huh? At least I strangle them after they're unconscious; no pain that way. If Roger found 'em, he'd have stabbed 'em and made them bleed to death. My guys don't feel any pain. If you were going to be murdered, wouldn't you rather be strangled, after you got high on some quality reefer? Or would you rather be shot, or stabbed to death, or run over by a truck? They don't suffer. They're faggots living in misery, lonely, poor, addicted half of 'em, rejected by their families. I just put them out of their pain. They're so beautiful when they die; lying there, their faces completely peaceful as I send them to the other side. Like they knew I'd make love to them as I send them away. And they never complain; they never say it hurts, stop, don't do that, I don't like that. And nobody knows, nobody finds out a fucking thing. It's priceless, man, I love it. Killing a man is the most exquisite joy you've ever seen—until you've killed twelve of 'em. I can do anything. I'm like God!"

After that bravura performance, Jamie looked back at the campsite where Mr. Ferguson's remains were recovered; and silently promised the man he'd do his best.

He sat back down on the picnic table and apologized to the police officer. "No problem, that was great. Puke-worthy, but eye-opening."

"The rationalizations, like he's doing them a favor. The twisted logic. His intimate familiarity with the victims' psychic pain. But most victims had family and friends who were concerned about them. So who is living in misery, lonely and rejected? Who's rehearsing his own death, committing suicide by cop?"

"The killer with a diseased mind. And I get to find him."

"Is it possible to induce the manic phase? Better yet, what phase is he in right now?"

"He just killed somebody. He's still manic?"

"So now's the time to nail him."

"Deal! You're great at this, Jamie. You'd be an asset to any department."

"Every resource I have is at your disposal. Please catch this guy, whether Ford or someone else. You can do it."

Kessler clasped Jamie's shoulder. "Thanks. Let's go. We'd better head to Jasper County."

"Is there a real task force now? Are you the head of it?"

"Yup, with the title of Commander, by order of Major Slaughter. Anything else you know about Ford?"

They walked. "Just odd details. He's foul-mouthed. There was a definite schizoid quality that first time."

"What do you mean, schizoid?"

"Zig-zag conversation. Jumping back and forth from topic to topic: Schmidgall, Crum, the strangulations, my coverage, IU vs. Purdue basketball—he's for the Chair Thrower, naturally—homophobic cops, Schmidgall, homophobic media, Schmidgall, how he'd watch the Jerry Lewis Telethon and get all teary, or the little Christmas cartoons every year; what a good job I was doing, and on the other hand I got it all wrong, Schmidgall had nothing to do with it. And he was very careful with his syntax."

"Break that down for me."

"Sorry, his choice of words. He'd be cautious, very polite, but at other times his speech was pressured, out of control. Manic. Foul-mouthed. Inconsistent. He's inadequate, frustrated, angry. The other thing I've been told is that he hangs out at a certain Gay bar in Indianapolis, one that passes for a leather bar."

"A leather bar? Motorcycle gangs? Gay Hell's Angels?"

Jamie smiled. "Not exactly; more like opera-queen toughguys." He had to ponder how to explain this one. "You've heard of sadomasochism?"

"People who like to get beat up?" Kessler curled his upper lip.

"Sort of. It's a lot more complicated. In the Gay community it's very ritualized, very safe. Not that there aren't a few crazies out there like Tommy Ford; but over time Gay men—a few women too—have created a subculture around dominance and submission, developed a set of rules for it. The theme is universal, where people fit in the pecking order. It doesn't mean the frightening things you think. It's consensual and safe."

"If you say so. That's one more of these things I'm gonna learn about. But I'll tell you, it—well, it sure sounds perverted to me."

"You're certainly allowed to feel that way. You don't have to like Gay people, you just have to realize we're human. You're doing a great job with your questions."

"So what's the name of this place where Ford hangs out, they wear leather and," Kessler chuckled, "safely beat each other up?"

Jamie smiled, "Chez Nous."

"Will you take me there?"

"Sure, if you want to go."

Kessler looked far away to a darkened high-rise. "If that's where my suspect is, that's where I go. What will I find there?"

"Guys who are looking for sex and will step into any stranger's car to do it."

"Gosh, that's dangerous."

"How does the killer gain control of the victims? A positive inducement. If he uses animal tranqs, he's not overpowering them with violence, there are no signs of a struggle. He uses a passive double-cross."

"He can't pick 'em up on his own?"

"He can't even fuck 'em till they're passed out. He snaps their neck at the moment of orgasm."

They both endured a wave of nausea. "Let's shove off for Jasper County. I want to see the sheriff's pictures."

They neared the squad car. Jamie, definitely cold now from the wind and the conversation, used his fastest New York walk, but Kessler said, "Wait."

Jamie stopped, turned around, squinted at the officer. The wind wasn't doing Jamie's contacts any good.

"There's one thing I don't get," Kessler said, stopping a foot from him. Jamie could smell Right Guard. Big hands grasped his shoulders.

"What is it?"

"How do you… I mean, why?"

Jamie looked at the trooper blankly. "Why what?"

Kessler stared, incredulous. He twisted away like a Brooklyn Italian, then back, his chin three inches from Jamie's nose. "Why do you do this?"

Jamie searched his files for the right answer, but all he came up with was, "Do what?"

Kessler let go, kicked a rock, made a fist and frowned, got back in Jamie's face, grabbed his shoulders again. "You little jerk, I get paid to be a target. I got a badge, I got a gun, I got a whole team of people behind me if I get in trouble. What have you got? You ain't got squat!"

Jamie looked right and left, trying to figure out the answer to an unknown question.

"Why?" Kessler shook him fiercely, Jamie's neck in a little whiplash.

He got scared. This cop was turning violent and there was no one else around. His heart started to pound. He searched the trooper's face.

Then the eyes told him—*oh, that why.* An old, quiet feeling replaced his fear. The man seemed to be caring about him.

Jamie's face softened. He stepped away, his mouth opened, his hands moved to help him talk. "Kent, it's because..." It felt good to say the man's name, but he shook that off and began again. "It's because of people fired from their jobs, bashers beating us to death with two-by-fours; 380,000 dead of AIDS while Reagan and Bush let us die so they could get the radical right off their backs. Now we've got this Yalie yahoo from Arkansas, who only talks a good game.

"It's because of Karen Thompson, who had her lover stolen from her by the courts after the lover was almost killed by a drunk driver; two women in Pennsylvania on a camping trip and some guy shot one of them to death because they're Lesbians. It's because of all those scrub-faced Gay folks in the military with perfect records, getting their lives ruined because of their thoughts, their feelings, they don't even have to do anything. It's because of Olympic Park bombers who target our bars, emergency personnel and abortion clinics, killing offduty police officers. Turn on the TV, read the papers!"

"But you could be in danger."

How to tell this ignoramus? "Kent, it's because of Gay kids like me, who grow up in places like this—Nowhere, Indiana in Nowhere, USA—with no one their whole lives long to value them for just one minute for who they really are. Getting called queer in Little League before they even know what the word means."

Kent looked befuddled.

Jamie tried this. "If you see a car wreck, you're obligated to try to help the people, right?"

"Morally, yes. Not legally, but morally, darn right. No matter who you are, Jamie. Call 911."

Jamie's hands spread out, palms up. "That's the only reason, Kent. Gay life can be a car wreck waiting to happen. Anti-Gay hatred kills people, worldwide, and it has for centuries—as everyone knows, but won't admit. But nowadays some of us fight back, try to put an end to all this needless destruction. We're stopping at the car wreck and trying to help."

Kent heard all this for the first time in his life.

Jamie glanced away a second, struggling to articulate a volcano of emotions. "This killer isn't just a wreck, he's a multicar pileup, only he gets to drive away—and he's still out on that highway, waiting to take out someone else. It's my job to follow him. I know what others don't, that he's a killer. I have a moral obligation."

"But what if he targets you?"

"Man, I don't want to do this; I just don't have a choice about it. I'm supposed to stop following a story because it's inconvenient?"

Jamie stepped away for a final glare at the woodpile where Glenn Archer Ferguson, a young man with a lover and the world laid out before him, had been strangled, dumped and left to rot.

It filled Jamie with rage. *There is no why, ultimately, only people to care about.*

Still Kent looked at him. "It's more than inconvenient. It's dangerous. And you do have a choice now, Jamie. I'm on it. You always had a choice maybe."

Jamie looked at the cop with the dark curly hair. All he could see was Riley Jones with dark curly hair, smiling in the photo, handsome with his mustache from the clone days. He disappeared from a club over the Indy 500 weekend, told his friends he'd catch a ride with someone he met there. His friends never saw him again. "Do you know how much trust that takes? 'Well, Kent's on it, so don't worry about it?' Shit. If ordinary cops could solve it we wouldn't even be here. Mr. Ferguson would be at home with his lover, arguing over the phone bill."

"Man, I respect what you've done."

Jamie snorted. "In some abstract way, I suppose there always was a choice. But when I learn about a massive injustice, I tell the world. I wasn't raised to walk away when someone's in trouble. Not by my mother, not by my father, not by this town. In a place like this you take care of each other when there's a crisis. My family was on the receiving end of it one cold December morning. My father totaled his car and his body, driving home in the fog. As soon as people found out, casseroles arrived every five minutes. You don't think that stays with a ten-year-old at his Grandma's house?

"It is the one fine thing about growing up in Nowhere, Indiana. The only fine thing—but a fine one indeed. I'm proud as hell to be from this fucking homophobic small-minded little town, where people still care."

"Will you be my partner on these murders? Help me with them, so we can give these families some peace?"

"Families and friends," Jamie insisted.

Kent touched Jamie's shoulder. "Families and friends."

"Glenn Ferguson had a lover who turned in a missing person report the minute your damn system would accept it. His lover is the first in line when it comes to bereavement. It makes no difference that he's a man. He is the one you solve it for—not the parents, not the sister; the lover, the one Glenn Ferguson was in love with. Listen to your victim. He'll tell you who's important. He'll tell you everything you need to know."

"Right, his lover. Okay, partner? I need you. Will you help me?" When Jamie didn't answer, Kent gave Jamie's shoulder another little rub. "I need you."

So Jamie found himself co-opted again, an hour after he didn't even want to be friends. He stopped kidding himself. "Sure, Commander. I'm here to help." He strode off.

"Wait." Jamie stopped, didn't turn around, but cocked his head to listen. "It's Baseball's fault you can't be open."

Jamie turned, looked into warm brown eyes; and threw him a pretend popup. The centerfielder shagged it and tossed it back to his shortstop.

17

Wave

They headed for State Line Road. Jamie was sorry to be leaving, he liked remembering his childhood. He gazed at the scenery dreamy-eyed. Suddenly he said, "Stop the car."

Kent did. "What is it?"

"See this ditch over here? This stream?"

"Yeah. So what?"

Jamie got out. Kent followed. They walked to the stream. Jamie said, "We think we know that the killer picked Campsite 16, in the water behind the woodpile, deliberately. But look at all these other good spots." He walked west along the streambank. "See, this flows under the road and into Illinois. The water is running fast. This stream probably meets up with the Kankakee at some point, and then goes into the Illinois River, Peoria and beyond. The Quincy Strangler has a history of dumping his bodies in water, but why go all the way back there?"

Kent thought about it. "If he just wanted to get off the main road, he could have..."

"It would have been just as easy. And the body could have ended up in another state if he worked it right. Illinois is thirty feet away."

"So?"

"So you're a serial killer. The more jurisdctions you involve, the less likely the local cops are to connect the murders. It's called linkage blindness, Steve Helmreich coined the term. This killer's taken advantage of it repeatedly. He knows cops don't really share information, that all crime is local, reporting is voluntary. The Illinois cops have never heard of these murders. If you're the killer, why not cross the road and send the body to Peoria? Why was he even here? Illinois would have been much better."

"These roads are deserted. Why go into the park, find the woodpile at campsite 16? It's a good question. But it doesn't tell us anything yet."

"We don't have to know why a killer does what he does, but what it is he did."

"And the fact is, he was here, he wasn't in Illinois. Sometimes you get so caught up in why here, not there, that you…"

"Fail to notice what is here?" Jamie finished.

"It happens all the time." Kent looked at the little guy. A bad feeling started in his gut.

"With all these options, how did he decide? Any one of them's perfect. If he had a hard time deciding, maybe someone around here saw something. How much talking to the neighbors has been done?"

"Not much yet. Not with any results."

Jamie watched a cardinal light on a tree, perch and stare at something. He turned back to the car. "Let's go. Oh, wait a minute. I need pictures of you."

"Okay. What for?"

Jamie got out his camera, touched his panic button slightly to improve the auto-focus. He got good shots, horizontal and vertical. "I would do this anyway, but you're good-looking. It's a Gay newspaper, you figure it out. You want tips, we're going to use every edge we've got. Now off with the hat, please. It makes you look like Smokey the Bear." He snapped half a roll, then stopped before he fell in love with photography.

"Can I ask you a question? Why do you wear a uniform? Detectives wear suits, not uniforms, it's part of your higher status."

Instant raw nerve. Kent was embarrassed, but finally smiled a little. "Ain't been to the laundromat lately. All my dress shirts are dirty. Everybody at the post teases me about it. I ain't much of a housekeeper."

You're single, then. "I'm not fond of laundry either."

Finally avoidance stopped working. Kent leaned over the roof of the car, staring softly. "There is a reason why here, Jamie. Illinois would have been better. He didn't want Illinois."

Jamie's gut turned over; he fiddled with his camera gear, put things back in his bag. "I know," he admitted, not looking up. "That stupid, dramatic little kicker."

Kent made State Line Road, put on his signal to head left. "Go right," Jamie directed.

Kent paused at the park entrance. "Okay, but we've gotta get to Rensselaer. This is originally their case. If I'm up here, I should fill them in. The longer I wait, the more likely that Johnson will be called out."

"All these roads lead to Rensselaer if you know where you're going. Do we play trooper politics, or do we find a witness? At least talk to someone, so the neighbors know we're interested. Screw the Rensselaer post, it's not their case anymore. You're the Commander. Command them to wipe their own butts."

Kent smiled, steered the Crown Vic right. Soon the pavement ran out, as Jamie had remembered, and Kent slowed the car to adjust for gravel. They drove a mile or so past nothing. "What are we going to find here?"

"This is Hopkins Park, Illinois, not so much a town as a mindset. There will be a cluster of houses on the left, owned by Black folk for a hundred years. Farmers, most of them; others work in Momence or Kankakee. They're surrounded by Whites. Very little money, some folks have more than others. They've been here as long as we have—Civil War or a little later, refugees from the South. Came up here looking for cheap land the same as we did, so they could raise their crops and feed themselves in the Land of Lincoln. The only thing any of us could afford was this old sloughland. Their culture is a lot like ours—but African-American too, so unique."

"I had no idea this place existed. Look at how lush their fields are. That corn's eight feet tall."

"Such a luxurious green. Are you the Kent in Kentland?"

Kent bit his lip a second. "My Mom's family."

"She was a Tanqueray. My family used to eat at the Nu-Joy."

"My great-great grandfather's house. He was the Kent in Kentland."

"These small towns must be deep in your bones."

"They are. Welcome home, Jamie. Look at what you made of yourself, coming from this no-account swamp."

Jamie chuckled. "What an odyssey. When I was eight, I promised myself I'd move to New York someday. And I did. Two decades later, I'm right back here."

"Given the tragedy that took place, you're the perfect guy to come back here and make justice."

Jamie felt a wave of closeness, gratitude, respect; Kent supported him. "Let's do it together." The first houses appeared; some were run-down, others well-kept, with bright geraniums and ceramic geese arranged in the yard. There wasn't much life around, though, no cars were parked in driveways.

Ahead of them rose a cloud of gravel dust. Kent slowed down, steered closer to the edge of the narrow road. A farmer, Black and aged, wearing a straw hat to protect himself from the sun, drove a tractor toward them. The two vehicles began to pass each other, and on impulse, Jamie waved big and slow to the farmer. Kent, cued, did it too.

The old man smiled and returned the big wave.

"Him," Jamie pounced.

Kent looked in his rearview mirror. The farmer was turning down a lane on the Illinois side. Its ruts led to an old red barn; further south, well back from the road, was a large Victorian farmhouse, white with black shutters, sheltered by tall old maples and oaks. In the back was a huge willow tree.

Kent found an opening on the right, Parking Area 16, State of Indiana, pulled into it and turned around. He drove back to the farmer's lane. The mailbox needed paint, but they made out the name WALKER. Kent eased the car over bumps and ruts, chose a wide spot to park.

Jamie jumped out of the car first. The farmer climbed down from the tractor, mopped his face with a faded red bandanna. He eyed Jamie and Kent. "Afternoon, Mr. Walker," Jamie called, smiling, approaching slowly. Kent donned his trooper's hat, then followed, hanging back a little, letting his partner lead.

"How ya doing, fellas?"

"I wonder if we could talk to you for a minute? My name is Jamie Foster. I'm from Morocco, and my relations have a farm outside Lake Village." It was hot here again on the other side of the lake. Jamie deliberately employed Hoosiertalk.

"Foster?" Mr. Walker said, folding his handkerchief and stuffing it into the back pocket of his overalls. "I don't rightly recall no Fosters. But then, I reckon I don't get into town much. Or over to Lake Village neither. How much land they got?"

"A thousand acres. Corn, beans, hogs, and the Nowak Brothers' Lime Service."

"Nowak. Now lemme see." He gazed at Jamie. "Yeah, I've run into Deed Nowak."

"You've met my Unca Deed?" Jamie's eyes shone.

"Nicest guy you could meet, heck of a farmer. I met his mama once, a fine lady."

"She certainly was, sir," Jamie choked. "She was my Grandmother."

"And this here's Deed's nephew, don't that beat all. What can I do for you boys?"

"Mr. Walker, we're here on police business. This is Sergeant Kent Kessler of the Indiana State Police. We're trying to find some information about a young White man who was killed over at the Slough. Found him not quite a week ago."

"Yes, I remember that. Terrible. You boys thirsty? I shore am. Been out in that field since 6 o'clock this a.m."

"That'd be real nice," Kent smiled.

"Well, come on in, then," Mr. Walker grinned. He turned toward the house. "Maw! Hey Maw! Comp'ny!"

They followed Mr. Walker up four well-trod back steps to the kitchen. Maw was a short, stoutish woman, gray hair neatly piled up on the back of her head, an old pair of dark-rimmed glasses slipping partway down her nose, a pink and yellow apron tied over a blue-print house dress. She smiled at the visitors, but it was her husband she talked to. "You ole hoss, I was wondering if you were ever coming out of that field. Child, you get over-heated, the next thing I know we'll be finding you keelt over that old tractor and making me a widow. You best heed what the doctor told you now, old man." To Kent, "You fellas want a cold drink?"

"With ice cubes!" Mr. Walker bellowed, heading for the bathroom.

"If it's not too much trouble, ma'am," Kent said, all teeth and smiley eyes. Jamie could see why he always got the Dillinger's mother assignment. Mrs. Walker moved slowly to an old steel cabinet overhead, white-enameled, next to the sink. Her kitchen was immaculate. On an old white stove, a pot of fresh green beans simmered, smells mixing with the aroma of fatback. A beef roast was done to a turn. Huge red homegrown tomatoes were peeled, thick-sliced, juicy and piled high on a platter. Jamie briefly stared at them, his mouth watered. He smelled cornbread too.

He gave Mrs. Walker their names. Glancing over her shoulder, she nodded and smiled. She handed down glasses two at a time and put them on the counter. At the freezer, she pulled out a steel tray of ice, which she took to the sink. The tray had a handle on top, which she yanked up to free the cubes. The old tray looked like it wouldn't budge, but she was stronger than it was. Jamie's Grandma Clara had ice trays like that.

Mrs. Walker put big cubes into each glass, then returned to the refrigerator to find Pepsi-Colas. The refrigerator was so stuffed with her food, only an architect could have fit in more.

Mr. Walker re-entered; he'd washed his face and removed his outer shirt. Brown eyes, old and wise, surveyed Maw's progress. "Sit down, boys, sit down," he said, scraping out his chair at the steel and vinyl dinette in the middle of the room.

Mrs. Walker brought two glasses of cola, laid one in front of her husband and one in front of the police officer. She returned to her counter for the others. "Believe I'll sit me down too, just for a minute. Now don't mind me." She sat down in her chair, but didn't pull it up to the table with the men.

"Mrs. Walker, Mr. Walker, thank you for your hospitality. We're sorry to intrude," Jamie began. "I know you've got supper on the stove, ma'am, so we'll just be a minute."

"Land, child, don't you never-mind. We've got plenty, and we'd be real happy if you could take a bite with us."

"You're very kind," Jamie smiled. "I'm afraid we can't, though. Sgt. Kessler has business in Rensselaer this evening. We're going to have to miss that cornbread of yours. I hear it's famous."

She put her head back and chuckled. "Just ole cornbread, same as I've been making for sixty years. You've been talking again, ole man," she teased her husband.

"Now Maw, they here on bidness," Mr. Walker growled. "You heard the fella, this here's police officers."

"It is kind of you both to let us into your home," Jamie said. "Ma'am, you keep a fine house." Mrs. Walker smiled. Jamie took a sip of cola. "The reason we're here has to do with a young White man whose body was found at the Slough a few days ago. Maybe you heard about it."

Mrs. Walker folded her arms over her bosom, looked down, shook her head sadly. "Poor baby. Tsk-tsk-tsk. Lord have mercy on his poor suffering mama."

The back door opened. A lithe young man in a white dress shirt, tie and gray dress slacks bounded into the room, suit jacket over his shoulder. He halted when he saw Kent and Jamie. "Mama? Daddy? What's going on?"

"LeRoy, now, where are your manners? Who taught you to come into a room that way?" Mrs. Walker jumped up to make a drink for her son.

"Daddy? Is everything all right? What's this about?" LeRoy hung his jacket on a hook next to the door, but he never took his eyes from the strangers.

"Now son, these officers is here concerning that young man was found over at the Slough a few days ago. They want to ask us some questions, now. You heard your Mama."

LeRoy continued to watch Kent and Jamie as he headed to the sink, where his mother handed him an icy glass. He swallowed thirstily, then said, "How do you do?"

Jamie got up, approached LeRoy, hand outstretched. "Mr. Walker, I'm Jamie Foster. This is Sgt. Kent Kessler. We're sorry to disturb your family. Nothing has happened, we're only looking for some help."

Kent stood. LeRoy shook hands with him too.

"Now will you let the man finish so's we can eat?" his father demanded.

"How was the bank today, son?" Mrs. Walker inquired.

"Fine, Mama," LeRoy replied softly. He was still watchful, but if his Mama said things were okay, they were okay.

"The body was found September 7th," Kent said. "He had been there awhile before anybody found him. We think he might have been put there of an evening, maybe around the Labor Day weekend. We were just wondering if you remember seeing anything unusual around then. Did you happen to see anybody near the Slough that you thought looked a little out of place? Anybody who caught your eye or made you wonder?"

Mr. Walker rubbed his chin thoughtfully. Mrs. Walker cocked her head, trying to remember. LeRoy moved to study a calendar, advertising a Watseka grain elevator.

"Maw, what night was it you had me go investigate that there foreign car?"

"I'm not sure what night that was, Henry," she said slowly. "LeRoy? You remember what night that was?"

Jamie asked, "What was the car doing that made you notice it?"

"Well now, Maw had seen it from the kitchen window there when she was finishing up the supper dishes. Driving up the road faster'n he oughten to, raising a big cloud of dust. And then coming back again. What for? Sometimes he'd stop over on the Slough side, pull into one of them parking areas, then turn around and go the other way."

"Up and down. Up and down," Mrs. Walker said. "Like he was looking for something but didn't know what it was. If you miss the Slough sign, you miss it. If you're southbound, Illinois don't show you a Indiana park."

Kent asked, "What kind of car was it?"

"Tuesday night. September the 6th," LeRoy said, finger on the date.

Kent's eyes met Jamie's. *Right time frame.*

"Is that when it was, LeRoy?" his mother asked.

"Day after Labor Day, Mama," LeRoy said emphatically. "Everybody came that day to get money or deposit their checks. We had the picnic the afternoon before at the lake."

"With all the bank people," Mrs. Walker told Jamie. "First Bank of Kankakee, yes sir. He invited them and everybody came, even though it's little ole Hopkins Park."

"You must be proud of him." White people seldom ventured into the historic Black settlement.

Mrs. Walker beamed. "Assistant manager there at the mall."

"Wow. Assistant manager already. Banking."

"Don't tell him I said so, but he's a smart little fella. Put First Bank on the Internet, yes sir."

Jamie knew what a huge achievement this was—not the Internet, but the family. "A college man?"

The farmer's wife swelled even more. "Yes indeedy. Univers'ty of Illinois. Mr. Walker scrimped and saved for that boy."

"Congratulations, all of you. What fantastic parents." Mrs. Walker sat proud as a mother hen.

"Let's see," Mr. Walker said, rubbing his chin some more. "A brown car, pretty beat up. What's the name of that foreign car, LeRoy? A Twyota? Yeah, Twyota. Ten years old at least. Maybe more." LeRoy grinned slightly at Jamie. "Anyways, I was sitting in the front room there, watching the teevee. And then I seen him going up and down the other way. Looked like he'd go into the Slough, then five minutes later back out again, up and down. I didn't like it. That's why I noticed him, yes sir." Mr. Walker nodded, certain of himself.

"Did you see who was driving it?" Kent asked. Jamie pulled his notebook out of his back pocket.

"Not right at first. After awhile we didn't see him no more, and I got ready for bed. I was going to turn in when Maw here comes saying that little brown car done turned into our lane and was right out there, and I had to go see."

"That's right, now. What was that man doing here? I didn't like it," Mrs. Walker scowled.

"So I put on my overalls again, and LeRoy, you come in asking what I was getting dressed for, so..."

"So Daddy went out the back door to talk to the man, and I went out the front and circled around," LeRoy finished. "I don't want no White man tramping around here at 10 o'clock at night." He looked at Kent, then Jamie. "I mean..."

"Absolutely right," Kent said. "You have to protect your family."

"Sometimes the hunters, they pull over and urinate on our property, right close to the house even, out there in public," Mrs. Walker said. "Don't give a care who sees 'em."

"Did you get a look at the driver?" Jamie asked.

"We both did. Didn't we, son?" Mr. Walker replied.

"We sure did, Daddy."

"Could you describe the person?" Jamie pressed, pen in the air.

"Well, it was a White guy, like I said," LeRoy began, glad the race thing was out of the way. "Maybe six feet or so? Medium build. In his mid-30s, or late 30's. Wearing Levi's and a blue and gold tank top with a basketball. Brown hair. Just a regular White guy's haircut. I don't think he saw me in the dark."

Jamie wrote, *blue and gold tank top, hoops.*

"Said he was lost, had a map out," LeRoy's father said. "I asked him could I help him find what he wanted, and he said no, he'd found it, he'd be moving on right now."

"And Daddy, you waited till he did."

"Stood out there in the driveway, trying to look stern, you know, even though I was in PJ's under my overalls." Mr. Walker chuckled. Then he grew serious again. "Don't like strangers coming here late at night."

Kent asked, "Did you see him well enough that you would recognize him if you saw him again?"

"Well, now. Yes sir, I think I might. I think I might."

"LeRoy?" Jamie asked.

"I can do better than that," he said with satisfaction. "I wrote down his license number. Now where did I put that paper?" He moved over to a kitchen drawer as Kent and Jamie exchanged glances. Kent got up to stand next to LeRoy.

"Child, is that the slip of paper I put in my special place?" Mrs. Walker asked. She told Jamie, "That's where I always put my important papers."

"Maybe, Mama."

She got up, went into another room, returned with a white slip, handed it to her son. "Is this the paper you mean?"

LeRoy unfolded the note. "This is it, Mama, 49R 772. I even got the expiration date. And the date and time it happened."

Jamie wrote the number down, *49, Marion County.* The plate was purchased in Indianapolis. Kent asked LeRoy to sign the paper and give it to him; Kent gave him a receipt and pocketed the evidence. Jamie said, "What else should we be asking? Any other details you remember from that night? Any little thing."

LeRoy declared, "That car stunk."

His father looked at him. "Shore did. Don't know how he could stand it. Like he was a hunter, 'cept he didn't have a pickup. And it ain't huntin' season noway."

Jamie asked evenly, "The smell of dead flesh?"

"Daddy, wouldn't you say?"

"He had animals in there for three, four days afore he cleaned 'em."

They had no other details; these were plenty. Kent handed his business card to Mr. Walker. "Sir, you've all been very helpful. We really appreciate it. It's the good people like you who help us out and give us a chance to catch the bad guys. Now you call me if you think of anything else. Or if you happen to see that car or that man again, you call the sheriff first thing, then you call me. Will you do it? It's an 800 number, toll-free. It doesn't cost anything. Will you do it?"

Mr. Walker took the card, studied it. "Sho' nuff. You think he might be the one?" He stood, scratched his neck, gazed up at Kent.

"We don't know, sir, but if he is, you've helped us so much. We have a lot more questions before we know anything, and I'll be back to talk to you again, show you a photograph and ask if that's the man. But you've been very helpful. All of you have," Kent said, turning to face Mrs. Walker and LeRoy.

"Thank you all," Jamie said. He shook hands with LeRoy, whose vibes had changed. Jamie smiled at him, and LeRoy smiled back.

Mrs. Walker held out her hand shyly; Jamie took hers in both of his. "We'll let you get back to that good supper, ma'am."

"I wish you could stay. We've got plenty. Man needs to eat regularly."

"You're so kind."

She reached toward her husband. "Now here, Henry, you give me that card. I've got a safe place for it."

"I'll see you to your car," LeRoy said, following Kent and Jamie down the back steps. Kent went on ahead, studying tire tracks; LeRoy fell into step beside Jamie.

This was pleasant. A stand of gladiolus was colorful in the late-summer air. LeRoy seemed to want to say something. Jamie glanced at him. LeRoy was smiling, but he was watching the behind of the officer in front of them.

"Oh," Jamie grinned.

"Oh ain't the half of it, you dog. Look at that hot bod." LeRoy growled like a cat, then whispered, "I don't know how you did it, but that is the handsomest cop since Erik Estrada." Then he held back. "But I do know how you did it. You are the most gorgeous man I've ever seen."

Jamie chuckled, they went on to the car. "Where did he park?" Kent said. LeRoy showed him. Kent crouched, studied the ground. "Between the rain and the tractor, this is a waste of time. We've got the plate number anyway."

Then Mrs. Walker came out carrying napkins and two paper plates. "Would you eat a tomato sandwich? If I'd'a known, I'd have fried up some bacon."

Jamie squealed. He took a plate from her, bit into white bread, mayonnaise, salted juicy redness; his mouth had an orgasm. "Fantastic. Thank you, ma'am, no bacon's needed. Tomato sandwiches are my all-time favorite meal."

Mrs. Walker cocked her head at him in mock accusation, "I knew I caught you looking at my 'maters."

"Busted," Kent laughed. "Tomato thief!"

Jamie wiped his mouth, shook hands again with his fraternity brother. "Thank you so much, Mr. Walker. It was great to meet you, and your information could be very important. Congratulations on such a fine family. Sgt. Kessler will be in touch."

"Hope so. Anytime," LeRoy replied with an eyebrow twitch. "Night, sergeant." The young bank manager turned back toward the house, arm around his Mama.

"What a turnaround," Kent said. "First he thinks we're there to beat up his parents, and five minutes later you're best friends?"

"Get in the car, Commander," Jamie ordered, grinning. "They're expecting us in Rensselaer." Before they reached the highway, Jamie devoured his tomatoes and Kent obtained a registration on the license plate.

They discussed that soberly. Then Jamie silently lusted after Kent's sandwich—never has a tomato been cruised harder—and after suitable suspense Kent finally shoved the plate over, accusing him of tomato larceny. Jamie gobbled up the evidence and went uncharged.

18

Jack

Kent dropped Jamie off at the sheriff's office in Rensselaer, then headed back to the state police post at I-65. Their contacts were still at work, staying over for them.

Jamie hadn't been to Rensselaer since he was 13. He was born in the hospital there, his whole family was; Rensselaer was a city of 5000, so big it called its high school Rensselaer Central, as opposed to the suburbs.

He pushed his way inside the new jail, told a woman dispatcher hidden behind smoked, one-way safety glass who he was and what he wanted.

A buzz, then a door opened off the small lobby. Lt. Jack Snyder was a compact man, 5'9", beginning to strain the seams of his brown uniform. His close-cropped hair had once been sandy; now it was going gray. His nose had been broken years ago and set by the town dentist. "Jamie Foster. We meet at last," Snyder boomed.

"How's business, lieutenant?" They shook hands.

"Drunks, drugs and domestics, we got 'em in 3-D."

"Full house next door?"

"Double-celled by court order," Snyder said proudly. "Our stars are a couple of Colombians from Miami Beach. Found them speeding on their way to Chicago. That wasn't all they were doing."

"How much did you pull in?"

"Estimated $175,000. Biggest bust in county history. Surrendered without a fight."

"That's great. Did you get the takedown?"

"McClatchey and me. What brings you up here?"

Jamie told him about Thelma, Kent, Mr. Ferguson and the Slough, as Snyder showed him to a desk and pointed him to a chair. The gray steel desk was piled high with file folders. A half-finished form ripened in an old Selectric. "I heard about that body at the Slough. They get an ID?"

Jamie described the victim. "We saw the crime scene, interviewed the naturalist and some neighbors."

"Is Suzanne Myers still working the geese there?" Jamie said she was. "Nice woman. Wonder why she never got married. I go hunting at the Slough every fall and see her. I look forward to those trips—a chance to shoot something and watch it drop right then and there. Not like this job, where it takes a judge and jury six years to let your prey off the hook." Snyder pictured his last kill. "Go out real early in the morning with my brothers-in-law. We have a hell of a time." He eyed Jamie, who was probably not a member of the National Rifle Association. "Not too mature, is it? Grown men chasing after Bambi?"

"Hey, you've got to let off steam."

"Hell. Wouldn't do it if I didn't want to. Where's Kessler now?"

"State police post. Talking to Johnson."

Snyder nodded, noncommittal, reached for a Marlboro Light, lit it with a scratched-up Zippo. "Good luck."

Jamie pulled out a cigarette too. He wondered how his mother was doing. After they were done he'd ask Kent to take him back to West Lafayette. But Snyder was telling him something. "What's that mean?"

Snyder leaned back and stared at the ceiling for a minute. "Nothing. Forget it. Maybe it's me."

"Jack, this may be our first meeting, but we've worked together for three years. Don't hold back on me now."

"You're right. I just think Johnson's lazy, a con man. Spends his time looking for lady travelers he can help out, in exchange for certain favors. Or hanging out at the rest stops by Roselawn and Remington, looking for Gay guys he can haul in for giving blowjobs in the woods at 4 a.m. Says he's protecting the decent people, but it's really that he enjoys it." *Hell, I got a blowjob from a queer once, at a rest stop. He was damn good.* Jack Snyder never disrespected a Gay man again.

"By the time he hauls them in the story's not 4 a.m. in the woods, it's sodomy with a 6-year-old, high noon at the courthouse square."

"And he's always playing the jealousy game, like the state police are God's gift to Indiana. They get a new piece of equipment, he'll be over here bragging about it. They get a decent bust, it's all over the paper. Hell, we've got a better arrest record in this county than they do. If we get one, we won't see Johnson for weeks. Then he comes in and wants to tell us how to run our department. Most of the officers at the post are good, solid, reliable guys—a couple of sharp gals, too—people you can turn to if you're in trouble. Johnson? He makes trouble."

"Kessler feels he has to schmooze him to cover his own backside, so he's making a courtesy call."

"Maybe I'm wrong. I hope I am, hope he's not wasting his time. Did you find anything today?"

Jamie told him about the Walker family. Snyder listened, made a few notes. "What was that plate number again?" Jamie read it back to him. "Forty-nine, huh? Did Kessler run a check? Who's it registered to?"

A voice behind Jamie answered for him. "Thomas Alan Ford, male White, age 36, Indianapolis." It was Kent.

That was a quick visit.

Snyder dropped his PaperMate, dropped his jaw, stared at Kent and then at Jamie, whistled long and low. "No shit." His adam's apple bobbed as he swallowed hard.

Jamie said, "Jack, Kent needs to see your photos. Or better yet, get them copied. All the ones with Schmidgall, Crum, Ford and Lash."

"Right." Snyder stubbed out his cigarette. Hands on the edge of his desk, he shoved back his chair. But he didn't stand up. Again he searched their faces. "Holy shit. You've got him at the scene of the crime."

"Don't tell your wife," Jamie cautioned. "Don't get her hopes up."

"No. No, I don't want that." Snyder rose with purpose. "This way," he called behind him, heading down the hall. In the dispatcher's office he picked a ring of keys off a hook, told his fellow officer where he'd be. Jamie and Kent followed him to the evidence room.

Snyder entered his code on an electronic keypad. They heard a buzz and a click. Snyder opened the door, switched on overhead fluorescents. Rows of numbered wire baskets lined the wall, storing the personal effects of two Colombians and a couple dozen locals at the county jail. A large table made of two-by-fours and plywood stood chest-high in the center of the room. A goose-neck lamp of brown steel, circa 1930, was screwed onto one end of the plywood. On another wall, lateral file cabinets stood shoulder to shoulder like sentries. Snyder found the year he was looking for. A silver key unlocked the cabinet. He opened a drawer, riffled through folders, hauled one out. "This is it." He led the way to the examination table. The file was labeled, block letters, "Doe 8/15/88 File #3, Photos." And then in cursive, "The Red-Haired Boy."

Jamie admired Jack Snyder.

Snyder lifted the manila. An 8 by 10 greeted them: redheaded, mostly nude, stabbed and rotting, dumped in a creek, his gut and chest gashed 24 times. Jamie swallowed hard. Snyder stared. "Fuck." He turned away. "I can still smell that smell. You know?"

Kent nodded. "Nothing like it."

More pictures, different angles; crime scene, vicinity, the farmer who discovered the body; the autopsy, the morgue, the pauper's burial plot.

Jamie spoke. "Jack, if you've got time, I'd like to go to the cemetery. Or you can give us directions."

"Really?"

"I brought something for him. Just plastic flowers and little flags to remember him."

"Jamie, you're a good man. By God, that one I'll tell Marie."

Kent whispered, "So that's what's in your bag,"

They found the photos they came for: Schmidgall being transported to enter his guilty plea in Kickapoo County; Dr. Crum outside the courtroom, on trial for murder; Schmidgall at a convenience store in Eastwood; Schmidgall in court at Crown Point and in jail fatigues in Lake County; Ford and Lash, in separate Indianapolis P.D. mug shots; Ford and Lash together outside the Indy Public Library; Ford dressed for his social work job; Schmidgall outside the Chez Nous bar; Lash and Ford coming out of the Six of One Tavern. Then older photos: Ford and Schmidgall with the veterinarian; Crum and Ford outside a fast-food joint; Ford and Lash at Crum's farmhouse. If Crum and Ford were involved in criminal activity, they both had a friend in Lash, he wasn't just Ford's associate.

Each photo was meticulously identified on the back. Jamie said, "These are great, Jack."

Snyder asked, "Can they help you, Kent?"

"Sure they can. Question is, how are we going to get them from here to there?"

Snyder lit another cigarette. Jamie said, "Jack, since Schmidgall's confession, how much do you need to keep these shots? I know you can't legally close the case without having questioned him yourself, but it's also 99% likely that Schmidgall did it and this is as closed as it's going to get. On his deathbed the man admitted it."

Snyder exhaled smoke. "True. Unless he had help."

"Can you let Kent borrow these for 24 hours, just long enough to get dupes made? If Schmidgall had helpers, Kent's going after them."

Snyder sighed, felt old all of a sudden. "Funny thing, you know? There's regulations; don't give them to you for even a minute. There's common sense; of course lend them to you. But somehow it's Marie I'm thinking about." His eye found Jamie's. "Marie and that boy."

Jack and Marie Snyder had not only buried the victim, they'd been the only visitors to his grave, every Memorial Day, every Christmas, tidying things up every year for the last ten. "Shall we ride?" Jamie asked quietly.

Snyder found an evidence envelope, selected photos, shoved them inside and tied the envelope's string. He jotted a note on an inventory sheet, put Doe's File #3 back in the drawer, closed and locked it. They headed out, Snyder turning off the lights, keypadding the door. "Let's go, men." He handed the envelope to Kent, started to follow them out. Kent was so happy to get the pictures he instinctively slapped Jamie's butt.

Jamie whirled around, eyes like saucers, "What the fuck was **that** for?"

Kent froze. "Um, good job?" He held the envelope up defensively. "My teammate done good?"

Jamie looked away, blinked a few times, "Oh." He nodded up at him very slightly; turned and led them out, his boots chomping the tile and concrete floor.

Jack said, "Man, fags can be touchy. Him especially."

"Tell me," Kent muttered. "Don't call him that, though. He's a skilled investigator, he ain't your epithet."

"I'm sorry, I didn't mean it. It's just a term guys use, I should never have said it."

Kent was surprisingly emotional, the first time in his life he'd defended a homosexual. "I know, no problem. But stay professional, don't ever call him that again."

Jamie heard Jack call him a faggot; it hurt a little, it always did. He didn't hear Kent's rebuke. But that wasn't the most important thing that happened. Neither were the photos.

Jamie's ass burned.

19

Pinball

They were quiet on the drive back to West Lafayette.

Kent found the cemetery visit touching—not because he was moved to see John Doe's little marker, but because the other guys were. Kent didn't allow himself to feel much over dead people, or he'd lose his ability to find the criminals and put them behind bars. Yet there was Jack Snyder, a tough cop and a good one, a little loopy over The Red-Haired Boy, even tending his grave. And Jamie, who seemed to operate on nothing but emotion—he was excited over today's progress, Kent could see it in his eyes.

But he heard the silence of Jamie's brainpower.

Jamie played Snyder like a piccolo. He'd obviously planned the whole thing. What did he write in his note to Marie from the cemetery?

"You could take a lesson from this kid," a voice told Kent. *Where did that come from?*

It was Rufus Snodgrass, his investigations professor, a retired Chicago homicide cop in the criminal justice program at Indiana University. Kent could hear his raspy voice: "Think on your feet, tune into people! Try listening for a change. You're playing catchup, Kessler.

You're down five runs in the bottom of the eighth. You gonna keep swinging at the same old shit?"

Snodgrass challenged him. Kent liked and respected the old bastard.

As they crossed the Iroquois River on I-65, Jamie spoke. "What did you hear from Corporal Johnson?"

Kent eased past a tractor-trailer and into the high-speed lane. All around him, drivers going 80 suddenly found they wanted to drive 62 instead. "Nothing worth hearing."

"Did he react that the car was registered to Ford?"

"He didn't know who Ford was. As for Mr. Walker, and I apologize in advance, he's just 'some old nigger who'd say anything to get you out of there.' How idiotic. The Walkers supplied us with the suspect's license plate."

"Just what we need, racist cops with guns."

"It's why I left. Man, that's an Indiana state trooper. I was so ashamed."

Softly Jamie said, "Always be proud of your badge, Commander. Someday you'll be in a position to fire guys like that."

"Honest, I don't think it's widespread. But this case makes me so much more aware. If they can't take a difference in skin color or language, they sure as heck don't like a different… sexual orientation."

"I'm sorry you have to be exposed to the ugliness. You're a kind, fair man. Other people are not."

They passed the first sign for the Remington rest stop. "He wanted to know why I was letting a queer reporter in on this case. Sorry, those were his exact words."

The sun was turning into a big red ball over Peoria. "And what did you say, Kent?"

"All I care about is solving the crime, and if that means having a Gay expert along, so be it. He looked at me with total pity. So as a sergeant, I gave him a verbal reprimand for using unprofessional language. Next time I'll speak to his post commander.

"Jamie, in this business you learn real fast to get along with fellow officers, 'cause you may need them someday. Then I told him..." The rest stop whizzed by. "...That you were the best darn partner I've ever had."

* * *

They didn't speak again until they crossed into White County. Kent picked up his radio mic, called in for messages; nothing urgent. Jamie asked if the technology allowed him to check Thelma's answering machine.

They heard touch tones, a phone ringing, Jamie's pre-recorded voice, a beep. "Hello, this is Hoosier Hospital calling Jamie Foster. Would you give us a call at ICU, please? It's about your mom." An automatic voice said, "Five fourteen p.m."

"Rats," Jamie muttered.

"We can call from here," Kent offered.

Another beep. "Hello? This is Terry at Hoosier Hospital ICU. Jamie, we really need to talk to you. Please call us as soon as you get this message." She gave a number at 5:52 p.m.

"Forty minutes later. Two calls," Jamie moaned. "I knew I shouldn't have left. I need to call." He dug in his bag for his cell phone.

Beep. A different nurse, probably Sandra the Mennonite, she didn't say. "Mr. Foster? This is Hoosier Hospital. Concerning your mother. It's urgent that you call us right away. Please call this number as soon as you get back." That was at 6:10 p.m.

"Oh, man! What is going on? That's three in one hour."

Beep. "Jamie? We've been trying to reach you all afternoon," Terry began. There was an edge to her voice, but she was under control; too much control at 6:51 p.m.

Kent flipped on his lights and siren, kicked the Crown Vic up past 90, scattering cars like pinballs.

Jamie stared, disbelieving, as they zipped past soybean fields. He pounded a knee. "Why did I have to come up here today? She told me to come, I swear she did. It's going to rain tomorrow, so I should do it today. Oh, God, why did I come up here? All because of some goddamn murderer!"

20

Mom

She was alive when they got there, but she slipped in and out of consciousness. Once she said, "You're back."

Jamie kissed her forehead. "I'm back and I'm staying. You're not alone, Mom, I'm here."

She breathed slowly, a sickening sound Jamie had never heard before, of liquid, of mucus gurgling.

He called his brothers, had to leave messages. "Call me here at the hospital, it's urgent. Don't call the house, call my cell phone."

A nurse came. "The doctor wants to talk to you."

"I'm here."

"He'd like to see you at the nurses' station."

"Ask him to come here. My mother's a medical professional, I won't have us hiding things from her. She's a participant here. Ask the state trooper to come too. I'm not leaving this room."

The doctor came. "Her heart's giving out. There are no good options. She's in pain. Fluid is filling her lungs. We can remove it but it's a very painful procedure. We can't take a chance on general anesthesia. If we give her pain meds, her blood pressure will drop dangerously. But it's already dropping without them. She's scared. She can't breathe, she's drowning. What do you want us to do?"

Jamie stared at nothingness. Once again he had responsibility for someone's life—his own mother's. He looked at Kent, whose eyes were full of compassion and strength. He looked like a state trooper in an emergency.

Jamie keyed in on the strength. "I'll deal with her fear. You save her life. Remove the fluid from her lungs. If she's unable to tolerate the pain, give her the minimum analgesic that allows you to continue the procedure. If you're still unable to continue, give her the pain meds. Do not allow her to die in pain!

"As for the blood pressure, perform a balancing act. If it doesn't work, despite your best efforts, don't let her die in pain. Thank you; good luck. Now get to work. Save my mother's life."

The doctor hurried out. Kent looked at Jamie. "You're amazingly poised. Those are the best possible choices."

"Hope so." Jamie went to his mother's side, kissed her cheek. Awake, she looked at him.

Then he had an impulse, brought Kent over to her. "Mother, this is my friend, Sgt. Kent Kessler of the state police. Kent, my mother Thelma Rees Foster, a clinical pharmacist and formerly Indiana's Junior Miss."

She looked at Kent a long time. "Hello, ma'am."

She said to Jamie, "Nice eyes." Kent stepped away.

A minute later she said, "Things are bad." And the sickening sound of fluid in her lungs.

"They have no good options, Mom."

"I know."

"Hang on as long as you can. I love you."

"You too. Stone, Danny."

"I've got calls in to them. Meanwhile, will it help you be less afraid to know what's going on?" She nodded a little. "They're going to try to remove the fluid in your lungs," he said, patting his chest. "It will hurt.

They can't give you much anesthetic because of your blood pressure." She blinked. "If they can balance everything and you get through it, you may be okay."

"No," she said. "Dying."

"Oh, Mom," he cried softly. But he nodded a little so they wouldn't be afraid. He held her hand. Her eyes, when they were open, looked fear at him; but she was also courageous and calm somehow, giving strength to him. They tried to give it to each other. "I've ordered that you not be in pain. If they can't do the procedure, they're to take away your pain."

"Good. Love you." Technicians came to wheel her away.

* * *

Kent and Jamie sat in a pseudo living room, not talking for a half hour. Jamie's phone didn't ring. Finally Kent said, "I should get you some food."

"Ugh. I couldn't possibly."

"I'll go down to the cafeteria. You want anything? Just name it."

"You go," Jamie said with a perfunctory wave. "I'll try a few bites of anything."

Kent brought back two plates, chicken and ham, had him pick. Jamie pointed at the chicken. The meat turned out to be lukewarm and greasy, awful. He ate mashed potatoes out of the box, a few bites of chemical-tasting dressing. He ate some green beans, picked at the chicken with fork and then fingers. Kent did better with his plate. "Eat," he urged.

"I am." Jamie ate three more bites of chewy chicken, unwrapped his apple pie, stared at it. Ate a bite or two, then felt full and heartsick. "I don't even want to look at this."

Kent finished his food, took the trays away, sat down again. Didn't know what to say; there was nothing that could be said. Jamie tried to push money on him. Kent wouldn't take it. They just sat together in gloom.

"Thank you for staying," Jamie said. Kent reached out a big hand, rubbed Jamie's back.

* * *

The operation didn't work, she couldn't tolerate it. They brought her back, "made her comfortable." Jamie sat with his mother while she lay dying. Kent stayed outside where Jamie could see him. Pain shots came every twenty minutes. Thelma's breathing slowed dramatically, just four or five a minute.

Jamie tried to think of what he could say that would most please her, the most important thing to say while he still could. Then he knew what it was, knew exactly; and had to think of whether if he said it, he'd mean it, be able to live up to it.

He wouldn't. *But maybe that's just pride.*

Could he concede? To the brother he hated and loved? He kissed her cheek, picked up her hand, leaned close to her ear. "I love you, Mom. I promise you, I'll try my best to get along with Stone."

She gasped. Tears flew out her eyes. He gave her what she wanted—and she died, she up and died.

21

Pallet

Kent drove him home. Jamie thanked him woodenly and hurried inside. He shut the door, leaned against it, and as soon as he saw her decorations he began to weep.

There was nowhere he could look without seeing her. Renoir prints, cut from old pharmaceutical calendars, hung in fancy frames. Porcelain birds, a cardinal, a bluebird, a yellow finch, perched on her coffee table. The hutch displayed every vase and pitcher he'd ever bought her. He cried. He just cried.

His stomach hurt, his eyes felt hot, his nose ran. He sank to his knees on her berber carpet. She couldn't be gone, she couldn't be. But she was. As soon as he'd promised her the one thing she wanted, she died.

He looked at his hand, at the knuckle where her tear fell. He hated his hand.

He kissed it, could still see where that tear dried.

His mother was dead. What's worse, he made the decisions that killed her.

He wracked for ten minutes that way. Slowly he became aware that this didn't accomplish much; that he had duties, responsibilities. He had brothers; he had a funeral to plan, he ought to call the priest.

He wanted to call Kent, turn himself in, be locked up, plead guilty. He wanted Kent to throw away the key.

Yet the doctor said there were no good options. Jamie'd done the best he could. His brothers wouldn't second-guess him; not even Stone would.

He cried anew. Why couldn't he reach Stoney?

He dug out his cell phone in case Stone called. Then he looked at it, not ringing, smug and silent.

He needed a tissue. He needed to wash his face. He trudged to her bathroom, yellow and cheerful, carpeted in berber, the towels hung just so, everything perfect. He'd shown her how to fold the towels in sixths so they'd look perfect.

He blew his nose, washed his face, dried it on one of her perfect towels, which he refolded out of rote. He watched his hand fold the towel and realized he'd just washed off her tear.

He avoided her bedroom, walked back the long way through the living room, into the kitchen with its Astroturf and its remnants. Her phone sat on the kitchen table. He had to call the priest. He didn't want to. He didn't want to tell anyone what happened.

He didn't know where she kept the phone book. He didn't know the priest's name. It was getting late, though. He'd have to call the priest at home. He should do it now, not wait till the man—he was pretty sure the priest was a man—went to bed. Where did she keep her phone book? Why didn't his cell phone ring?

He found the book. Opened the yellow pages under Churches, found Episcopal, found the man's name. Found the listing in the white pages, called. "My name is Jamie Foster. I'm Thelma Foster's son." He broke a little.

"Yes, she's in the hospital, I visited her. How is she?"

What to say? How to get the words out? *Report them, straightforwardly.* "She died tonight." The priest said he'd come within an hour.

* * *

Jamie had to talk to someone close. He tried for ten minutes to get his voice together, but as soon as he heard Casey's he went wobbly again. Choked out his news, a junior Walter Cronkite reporting the death of the President.

Heard Casey's shock, his sorrow, his mourning voice. "Fucking diseases. When did it happen?"

"This evening, um, 9:12 p.m. I was out with my cop, up at the crime scene. My mother told me to go, I swear she did. Then this happens. The hospital called and called this afternoon, while I was looking at pictures of murder victims. Casey, we were getting somewhere, the cop and I, she was feeling better, and God, Casey, I'm an orphan. In six months I've lost everything. My poor Ricky. Now my Mom. I have a brother who hates me 200 miles away; the only person who loves me is 2000 miles away.

"In Columbus people look at me and say, 'He's cute, he's blond, he's smart, he has everything.' I have nothing! It's all been stolen from me. It took me years to finally get a little family. And now they're gone. My poor mother."

He couldn't help it, he sobbed. "Let it out, child. Go on now, don't hold back." Jamie found himself wailing over the telephone. He pulled himself together somewhat, only to lose it again. "That's it, baby. Cry your eyes out, I'm here." Casey's tenderness threw Jamie into another spasm. "Poor baby. You did everything you could."

"No, I didn't, Casey. I went chasing after a story when I should have been at the fucking hospital!"

"James, listen well: you did everything you could for her. You were there for her, not Stone, not Danny. You couldn't know this would happen. She sent you up to that slough, right? And you were there with her, mowing her grass, smoothing her skin, getting her the pain shot they didn't want to give her. It wasn't your brothers who were there, man, it was you. Come on, Jamie, stay with me."

Jamie sniffled, couldn't talk for a minute.

At last he said, "Thank you, Casey. I love you." Another dam broke behind his left eye.

"Whoever told you WASP boys about that stiff upper lip bullshit was a liar." Jamie chuckled slightly. "Man, I'm sorry. We loved your mama. Even Louie did."

"I know," Jamie said, sniffling a big one. He realized it wasn't too entertaining to listen to someone blow his nose long distance, so he managed to say, "You gonna be there awhile? Let me call you back, man. I'm sorry for this. It's just, it's so unexpected and I can't handle it and it's my mother. This is Thelma R. Foster we're talking about!" He had to add the next line, but it tore him up to say it. "Indiana's Junior Miss."

"Tell you what, James. I'm going to the store right now to buy cigarettes. It's only a five minute walk, and I'll be here for the rest of the night. Okay, Jamie?"

Jamie nodded six times before he could answer. "Yes, Case," he croaked. "Thank you, I'm sorry."

"No never mind, James. You know better than that. I'll be home in five minutes."

"Okay. See you." Even to himself Jamie sounded three years old.

* * *

Thirty minutes later, having paced every square inch of his mother's berber and dialed answering machines repeatedly, he called Casey back. "How you doin', baby?"

Haltingly Jamie said, "I wanted to get back with you, I didn't want you worrying and wondering, hanging by the phone. I'm not any better but at least I'm functional enough to call you back."

Casey could tell he had written it down. "It's okay, man, call me anytime. I'm here for you. If you want to call at 4 a.m., you call, now. Any luck reaching your brothers?"

"No. I'm still on my own, but I did reach the rector, he's going to be here in 30 minutes and that will help. The rule is you call the priest first, then he helps you figure everything else out, so you don't blow ten grand on a casket to put in the ground because you're grief-stricken; but we don't need a casket, she didn't want that. But still I suppose they're trained people; am I making any sense?"

"Sure. You haven't got hold of Danny or Stone yet, but you did reach the priest and he's on his way. I'm glad. You have to have someone with you. I wish I could be there. What can I do to help you, long distance?" Casey's honey voice, always sweet to the ear, broke Jamie's heart again.

"There's nothing to do, really. I donated the transplantable organs."

"Good, Jamie. Your Mom will live on that way."

"That's a comforting thought. Thank you, Casey, I needed to hear that. I guess the next step is IU. She always had this idea from her college days that the body is just a shell and why not give it to pharmaceutical research? So I call Indiana University—they're the ones with the medical school—to arrange for it. There's probably a document about it in her computer, she always was great with the paperwork, but it's an IBM-compatible and God knows how long it will take me to figure out how to work it." Casey groaned in sympathy and IBM ignorance. "As many times as I told her about Macintosh, she went through two computers but she never would buy a Mac." Jamie knew this tangent was quite crazy, but he said whatever came into his head. "Of course, the operating systems are becoming more similar. And she does have Windows, the poor man's Mac. But still, I don't know nothin' 'bout birthin' no IBMs."

"I wish I could help."

"She's got financial stuff in there, I'll have to go through that at some point. And go to the safe deposit box first thing tomorrow before they lock it up. She died in the hospital, so the local paper will call them right before deadline, they may have her name in tomorrow's paper, in which case fuck the safe deposit box. Casey, I'm babbling so bad."

"No, you're not, you're thinking things through with me. I'm listening to every word."

"Father Jim's on his way, and I've got the disposition of the body to go through, but we can have the funeral whenever we want. Once IU's done, they cremate them. Then we're to bury her ashes in the garden at St. John's."

"That's a sweet thought, the church garden. Father Jim will help, you'll be glad he's there. And take care of yourself, now. Have you eaten? Think about eating."

"I ate tomato sandwiches this afternoon." Thelma didn't keep food in her refrigerator. Could he bring himself to eat the frozen lasagna he'd made for her? "The worst part is I'm going to be here by myself tonight, and I hate the thought of that. What am I going to do with myself?" An idea came to him. "Once I reach Danny maybe I can try to work. The prose will be incoherent, but I'm going to need something to structure my time, and that's what we pay editors for, right? All I'm doing here is wearing holes in the carpet."

"Don't worry about work. This is unnecessary, James. I mean, if you get hit by lightning and want to work, fine. Otherwise don't give it a second thought."

"I'm just trying to think of something to occupy my time, I'm this total tilt-a-whirl of thoughts. We did good today at the Slough, did I tell you? We really did good."

"Will it help you to talk about that for a minute?"

"Maybe it would. Help me get rid of this jumblehead." Jamie lit a cigarette. "The cop's excellent. He got an ID, Glenn Archer Ferguson of

Indianapolis, report filed by roommate or lover Gary Tompkins. Victim strangled, ligatures, no sign of struggle, no physical evidence—and the cop's a crime scene expert. But we found great witnesses: neighbors can place an old brown Toyota at the scene, registered to Thomas Alan Ford." Casey dropped the phone. "Are you there?"

"I'm here, man. Blown away, but I'm here."

"Now you know why I'm such a complete french-fry brain."

"Boy, you got me extra crispy."

Jamie smiled. "So it is a story, Case. And here I'm a total wipeout, my mother's dead, my brothers are hundreds of miles away, I'm pacing all over the place, I barely know where I am, this isn't the time to be thinking of this; but for the last four years we've thought of little else. I won't be able to write anything useful. I suppose it can be postponed a week. But when we're going for tips we ought to strike while the trick's still dripping. Now we're not gonna make it. Damn, I can't believe all this happened in one day."

"You've got way too much on your mind. So I'll give you some directions, okay? Take some quick notes?"

"Let me find paper. Okay. Go, chief."

Casey snorted. Casey as Jamie's boss was a fiction they maintained only when it suited them; it seldom did. Tonight Casey was Jamie's caregiver. Otherwise they were soul buddies, fraternal twins, close as sardines. "Headline: Jamie's Goals Tonight."

"Goals Tonight."

"Number One: Talk to priest."

"Right."

"Number Two: Reach brothers."

"Yes. Oh God."

"Number Three: Eat something. Did you write that down, James?"

"Eat something," Jamie mumbled, unable to imagine it.

"Number Four: Focus on Jamie's needs only. Underline 'only.' Nothing else matters. Read 'em back to me."

Jamie did. "Thanks, Casey, that's a big help." He re-read the list, his lips turning into a semi-circle, quivering, pointing to the equator. Six months ago Number One was Talk to Priest. "But what I really need, and I'm so ashamed?" He hesitated. "I want someone to hold me. I want a man to fuck me silly and make me forget everything. And sleep with me and be there for me the next day and the next."

He began to cry again.

Casey got alert; Jamie had never been fucked in his life. He was the aggressive type, but also open and curious; Rick was the one who needed rigid roles. Casey and Jamie had discussed in great detail the thrills Jamie got from being Rick's little blond musclestud—all of which lasted one year, not five. Casey would never have put up with it, but he hurt for his friend. "You need someone to take care of you tonight. Imagine your new lover's there right now, his arms around you, kissing you, keeping you safe."

"My new lover? Will I ever find a man I can trust?"

"You've had a standing offer from me for five years." But they'd had that conversation many times, so Casey said, "You'll find someone. He's waiting for you, and he'll be fifty times better than Rick. If you're lucky, he'll be half as good as me."

"I can't work for you and be your lover."

Casey sighed. But here was Jamie, needy and bereaved. "Invent someone tonight. Invent your new lover."

Jamie stopped crying, shut his eyes, picturing him. "He's tall. Black curly hair. Emotional brown eyes. Handsome as hell. Very macho, built like a major league athlete. And yet what gives him pure raw sex appeal is the contrast."

"Pure raw sex appeal?"

"I wanted to fling myself at him. Macho's great, but it's also limited, ossified, predictable, selfish, oppressive. But this man gets a look that is… tender. Gentle. Loving. At first glance his face is 100% butch, as in 'Hey buster, what do you think you're up to?' But then you look again, he hasn't moved a muscle, and you see generosity, open human feeling. That's what makes him overpoweringly sexy. He is a gentleman. You want to crawl into his arms, you'll find solace with him. I've never in my life seen beauty like his."

Casey thought, *He sounds a lot like you.*

"He's a bundle of contradictions; intelligent, physical. Serious but fun-loving. Courageous, careful. Violent almost, but self-controlled. And principled, the finest thing about him." Another tear coursed down Jamie's cheek. "Casey, don't let me indulge this, it will only result in pure pain."

"Why? Is this that cop?"

"You should have seen him tonight. God, he was wonderful to me. As my mother lay dying. But I can't have him, I'll never have him. He's Straight. Why can't I get that through my fucking head?"

Casey breathed deeply. "Jamie, it doesn't hurt to indulge a fantasy. We'll label it a fantasy, it will never come true. He'll never know. Therefore it harms no one."

"He's easily the most exciting man I've ever met."

Softly Casey said, "Imagine he's there tonight. He holds you in his arms, he kisses you. He comforts you, makes love to you."

"You don't understand! Indulging this will change my behavior towards him, cloud my judgment. Casey, pull me off this story, I can't take serial killers anymore. They're killing everyone in my own life!"

"No, buddy. This is your Pulitzer story, James R. You have to play it for all it's worth."

That made Jamie a little more resolute. "I'll follow it. I'll be attracted to the man but it goes no further."

"What did you want to do with him, when you met?"

Jamie'd never felt such attraction before. But he was talking to his best friend, with whom he was always honest, and he finally said, "If he'd been open to it, I wanted… to touch his face. To learn about him."

"Is that all, to learn about him?"

"Kiss him, if he'd let me. Run my fingers through his hair."

Casey struggled to understand Jamie's sexuality. "What is it about this guy?"

"He's total masculinity and yet, the purest gentleness. What I'd like to be as a Gay man. But he's Straight. I don't go for Straight guys. This is ridiculous, Casey, I'm out of control. I'll be hurt if I indulge this."

"Indulge it tonight, just once. Tomorrow he'll make some redneck remark and you'll see him for what he really is. Tonight, be Gay. What if he were too?"

"Indeed he will not make a redneck remark. He enforces our civil rights because he believes in them."

"Jamie, what would you do with this paragon?"

"I'd kiss him. A thousand times I'd kiss him."

"Kisses, touching his face. Get to the good parts! Jamie, have you never objectified a man? Never looked at a man and said, Now **that** I want to fuck?"

"Yes, but a person isn't a that! Everything depends on our interaction, what he shows me, his wants and needs and feelings as well as mine."

It was a philosophical and sexual difference between them. Casey turned men into body parts, while Jamie had been objectified since childhood. Jamie never considered sex outside a committed relationship. Jamie was monogamous and Casey was… well, it wasn't a point in his favor. "Suppose you did get physical with him."

"I'd love to see his skin. Touch his body, feel his muscles. Soothe him. Sleep with him someday. It was certainly physical, what I felt; chemical. I broke out in a sweat over that man. But it was emotional too, not just sexual. Sure, I'd love to fuck, but I want to get to know him. His eyes—he's very strong, but there's a gentle soul in him that's pure beauty."

"Then let his soul make overpowering love to you."

"This is terrifying. Don't let me fall for a Straight man."

"I won't. Tomorrow I will bitch you up royally if you ever play the fool. I'll be the first to tell you that what you're really doing is projecting your own desires onto him, seeing what you want to see."

Jamie stopped crying immediately.

"But that's tomorrow, STG. Tonight you're in need. Reality doesn't matter tonight. Jack off if you feel like it. And later on, eat, you hear?"

Jamie said he would. Didn't, though; got buzzed on Thelma's booze instead, ashamed of everything he'd done the last few hours. It was indeed like him to see what he wanted to see; to try to make over the world.

* * *

Father Jim was a comfort; they looked at the Prayer Book and designed an uplifting, pastoral liturgy. Danny called, promised to fly in tomorrow morning. Jamie was able to take care of his big Bro when he cried, be the strong one again. Later Jamie tried Stone one last time, but had to settle for another urgent, nondescript message. He felt like Sandra the Mennonite.

At midnight he made a pallet on the family room floor, sheet, blanket and pillow between his mother's La-Z-Boys. No way he'd sleep in her bed tonight. The phone he placed next to his pillow. Then there was nothing else to do but drink.

He was alone in the house; alone in life. He was alone.

He sat at the kitchen table and his heart started racing. His breathing went erratic. He fought a losing battle against the terror.

Anxiety attacks usually happened when he was physically down; he hadn't eaten or slept that well in days. He wondered if he would die; which he knew was ridiculous, but he was seized by fear. His heart pounded so hard it might well explode and kill him.

He put the booze away, then sat there keening softly, hands clutched around his chest, trying to talk himself down. "You're okay, you're safe here. It's only because of Mom. You have to not drink when people die. You're at your most vulnerable at times like this. Don't make yourself more so."

"I'm always alone when anxiety attacks happen. That's what's so terrifying, I'm always alone."

Then he split again, "You won't die, Jamie. You're healthy. Your fear is real but you won't die. Mom wouldn't want you to. Danny doesn't, Casey. Visualize your friends, all of them here in the room right now. New York friends, Chicago, Europe. See them? They say ease up, Jamie, you're okay. They touch you. They love you, Jamie. You're okay." His heart pounded worse than ever. He visualized his mother being dissected by med students.

The doorbell rang, of all things, a new panic, "Who the fuck is this?" Now he had to pull himself together for someone else's benefit?

He suppressed a scream, imagined himself collapsing to the floor, having to crawl. But he stumbled to the door, flipped on the light, and there stood… the man of his dreams or his projections; the man he would never have.

"I saw your lights on. I wanted to make sure you were okay."

Jamie shook badly, turned away, didn't want Kent to see him like this. "I'm not exactly."

"I got to thinking, you're here all alone. I didn't want you to be by yourself."

"Thank you," Jamie managed. "Come in."

Kent did, Jamie shut the door, then he couldn't solve the mystery of where they should sit. Kent held up a little paper bag. "I made you a sandwich. Did you eat?"

"No." They found their way into Thelma's kitchen. Jamie unwrapped the sandwich and put it on a Corelle salad plate, then stood there staring at food Kent made for him. "Um, something to drink?"

"Ice water's fine."

"Ice water. I remember how to make that."

They sat at the kitchen table. Jamie couldn't make conversation and he certainly couldn't look at the man. He nibbled on his sandwich—salami and sharp cheddar, mayonnaise and big salted slices of home-grown tomato.

"When my Dad died," Kent said softly, "I couldn't have stood it if I'd been by myself."

"I'm very grateful, I'm not standing it well either."

They were silent as Jamie ate.

The cure for anxiety is feeling safe. He breathed more deeply, gradually calmed down, his symptoms faded. He wasn't alone. He had a new friend, here with him. He felt safe.

Kent said, "What's with the blankets on the floor?"

"That's where I'm going to sleep. There's only one decent bed in the house, my mother's, and I don't want to sleep there. Not tonight. Never again."

"That's strange, I sleep in my Dad's bed every night. It makes me feel closer to him."

"I'm glad you feel that way. Maybe I'm in denial. Whatever the fuck that means."

"Did you talk to anybody?"

"My best friend Casey. My brother Danny's on his way tomorrow. The priest."

"But nobody to be with you till tomorrow?"

"No."

"Where are your cousins, your aunts and uncles?"

"I haven't any. Both my parents were only children."

"What about your Unca Deed?"

"I didn't call him, he's been in bed for hours. We're not related by blood, just hearts."

"Gee, no cousins even. You're all alone." Then Kent wished he hadn't said that.

"I sure am."

"Did you cry, Jamie?"

"Man, the Wabash is at flood stage."

"Good. I didn't cry at first over my Dad. Which only messed me up later."

"How long ago?"

"Four and a half years. I miss him every single day."

"Why do parents die?"

Kent frowned; the quiver in Jamie's voice got to him, the poignancy of his question. "Don't know. I'm sorry, Jamie. But I know exactly how you feel."

"Upside-down crazy?"

"At the very time you're trying to be strong for other people."

"What was your Dad's name?"

"Big Stick Kessler." Kent smiled a little. "James Earl."

"A player too. A home run hitter?"

"Homers and doubles. You knew about me?"

"I knew about you."

"Can I stay?"

Jamie was stupefied. Was the man coming on to him? Was he just unbelievably kind?

Did it fucking matter? "Would you?"

"Someone to be with you in the house. I don't want you here alone at a time like this. Unless you want to be."

Jamie sobbed a little. "Don't want to be. Can't stand to be."

"Me neither. Let's pretend we're boy scouts, camping out on the floor."

Jamie was so overwhelmed that he sat there and cried. "I felt so afraid."

Kent rubbed Jamie's forearm. "Sometimes the way gets dark and scary."

"Then someone comes to help you through it. Kent, thank you, dear God."

"All I know is people need each other. When I saw there weren't any cars in your driveway, I knew you had to be by yourself. And I didn't like that at all."

Jamie dried his eyes finally. "I'll never forget this, man. Never in my life."

Kent shrugged, made Jamie finish his sandwich. Jamie mumbled, "These tomatoes are really good."

"I wanted like anything to bring you a casserole. But I don't know how to make one, and it was too late to call my Mom and find out how."

His caring cut Jamie so deeply, he stabbed at levity instead, "No merit badge in cooking, huh?"

"Man, cooking-wise I'm a tenderfoot."

"My sandwich says it all."

* * *

Jamie blew up an air mattress, bigger, nicer, placed it four feet away from his little pallet and made up another bed. He showed Kent the bathrooms, turned on the overhead fan, and they slept together—not sleeping together, but together in their underwear, one light on as they got out of their clothes, backs turned, no looking, then lights out.

Jamie lay there in the dark, staring up at the fan. Kent's smell was distinct; deodorant soap, but another scent that seemed to come from inside him, sweet as baby powder. Jamie had never smelled anyone like him. It was as if he could smell the man's soul.

Gradually Jamie heard a soothing sound; a quiet, gentle snore. It made him smile a little. Rick used to snore too.

In a way it was every bit like sleeping together. Jamie loved that snore, and the sweet scent of a man who slept on a pallet so he wouldn't be alone.

Jamie wasn't projecting. He saw Kent as he was; a kind man, open and brave enough to come to a Gay house, take his clothes off and sleep in the same room, because Jamie needed him. Two hot tears escaped, aching for such tenderness.

He didn't need to be fucked silly. He needed the comfort of a friend.

Jamie turned onto his chest, hugged his pillow like a lover, matched his breathing to the snoring, and slept.

22

Glenn

Kent was gone the next morning, but left a note: "I didn't bring work clothes. Call you today." His handwriting was tight, compact, masculine and eye-pleasing; there was no mistaking that long-tailed K. *Don't indulge this, let last night's magic be what it was.* Just having Kent in the house made the Day After more bearable.

But five minutes later Jamie lay on Kent's sheets, soaking up nature's baby powder, letting his cock do what it was built for, as he clutched the pillow Kent snored on.

*   *   *

Jamie retrieved the morning papers; no Mom. When the bank opened he would inspect the safe deposit box, pick up the bonds, leave his raw notes of Ford's calls, max out the ATM card and say nothing.

He made coffee. He poured himself a cup but let it go cold. *Might as well try to work.* There was so much to do.

He learned to negotiate his mother's computer. He was appalled by Microsoft's clumsiness, but he located the legal and financial information he needed. *Jeez, Mom, plug in the Bunn!* She held onto her stock in infashion.com and did very well with two local corporations and several mutual funds. A document called "My Dear Sons" explained the first steps to take; every asset she had was divisible by three boys. She made a pitch for contributions to Purdue, and she told them that she loved them.

He sat in his mother's office, reading, occasionally tearing up, but mostly trying to get an old dot-matrix printer to work. It finally did, racing back and forth on its track, a noisy, bizarre little machine that somehow typified his cheapskate, adorable mother.

Danny called to say he couldn't get plane tickets closer than St. Louis, so he and Lynn were driving in from Colorado and would arrive tomorrow. Jamie's heart sank, but he didn't show it. "Be safe, Bro, don't push yourself if you're tired. Stop and get a hotel room." Danny said he would, but they both knew he'd drive straight through.

And still Stone didn't return Jamie's call. Later Jamie would learn that was because Stone was drunk 24 hours a day.

Jamie signed a paper and faxed it to the Indiana University School of Medicine, allowing it to take control of her body. The funeral home people wanted to know what to dress her in, and how her hair should be done. He called Connie, her friend and hairdresser. After receiving her shocked condolences, he said, "My thought is we're not burying her in a favorite outfit; it's a different sort of occasion, like she's going to work at her volunteer job at Pharmaceutics Research. I think she should dress down. And since we're sending her to IU, I'm thinking of decking her out in Purdue sportswear."

"She'd love that. And I'll do her hair one last time. Please let me, it's my gift to your family, and to her."

He accepted her gift and headed down to the Village, West Lafayette's shopping district. At the Purdue Spirit store he picked out gold sweats. At the checkout counter he spied a little $5 trinket, pushed its button to activate a computer chip. "This," he cried, "we must have this."

He ran to a nearby copy shop, made up a little sign to pin to her sweatshirt: "IU MED SCHOOL, PUSH HERE," with an arrow to the button. Then he delivered the outfit to the funeral people, specifying that his mother's body wasn't to be moved until his brothers arrived.

It would be a good memory in future years; they'd send her to IU singing "Hail, Purdue!" He remembered her singing the Fight Song to him as a child, solemnly teaching him all the proper etiquette. All the little Foster boys knew that cheering for Purdue was like cheering for their Mom. So they cheered like crazy. *Alma mater; dear mother.*

Back home he fired up his laptop, tried to organize his information. It was better than playing 99 games of solitaire, the only alternative he could think of.

His sadness turned to anger as he read his notes about the murder of Glenn Archer Ferguson. Anger was often Jamie's fuel; now he deliberately channeled it into the one thing he could do to make sense out of this irrational world.

Later he made another phone call, got what he needed. Ate, went to the bank, then drove to Indianapolis.

That evening he e-mailed Casey:

ED. NOTE: Six (6) photos sent in .JPG for download: Victim Glenn Ferguson (1), lent by lover G. Tompkins; Crime Scene (2, 3) at Willow Slough, Morocco, Ind.; investigating officer Sgt. Kent Kessler of Ind. State Police (4, 5); Kessler with state Conservation Officer Suzanne Myers at scene (6); she discovered body behind woodpile.

Call if you have ?s, Case, it's okay to call despite everything. Edit for tightness & coherence, I guarantee the veracity but not that I make sense. Not much sleep last night so watch out. I think we should copyright, don't you? Our exclusive, don't let AP steal it. Love & thanx, J.

P.S. See what I mean about the cop? If you run him I recommend no hat, let that face be seen. But maybe the hat adds credibility. (And no you can't have a copy of the print, you nasty boy.)

Quincy Strangler: Body in NW Ind. Linked to 12 Others
Death of Young Professional Alters Serial Pattern

By James R. Foster

MOROCCO, Ind., Sept. 10—The Quincy County Strangler has struck again.

Indiana State Police confirmed today that the mostly-nude body of a Gay Indianapolis man found strangled in a park near here is linked to twelve other murders over a 14-year span.

Sgt. Kent Kessler, detective in charge of the investigation, said, "We believe this case is connected to a string of Gay-related murders in Ohio and Indiana." No arrests have been made.

Forensic specialists in Indianapolis identified the body as that of Glenn Archer Ferguson, 29. He was a marketing manager for concessions for the Indiana Pacers of the National Basketball Association.

He had been missing since Sept. 6, according to his lover, Gary Tompkins, 26. The two men shared a luxury apartment at Riley Towers in downtown Indianapolis since April 1995, Mr. Tompkins said.

He filed a missing person report on Mr. Ferguson Sept. 7, police records show, a day after he failed to return home from work.

Mr. Ferguson's body was found in the Willow Slough State Fish and Recreation Area that day by a conservation officer near this small town in northwestern Indiana, outside Chicago.

Police believe Mr. Ferguson was killed elsewhere and his body dumped here in a deserted campground behind a woodpile Sept. 7.

An autopsy performed by the Marion County coroner's office named the cause of death as strangulation, according to Sgt. Kessler. Further test results are not yet available.

Disbelief

Mr. Tompkins was in shock after learning of his lover's death.

"Glenn never picked up guys in bars," he told The Times. "I can't believe he'd be victimized this way. He was a professional with a lot of Straight friends as well as Gay ones. He didn't go out (to Gay bars) much, and then only if our schedules kept us apart. If he did go out, he always came home alone. Ask anybody who knew him. He loved sports and the arts; otherwise he was a homebody, we were in love. He was a guy with a future, not the type to put himself at risk."

The night of Sept. 6 was different somehow. Police are trying to determine what changed Mr. Ferguson's pattern.

He visited two downtown Indianapolis Gay bars prior to his disappearance, according to bartenders interviewed by The Times. "He got here about six, had a beer, and left sober and in a good mood about an hour later," said Russell Dixon, manager of the Six of One Tavern. "He was always quiet, cool, never caused any trouble, never picked up anyone or tried to drive drunk. A good customer, a nice guy, handsome and popular, the last person you'd expect to find murdered."

Later Mr. Ferguson traveled to the Chez Nous bar on 16th Street. Bartender Jimmy St. John remembered seeing him that night. "He had a Miller Genuine Draft, which was usual for him. He played a couple of games of pool. Then I didn't see him. But he wasn't the type to pick up people. He flirted a lot but he loved his lover, it was obvious."

Mr. Tompkins, a real estate agent, said he had early-evening appointments to show a house in the northern suburbs, followed by shopping at a nearby mall. Clients and friends confirm his account. At breakfast that morning, the two agreed to eat dinner separately, then meet at their apartment later that evening.

Mr. Tompkins waited in panic when his lover never came home.

Linkage

Police linked Mr. Ferguson's murder with 12 others in Indiana and Ohio dating back fourteen years, based on the cause of death, the victim's place of residence and the rural, watery location where his body was discovered. When they learned that Mr. Ferguson was Gay, the linkage was complete.

Most of the other victims—all young men "with ties to the Gay community in Indianapolis," according to authorities—were strangled and dumped in isolated, rural bodies of water. Four were found in Quincy County, Ohio, more than any other location, leading The Times to dub the killer "the Quincy County Strangler."

Times stories have been picked up in Dayton and Cavendish, Ohio and Richmond, Ind., but have not played in Indianapolis, where all 13 victims originate. The Indianapolis Sun still has not reported Mr. Ferguson's murder.

Mr. Ferguson has one similarity with—and one glaring difference from—the other victims. He generally fits the physical profile, being a trim, handsome young man, six feet tall, with dark brown hair. But his job set him apart, according to police.

"Most of the other victims were more or less street people, or at least individuals familiar with street life," said Indianapolis Police Lt. Phil Blaney, who is assisting Sgt. Kessler with the investigation.

"Some of the others were hustlers, or guys who hung out at the bars a lot, maybe had a little drug involvement, minor police records. One was a practical nurse. But Mr. Ferguson was a college graduate, had a professional job and a very good income. He never even had a traffic ticket. He was well-known in the community. That makes him very different from the other victims."

A few of the Strangler's earlier victims were loners who went unidentified for years after their decomposing bodies were discovered. Other victims' survivors have pressed police for answers for over a decade.

Task Force

Indiana State Police are now in charge of a "task force" of officers from seven counties in the two states. An FBI conference was convened in Greenfield, Ind. two years ago to discuss the cases and to circulate a psychological profile of the killer, which has never been released to the public.

But as The Times has repeatedly noted, until this week the "task force" has existed only on paper. It has had no staff, no budget and only three officers doing part-time investigation. In police terms, these are cold cases.

However, Sgt. Kessler of the West Lafayette State Police post may symbolize a renewed effort to find the killer. The post in Rensselaer, 10 miles from here, would ordinarily be in charge of Mr. Ferguson's murder; but in a highly unusual move, top officials in Indianapolis have assigned Sgt. Kessler as the task force Commander, saying that "new blood" is needed to solve the serial cases.

West Lafayette is halfway between the crime scene and Indianapolis, noted Deputy Superintendent for Investigations, Major George F. Slaughter.

"We are doing all we can to energize the task force and see that the killer or killers are caught," Slaughter told The Times. "We will not rest until this killer is brought to justice. It doesn't matter who the victim is—Gay, not Gay, his family and friends have a right to know that the state of Indiana is doing all it can to find the killer and lock him up. That's exactly what we intend to do."

Sgt. Kessler, a nationally certified investigator, urged all citizens who may have information about Mr. Ferguson's actions and whereabouts on the night of Sept. 6 to call this toll-free number: (800) 555-TIPS. Callers' names are kept confidential.

"The Indiana State Police will not discriminate on the basis of sexual orientation, or any other basis, in investigating these cases," pledged Sgt. Kessler. "I want the killer, not the informants."

-30-

Jamie tried but failed to bring out his usual ebullience over getting the story. All he could see was Gary Tompkins, sobbing in his arms a few hours ago.

Jamie was able to give to Gary as Kent gave to him. Jamie heard all about Glenn and Gary's vacations, the house they were building that Glenn would never see; their parents' reactions. Glenn's were okay; Gary's were hateful. Gary had pulled himself up from rural Hoosier poverty and found the man of his dreams, an athlete, starting point guard for the Saint Louis Billikens—a topman for poor, insecure, over-achieving Gary. "He was so sexy standing there in the bar, no shirt, great body, tight sweatpants, I could see it right there. He saw me looking at him, so he touched himself, then walked right up to me. I couldn't take my eyes off him. He said, You want it, don'tcha. Did I ever. Then he turned out to be nice, sophisticated, everything I wasn't. He took me to my first art museum, my first play, my first NBA game. All I had to do was be faithful to him, mind him, cook for him and put out. What a hardship. I wanted him 24/7."

Seeing Gary's bereavement, Jamie could be quiet with his own.

* * *

Kent called while Jamie was down in Indy, didn't leave his number, and wasn't in the book.

Jamie sat in a La-Z-Boy with only the stove light on, listening to Bach, drinking sour mash, waiting for Stone to call; half-hoping the doorbell would ring, but knowing it wouldn't.

When he'd had too much to drink, he put himself to bed on the air mattress. The smell of Kent's sheets cheered him. *Danny will be here tomorrow.*

Kent was here last night.

23

Danny

The next day Jamie tried Stone one last time, "Get your ass up here right now."

He showered and shaved, then straightened up the house for Danny and Lynn. He looked in the refrigerator. They would need food. What to buy? He made a list on an old Navane note pad.

Beer; Michelob, he thought. They could always send out for pizza; no one would expect him to cook at a time like this. Breakfast food; he wrote down a loaf of bread, eggs and bacon, sausage and fruit. He couldn't find an onion, and added that to the list, along with sour cream. Soft drinks; all she had was Diet Pepsi for Arnie.

Arnie! He was sitting down in Indianapolis and didn't know about Thelma. How to get in touch with him? How to deal with Mrs. Arnie if he reached her instead?

Arnie's number wasn't on Thelma's speed dial. Where would she have put his number, or would she have kept it in her head, or did she never call there because of Mrs. Arnie? Should he wait until Arnie called him?

Somehow this was more nerve-wracking than anything else. Jamie remembered how Ronald's wife #5 hadn't bothered to call his sons after he died, pissed off because none of them had kept in touch with their abusive father. Then they'd had to buy her off to settle their grandparents' estate and *God, what a mess.*

Poor Arnie. Jamie would call him when he found the number, screw Mrs. Arnie.

The day grew longer. He worried that if he left for a half hour to go to the store, Danny and Lynn would arrive and he wouldn't be there. Wait, go, who knew? The phone rang. It was Kent. He asked to help. Jamie faxed him the grocery list.

Then he cried again. Kent was too solicitous, which felt wonderful and miserable at the same time.

*　　*　　*

A black, late-model BMW sports car was parked in the driveway when Kent came by. Jamie was hugging a blond man; a blonde woman rubbed Jamie's back and had a hand on the other guy's shoulder.

Kent slowed the pickup to a crawl, wishing he'd arrived either sooner or later. Slowly, quietly, he parked and switched off the ignition. The hug ended with the older brother still holding Jamie by the shoulders and talking to him. Kent wished he had an older brother.

Danny said, "We've got company." Jamie looked up, saw Kent. Jamie's eyes were red. Kent felt his lips frown. He unlatched his door, climbed out of the cab.

Jamie said, "This is the detective I was with when we got the word about Mom. He stayed with me at the hospital and the whole first night."

Kent stepped over to meet the people. Jamie said tremulously, "Lynn, Danny, this is Sergeant Kent Kessler of the Indiana State Police. He's an elite homicide detective and task force Commander. He volunteered to do grocery shopping for us. Kent, I present my sister-in-law Lynn Evans, the acclaimed illustrator of children's books; and her husband, my big brother Dan Foster, who writes for the Denver Rocky Mountain News."

"How do you do, sergeant?" Danny said, reaching out to shake his hand. "We appreciate your getting this stuff."

Perfect grammar, just like Jamie. He was five years older; his blond hair was darker, not as thick, he was three inches taller, 40 pounds heavier, husky almost, built nowhere the same; but the family resemblance was striking. He lacked Jamie's ability to stop traffic, but Danny looked just like him. It was amazing to see them together.

Danny loved his little brother, it was obvious. Jamie loved Danny with all the hero-worship a little brother can summon. A Gay guy, a Straight guy, they were Bro's.

Which made the Stone thing all the harder.

Kent shook Danny's hand, said hello to pretty Lynn. "Ms. Evans, I'm sorry we have to meet like this. You must be tired after that long drive. I hope it was uneventful?"

She said ruefully, "For fourteen straight hours."

"You need help with those?" Danny asked, moving toward the 250's passenger door.

"No, please, Mr. Foster," Kent protested. "You just got here. Relax, visit, I can bring this stuff in."

"Come on, honey," Lynn said. She turned to Jamie, standing by himself, immobilized. She slipped a hand on his elbow. "Cutie, you got a bathroom in this place?"

"Yes, sure." He led her into the house, pausing to prop the storm door open so Kent and Danny wouldn't have to fumble with it.

Danny unlocked the sports car's trunk, surveyed assorted suitcases, picked up Lynn's dress bag, a carry-on and a shopping bag full of shoes. "Kent Kessler. Big Ten Player of the Year—for the Wrong School." Kent smiled; Purdue fans were all alike, they hated IU, which hated them back. "Two and a half years with the Braves. All-Star team, that game-winning catch in the LCS in '93. I'll never forget it. It summed up the grandeur and tragedy of sports."

Danny gathered himself. "I saw you play against the Rockies. You had a great game, a triple and a home run, five RBIs."

"Against Sant'angelo? I remember that game."

"I'm a sportswriter. I cover the Broncos mostly."

"Dan Foster. Hey, I've seen you on ESPN."

Danny was amazed to meet Kent this way, a star athlete who became a police officer. The guy could have lived off his signing bonus, lent his name to a car dealership and a restaurant and loafed for the rest of his life; every other ex-jock did. "Thanks for coming, man." It was forlorn but Danny didn't know what else to say. "Thanks for taking care of my Bro." Kent, with three bags of groceries, followed him into the house. The famed Dan Foster was Jamie's big brother. "Kitchen's to your right."

"Got it." Kent knew where the kitchen was.

A minute later he helped Danny with the suitcases and deposited a covered plate on the kitchen counter. *Jamie, I'm sorry. And your brother's a reporter too.*

But sports, fantasyland, not homicide. Puts things in perspective, don't it? I know who the star is in this house. Gosh, little man.

Jamie unpacked groceries, was in charge of the kitchen. Water ran elsewhere. Jamie saw the plate. "What's this?"

Kent looked down at the floor. "A pie. From my Mom."

"Oh, Kent. That is so nice." Jamie took the lid off the Tupperware, stared at golden-brown latticework made by hand. "It's beautiful. Please thank her for us. She didn't have to do that." He looked at Kent, then held onto the counter, looked away. "Casseroles every five minutes, Hoosierman."

Kent made a fist, studied a carton of eggs. "Whatcha got?" Lynn asked, entering the room to look at the pie.

"Homemade," Danny said. "From Kent's Mom."

"What kind is it, cherry?"

Kent said, "Cherry's the pie she's most famous for. She grows the fruit herself. Stay out of the way when Mom's pitting cherries."

"It's very considerate of her. Jamie told us how you sped down the highway the other day after you played back the messages on the answering machine."

Danny said, "And stayed with him at the hospital, when he was all alone, and we couldn't be there. Thanks, man."

Kent just felt glum.

"Um, should I make coffee, tea?" Jamie asked. "What do you all want to drink? Lynn? We've got beer, wine, booze, soda, juice. Kent, what can I get you?"

"Coffee, I think," Lynn said. "I can make it."

"Nothing for me, thanks," Kent said. "I've got to get back."

"Honey, you want coffee? Or a beer?"

"Beer sounds good. You sure you can't stay?" Danny asked Kent. "We appreciate all you've done for us."

"Lord, it would help if I'd pay the man," Jamie scowled. "I'm such a scatterhead. Where's my checkbook? Lynn, find the receipt." He went off to the dining room.

"I have to be going," Kent said. "Jamie, we can do the money later."

"No, at the rate I'm headed, I won't remember it two minutes from now and you'll be out eighty bucks. Here's my checkbook. Lynn, did you find that receipt?"

"Fifty-four dollars and twelve cents."

Jamie wrote the check. The phone rang. Danny stood in the doorway. "Jim DeShaies, asking for you."

"That's the rector," Jamie said. "Tell him who you are. Ask about the string quartet." He handed Kent the check. "The pie symbolizes all you've done for us. Not just the groceries, but the hospital. And the camping trip."

Kent put a hand on muscled shoulder for a second. "You should have told me they weren't getting here till today. I'd have stayed with you last night."

Their eyes met. "It meant so much that you came the first night. I didn't want you sleeping on a hard floor two nights in a row."

"I'd have come. You shouldn't have been alone at a time like this."

"Kent, all day yesterday I took comfort in the fact that you came the first night. And now I'm not alone. But I'll never forget what you did. Never."

"Call you tomorrow?"

"Would you? I'd like that." Jamie walked him to the door, then Kent was gone.

Lynn said, "He seems like a real nice guy."

"He's a prince. Lord, I'd better talk to Father Jim."

"You're having a string quartet?"

"I'm paying for it. Something classy, you know? And afterward a sound system in the parish hall, playing Julie Andrews." Jamie hurried to the phone.

Lynn poured coffee. Danny came behind her, put his hand on her shoulder. "String quartet," Lynn told her husband. "And Julie Andrews. Is that Jamie or what?"

"Mom deserves it. She loved Julie, he does too. I remember the day, he was maybe five, when he realized Eliza Doolittle sounded just like Queen Guenevere and Mary Poppins and Maria von Trapp. The little shit ran around screaming, 'See, Mommy? See, Danny? Juwie Andwews, Juwie Andwews!'

"He was so cute—and so obnoxious. He played Mary Poppins so much I told him I'd shove that spoonful of sugar up his ass. Mom finally banned 'Super-Cali-Fuck-You-Julie' every day but February 29th." Danny clapped his hands, dissolved in laughter. "It took him years to catch on. He got totally pissed. Then every leap year, the goddamn cast recordings blasted 24 hours a day."

Lynn loved hearing stories about Danny's childhood. "The quartet will be nice. I'm glad he thought of it."

Sadness came quickly back; they were talking about Danny's mother's funeral. Lynn said, "I wonder if he's heard from Stone."

"Don't know. With Jamie, maybe Stone doesn't return messages."

"You call, then."

"No," Danny spat. "He finds out from Jamie, or he doesn't fucking find out."

24

Trophy

Stone made the funeral. So, to Jamie's surprise, did Casey. Danny met him and said, "I know Jamie gets the credit, but the Pulitzer finalist was The Ohio Gay Times. It goes on your résumé too."

Kent wore a dark blue suit; Jamie asked him to keep Arnie company. Arnie, a retired Army colonel, appreciated having the trooper there. Jamie asked them to sit with the family, but Arnie preferred the row behind. Jamie wrote Thelma's obituary in the Union-Gazette and the paid ad, where he made Arnie a "special friend." Arnie liked that. He'd gone with Thelma for fifteen years. Casey glommed onto Kent the minute they met.

The big, stained-glass church was half-full. As the liturgy began, an older couple took a back pew, looking uncomfortable. At the passing of the peace, the Fosters found them and brought them up to sit with the family.

The string quartet was lovely, the pipe organ was impressive, Father Jim was pastoral, and the *Book of Common Prayer* took care of the rest. A life was celebrated; a death was solemnized. Everyone moved to the parish hall, while the family stopped in the side chapel to make their communion and, as asked in the letter "My Dear Sons," say together a favorite prayer of thanksgiving for their mother's life. The older couple were there, but not Arnie, so not Kent.

*　　　*　　　*

In the chowline, the first number was "Crazy World." Casey told Jamie, "You should have flung yourself."

"I still might. He didn't have to come today. This is pure kindness."

The worst of the reception for Jamie was having to talk with Thelma's friends. If he knew their names, they had good stories to tell. If he'd never heard of them, they slapped him upside the head with the same 10¢ greeting card. But he was grateful they came, and they had a need to express themselves. Finally he broke away and joined the family party.

A few minutes later he came and got Arnie and Kent, and proudly introduced them to Norman Nowak, a homely man in a suit that didn't fit and dentures that slipped. But inside him a gentle radiance could only be called beauty.

Kent smiled, shaking hands, "Hello, Unca Deed. Henry Walker in Hopkins Park sends his respects." Jamie set about taking photos of his close people with Unca Deed, who wanted to know how Mr. Walker's corn was doing, ten miles away in that foreign country, Illinoise.

Kent learned that Thelma became Deed's stepsister as young adults, that he'd watched the Foster boys grow up; in high school Danny was a farmhand under Deed, and once little Stoney ran away from home by riding his 16-inch bike ten miles from town to the farm; but Jimbo always stayed in the house with his Grandma, and was scared of the pigs. He didn't even like gathering eggs from under the hens, easiest job on the farm. "He could do it, but he didn't like it. He was scared of the chickens too! But why do you think they're called chickens?" Deed's eyes lit up, laughing. "My Jimbo's smart, though. Went to college at 13 years old, up in Chicaga, all by himself. I couldn'ta done it; neither could you. It ain't right to keep a boy like that on the farm. A boy like that, you got to do right by him."

"He's still got a lot of farm in him. He's got a lot of his Grandma, and his Unca Deed."

"The smart one spent his time with my Mom. That proves how smart he was. I'm sorry these boys have to go through losing their mother. I know what it's like."

Kent had his mother but not his Dad. Then Deed had to get back, so Danny talked sports with Kent, told Arnie who Kent was. Arnie was more interested in law enforcement. Then he cut out too, and though Jamie was disappointed, he knew that was Arnie's way.

So Danny and Kent got to talk more, and afterward Danny came up to Jamie. "I want to do a column on him, he's a heck of a guy. The last thing most retired jocks do is put their butts on the line for 26 grand a year."

"I'd love to see that column. He utterly deserves it."

"He had an offer to anchor sports on local TV. Didn't take it, and the way he explains it I don't blame him. He asked himself what he most missed about baseball—his teammates, the camaraderie. Should he work at this lousy entry-level TV station, or fall back on his other career like he always planned? Lots of teammates with the State Police; challenges every day. Besides, maybe it was time to give something back, after all the free rides athletes get."

Jamie looked away. "Values. Clear-headed thinking."

"He's a typical athlete, an overgrown kid, always ready to play. But there's more to him, an intelligent adult who wants to contribute. TV wouldn't have satisfied him."

"I've seen his intelligence. He's working a serial murder, but won't fit his facts to a pre-existing theory."

"He told me how poised you were at the hospital, making the toughest decision a son can ever make. He thinks the world of you, Jamie."

"Don't make me cry, Bro. I don't go for Straight men."

So Danny understood what Jamie was struggling with. "I respect what you do, Bro. I could never do it. Be safe for me, okay? And thanks for taking care of Mom. I know you excelled at it. You always excel. Thanks for being with her. I'm sorry you had to do it alone."

They hugged hard, as Danny made them both cry. Jamie loved being held by his brother.

* * *

Stone and Jamie didn't talk, till Stone crooked his arm around his little brother's neck, "You done good, Bro," as Stone headed out the door for southern Indiana.

They were the first words he had uttered to Jamie in a dozen years. "Bye, Bro!" And Stone, escorting his chippie-of-the-month, threw him a little wave over his shoulder. *Poor Stone. You're the most bereft of all.*

Then dancing broke out, Casey and Jamie together for "Le Jazz Hot." Kent grinned, watching them. For the first time he figured that Gay must mean happy.

Or sad, just trying to dance through it.

* * *

At Father Jim's suggestion, the family toured the garden where their mother's ashes would be buried. A small but grand Gothic arch separated the courtyard from Ferry Street, and a plaque on the church wall recorded people's names. There would be room to lay flowers when the time came.

Back inside, Jamie sipped tea until the music got much louder, commanding attention. The song's opening flutes made him wince. Jamie broke away, his back to everyone as he felt every note. At the dramatic change in the third verse—no more breves, building up to the climax—Danny clasped him on the back and they sang together, while in

London Julie gave the stereophonic performance of a lifetime, "I Could Have Danced All Night."

After that, there could be no more music.

Kent finally approached Jamie. "I know it's family time, but I'm the only person you didn't talk to."

"I'm sorry, I wanted to. I'm deeply pleased you came. This adds even more to the hospital and the camping trip."

"You put on a beautiful service, Jamie, a work of art. I've never been to anything like it."

"Thank you for being with Arnie and Unca Deed."

"I liked them. Deed's never lost his innocence."

"He's the closest thing we have to Grandma. What I wouldn't give to have back those days with Grandma."

"What was best about her?"

"Her kindness. She was selfless. She loved children."

Kent glimpsed a child who wasn't always loved.

"Unca Deed lost his dad at a young age, the middle of five sons; but he took over as Grandma's breadwinner. He never left her. We see her purity of heart in him."

"We're lucky in our families, huh?"

"For the most part." Jamie's eyes shone moistly. "And our friends. Very lucky."

Kent hugged him, a few seconds of bliss in male arms. "I'm not like you, Jamie. I want to be friends."

"Stupidest thing I've ever said. Man, you're priceless."

They stepped apart, and Kent went to shake hands with Danny, say goodbye to Lynn. Casey handed Kent a copy of The Times with Jamie's story. "Thanks, I'll read it as soon as I get home."

Jamie watched Kent go; then Lynn came up and said, "How 'bout we all get drunk?"

So they went home and told Mom stories and laughed and cried and ate casseroles and cherry pie and got totally wasted. Maybe they had to get drunk to get through the final ritual—watching an old video of the pageant. Her sound didn't compare to the great star's; it was throatier, without the amazing range. But by changing the key and the phrasing, and visualizing her joy if she got to go to college, Indiana's Thelma Rees nailed the high note and brought down the house with "I Could Have Danced All Night."

Danny and Jamie bawled like little boys.

* * *

The next day they visited the lawyer and signed new signature cards at the bank, but Danny wouldn't take anything of Thelma's, had no interest in profiting from his mother's death. Finally Lynn shyly admired the fancy sewing machine and stand, which Jamie, in charge of the trust, gave her on the spot. It was a good few days for the brothers, but soon Danny had to get back home to cover the Broncos game. So everyone left and Jamie sat alone in a La-Z-Boy all weekend, staring into space. On Monday, all he could do was work.

He woke his PowerBook as Casey called to say that a report of Jamie's story moved on the AP state wire for Sunday morning, but only the Dayton Tribune and a second-tier chain printed it. The Tribune credited The Times and added original reporting, which was fine; Casey read him the wire version, which mentioned The Times in the second graf, along with the serial connection.

They hung up so Jamie could check the Indianapolis Sun—nothing; amazing. The Lafayette paper had two grafs in the agate, page A-8:

Slough Victim Named

A body recovered in Willow Slough State Fish and Game Area a week ago is that of Glenn Arthur Ferguson, 29, of Indianapolis, according to a published report quoting Indiana State Police Sgt. Kent Kessler. Ferguson, a marketing manager for the Indiana Pacers, was strangled, and police believe he was murdered elsewhere, then transported to the isolated Newton County park.

The report, in a newsletter catering to the Gay community in Columbus, Ohio, could not be directly confirmed, but a state police spokesman in Indianapolis told the Associated Press it was "substantially accurate." Kessler, of the West Lafayette post, could not be reached for comment.

"'Substantially accurate'?! A newsletter? Try getting the victim's name right. And no mention of the serial connection! How can you call yourselves reporters?"

He called Casey back for a joint fume session. "There's only one thing to do, Jamie."

"Right, man. Go out and beat 'em."

"That's m'boy."

* * *

"I read it right after the funeral. You reconstructed his movements prior to the crime," Kent said, setting the clipping on top of the fast-growing Ferguson file. "One day after your mother dies? That's awesome."

"There's a lot more to learn, and for that I need to go back to Indy. What have you been up to?"

"Taking phone calls from reporters. Your article really had an impact. Papers in Dayton, Cleveland, Toledo, Cincinnati, Akron, I don't know where all. TV and radio stations. A ton of people from Columbus. Oh, and the paper in Richmond, but they're the only ones in Indiana."

Jamie frowned, "Richmond is in Dayton's TV market."

"The reporters all know you. The AP guy said, 'What's Jamie onto this time?' You're famous there, aren't you."

"I report news, not make it. Who called from the Dayton Tribune?"

"Josephine Hansen. She knew a lot more and asked much tougher questions. She congratulated you on your scoop—then complained about it. 'I'm a police reporter, when did that turn into the Jamie beat?'"

"Go Jo. She's a dynamite writer, the only one who's cared." She was also Bisexual and working on a series of detective novels featuring a beautiful blonde Lesbian insurance investigator. "Any other progress?"

"Two things. We have proof that Mr. Ferguson was not killed on-site. Um..."

Jamie shuddered. "Forensic entomology?"

"A guy at Purdue's a national expert in it. Those were southern Indiana bugs."

"Southern? Start from Indy, kill him south, then drive him north?"

"The hills down south have a different soil composition."

"Gruesome. Go to point two."

"Trooper Campbell and I interviewed everybody who lives on State Line Road; Mr. Walker and LeRoy gave us separate positive I.D.s on the photos of Ford. Plus we found a teenaged girl who remembers an old, brown Toyota without prompting."

"Great. Did she have the date?"

"Day after Labor Day," Kent said emphatically. "Not bad, huh? He was out late. That and White skin made him noticeable. Nobody else goes into the park at night."

"Great work." Jamie made a fist and blew into it. "I find myself wondering why he picked Mr. Ferguson. He doesn't fit the pattern. This killer has relied for years on the obscurity of his victims, it's part of his plan."

"We're getting a lot more data on him than we've ever had before."

"Given the pattern, why divert from it? Why take a chance with a rich guy?"

"Physical type?"

"I don't believe in the physical type explanation. Too Hollywood. It's more a feeling that he can get away with killing this one." Jamie paced. "Just because Glenn was young and handsome doesn't answer why him. Most Gay men are attractive. A million of them are his type."

"If a man's handsome, he's Gay?"

This was provoking, and also off-goal. Jamie confronted the undercurrent. He looked Kent full in the face. *God, what a face.*

Jamie said gently, "No, Kent. There are plenty of handsome Straight men and plenty of ugly Gay ones. But Straight men get married, take sex for granted and start putting on the pounds. Gay men work on their grooming, their clothes, and increasingly, their fitness; as a group we're good-looking. Can we focus on Mr. Ferguson now?"

"Sorry. I just don't always know what you mean." Kent's cloudy look came back. "So answer me this. I always heard Gay guys are sissies. You ain't. Why not?"

Of the 5,000 possible replies, first of which was *Yes, I am,* Jamie said, "All people combine softness and hardness in individual ways. You do; I do. I hope we can still work together."

"We can. Are there many masculine Gay guys?"

"Depending on your criteria, all Gay guys are masculine. Some of us toughguys even hate opera."

Kent laughed, "Thank God, I hate that opera crap."

Jamie backhanded him again, for disrepecting opera, and got pounded back. "Let's move on, buddy. What was different about Mr. Ferguson that night? Let's see the clothing list." Kent shuffled through photos, notes, handed over a list, "Gray, summer wool suit by Perry Ellis, sports cut," Jamie read. "Blue and gold tie. Black Italian loafers. Kent, this isn't right."

"He wasn't wearing that?"

"If he was wearing Perry Ellis the killer wouldn't have touched him in a hundred years. Rich guy, too many clues. Glenn disappeared on a Tuesday. Where are the white socks? He lifted weights three days a week, Tuesday, Thursday and Saturday. Gary said in blizzard or tornado, Glenn always worked out."

"If they're his, the socks prove he changed."

"Maybe Gary can identify them. How did it go? After work, Glenn's downstairs in the weight room, he's showered, he's getting dressed, going out for a beer. Would he put his business suit back on to go to a Gay bar? No. He keeps casual clothes in his locker to wear home, he and Gary are going out to dinner the next night so he doesn't have to wear the suit. What is this list, anyway?"

"Tompkins' initial missing persons report."

"Is there another list with the last known witnesses' description? The bartenders and anyone else who saw him? I didn't ask them, did you?"

Kent shuffled through his papers again. "White crew-style socks, mid-calf. Blue and gold stripes around the top. That's the description of the body on discovery. None of our witnesses saw what the guy was wearing?"

"You don't think the killer put those socks on him, do you? What kind of police work is this?"

"It's possible the killer put the socks on him, but not likely. Forensics said the socks had been washed multiple times before, they're a better brand. Maybe the witnesses' descriptions are just contained in the interview reports. There isn't a separate document."

"Have we interviewed the other customers or just the bartenders? Did we take Ford's photo in to show people?"

"Indy PD interviewed bartenders. Nobody showed any photos."

"Jeez, there are people who hang out in those bars every night. Why don't we have anything from them?"

"'Cause I'm not in control of the interviews. That's going to change."

"And because IPD doesn't want to interview Gay people. God damn. So we know he wasn't wearing the suit. Did anyone look at the locker?"

"I don't remember seeing anything on it." Kent tossed aside photographs and lab reports. He told himself, "Time to command, sergeant. We've got too much task and not enough force."

"Call IPD. Better yet, call the Pacers too. Have them…"

"Seal that locker," Kent said grimly. He picked up the phone, pushed a button on the speed-dial. Jamie heard him bark, "Sealed. Dusted.

Inventoried. Photographed. Receipted. And then all contents locked up. Got it? Or should I ask Captain Brown to do it for you?"

Jamie paced. "After his workout, he puts on casual clothes—jeans or sweats, a T-shirt, white socks, old Reeboks. He walks or takes a cab to the bar, it's a short walk from home to the arena so he doesn't have his car with him, his lover's out shopping at the mall. He's dressing for the bar now, he puts on—oh, no."

"What?"

"He's in sports marketing, so he's wearing a Pacers T-shirt. Just like he was wearing team colors in his tie earlier, even his socks. But that T-shirt's what started the conversation. Our killer—if he's our killer—is a basketball nut. Remember his call to me, IU vs. Purdue? How much he's in favor of the Chair-Thrower?"

Kent smiled. Jamie wouldn't even say the IU coach's name. "Hoosier Hysteria. Like everybody else in this state."

"The clothes and no car are what convinced the killer that Glenn Ferguson was no big deal, that no one would miss him. Especially if Ferguson was non-committal in a bar conversation, didn't give out much information."

Kent frowned. "How did he get him in the car? Everyone says how cautious Ferguson was."

"The killer's persuasive, we know that. How he does it we don't find out till after he's caught. Don't focus on the killer, focus on the victim. The victim tells us who killed him, if we figure out how to hear him."

Kent was silent for a minute. "I don't know how you know the things you know. But you're right, I know you are. Besides, we still don't have the drug screen yet."

"You want a theory? Worthless speculation, but Glenn hits the bar for a beer, then he's going to get a bite to eat at a nearby restaurant and head home. The killer offers to drive him to the restaurant, says he's going that way and takes it from there. Maybe he's got some added enticement. Maybe Glenn liked to get high."

"Did you ask the lover?"

"No, it was too loaded a question for a first interview. But what about his watch? That's how we know he changed his clothes and the socks are his; therefore he wasn't wearing the suit, therefore the killer got fooled. He had an expensive watch which is still inside that locker."

"So he changed watches, he was going out for a beer, and there's no reason to flash a lot of money at the bar, he's got a loved one at home and he doesn't need to impress anybody, but he's the professional type who feels naked without a watch, so he's got a cheap one he wears sometimes. Call the lover and check."

Jamie pulled out a pocket-sized address book, dialed, waited. "Gary, it's Jamie Foster of The Ohio Gay Times. How are you getting along?" He listened for a few seconds, slowed down. "Gary, I'm here with Sgt. Kessler, and we got to thinking. What kind of watch did Glenn wear to work? And did he have another watch he wore at more casual times?" Jamie held up two fingers. "And do you have both of them there, are they among his things? Either one of them?" Jamie shook his head. "Did you ever know him to change clothes after his workout? What kind of clothes would he put on afterwards?" Jamie gestured for note paper. Kent ripped off two sheets and tossed him a ballpoint. "It won't go in the paper, Gary. No one needs to know except Sgt. Kessler. It's private. What kind of T-shirt designs?

"That many, eh? Always promoting the team. Have you cleaned out his locker? What about his desk and his office?" He made notes.

"Gary, there's one other thing. I wouldn't ask you, but it could be terribly important. Can I ask you a tough question? Did you ever know Glenn to use marijuana, or any other drug, or talk about it? It can't hurt him now, and don't worry about the legality, just tell me frankly. It won't go in the paper, I promise."

He listened, looked at Kent, slowly stuck a thumb up.

"Thank you. I know it wasn't an easy thing to say, and I don't judge. I'm not sure that it's relevant, but every little thing helps. Are you flying or driving to St. Louis for the funeral? Give me the phone number where you'll be." He wrote it down. "Gary, I really appreciate your help. I know it's a horrible time right now. It's a great big hurt you're going through."

A minute later: "You know the only thing that works for me? I lost my lover six months ago and my mother a week ago. I tell myself, 'Just put one foot in front of the other and keep going.' Otherwise I'd shut down, just stop functioning." Jamie talked with his hands. "If I space out in grief I'm dead meat. And I can't walk a mile or even a block; but I can put one foot in front of the other, take one little step. And then at the end of the day, the hurt's still there, but somehow the walking has improved me." He handed the notes to Kent. Another line rang, Jamie said goodbye, handed the phone to Kent.

"Kessler." He listened a few seconds, flashed an OK sign to Jamie. "What did you find?" He jotted his own notes. Kent was a southpaw, his wrist curled up above the line; it was a tiny thing to focus on, but Jamie was fascinated by watching Kent write. "Anything else? No, keep them for me. I'll return them to the roommate when I can. Thanks." He hung up and smiled crookedly.

Jamie suggested, "Trade notes."

They learned that on Tuesdays, Thursdays and Saturdays, Glenn Ferguson changed to sweats or tattered cutoffs, a Pacers T-shirt, a $2 plastic watch, jock and "thes ol stnky BB shos I kept begg. hm 2 gt rid of (our fant, bt shwr, sweet)." Every Wednesday they went out to dinner. And Gary didn't have either watch in the home.

Kent didn't ask what the fant was about. But Jamie understood Gary perfectly. If Glenn was wearing his old, stinky, favorite basketball shoes from college, Gary could expect a nifty pass from his all-conference point guard.

And it was those old, stinky shoes that made the killer think Glenn Ferguson was broke.

Meanwhile Perry Ellis, Italian loafers, a Rolex and used jockstraps crossed the street from Market Square Arena to the City-County Building, to be inventoried and stored in IPD's evidence room. Jamie said, "I know where to find the shoes, sweatpants, cheap watch and jock. They are folded, but unwashed, in airtight bags in a bedroom closet in Indianapolis, along with assorted other trophies."

"Trophies. Why airtight?" Kent's lips curled up in dawning disgust.

Hollowly Jamie replied, "Except for the shirt, he wants to keep Glenn's smell on them as long as he can."

"Why not the shirt too?"

"Remember LeRoy's description? Blue and gold tank top with a basketball on it. He got to secretly proclaim himself to the world as Glenn's killer. If people only knew, hee hee hee."

"Man, that's sicker than cancer. You think he looks at his trophies sometimes?"

"He doesn't just look. He jacks off over them."

Partners exchanged looks of loathing. Kent shoved away from his desk, stood up tall. "Indianapolis."

25

Rolex

They rode, silent with their thoughts. Jamie wondered what he would do, now that he was alone in the world.

Go back to Columbus, of course; but for what? The job? Casey? Louie, for God's sake? With Rick and Thelma both gone, there was no reason Jamie had to stay in the Midwest.

With his credentials, a Gay paper in Columbus wasn't where he should be; in fact it was a dead end. Maybe he shouldn't have quit the bigoted Telegraph in such a righteously indignant huff; it wasn't a smart move, but it was the right one.

Maybe he should have taken the New York Times job. Maybe he should have gone with Newsday. But he had too much reputation in New York, couldn't make his career jump there.

He thought about the offer he never got, for the job he really wanted, at The Post. To be in Washington, at the center of world power, was exactly where he wanted to be. But he got cut at the last minute, too many queers in the newsroom, a "controversial issue." A discrimination complaint wouldn't help his career move, and his entire plan was to make that jump.

So he accepted the lesser-tiered, general assignment job in Columbus. Walked out in a huff and into Rick's arms. *Fuck it, you do the best you can.*

He should be pro-active with his career; he was a Pulitzer finalist, where did he want to work? He had contacts at The Plain Dealer; he wouldn't lose his sources, staying in Ohio. And there was always The Pinnacle.

What did he want? He wanted to write important stories and live in a nice suburb with Rick Lawson. Those were the happiest years of Jamie's life, but now they were over.

When this story was done he'd start looking for another job.

They passed Wrecks Inc., a junkyard landmark outside Zionsville. Kent said, "I have to mobilize my organization and get control of this investigation. It's too fractured."

Jamie switched mental gears. "That sounds right, Kent."

"If Indy PD doesn't see me there, we'll continue to get this haphazard work. After all, it isn't their case, they're just doing what they can. I need to use the state police more effectively, my own organization. They need to see me in action, exercising authority, coordinating things, getting everyone's input. Otherwise it's every one for himself."

"Call a formal meeting of your task force. Bulldog and Hickman and Blaney will be there, all you have to do is ask. And I suggest you get Dr. Helmreich in as an outside consultant. He consults with Scotland Yard. Have you ever worked a serial case before?"

"Serial rape, not murder. Does that mean I can't do it?"

"No, Slugger, it means you need an expert coach. But you're the one in the batter's box."

Kent looked at him, pleased. "Deal. Then how do I synchronize schedules in nine jurisdictions? If Quincy can make it, Hancock or Hamilton or Shelby County will say, 'We've got this other thing scheduled.'"

"Forget them. Just convene your meeting, get fully organized. The cold counties will sit on their butts and let you figure everything out.

The issue isn't the cold cases, it's Mr. Ferguson and this active investigation. Narrow your task force to the state police, Quincy County, Jack Snyder and Phil Blaney. Make it obvious, you're the leader."

"Maybe that's what was wrong with the old task force, the membership was wrong. Too unwieldy, too many jurisdictions."

"And no leader. Take control, Kent. Solve the current crime, close our their cases for them. Do you have the backing of the state police hierarchy?"

"Yeah. But it would be good to have the deputy superintendent there at that meeting, or a symbolic appearance with me later today at Indy P.D. I better call him."

Kent radioed headquarters. Soon George F. Slaughter's deep voice came booming through the car. "Commander Kessler, Slaughter here."

"Yes, major, thank you. I'm coming in. I've done all I can do in northern Indiana, I need to be in Indy from here on out."

"Right, sergeant, what do you need from me?"

"It's time for the commander to command. I need to get control over the investigation, and be perceived by my fellow officers as doing so. I'm visiting IPD Homicide, Capt. Brown, Lt. Blaney at the prosecutor's office, forensics and the prop room. We're too fragmented, we just came up with another example of poor followup, lack of coordination, and I'm putting an end to that right now. The victim's locker had never been searched. I've got my Gay smart card with me, chief."

"Hello, Mr. Foster."

Jamie smiled, "Hello, major."

Kent said, "So if you have time this afternoon, I want to invite you to sit in with Capt. Brown, back me up a little. I need workspace, personnel and hardware, and I think if the local post commander and IPD Homicide see that we're doing this in a coordinated way with your support, it will be easier for them to assist."

"Good plan, Kent. I'll contact the commander of Post 52. I've already arranged for space and hardware. Major Jenkins-Harris assures me that

'936' funds are available. If we need more, she's going to be looking over your shoulder that much harder, and that always brings in the colonel. Beyond that it's the governor's office, but I've mentioned this operation to his chief of staff."

Jamie pumped his fist.

"Thank you, sir, that's great. I appreciate you laying the groundwork. Do you have any time available this afternoon if I can get in to see Capt. Brown?"

"I'll tell Harvey to expect your call later today."

"Appreciate it, chief. Talk to you later." The radio crackled and went dead.

They passed the forest at Eagle Creek Park and bits of city began to appear. Traffic grew heavier. Shortly before 38th Street, they passed under Kessler Boulevard, and Kent honked the horn twice, sending long, loud echoes through the underpass. "Sorry," he said. "For my Dad. I do it every time I come this way."

Jamie grinned. "My mother did that when she got to the big Purdue sign on I-65. Now she's got all of us doing it. Stone too, and he's an IU grad." *Of course.*

The former INB Tower came into view; Jamie didn't know what bank owned it this week. Indy had acquired a modest skyline. Kent got off at Ohio Street, turned onto Alabama; Market Square Arena was on their left, police headquarters on their right. He parked in the crowded Police Only lot. "I thought we'd make the first stop at the property room."

"Great. But what do you want me to do while you're having this meeting?"

Kent flushed. He didn't really want Jamie along for it. He wasn't sure how other officers would react to having Jamie tag along. And securing the right reaction was what Kent was there for. "Let's see the contents of that locker, then we can figure things out from there." He opened the door for Jamie. Jamie frowned but said nothing.

The Rolex was tastefully gaudy. He hoped Glenn Ferguson didn't wear gold neck chains. The jocks probably had Gary's lip-prints on them. The only pair of sweats read "Saint Louis University." There should have been more sweats.

There were no stinky old basketball shoes.

They found nothing else remarkable; the Perry Ellis had been folded with more than the usual care, and otherwise there was the rest of the business outfit, a weightlifting belt, two handball gloves, two weightlifting gloves, a headband, a rank Pacers T-shirt, a golf scorecard from two summers ago with 79 written in red ink and circled. Glenn Ferguson earned his jock. Jamie peeled off plastic gloves. "It's what's missing that's the point."

"Let Gary know you've seen it and where it is. And give him the receipt. Tell him we'll get it to him as soon as we can. Thanks, corporal," Kent told the guard.

In the corridor Jamie leaned against the wall, out of traffic. "So, I leave now, right?"

Kent felt embarrassed, tried to think of what to say. "Hey, it's okay," Jamie said. "Don't think I don't know what's happening. You want to set up a rendezvous, or am I on my own now without a car? Don't worry, I won't slow you down."

"I haven't thought that far ahead. We'd better get a hotel room. I have to stay at the Ramada on Washington Street, that's what the state pays for. You want me to make reservations? I can put it on my credit card."

"Two rooms, so we've both got workspace. Here's my credit card. Then check in after work and change clothes, take a cab and meet me at the Victory Lounge, 12th and Pennsylvania, at 7 p.m. We'll have dinner. Meanwhile I'll go see Gary, drop in at the Six of One Tavern."

"Victory on Pennsylvania. Okay. Um, Six of One?" Kent was glad to be off the hook.

"Half Dozen of the Other. I'll get Gary to give me a picture of Glenn, and I'll talk to the late afternoon crowd IPD was reluctant to interview;

see if the regulars saw him that night. With luck the same bartender will be working, too. I'll get much more than a clothing list. I'll find out what sexual message Glenn sent out and who picked up on it. Did he wear that tank top in the bar, or did he walk from the arena on a hot day without it? He first picked up Gary shirtless in sweats, showing off that pumped body. Maybe our image of the killer as someone who lures the victims is wrong. Maybe Glenn was luring him."

Jamie headed out the door. Kent stared at him. *When am I going to get a step ahead of this guy?*

26

Catfish

The Indy FBI office called West Lafayette for Kent, but he was out with the CI, so Campbell took the call. "Trooper Campbell, this is Agent-in-Charge Frank Carson. How are you, Julie?"

"Great, Frank. What's up?"

"I wanted to see if Sergeant Kessler is making any progress on that body up in Willow Slough."

"He sure is. He's got two witnesses who can place the suspect at the scene of the crime. Four can place the vehicle."

"Indeed. How did that happen?"

"His witnesses live across the road from the park, and the suspect managed to find his way into their lane. They spoke to him, got a good look at him. And later I found a witness to corroborate on the vehicle, too."

"Good work, both of you. I'm sure you'll get to the bottom of this. These cases have never had witnesses before. How did Kent come up with them?"

"Aw, he's got some fag reporter he's chasing around with. They went up there to the scene a few days ago, and the queer latched onto these neighbors, knew how to approach them. But God, I don't know how Kent can stand to be in the same car with him. I'd be scared of getting AIDS just being near him."

"Is this just a one time thing, their working together?"

"Hell no, they're out together again right now. That faggot's hanging onto Kent like barnacles on a boat."

"I sympathize with him. I wonder why Kent's allowing it. Homosexuals aren't trustworthy informants."

"Kent's encouraging it, they're thick as thieves. He even calls him his partner. Can you believe that?"

"No. What's gotten into him? A police officer doesn't call a civilian his partner."

"Well, that's what he calls him. A partner who's queer."

"You know, a thought just occurred to me. Oh, I almost hesitate to say it."

A red light went off in her head. "What do you mean, Frank?"

"I hate to even suggest it. Still, we have to consider all the possibilities."

"Tell me what you're thinking. Whether he knows it or not, he's my partner. I'd better have all the info I can."

"Would you please keep this confidential?"

"Sure, Frank, spill it."

"I was trying to think whether Kent had a woman in his life. Here he is in his late twenties, and still single, isn't he?"

"He's 26. The woman in his life is me."

"Oh, you're seeing each other often?"

"Well, it's not that often," she stammered. "But I know he's not going with anybody else. He and I kind of have an arrangement. We let each other know when we date other people. We kid around about it, 'cause it's always the date from hell."

"It's good you're close. When's the last time you two dated?"

Her gut twisted into a knot. "It's been awhile."

"How long, if you don't mind my asking?"

It's none of your business. I'm the woman in his life!

Carson continued, "You're his partner, you should be helping him on these cases, not some homosexual. Kent could be very vulnerable. Foster is deemed extremely attractive among homosexuals."

"I've seen him myself. He has cocksucker written all over him."

"Julie, we must talk more about this, off the record. I think I can help you."

"Maybe you're right. This is sensitive territory."

"If Kent falls prey to a homosexual, this investigation could be completely compromised."

"Kent ain't about to fall for no queer," she scoffed. "For God's sake, he played major league baseball."

"Baseball. Around other young, athletic men." Carson paused. "I can help you, Julie. And your investigation. I have information you need to know. Foster isn't what he seems. The alleged reporter is the target of a Federal investigation."

"God, that could screw up everything."

"This is extremely important. The Bureau needs your help, Julie. The American people do."

"Sure, Frank, anything."

"Let me take you to dinner tonight. I know an out of the way place with catfish and great steaks. Shall I pick you up?"

With drinks, some deep, confidential sharing, a few well-planted fears and sex later that night, Agent Carson sewed up Campbell with a ten-dollar plate of fish.

27

Victory

Kent was late for the Victory Lounge. He wore DKNY jeans, a commemorative V-neck from a golf fundraiser for the Boys and Girls Club; 46 eyes followed his muscular progress to the back.

He found Jamie at a table in a small room on the right. Two salads with low-fat dressing and two glasses of white zinfandel awaited his arrival. Jamie spied the gold chain this time. "Hey. Sorry I'm late."

"That's okay, I knew when you got here."

"How's that?"

"I'm a reporter, news travels fast."

"This joint's gone to seed. How's the food?"

"The cook won't be drunk for another hour." Jamie hated the place, its butt-sprung booths and passing-for-Straight décor a perfect symbol for India-noplace; but it was easy to find in a city hard to drive in. A waiter came. "Chicken piccata. Beg them to make it lite."

"Bacon double cheeseburger," Kent declared.

"How do you want that cooked?" The waiter moved to within three inches of Kent's biceps.

"Uh, medium." Kent snapped the menu shut, handed it back and looked elsewhere. Anywhere.

"Thanks, fellas," the waiter said, sashaying his retreat.

Kent followed with his eyes for a second. "Takes all kinds, I guess," a casually homophobic remark that Jamie registered. Kent tried his wine.

"How did it go with IPD?" There was an unusual amount of activity in their direction, as customers stood at the end of the bar to drool.

"Good. It helped to have Major Slaughter there. The meeting with Quincy and Stillwater is set for Monday morning. Bulldog is coming but not Hickman, with a Stillwater deputy. Post 52 commander'll be there. I left a message for your Dr. Helmreich."

"Good work, Kent. Where's it going to be?"

"My new office at state police headquarters. And it's not just my office, Quincy and Stillwater and anyone else can use it as their base when they're in town."

"How's the computer?"

"Not the newest but it'll work. I'm going to put Julie Campbell on it. She and I complement each other real well. She came back from training last year with the best scores in her class on computer analysis. The program can pick out any little similarities I'm missing, and the database will be a big help."

"This can lead to thousands of leads, tips, wild goose chases—guys who suspect their ex-lovers because 'he got drunk in 1984 and said he'd kill me, the sumbitch.' After awhile you don't remember half the people you've talked to. The computerized Rolodex alone saves you time."

Jamie tried his salad—mostly iceberg, with some onions and carrots. But the tomatoes were homegrown and delicious. A voice at the bar said, "I don't care if they are. The blond looks like Troy on 'General Hospital,' to die for, 'cause he's heaven. And the brunet he's with, don't they make a pair."

Jamie raised his voice, "I saw Gary. He was glad to get the receipt and know Glenn's belongings are safe. The one thing he wants right now is

Glenn's desk photo of the two of them." Glenn Ferguson, with a job in pro sports, kept a picture of his lover on his desk—and was still well-liked. Jamie admired that. "I told him I'd ask if you can spare it, but everything else is evidence."

"Sure, we'll get it to him. Poor guy, he really seems devoted to Glenn."

"He was. Now he's just numbed out. As long as Glenn was missing he could hope. Now he doesn't have that anymore. I hate that he had to ID the body by himself. Those ligature marks on the neck will haunt him the rest of his life." Jamie looked sad, angry, then determined.

"We didn't run it that way. I had Lt. Blaney pull out the drawer, take a Polaroid of the face only, and walk it back to Gary. He never saw those marks."

"What a sensitive, caring, thoughtful way to do it. My goodness, Kent. Thank you."

Kent shrugged, "Most people don't want to see the trauma. Phil said Gary was a nervous wreck."

"Did you have him bring in duplicate socks?"

"No. Good idea, though. Did you get anything else?"

"Background on the victim. And I hired a hustler."

Under his breath Kent said, "Oh my God, look at that!"

Jamie turned around, didn't see anything. "What am I looking at?"

"There's two guys up there kissing each other! Say, what kind of a place is this, anyway? There's nothing but guys in here. Why, you…"

"We're here, Kent." *We're queer.* "Get used to it. Two guys kissing, what a novel idea. I wonder why Glenn and Gary never thought of it." Jamie laughed, "Eat your salad, lunkhead." Kent gulped his wine instead. "Slow down, tiger. That metal thing is called a fork. And it's not polite to stare."

Kent said quietly, almost angrily, "The least you could do is warn me you were taking me to a gaybar."

Jamie set down his elbow, pointed a finger at him and sneered. "Sergeant, if you think you're going to catch a Gay killer without setting foot in the Gay community, go back to rookie league!"

Their eyes blazed. Jamie turned the intensity down a notch. "If you have to work your way up to it, you're as bad as Hickman, barreling in wearing a neon 'COP' sign. Be better than that, man; look around you. This is the tamest place in town. It may have been where Glenn was headed to eat the night he was killed."

Kent glowered, but took a big chomp of salad. Slowly he said, "I never thought of that. I've just never been to one of these places before."

"Nothing is going to happen in one of these places that you can't handle, big man."

"If you say so, little man."

They ate in silence until the waiter returned with their plates. He set chicken in front of Jamie, then sidled over to Kent with an enormous greaseburger. "How are you boys doin'? Can I get you anything, hon? Ketchup, wine? A date for after work?"

Kent cleared his throat while Jamie suppressed a smile. "Uh, no thanks. Uh, maybe some iced tea?"

"Whatever you want, sugar. My name's Miles. I am definitely your server tonight."

"Thank you, Miles," Jamie answered. "Server is fine, servant is not." He smiled, his voice had just the right degree of acidity. Miles frowned and left.

Kent rubbed his face. "Thanks. First time in a Gay bar."

"And see, it's over now. He won't bother us again."

Kent nodded. *"It is no reflection on your masculinity, Kent. In fact, it is the most macho thing you can do."* He said softly, "Maybe you were right to bring me here."

"I'm sorry. It never occurred to me to warn you that you might meet guys like me."

"I didn't mean it that way! Darn it, Jamie, I hate fighting with you. I want us partners."

"Forget it. Lighten up, you're doing great. Don't misplace your sense of humor. If you're going to watch guys kiss, rate them on technical difficulty and artistic merit. Did their tongues nail a quadruple axel? It's never been done in competition."

"I predict it will be completed by a guy named Todd."

"That only eliminates three guys."

Kent smiled his big open smile. "Now what's a hustler exactly? What I think it is? What do you want one for?"

Jamie took a sip of wine. "A male prostitute. His name is Rocky, I gave him lunch."

Kent choked, "What do you want with some prostitute named Rocky?"

"I want him to keep an eye out for a beat-up Toyota, a license plate and two guys in a photo. Remember, some early victims were known hustlers. If your killer were capable of forming a relationship, he wouldn't need a prostitute."

"But he ain't capable. Can't compete, no self-esteem."

"IPD and Quincy surveilled the library a year ago, videotaping. All they caught were truckers and teachers in line for a quickie. You should have heard poor Bulldog. 'Why, there was married men and everything.' Gee whillikers, Sherlock."

Kent chuckled. "Why the library?"

"That's where hustlers hang out. You thought it might be the Hyatt Regency?"

Kent was chagrined. "You think this Rocky will do it?"

"It's worth a shot. I gave him fifty bucks and told him I'd give him another fifty the next time I see him. He's the smartest one there. Goes to college and shows up in late afternoon for the businessmen. I talked to four of them, once I got them calmed down."

"What were they upset about?"

Jamie looked right at him. "Competition. Loss of revenue."

"Oh, gosh. You're a surprise a minute."

"I told them not to go with him and not to let anyone else if they could help it. If they did see him, to remember the time and date and license number. Rocky carries a sketchpad in his backpack, so he can write it down."

"Good idea, I guess. I hope it works and he doesn't just take your money."

"It beats having no observers at all. He said he'd been on the scene for two or three months—which probably means eight or ten."

"Earning tuition money?"

"Why not? He also hitchhikes on Washington Street, but Monument Circle is hot right now."

Kent took a bite of his burger. "This is good," he said with his mouth full.

"Enjoy it while you can."

"What's that mean?"

"The heart attack comes later."

"I work out all the time."

"Good, it'll make your recovery go faster."

"Want to compare who's healthier here, little man?"

"I'd smoke you in a cholesterol test and you know it. Bacon and cheese, mayo and a half pound of fatty beef? They'll have to pump Liquid Plumber in you to get out the clogs."

"I am not a vegetarian, Mom," Kent growled, wiping grease from his lips. "I eat meat and dairy products. I'm a Hoosier. My family raises the food that keeps your skinny butt alive." He tried to act upset but his eyes crinkled fatally.

Jamie plunked his elbow on the table like he was going to Indian wrestle, then cocked his arm backward, "Whoa, copboy do bite back."

"I'm tired of you know-it-all city guys," Kent reproved. "Think you're hot stuff 'cause you got running water."

Jamie laughed, sliced his piccata. *His smile, the way his eyes look; it's not just how attracted I am. This guy is fun to be around.*

"It's funny," Kent said softly. "You're the one with the walls, Jamie, like I won't accept you; when I have to fight so that you'll accept me."

"I've always accepted you as a police officer. Since my mother died, I've welcomed you as a friend."

"You don't accept me as a man."

How can I, when you're shocked over a kiss? How can I, when your purpose is to use me?

How can I not, when we were boy scouts on the floor? "Damn, you're good. Call me Dillinger's mother."

"Tiny lady, she lied about her height too. Buddy, you're not five-ten. That height chart must have been put up crooked."

"I am too, darn you. Don't be telling that. I'm five-ten."

"Never lie to a police officer."

"Never lie to a reporter! You got the case because Slaughter didn't want that bigot in Rensselaer on it. Every state police post investigates every type of crime."

"Oops. Didn't know you knew that. But it was too soon to tell you it was a special assignment."

"I understand. And by God, I'm five-ten."

"You only let me get away with lying for ten minutes."

"It's my aggressive interviewing technique. Mrs. Dillinger would have served me up on toast points. Here, she'd say, have a cuh-nape." Jamie found this hilarious. "That's Eye-talian for little bitty samwitch."

"Do you really think you're five-ten?"

It was a joke, but Kent almost wanted to establish something. Control? The truth? Truth was what Jamie dealt in. "Perhaps I'm not quite. Years ago I was five-nine and three quarters. But that little quarter-inch lie made all the difference in the world. I used to have a job with height and weight requirements."

"Doesn't matter, man, I'm glad you finally told me. I knew there was a reason. There always is when people lie."

Jamie looked down. "I'm sorry if I lied to you."

"I'm sorry too. No more lies to each other, okay, partner?"

"Got it, Commander."

"Heck, Jamie, I'd hire you at five-nine."

"And three quarters! Don't you steal my fractions."

* * *

After that, Kent began to notice new behavior in Jamie; he finally relaxed. Through the rest of the meal Jamie unconsciously went through a series of moves, loosening every joint, stretching every muscle. He threw his shoulders and elbows back, stretching his pecs; he crossed his arms in front of him, stretching his lats. An elbow in the air stretched his triceps. He put an ankle over one knee and bent his foot backward, then forward, stretching his gastrocs; then the other leg. He was living in his body, which he hadn't done before; no longer pure brainpower.

Kent did those things himself all the time, brainless stretches that athletes do. It pleased him, though, something in common. Jamie was finally being his full self. Kent wondered what sport he played; then decided, *basketball.*

"The hustler was a good idea—if he follows through."

"He's studying at the Art Institute. It's tough to get admitted there. He has talent."

"Is this Rocky some big bruiser?"

Jamie chuckled, "This Rocky is thin and bespectacled."

"What's an art student doing hustling at the library?"

"College is expensive. A lot of students dabble in prostitution."

"Does he know why we're looking for these guys?"

"I just told him they were violent, and gave him your 800 number."

"It would be better if my task force had its own 800 number and voice mail. Let callers know they've got my task force as soon as I pick up the phone. Don't make them get transferred all over the place, some of them will hang up."

"Were people pleased with your progress?"

"Yes, but the prosecutor wants more. I saw his chief criminal assistant today. The bottom line is they don't want another Dr. Crum."

"Rats," Jamie said, wanting to throw his fork at something. "If Kickapoo County had a decent prosecutor they could have convicted Crum. That whole trial was political, a prosecutor with no commitment except to embarrass the previous prosecutor, for making a big deal out of why the prosecutor before **that** never tried to nail Schmidgall the first time. But it was Studer who got the confession out of Schmidgall, then Studer lame-ducked out before he could get Crum to trial." After this outburst, he patted his mouth with his napkin. "Listen to me, using words like 'lame-ducked' and 'surveilled.' This case is ruining my vocabulary. And I'm done with this food. Hail your waiter friend for me."

"It's going to take me awhile to get used to this. Like a year maybe."

"You're just feeling threatened. Nobody here is going to harm you; no one at the post will ever know. You're on home turf for both the victim and the killer, and you blend right in. Be proud you had the guts to come here and learn something new."

Kent was silent awhile. He finally said, "Thank you."

"Takes a stud to catch a killer. Hi, stud."

Emotions played on Kent's face. "It sure does."

"Finally I'm looking at one. I admire you, man. Meanwhile I take it we need proof. We need to make the prosecutor's case for him."

"Speaking of which…" Kent interrupted his speech with a last, giant bite of burger, "I asked what they'd be comfortable taking to the grand jury. It's not just that the Crum trial turned out the way it did, it's the likelihood that these cases are related. They agree with you, Crum had a heck of a legal team. Nobody knows who was paying them, but it probably wasn't the meek little veterinarian. We know how much money he makes from the earlier search warrants. The same lawyers defended Tyson. There was big money changing hands."

"If there is a conspiracy, why did FBI Quantico tell me there's no such thing as snuff films? What other explanation is there? Somebody's financing this stuff. Was that agent lying? Do snuff films exist or not?"

"They definitely exist, but there's no commercial market for them. Too much risk. Get me the agent's name, though, I'll double-check with him."

Jamie pulled out his notebook. "Kent, put Helmreich on the payroll. He's my main resource in the serial phenomenon, a street cop who went back for his Ph.D. He'll keep you from reinventing the wheel. He's seen the investigative mistakes as well as the successes. A great coach for a great player."

"Dr. Street Cop, huh? Sounds great. When are we going undercover?"

"You can barely function here and you want to go undercover already?"

"Listen, partner," Kent said, propping his elbows on the table, leaning forward. "I'm your Commander. I'll dress up as the Queen of England if I have to to catch these guys. You're tough, all right, but you ain't gonna out-commitment me."

Jamie got lost a little. The brown pools staring at him also contained fire.

"Thank you, Kent. That's what I want."

No reply.

Kent loosened his shoulders. "So hey. I might look swell in a tiara."

"Just think, Commander, you could carry your gun in that little purse. If you didn't kill 'em with hauteur; that's how she does it."

Kent tried looking down his nose at a peasant. "What did you find out about Mr. Ferguson?"

"He was more complex than his up-and-coming sports marketing image. He showed off his body at the bar that night, then put his jersey on later. Nor was that uncommon, he always showed off, especially if he was with Gary. It was one way Glenn controlled him. Gary knew the other guys wanted Glenn. Glenn rubbed his nose in it, 'See, I don't have to be with you.' It made Gary proud and excited that his lover was good-looking, but scared at the same time."

"Like an exhibitionist?"

"That's too strong a term. Listen, I don't want to make you uncomfortable. How explicit can I get with you?"

"Feel free. Think I don't know what a blowjob is?"

Jamie was taken aback. *I'm sure you do.* "It's common enough that young Gay men with good bodies don't wear shirts at the bar. We dance, we sweat, we use looks to attract a friend or a one-night stand. The bar manager, Russ Dixon, was a friend of Glenn's before he met Gary. Glenn was always a cocktease. When Gary came along, Glenn didn't change. He used other guys' attraction to keep Gary in line. Glenn wanted to be waited on, have everything at home just the way he wanted. As long as Gary did that, Glenn was monogamous. Unless he went out of town."

"Like he dominated the guy?"

"Too strong. We have our own terms for it, tops and bottoms, and bottom men rule. Those are sexual terms, it's complex. Remember the natural pecking order?"

"Glenn was the man, and Gary played the woman's role?"

"They were both men, that's the point of Gay life. If Glenn wanted a blowjob from a woman he'd have gotten a woman. Not that women are any good at it. It takes having a dick to know how to take care of one."

Kent gulped. "You're right, it's complicated. Who did Glenn talk to?"

"His usual admirers. They were eager to talk to me, his murder is the lead topic of conversation, and everyone knows The Ohio Gay Times."

"Was Ford there that night?"

"No, but Russ recognized his photo. Right away he said, 'Schmidgall's ex-lover.' He supposedly hasn't been there in over a year."

"So Ford's got a rep. What's the plan?" Kent gestured for the waiter.

"Hit Chez Nous at 10 o'clock, learn how to handle yourself. We're not going to be together all the time so I can save you from every guy that happens by. Lord, I'd be doing nothing else."

"How do I do it, then?"

"Real simple, Nancy Reagan: just say no. Spare yourself these dueling stereotypes—on the one hand we're all sissified faggots, then magically we turn into brutal rapists. Look around you, these guys are gentle. God, you'd think Gay people just landed here from Mars."

"Up Uranus."

Jamie stared, open-mouthed.

Kent grinned, embarrassed. "Sorry, guy, it just slipped out. I had to say something to keep up with you. Man, you're fast."

The waiter removed their plates. "What can I offer you? Dessert maybe? Something sweet and creamy?"

Jamie said, "If we wanted sweet and creamy we'd go to Roselyn Bakery. It'd be more expensive than you, Miles, but we'd know the health department inspected it before it shut the place down."

"Ooh, you're gorgeous too, even if you are the blond bitch from hell." Miles flounced away.

Kent grinned, "I need you to be my bodyguard in these places, not my lightning rod." Jamie weighed 499 replies. They paid and headed for the door. "Why do we have to go to the bar so late?"

"Because, Your Majesty, queens only come out at night." Then Jamie had to take off to escape the fist flying in his direction.

Kent sniffed, "Should have hit you with my dainty handbag," since he hadn't yet mastered hauteur.

28

Fender

Kent had set up an interview with Glenn Ferguson's boss at her home after dinner. They drove to an address in Broad Ripple, which passed as the artsy section of Indianapolis, Indiana, meaning the last spark of life hadn't been stomped out of it too.

Parking was at a premium, but Kent found a spot two blocks from the house. He and Jamie started up the busy avenue. A man called out, "Look at that blond! Have you ever seen a prettier ass? Hey, guy, you busy tonight?"

"Ooh, and the stud he's with," cried a passenger. He made kissing noises as the driver blared his horn. Blood rushed to Jamie's ears; he stared straight ahead. "Look out!" yelled the passenger. Tires squealed, Jamie winced and quarter-panels crumpled under the impact.

"What the heck?" said Kent, staring at the collision. A woman driver, trying to pull away from the curb, jumped out and gaped at her side-swiped car. Then she saw Jamie and gaped at him.

Jamie glared ahead, boots chopping concrete.

"Guess I should report the location," Kent said, fumbling with a cell phone. "This is a new one on me."

"Let's interview the witness, Commander."

"You're a human traffic hazard."

"I'm an innocent bystander. He's a reckless driver."

"Well, a bystander at least."

Sharon Sachs came to the door. She was attractive, a little chunky, maybe 37. "Ms. Sachs, I'm Sergeant Kent Kessler of the Indiana State Police. This is my partner Jamie Foster." Kent showed his badge.

"How do you do, officers?" Two handsome men were standing on her porch. She stepped out. "Can we talk here? I don't want the dog to get loose."

"That's fine," Kent smiled, showing lovely teeth. "We wanted to ask about Mr. Ferguson's work habits, whether you were happy with his performance."

"I was ecstatic with him. His sales were up 16% last year, when ticket sales were only up nine. He had great work habits, everyone liked and respected him."

"We always get good reports on him. But let me ask, did you ever see any behavior out of him that was uncharacteristic? Were there times that his private life had an effect on his job?" Kent rubbed his chest briefly.

"No, he was very disciplined, a real go-getter. Sure, everybody knew he was Gay, but that has nothing to do with selling beer, nachos and programs. He was a whiz at that, sergeant. He managed the staffing and vendor contracts flawlessly. He'd be in line for a major raise when we get the new fieldhouse open."

Jamie asked, "What was he like, the last day you saw him?"

She shrugged, "Happy, optimistic, working hard."

Kent widened his stance. "Did you ever socialize with him away from the job?"

"I've often had him and Gary here for dinner, plus the occasional cocktail party for a client."

"Oh, you live alone?" Kent twitched his eyebrows.

"Yes, sergeant. Except for the dog, quite alone."

"Do you think Glenn ever used drugs?" He hitched up his jeans, put his thumb in the waistband.

"No. In season the whole staff's randomly tested along with the players. I never knew him to use drugs."

"But it's possible he could have, in the off-season," he winked.

"It's possible, I suppose. But I never saw him under the influence of alcohol, either. So I don't think so."

"Straight and narrow, huh?" It took less than a second, but he adjusted himself. "Well, maybe not those words exactly."

Jamie said stonily, "You're lying, Ms. Sachs. He smoked marijuana and you knew it. You smoked it with him."

She looked off to the street. "Not for years. It was years ago. We're tested, I told you. We always pass."

Kent glanced at Jamie, a signal to keep going. Jamie growled, "When's the last time you smoked together?"

"I don't remember."

"Please, Ms. Sachs, we don't care about your behavior, we care about Glenn's. Can't you see we need to know the truth? When was the last time you two smoked?"

She stared at the handsome, hard young man. "A week after the playoffs," she confessed. "Our financial reports came out after the end of the season, our numbers were great, and Glenn wanted to celebrate. He bought a joint off some dealer down by Riley Towers. One little joint, one time a year. We made the playoffs. We made a profit."

"Thank you. We don't judge, but we need to know. Lies keep us from finding Glenn's killer, so don't ever lie to us again."

She hung her head, enough to glance at Kent's thighs. "I'm sorry. The NBA's a highly-publicized business. I'd hate for one little slip to reflect badly on the organization."

Kent said, "I respect that. Players are under a microscope. So's the front office."

"We sure are. And what kind of company is this organization? One that employs a Gay executive like Glenn, in a management track that doesn't discriminate, that only cares about performance. A Jewish woman from New Yawk supervised him. I'm proud of that. So was Glenn."

"So am I," Jamie said. "Ms. Sachs, how did the NBA lockout affect Glenn's state of mind the last time you saw him? Was he upset about anything? Depressed, anxious, pressured? What was he feeling?"

"His vendors are directly hurt by any labor action, so he consulted closely, kept them fully informed. They're anxious, but they appreciated his consideration, and we're getting through this with a minimum of fuss. He's loyal to them, they're loyal to us. We're all eager to play without bankrupting the teams, and Glenn was holding the vendors. The GM praised him in writing for it, so Glenn was feeling good."

"When is the last time he fought with Gary?"

"He never fought with Gary. In a conflict he simply told Gary what to do. Gary's a little pudgy, see? A little feminine. To him Glenn was a masculine athlete with a beautiful body, the man of his dreams. Gary idolized him; Glenn ate that up. Gary made him a wonderful home, the perfect mate, even though Gary's immature at times. They weren't quite Ozzie and Harriet maybe; who is? But they were close to it; they got along better than most Straight couples. He was faithful to Gary, in love with him." She faced Jamie. "Something about playing the point guard?" He nodded. "But no other drugs, never during the season, it would mess up his performance. He knew that. He was committed to success, an athlete himself. One night a year, one lousy joint, isn't that allowed?"

"Of course," Kent sympathized.

Jamie said, "Then what else must we understand about Glenn to get inside his head?"

"He was so juiced about the new fieldhouse. We're going to blow the lid off this town with new amenities, fabulous food. He couldn't wait.

Young, dynamic and successful, that's Glenn. We adored him. He could have been a general manager one day. I miss him terribly. It's so unfair." She suppressed a sob.

Kent said he was sorry, thanked her. They walked back in silence, frowning over the likelihood that one little weakness for marijuana, once or twice a year, cost a gifted man his life.

* * *

Jamie shook his head as apartment buildings glided by. "What from here?"

"Shoe leather. That's what solves cases 95% of the time. Like you said, re-interview the bartenders, chat up the regulars, what was Glenn wearing, did you see who he talked to? Show the photos. Police work's real glamourous. On TV."

"This is depressing. He had everything going for him."

"Don't get down. You did great back there."

"Me? You turn it on and off like a spigot."

"What are you talking about?"

"Sex appeal. I figured I'd walk the dog while the two of you fucked on the floor."

Kent grinned. "You're seeing things."

"You have the subtlety of a commercial for used cars. You all but groped yourself like a centerfielder."

"I would have, if need be. To see what someone's thinking, watch their eyes. She undressed you, too, don't think I didn't notice. But she was on cruise control till you broke her down. For a bad cop, you're pretty darn good."

"Just get me to the hotel, okay?" *Without any more demonstrations of your heterosexuality.*

"Lighten up. I didn't cause any fender benders."

"We're in Broad Ripple. In Speedway you'd have caused a ten-car pileup, they'd have had to stop the race."

"You're the walking yellow flag. You ought to get liability insurance on that hair."

Jamie flipped his liable hair and his middle finger. They both competed, both smiled, both liked to be teased.

But Jamie had a reason to hurt. One of his own was killed, a talented young man with a devoted lover.

And Jamie had a reason to let go; he was friends with a caring, handsome, Straight police officer who knew all about blowjobs. Jamie couldn't sort it out, and stopped trying.

29

Centerfielder

Kent hadn't rented them two rooms, just one. "Why not?" Jamie asked.

"Why waste the money? It's got two big beds. You can run your laptop on the table."

"But I'm on an expense account."

"I'd share with any other guy, Jamie. Or did you want to…?"

"No, I'm not that way."

"We've gone camping together, we can sure as heck share a whole room. It makes up for the night I should have come after your Mom died."

That silenced Jamie. He fired up his laptop while Kent took a shower. At 9:45, he appeared in the doorway in his BVDs. "What should I wear?"

Jamie's sweat popped out.

He was shocked to see Kent in the flesh. At only 225 pounds he wasn't a stereotypical bodybuilder, he was just all muscle, like an athlete. His pecs and shoulders were big, his abs perfectly defined. His nipples were the size of half dollars. His arms belonged on a giant, his quads bulged. But his skin was the revelation, thin, taut, dark, flawless. Jamie was very proud of his own body, but this man made him feel like a skeleton—a short one at that. He forced his eyes to return to the screen and stay there. "So that's what a home run hitter looks like."

"Well, uh, yeah." Kent scratched his chest hair.

"A sweatshirt will be best. Long sleeves will cover your arms, and you want to fit in, not stand out. Don't draw attention to yourself. You're there to look. Wear a baseball cap. It will hide your face and eyes, so you can observe others more easily. Wear sunglasses too, people will think you're acting cool, but meanwhile you're observing."

"Okay." Kent turned away. Jamie's eyes feasted on ass, narrow, high, round and built for love.

* * *

They headed through the lobby toward a cab when Kent stopped in his tracks, grabbed Jamie and pulled him over to a TV. Onscreen, Jamie was mouthing words while a reporter did a voiceover. Superimposed on Jamie's chest were the words, "Quincy County, Ohio, 1994."

They listened. "...broke the story four years ago when he linked the murder of Aaron Haney, a Richmond, Indiana native living in Indianapolis, to three others here in Quincy County during the 1990's. And now, police confirm, the killer has struck again." Jamie recognized the voice.

"What is this?" Kent asked.

The picture changed to a map of northwest Indiana, showing Willow Slough, then footage of Haney's crime scene, the bridge over Sevenmile Creek. Jamie turned away. But Kent caught his arm again, made him watch. The clip ended with the woman in front of the Quincy County Courthouse and the words, "still at large. Darla Collins for ABC News, Cavendish, Ohio."

Next came a live report about a house fire in the suburbs. Kent and Jamie headed for the door. "How did Channel 5 get that?" Kent asked quietly.

"It's nothing but file footage. The Dayton station heard about my story from last Thursday, so they rehashed it, you can tell by their focus on me. Then Darla did a retake on the voiceover 'for' the network, and the ABC station here pulled it off the satellite. It looks like news, but it's really cost-cutting. It's cheaper for the Indy stations to pay Dayton than to do it themselves, even though it should be their own local story. Knowing Darla, she sold it herself for the residuals. God, I hate local TV."

"You're really well-known over there, aren't you?" Jamie didn't reply. "I can see why. So, what do you think it means?"

The cab was waiting for them. "Every station in town will mention it at 11:00, and The Sun might give it a graf two days from now. That was Channel 7's 11:00 program at 10:00 on Channel 5. That means the competition gets a preview of what Channel 7 has, and they've got an hour to see if their own affiliates have the story, since it was 7's lead. Soon it will be on all five stations. That means our killer's been put on notice. Ever since he dropped Glenn off at the Slough, he's been waiting for his reviews."

"Jeez, that's sick."

"Why kill a bunch of people if you don't want to be famous? But Ferguson witnesses, if any, are also alerted. Poor Gary, I hope he's not watching."

"The 'put on notice' part bothers me. I hate for him to know we're onto him. Darn."

"Hope for witnesses, man," Jamie replied, peering unseeing at the darkness as the car took off. "If people have a right to know anything, it's that there's a serial killer in town."

They talked about the conflict between police work and journalism. Then Jamie prepped Kent for the bar. "Let's review why you're going undercover at all."

"To familiarize myself with the Gay community."

"Good. But more than that, Chez Nous is where Mr. Ferguson disappeared from. Your suspect hangs out there, it's a place he and Glenn had in common. You're in 'A' ball now, no more rookie league."

"Thanks for the promotion, coach."

"It's a Monday, so there won't be much crowd, a perfect night to initiate you. An impulse tells me our killer does not come out on weekends when the bars are crowded. Like with Haney, a sweet, lonely drunk in the corner, it's easier to pick someone up during the week when there's less competition. And Glenn was picked up on a Tuesday after a holiday. Now be forewarned: this place is cruisy, with sexual overtones. They'll assume you're Gay. Don't take it personally, you're here to do a job."

"Right. Should we stay together or stand apart?"

"Apart. If we're together they'll think we're a couple."

"There are couples in Gay life? Is that common?"

"Puh-lease, this is A-ball," Jamie demanded, incredulous and impatient and, as he looked at Kent, less impatient. "Sorry, man. Of course there are couples in Gay life, 40% of us. You don't think Gay people fall in love? Glenn and Gary did."

"I never thought about it before. They weren't just roommates, huh?"

"Kent, Gay people are exactly like everyone else, except that… we're not. Know what I mean?"

"I'm trying. So it's not all just, um, one night stands?" *At the rest stop?*

Jamie rubbed his face, looked out the window. "Please, Kent, try to understand. I was with my lover Rick through vasculitis, amputations, wheelchairs, chemo, prostheses, heart attacks and death at 34. Does that qualify as love, or not?"

"It sure sounds like it."

"We're just like everyone else except we're Gay. It's two men or two women, and that changes things, but we want the same picket fence, shaggy dog and IRA as everyone else. We have the same loyalties, the same virtues and problems. Rick was with the Marines in Beirut, for God's sake. I'm proud to have known the man."

Kent looked out his window. What could he say? *A Marine, in Beirut.* "I'm sorry."

Jamie couldn't handle doe-eyes right now, there was a killer to catch. "Don't worry. Keep asking questions, you're doing great. If I react testily, please forgive me, it's only because… I so want you to understand. I need that. These victims do."

"You're very patient with me. I need to start thinking of you guys as normal, don't I?"

"That's the best thing you've ever said. Don't focus on the difference, focus on the similarity. Mr. Ferguson was a happily married man. His homicide is like every other one you've ever worked."

They arrived at the bar. Jamie went in first. Kent waited a minute, then walked into pitch darkness. Slowly his eyes adjusted through his shades. Dance music was subdued but bouncy. The bar was straight ahead. Jamie took possession of a Bud Light, said a few words which brought a laugh from the bartender, and headed to his left, toward pool tables. Everyone in the room watched him walk away.

Then they looked at Kent. He felt conspicuous. It wasn't his clothes, Jamie's suggestions were right on target. He felt conspicuous because he was in a gaybar.

Don't think about it. He ordered a Miller Lite, and tipped big as he'd been taught. Overhead was a huge rainbow-striped flag, just like the little one Jamie had put on the Red-Haired Boy's grave. Kent wondered what the flag meant.

These people aren't too bad. Kinda weird-looking, some of them, but okay. Half of them look normal even. I wouldn't have guessed if I saw them on the street.

They hug each other a lot. And they laugh, they seem to enjoy each other. Nothing wrong with a little show of affection in their own bar, he decided.

In the corner were two guys wearing leather jackets, tank tops and longjohn underwear designed to outline their equipment. Blatant, like homosexuals on the TV news. One was okay-looking in a grungy, street kind of way. The other was fat and had tattoos. Kent stared briefly. *Dressed alike, maybe they're lovers.* He turned away.

The music sure wasn't his style, but he noticed he was tapping his foot.

Jamie moved through his field of vision, opened a glass door in the back and went through it. Thirty guys followed him, jockeying for position. *There is more to this place than I realized. I better start moving around, they'll think I've taken root here.*

* * *

The guy at the pool table is a hustler. Long hair, the bored look of the not too bright; a little chunky in the middle, are there a lot of customers for that? There was one tonight; a bald man was plying the guy with drinks and using every opportunity to paw him as he lined up a shot. Kent tried not to curl his lip at the display.

A test at 11:13: he had to go to the bathroom. *Where is it here?*

He saw a guy coming out of a swinging door at the back of the pool room. No one else headed that way. Kent waited a minute to make sure. He set down his bottle, walked with casual wariness, pushed through the double doors. Two urinals, a partition between them, *thank goodness, nobody.*

At 11:20, a man in his twenties came up to him, sporting a buzz cut, earrings, Spandex trunks and a T-shirt reading "I'm Not Gay But You Sure Are." Kent heard his own blood circulating.

"How ya doin'?" the guy asked.

"Pretty good," Kent replied evenly. Then, "How are you?" The guy looked normal enough for what he was, maybe a student.

"Tired of this place," Not Gay said. "You're studly. You wanna come to my place and fuck?"

Kent swallowed and recited his lines. "No thanks, I've got a lover waiting for me. I'm headed home myself." To his huge relief, the guy wandered away.

At 11:40, another man struck up a conversation with some comment about the crowd tonight. Kent decided on a light but friendly reply. This man looked like he had his act together, a bank teller or an insurance worker. "Do you play pool?" Jamaal asked.

Kent played pool. Easily beat the guy, who came up and shook hands. "Nice game," said Jamaal. Then he moved away to give Kent space.

Kent relaxed.

*　　*　　*

It was getting late when two guys across the room caught his attention. Slowly his blood ran cold.

They were in love, it was obvious. No one else existed. They talked only to each other; they touched constantly, one sitting on a stool, his lover behind him, arms around his chest, kissing his neck, his ear, his hair. Then they'd shift, take a drink, and touch again, a hand rubbing a thigh, a knee; little kisses on the lips. And no one around them thought a thing about it.

Did the sight of them arouse him? Not in the least. They terrified him.

He'd never been touched that way. He'd never been loved by anyone the way these two loved. But for some reason—*here, now, panic time, in a gaybar?*—he could start to picture being loved like he wanted to be.

He stood stock-still. He couldn't look at them, he couldn't not look.

They couldn't see him stare because of the sunglasses, so he was safe; not that they had the least awareness of his existence. Only one person mattered, and it wasn't him.

Jamie walked past them. Kent instantly broke the stare, forced himself to take three deep breaths. And his feet started walking to the other room. Why on earth should he key in on those two? He didn't want to. When he calmed down, though, he realized Gay men could love each other, like Gary and Glenn did; *like Jamie and Rick.*

*　　*　　*

At 12:30 Jamie came up to him. "Hi there. Come here often?"

"Nope, this is my first time. What's your sign?"

"Burma-Shave. Look at the man on the fourth stool from the end. He looks vaguely like someone you've seen in a photograph."

"I'll do that. Can I buy you a beer as I head past?"

"Mineral water would be nice."

Kent left, came back in a minute. "Sort of like Lash but a lot heavier. And older."

"Our photos are older. It's probably not him, but he's been following me the last half hour. But not talking, not approaching. I'm uncomfortable. If it doesn't bother you for me to say this, often enough guys want to talk."

"I noticed. You're a magnet to these guys."

"I want to cut out."

"Thank God, I'm tired."

"The bartender's calling us a cab."

Kent smiled. "We're a cab."

Jamie grinned back, then went outside to wait. Kent watched the man on the fourth stool from the end. He didn't seem to notice that Jamie left.

Kent walked out. They discussed it; Kent made calls, ran nearby license plates through the computer; no matches. "Lash is an unusual name," Jamie said. "Can you get his address that way?"

Kent tried, got an address in the 800 block of Pennsylvania Street. "Walking distance," Jamie told him.

"I'll assign a plainclothesman to follow him home." Kent made a call to Post 52—and 30 minutes later, nobody showed up. He was stunned. "'Cause it's a Gay bar? Those bastards. They don't even have to go inside, just follow somebody, see who he's with."

Jamie patted Kent on the back. "You said you wanted to learn about the Gay community. Buddy, you just did."

"It's discrimination, Jamie. It ain't right!" Kent got pissed. "My own organization lets me down. Sgt. Gillespie's going to hear about this tomorrow morning, by God. So will Major Slaughter." He called the post again and ordered the shift commander, a corporal, to assign someone. As he did, the man on the fourth stool from the end walked out alone, headed for Pennsylvania Street. They hid. "At least he didn't see us," Kent said in disgust.

What played in Jamie's head was, *"It's discrimination, Jamie. It ain't right!"*

During the cab ride Kent told Jamie about Not Gay. Jamie shrugged, "He said the same thing to me. He memorized his lines better than you did."

"I can't believe guys would say things like that to each other. That's as blatant as any Straight bar I've ever been to. And you'd be amazed at how crude Straight guys can be. Girls too. Some of them are just as bad or even worse."

"The only difference is that it was a guy who was trying to pick you up, not that he was Gay or Straight or Green. Besides, there are 99% fewer fistfights in Gay bars."

Kent didn't have any reply. But he knew guys had to fight sometimes, it was nature's way. "How do you do it, then, when somebody gets drunk? How do you fight if you don't use fists?"

Jamie timed his reply. "We engage in polysyllabic debates over exactly which ten movies Bette Davis got Oscar nominations for."

Kent chortled, "And you always win."

At the door to their hotel room, Jamie said, "Good job, Majesty. You did great tonight. No one knew a thing, and we want to keep it that way. Good job."

Kent amazed himself. "Bet you say that to all the queens." His teeth flashed.

Jamie mumbled, "Yeah yeah yeah," and pushed inside.

Kent hit the sack immediately, but Jamie had computer work to do.

Half an hour later he stepped outside, pulled his cell phone out, dialed. "Here's the progress report you asked for. There won't be another one," he told the voice mail. "We hit the bars tonight and he did fine, no panic attacks and no neon. Cool, smart, funny, as flexible as you said. He's quite remarkable. We got discriminated against tonight and he responded perfectly. He's the best possible cop for this case.

"He's completely ignorant about Gay people but willing to learn. He also put me in my place a bit during dinner—he's the Commander, not me.

"There was a possible Lash sighting, but we're not sure.

"He's pulling Julie Campbell onto his team, and I've suggested that he hire Dr. Steve Helmreich as task force consultant. Steve can keep the group from falling into the jurisdictional jealousy trap. An older, neutral guy might also show the other departments you're not saying Kent's better than they are, when Bulldog's got twenty years' experience on him. All departments are competent in investigation, it's the rapid team-building that's essential. Therefore an outside consultant.

"Most of all thanks for your help all these years. I'm looking forward to seeing you and 300 other hot men at the Midwest Fun Run next month. Oh, but buddy? The next time this happens, do me a favor; assign an ugly dude. Kent is driving me nuts. I saw him tonight in his underwear—wow. I knew you were into psychotorture, but this is ridiculous. You will have hell to pay when this is over. And don't forget—I'm young, hung and mister, I'm blond, I know exactly how to torture you back!"

He cackled a full ten seconds on Major Slaughter's voicemail.

30

Message

Kent knocked on the bathroom door at 7:32 a.m. "You ready?"

Jamie, just out of the shower and naked, grabbed a towel in panic, got it around himself, turned his back to the door. "Ready for what?"

Kent leaned through. "For breakfast. I'm starved."

"No, I'm not ready. I'm not even awake. We worked last night. You said to sleep in!"

"Man, it's almost 8 o'clock. Half the morning's gone."

"What does sleeping in mean to you, ace?"

"Seven o'clock. What's it mean to you?"

"Ten!" Jamie gave heaven a hand gesture. "Which means I don't function till noon. Will someone teach this man about Gay time?" Then he chuckled, the guy was just up from rookie league. "Go on, give me 30 minutes. I'm not going anywhere with wet hair."

It wasn't wet hair that Kent noticed, but a dramatic, V-shaped back. Athletes always compare and compete. It wasn't huge, but it was a darn good back.

*　　　　*　　　　*

In the coffee shop they traded plans. Kent would call FBI/Quantico to get a copy of Behavioral Sciences' profile of the killer. He would release it to The Ohio Gay Times; Jamie would have another exclusive, and that would get Louie off his back. "Is your boss going to be a problem?" Kent asked over the last of a tall stack of pancakes, eggs and biscuits with sausage gravy.

Jamie sipped heavily-doctored coffee, moved a croissant around on his plate, ate a strawberry. "Louie Mascaro is always a problem. To stay here I'm going to need story out of this every issue, Kent. Something beyond 'the investigation is continuing.'"

"We'll come up with something," the trooper said, his mouth full of wheatcakes, maple syrup and real butter. "We're a team, you and me."

"Not if sleeping in means 7 a.m., we're not. If country people had running water you wouldn't have to get up so early."

"Maybe we can download some over the Internet."

*　　*　　*

Kent left for his new office—and a telephone harangue with the commander of Post 52. From the hotel room, Jamie checked his mother's answering machine. It was long distance, so he used his cell phone instead of charging it to his room. "One moment please. You have three messages." Tape spun; the first was from Casey, just checking in and being thoughtful.

Then: "Hello, Jamie. This is your friend down in Indianapolis." Jamie sat down on the bed. *The same brittle voice…*

"I hear you're casing the bars now. You want a confrontation, we'll have a confrontation. How's life on Tad Lincoln Drive? Did you get your mom's yard mowed?"

A hole opened up in Jamie's stomach and acid dripped in.

"I just wanted to tell you I know where you are. I read your mother's obituary in the Sun. Survived by three sons, Daniel of Denver, Stone of

Bedford, James of Columbus, Ohio. So that told me where your mother lived and where you are these days.

"You know you've written a million stories about Roger's so-called victims in Newton County, and that red-haired guy, and how you're from there originally. That was very foolish, Jamie. That was a mistake."

Jamie reached for his smokes. *We were naive then, we thought it would add power to the story. It did add power. But it was read by a killer.*

"I must compliment you on your mother's funeral. Very classy, with the string quartet and all. Of course, I prefer an open casket myself, but I know you fucking Episcopalians have other ideas. Let the corpse be seen, that's what I believe in!" An obscene giggle.

"Your brother Danny is looking good for his age. But Stone's about ready to go to seed, don't you think? Old Straight jocks always do." Jamie's hand clutched his mouth. He flashed on his phone tap and cassette recorder—useless in his suitcase, then he realized he didn't need them, this was already recorded. He'd call and play this back from Kent's office. *Jesus Christ. This son of a bitch was at Mom's funeral? I even looked for him.*

"So, Mr. Bigtime Reporter, or at least you think you are, Mr. Award Winner, you weren't content with finding that Ferguson guy—was that his name?—in the slough. I can't believe you're this stupid. Don't you know why I fucking planted him there? Don't you know I was trying to warn you off? It was your last chance, after you printed that pre-Labor Day 'Strangler' shit.

"It's that time of year, all right. But no, you've got to play the big Gay activist, show the world what a fucking caring person you are, when anybody else would have taken these murders for what they were and left 'em alone. But no, not Jamie Foster, the best Gay reporter of the year. Hell no. Jamie Foster wants to be a hero."

"No, I don't," Jamie told the tape.

"Yeah, you want to be a fucking hero. You think you've been a hero for the past four years. So I thought about it and I decided, okay, what's it take for him to get over this? Dump a body on his doorstep?

"But I went easy on ya. Besides, you weren't on your doorstep, from what the neighbors told me; there wasn't any mail in your mailbox in Columbus. Jamie's on vacation. Where'd he go? How about his Mom's?

"So Labor Day came, and I took pity on ya. Did I dump John Doe in Columbus? No. In West Lafayette? No. See what a nice guy I am? I always told you I was, and Roger too, and you never could get it right, you asshole.

"Okay, what's the next best alternative? How about the slough up in Morocco? It's got water, it's isolated, it's another jurisdiction, the county sheriff there doesn't investigate anything, it all goes to the state police; and I happen to know the Rensselaer troopers couldn't find their ass with a roadmap. Perfect. Now maybe Jamie will get the picture and get out of my life.

"And what do I get for my trouble, my time and consideration? Another goddamn copyrighted story while Jamie tries to win the Pulitzer Prize."

The voice hardened. "I'll tell ya, I have fucking had enough of you. You leave me with only one alternative. I've already got the bridge picked out I'm gonna dump you off. You'd love it if you knew where it was. It's very à propos. You stupid faggot. I can't believe you went to all those hotshot colleges and still root for Purdue.

"I'm gonna dump you off a little one-lane bridge—that road out of Battle Ground?—smack dab into the Wabash River! You can float your way to campus, Jamie.

"So I'll see you at the bars this week. I'll be wearing my Muscular Dystrophy Telethon T-shirt, just for you. I hope you've got your will together since Rick died on ya. You're gonna need one. And ol' Danny will be back in Lafayette for another string quartet, and I'll take it from there."

Jamie hadn't rewritten his will. Everything was still in Rick's name. *You keep your hands off my family!*

"Oh, I forgot. You really should have changed the default code for playing back the messages on this machine. You are such a fucking fool. I punched in 1-2-3 and it plays back everything you've got on this tape. By the way, who's Casey? Is that whose dick you're suckin' these days, now that Rick checked out on ya? Sounds like a nigger. Christ, Jamie. You're not only a cocksucker, you're a nigger-lover. That's really disgusting, you know that? Were you suckin' him off while Rick was in the hospital? Don't you know niggers stink down there? I mean, we're talking rank."

How would you know, unless you had your nose down there? Faggot!

"So I'll be able to erase this evidence before you even get a chance to preserve it. My computer is going to be calling in every three minutes. I reach two busy signals on your line and you're dead meat, because I've already talked for five minutes. I'll know you got the message, and I'll know where to find you, and then you're history. I'm going to have a great time with you. I've looked forward to this for a long, long time, you nigger-loving faggot hero in his own mind, incompetent asshole. Oh yes: Have a nice day."

A pre-recorded voice said, "Tuesday, 4:22am."

Jamie listened numbly to the last message, a brief one from Father Jim, who wanted to know if he was all right.

He wanted to hang up, but then he punched another code. "One moment please," said the pre-recorded voice. "I will replay messages." Jamie heard the whir of tape rewinding. *I can replay forever!*

He grabbed his camera bag. Notebooks, pens, cassettes flew out as he searched for his tape recorder and the tap. He found them and dashed back to the phone. Ford's voice. *Still time.*

He placed the tap's suction cup near the receiver's ear, hoped he had it in the right place. It had been a long time since Bulldog bought him the mic and taught him to use it. He popped a new cassette in the recorder. The answering machine was now replaying Father Jim's message. Jamie plugged the jack into the cassette player and punched Record. This would be tricky.

Tape recorder in one hand, phone in the other, Jamie heard, "That was your last message." He re-entered the code for the machine, soon heard rewinding sounds. He switched off the cassette, hit Rewind. Three seconds later, he hit Play.

Father Jim's voice on his cassette in Indianapolis, soothing. "Yes!" Jamie shouted.

The answering machine was just about done rewinding. Jamie reset the tape recorder, hit Record. First Casey. Then "Hello, Jamie. This is your friend down in Indianapolis."

The next five minutes were agonizing. This week! At "the bars." Which one? What had Ford planned?

Danny, Jamie's beloved big Bro. *Keep your filthy hands off my family!*

Once the answering machine got to Father Jim again, Jamie hit Stop on the cassette, then Rewind, then Play. "... you've got your will together since Rick died on ya. You're gonna need one."

Jamie wasn't the only one who'd made a mistake. This was two now. Besides the recorder in his hand, there would be phone records of Ford's original call, and all those calls from his computer to West Lafayette if he made them, plus the one where the computer hit Jamie in the act of retrieving; the answering machine itself.

Maybe not, if Ford called back and hit Erase. Jamie punched in more Touch-Tone numbers, ordered a new access code for the answering machine, then replay again. Ford could try all 1000 three-digit combinations, but that would take time or, more likely, programming. Jamie could stay on the line until West Lafayette troopers got there to yank out the machine.

The records on Jamie's cell phone would also be admissible. *I've got you at last, creepface! This cassette itself is enough to convict. Voice-prints, baby.* He punched the air like he'd just won the Gay Super Bowl.

He had the recording now and felt like hanging up, not wanting to hear it again. Then he had another idea. Still connected to West Lafayette on the cell phone, he picked up the hotel phone, dialed. "Stonewall Task Force," Kent boomed.

"Get back to the hotel now. Message from the suspect on my Mom's answering machine. I've made my own recording of it. Order the West Lafayette post to enter my Mom's house and grab that machine. Key's on the ledge, above left of the door. You come and listen to this filth."

"Be right there. Stay calm, partner."

Jamie was right, he could replay indefinitely. Maybe it would be a stronger case if Kent also listened first-hand and made his own recording. They could both testify.

In less than one cycle from the phone machine, Jamie heard a siren approach. Soon Kent burst into the room, ready for war.

31

Sister

Jamie screamed, "What do you mean it's not enough?"

"If you're asking," said chief assistant prosecutor Rob Willingham, "is it enough to convict for phone harassment, yes. We could get stalking. Terroristic threats, a felony at least. Accessory, yes. But for murder, it's way too chancy."

"What more do you need? I can identify his voice; you can make voice prints. You've got him on tape describing the place, the time of year, references to the serial string, the Schmidgall connection. He admits he dumped Ferguson off at the Slough. That isn't a confession of murder? Now you're telling me you want video of him doing it? Why not wait for the goddamn Broadway musical?"

"The reference to Ferguson is not enough. I want enough evidence to get a conviction for murder, kid, not phone harassment or accessory after the fact. We don't want another Crum here, walking away scot-free."

"You want a goddamn video for cases Marion County has never cared a fuck about."

"Jamie, settle down. Try to listen," Kent urged. Jamie glared at him, felt a little betrayed. "No one wants to lock this guy up more than we do.

But what if he's not the only one? What if he's like Schmidgall, and the vet is in on it, or Lash, or who knows how many? Picking up Ford, assuming we get a conviction, doesn't lead us to the rest of them. If we're really going to stop it, we need them all."

"Why don't you pick him up, play him the tape and manipulate the truth out of him? Isn't that what you guys are so good at?"

"What if he doesn't break?" Major Slaughter asked.

Jamie snapped, "Major, you won't know if you don't try."

"So we're supposed to Rodney King this dude, is that it?" the prosecutor asked. "Beat the truth out of him? Whatever it takes?"

"Get a killer off the streets and use psychology, not beat his head in," Jamie slammed back. "Don't insult my Commander that way. This is twice now you've used all-or-nothing thinking."

Slaughter noted, "He's right, Rob. Anything short of a murder conviction, you had Ford walking away scot-free."

Kent said, "We all need to calm down and look at this thing rationally. Okay, Mr. Prosecutor?"

Jamie said, "Commander, based on your experience and knowledge of the suspect's emotional state, what interviewing technique would you choose with him? Would you be empathic or confrontational?"

"Empathic. Get him to open up, tell me why he hurts."

"Major, Mr. Prosecutor, this trooper excels at being empathic. Ford won't stand a chance. The face will soften him up, and the genuine kindness will tip him over."

Slaughter said, "That's a powerful point."

"Interview him. Maybe he'll confess to everything in five minutes. Dahmer did. All they had to do was ask him. This guy's number two obsession is the day he gets caught. He knows he's out of control. He can't wait till he sees your lights. The suspense is killing him. Why else is he calling me all the time?"

"Dahmer acted alone," Willingham said. "Even if we did get Ford to confess, it doesn't guarantee we get the accomplices. Confessions are worth diddly."

"That's your problem, you want guarantees," Jamie sneered. "Would you need guarantees if the victim was your sister?"

The prosecutor's face turned red. Jamie didn't back down, but he did finally allow a standoff. "Major, tell me this is not because Glenn Ferguson was Gay."

"It's not about that, Mr. Foster."

The prosecutor yelled, "No, we just want a jury to convict Ford of something besides a goddamn traffic ticket! Jesus, George, your CI's a fucking prima donna."

"No, asshole. I'm a reporter," Jamie spat. "Who's actually managed to get some evidence on this creep, unlike anyone else in this room."

Slaughter closed his eyes, sighed. Kent shook his head. Jamie stared into space. "I'm sorry, Commander. You got the Walkers. And the teenage girl. I spoke out of turn."

"Forget it, man. We both got the Walkers. You did, for that matter."

"So these are my choices, Mr. Prosecutor: let myself be stalked so you can get your guarantee; or you do nothing?"

"Jamie, now you see what police work is really like," Kent urged. "We have to face these questions all the time."

"Don't turn on me, partner," Jamie warned. "You won't like the consequences, partner."

Slaughter intoned in his deep, controlling, calming voice, "You're upset, Mr. Foster. It's understandable. All of us are."

"Yeah, right. This prosecutor isn't the one who got the call. Ford knew about the music at my mother's funeral! That wasn't in the paper. He had to be there to know."

Slaughter shoved back his chair and jumped up. "It's not a crime to attend a funeral! Think, Mr. Foster. We are all upset. We just handle it differently. I'm sure you do not want to impugn these officers' motives. You're not the only caring person in this room."

Jamie was quiet for a time. He looked at Slaughter. "I respectfully disagree," he said softly. "It's very much a crime for a murderer to attend my mother's funeral."

"Jamie, I didn't mean to undermine the dignity of your mother or the solemnity of her service."

"And I don't mean to impugn anyone's motives. But if your department had a better record of working these cases for the last decade, the trust issue would never come up. If I'm out of line, I apologize. Otherwise it's my job to push you to make an arrest."

"The question is, what's our best hope of success? Isn't that so, Mr. Foster?"

"I want a cigarette," Jamie scowled.

Willingham tossed a pack across the table. Jamie jerked his jaw up an inch in acknowledgment, took out a smoke and lit up. He inhaled deeply, exhaled, looked out the window at nothing.

Somehow I've become the key to this whole case.

Wished he'd brought menthols. *This cigarette is for shit.*

Six months after Rick. My mom not even dead two weeks. And now I'm supposed to give it up for the Straight man's law, which says I'm a felon in 23 states, a non-person in all but nine. Welcome to Amerika, boy.

He faced the prosecutor, put his hands on the table and leaned forward. "Assuming you're right, which I do not assume: Is there no value in getting him off the streets for six months or a year? If you can get terroristic threats, that's a longer jail term. No one dies during that time. That counts for something important. And you start to tighten the noose for when he gets out. Assuming that you can't nail him for life, which I think you can."

"Sure," Willingham conceded. "We can take him out for a short period at minimum. Maybe more. The felony's six years. Doesn't mean a judge will keep him that long."

"If that's how you want to play it, Jamie, that's fine," Kent said. "I thought you wanted to catch a killer."

Jamie didn't know whether to laugh or cry. "I thought I just did," he said, exasperated and furious. "Why are you turning on me, partner? Surely you're not as bad as the rest of them."

Kent was torn, didn't know what to say. Doe-eyes finally got to Jamie. "I'm sorry, Kent. The last thing I want is to impugn your motives. You've been great, man. I'm not being objective, Major. Mr. Willingham, I'm sorry, I guess I don't understand the law."

"Jamie, forget it," Kent scowled.

"The way to do it," Willingham said, "is to wire the CI."

"No way," Kent insisted, "I won't allow it. He's in too much danger as it is. Let me try talking to Ford. We can videotape the whole thing and prove any confession wasn't coerced."

Willingham said, "And if that doesn't work, we're stuck charging a killer as a mere accessory."

Slaughter sighed at the dilemma. "It does come down to what you want, Mr. Foster. What your goal is. You are the one being stalked. I don't doubt Sgt. Kessler's interviewing powers; but it's a gamble. Absent a confession, I think the prosecutor is right if we go for murder. Meanwhile this is an extremely valuable tape."

"How nice of you to acknowledge that," Jamie muttered. "Pardon my sarcasm, I know I'm overinvolved, but God. Maybe you can get Tommy Tune to do your choreography."

Slaughter chuckled, but he wouldn't be diverted. "It is a great piece of evidence. It could be the centerpiece when we nail the guy, if we do. But it's not a stand-alone. It's a **piece** of evidence, Mr. Foster. And we may be up against a very powerful force here. It's probably not just one guy. You know that." Slaughter looked away. "I'm sorry. But he doesn't give any information that only the killer would know; and that's what constitutes proof. There's nothing to keep him from claiming he only transported the body. What happens when we haul his ass into court against millionaire lawyers and a possible organization behind him? Can we make it stick? If this were any other case, maybe we could. Isn't that right, Rob?"

"Sure, if this were an isolated case. You voice-print the tape, confront him and say, 'They're your own words.' It's a great tape and you've done a brilliant job, Mr. Foster. I give you that willingly. You alone got this evidence. But this is not your normal killer."

"The question is the others, Jamie," Kent said. "We take down Ford, even put him on Death Row, that doesn't guarantee your people stay alive. It just gives you the Schmidgall result all over again; one in jail and two or three others still on the loose. What if there really is an organization? They'll just find themselves another Ford."

Jamie hadn't thought of that. But he knew the Schmidgall cases better than anyone. "Consider the alternative on Schmidgall. Maybe it's for the wrong crime, but Chicago gets Schmidgall, subtract 21 unsolved cases and one killer. Criticize Chicago and Kickapoo County all you want for not getting Crum; I've made a career out of doing that. But with Schmidgall in prison, they can still close those cases, and he doesn't kill anyone else. For which even I have to give Chicago credit.

"Rob admits you can get Ford for a felony in the Ferguson case; what about Gary Tompkins, Kent? Doesn't Gary have a right to get on with his life after his lover was murdered? I would think that would be the first consideration. But no, you guys want guarantees, you want to bust the whole Mafia in one fell swoop. I know you're the studs of the world, but even Eliott Ness broke a complex case into pieces."

Slaughter thought. "Mr. Foster, that's helpful. Gentlemen, we cannot make this decision at this level of authority. Let us meet as soon as possible with the top brass, play them the tape and go from there. Mr. Foster, we'll need you to be present for that meeting."

"If I might be wired up, you better believe I'll be there. I have two side issues as well. One, what if this is a red herring? What if we focus on the bars in Indianapolis, and meanwhile he's in Chicago or Cincinnati or Fort Wayne? If I were he, I sure as hell wouldn't run the risk of finding any more victims in Indy."

Kent said stonily, "If we take his threat at face value, he doesn't want just any victim anymore. He wants you, Jamie. He's already got your bridge picked out." Inside Kent recoiled, but he was a cop. "He figures that if he takes you out he's home free."

"Till you came along, he would be. Point two: do we have anyone watching this guy? I know events are moving fast, but we don't want to be sitting around a table without someone watching his every move."

"When we find out where he's staying, we'll surveill him 24 hours a day," Slaughter said. "The phone company's getting us the number and location right now."

"If it's his home number."

"True."

"That's a pretty big if, major."

"True. But we'll know in ten minutes. Sergeant, do we have the original recording from the answering machine in West Lafayette?"

"Yes, sir. Jamie gave us permission. The machine records on a regular cassette, not a computer chip, so all we did was remove the evidentiary tape and replace it. If the suspect calls again, he'll get the same outgoing message, like nothing happened."

"Excellent."

Jamie agonized in silence. He had to work to keep from imploding. "Damn," he finally said. He stubbed out the lousy cigarette. He was so weary.

Tiredness he could shake off. Fury at the Strangler he could not.

He straightened his back and said, "If the brass agree that this is their best recommendation, then I will consider doing it. And you people..." he looked at the prosecutor, then at George, and finally at Kent, "you better act like Glenn Archer Ferguson is your brother or sister."

Willingham nodded, "Fine." He reached into his wallet, pulled something out, tossed it to Jamie. "Keep it for the duration."

Jamie gazed at a photo of a young, pretty woman. "What's her name?"

"Cassie Willingham. She's my sister."

Jamie put the photo in his shirt pocket, nodded pure respect. "I don't mean to be a prima donna, Rob."

"You're not, I spoke out of turn too. I swear I'll treat Mr. Ferguson like my brother."

"That's all I need."

Slaughter grimaced, "This meeting is over."

Kent stood, trying to look more macho than he felt. When the others left, he grabbed and hugged the little guy. "I'm sorry."

Jamie broke the hold in 1.2 seconds and strode out of the room.

32

Summit

Jamie darted into an elevator just as the doors closed. Slaughter was the only other person aboard. He punched the Stop button.

Jamie slumped against the wall and wailed, "George, I'm so tired of this."

Slaughter stepped over and opened his arms. "Let's give Jamie a hug."

Body contact was what Jamie needed, despite his rejection of Kent. Slaughter held him a long time. "You've been under so much stress. And still you got us that tape. You think so well, I don't know how you do it. You've always amazed me, James."

"Thanks, chief. My brain be 'bout to short out."

"Let's get Jamie's needs met. What do you need? Food? A nap? A massage?"

Jamie slowly released his friend; Slaughter re-started the car. "All of the above," Jamie said. "But most of all I want to work out."

"Excellent. I'll call my club and arrange it, and also a massage afterward."

Jamie's shoulders dropped a yard in total relaxation. "That does sound nice."

"You need it. My treat."

Jamie was used to paying his own way, but he didn't argue. "I love you, buddy."

Slaughter smiled, "I have this weakness for blonds." The doors opened.

Kessler was waiting for Slaughter in the lobby. Seeing Jamie, he motioned him over. Reluctantly, Jamie came. Kent whispered, "You mad at me?"

For Jamie, it was another look at long-lashed brown eyes full of concern. He sighed, weary of this too. "No, Kent. You're doing great. I'm just mad at this situation. Sick to death of it. I'm sorry I attacked your motives. You're a fine trooper, the best these cases have ever had."

"No problem. If I'd been working a case for four years I'd get frustrated too."

"But hey," Jamie said, more energetic. "I get to work out. I need to do something to get this stuff off my mind. While you guys chat up the top brass, I'll be filling my lungs with fresh air and sunshine, pumping iron, and then a massage afterward. Bliss! I'm going to float up to heaven."

"Ooh, I wish I could work out with you."

"Yeah, right. So you can beat me in every category?" *Don't add to my frustrations.*

"That ain't why, it would feel good. Can we have lunch together at least?"

"Major," Jamie called, "where are we going for lunch?"

"We'll meet you at the club, Mr. Foster."

"Cool," they said.

*   *   *

Jamie called Columbus. Casey was laying out the front page with the psychological profile, as well as dummying an Extra since the story was hot. The office was on high alert, exhilarated and scared and nearing deadline. Jamie told his editor the morning's developments. Casey cried, "Child, you make my heart stop!"

"It won't affect this issue, though. We can't report the tape, it's too dangerous. But the minute you're done, get over here."

Casey would hop a plane at Port Columbus that night. He'd also bring Kenny Dyson. If there was a bust, the portly Straight antique dealer/secret Gay stringer deserved to be in on it; and The Times would need all the editorial help it could get. "Don't get your hopes up, Case. We've been down this road before. We can still lose him."

Louie was anxious but subdued with Jamie. "Don't get yourself killed, hotshot. If something happens they'll raise my insurance rates. Where would I find another stud reporter at this rag? Anyone near as good as you."

"Why, Louie, I didn't know you cared."

"Aw, I'm over you, prettyboy."

"That's 'stud reporter prettyboy' to you."

Louie didn't rise to the bait. "Be careful, James."

Jamie got quiet. "Right, Lou. Thank you for all your help. I know I'm spending your money, but it's for a good reason. Look at what you're financing, tracking down someone who murders Gay men. I have nothing but respect for you."

"Works both ways. Now get off my phone."

* * *

His body liquid after the massage, Jamie flowed into the club dining room, ornate in its carved wood and simulated English atmosphere; not half-bad. He found George and Kent at a table. They stood up for him. It was odd, but an honor, and Jamie liked it.

They ordered, and Jamie learned the time of the bigwigs' meeting. "You'll even have time to take that nap if you want," George noted.

"Great. It would make up the deficit between sleeping in and sleeping in."

Kent smiled, started to go into some discussion of the case, but Jamie held up a hand to slow him down. "Kent, is this essential for us to know before the meeting? If so, then lay it on us, but if not, I'd rather talk about anything else. The chief here just got me feeling good."

Slaughter asked, "How was André's massage today?"

"Wonderful." Jamie closed his eyes to feel it again. "He loosened the fascia in my back, did the most amazing things to my abs and feet."

Kent grinned, "Go with the flow, buddy."

"I even wangled my way into a pickup basketball game. I love playing old men. Suddenly I'm Michael Jordan."

So they chattered about sports, movies, Slaughter's recent trip to Mexico and Cuba, Kent's plans for hunting season. Jamie tried to act non-judgmental at that topic; Kent invited George to tag along on his Dunes trip, and the chief said he'd go. They rehashed their water skiing adventure on Lake Shafer, and Jamie said he'd never done it. "Come next summer," Slaughter invited. "Both of you. We'll have a great time."

Jamie happily accepted. *Does this mean I get to see my guy in swimming trunks?*

Kent accepted too.

* * *

After the meal Kent told him, "Working out agrees with you. This is the first time I've ever seen you clean your plate. I was starting to think you were Karen Carpenter."

"I can pack it away with the best of them if I'm getting my…" (physical) "…needs met. Like a return to normal life."

"How often do you work out at home?"

"Weights three days a week, light, medium and heavy; bike and abs six days. Sundays I read The New York Times and vegetate."

"Six days a week? That's a great program."

"I'd love to get back to it. To enjoy positive health, the uppermost level, I have to work out. Otherwise I don't have enough appetite. Workouts are essential."

"All things in balance, you're right."

"One way or another, it'll be over soon," Slaughter assured them.

"It's the one way or another I'm concerned about," Jamie replied.

"It's your rule," Kent said, pointing his finger. "Don't think about the case. You're off duty. Go grab that nap."

"All right, Mom."

Kent grinned, glad they were friends again.

* * *

First there was a cops-only meeting for team-building, run by Dr. Steve Helmreich. Then Kent and Jamie sat alone on a bench in the lobby of state police headquarters before they went up to the conclave. Kent said, slowly and deliberately, "We got his address, we're watching it but he's not home, we don't know where he is. I may not get the chance to interview him before tonight. But it might come down tonight. If so, are you willing to help lure him out?"

Jamie thought and felt before he spoke. "He has to be stopped. If you'll help me, and the plan is good, then yes."

"I have to say these things to you, both as a police officer and as your friend. Don't be an excitement freak, Jamie. Don't be a hero."

They looked in each other's eyes a long time. Kent's questions forced Jamie to make a conscious choice. "I won't be. Thanks for the warning. Don't let me get killed."

"I won't. But know your motivation. It's an exciting, special status, being a police informant in a big case."

It was a lot more exciting to be a reporter with a great story. But Kent was warning him of the danger; and dead war correspondents stop filing dispatches. "It's not worth dying for. I have a simple motivation. I want him stopped. No one is allowed to murder my people and get away with it."

"Then partner, let's stop him." They shook hard and headed upstairs.

Slaughter's office was well-lit in the afternoon. "Right this way, Mr. Foster," said Harvey, his assistant. "The conference room is right down this hall."

They presented quite a picture at the double doorway: the dazzling blond guest of honor; the impressive deputy chief next to his tall, handsome task force commander. They took places at the head of the oblong table, the major in the power position, Kent and Jamie on either side. Dr. Helmreich sat at the foot of the table in the other power position. Harvey had arranged everything perfectly; Jamie knew he would.

Slaughter made introductions: state police superintendent Colonel Jackson R. Potts; Post 52 Commander Sgt. Eamon Gillespie; City Police Chief Melvin Watson, County Prosecutor Sanford Brown, County Sheriff Richard Grumwald; chiefs of staff for the governor, mayor and U.S. attorney; members of the interagency task force, Detective Homer "Bulldog" Sauer and his partner, Sgt. Barry Hickman of Quincy County, Ohio; Trooper Julie Campbell of West Lafayette; Jasper County Lt. Jack Snyder and IPD Lt. Phil Blaney; Dr. Helmreich, serial murder expert from the University of Illinois and task force consultant; and FBI Agent-in-Charge Frank Carson.

Jamie studied Gillespie, old-fashioned, barrel-chested, pushing 50—and the same rank as Kent at 26.

Slaughter framed two issues: "Is the evidence already in hand against Thomas Alan Ford sufficient to charge him with the murder of Glenn Ferguson? If so, given that Ford is a suspect in twelve other murders and is the ex-lover of convicted serial killer Roger Schmidgall, and both are connected to suspect Dr. Randolph Scott Crum, is it best to take down a bird in the hand or two in the bush?"

Jamie prepared to play the tape. "It's graphic, I have to tell you. There is homophobic content, and he's quite viciously racist. Chief Watson, everyone else, it's ugly."

"He's a killer," Watson snorted. "What else would he be but ugly?"

Jamie hit Play. But afterward, faces were ashen.

Col. Potts was the first to speak. "I'll be damned. What do you think, Sandy?"

Prosecutor Brown frowned and shook his head. "It's risky all around."

"What does that mean?" Jack Snyder asked.

"The tape itself is clearly chargeable, especially with those phone records. You've got terroristic threats, aggravated menacing, phone harassment, stalking, transporting the body, all felonies. But light ones, six years maximum. We can't hope for consecutive sentences unless we can tie him more closely to the murder. If this is your killer, you want to put him away for life, not six years. On the question of a conviction for one murder, I'd rate it possible, perhaps even probable, depending on results from a search warrant and what kind of defense team he's got. On the question of conviction for multiple murders, nowhere near. What is our evidence on those?"

George signaled, and Jamie played the Schmidgall videotape. Jamie then explained how the suspects were intimately connected, discussed Crum's acquittal, the lawyers who represented him and the theory of "murder for profit as well as fun."

Hearts sank, as Kent passed out copies of Snyder's photos from Jasper County, showing the suspects in various groupings. Agent Carson said, "Commercial snuff films don't exist."

Jamie asked, "Then how did Crum pay for those lawyers? You forget the anonymity of the Internet, the compulsive need to share sexual fantasies. Killers can't help but brag, murder is too big a secret to keep inside."

No reply. So Jamie asked Bulldog to reveal Quincy County's old physical evidence. Jamie had waited four years to hear this. Bulldog said, "We have a tire track from one of our crime scenes that perfectly matches one we obtained on Ford's Toyota—the tire was almost bald, just a little tread on the inside, so there's no mistaking it—plus an eyewitness who places Lash and another unidentified man at a fast-food joint in our county within the proper time frame on our third body. It was never enough for us to charge them, but that's why they've always been our prime suspects."

He looked at Jamie, who gave him a thumb up. If a Straight man and a Gay man could be friends and use each other, they were fast friends.

"So what are our alternatives?" IPD's Lt. Blaney asked.

"You can do the others, but there's only one best alternative," Carson said.

"Catch him in the act," said Bulldog, a little worried. Kent looked at him instead of at Jamie.

"It's a terrible thing to ask of a man," Phil Blaney observed.

Then everyone in the room looked at Jamie. They were waiting on him again. *Jamie, the sacrificial lamb.*

"There's another question," Carson said. "This is an awfully big operation to hang on this type individual." Jamie stared. "No offense, kid."

Potts seemed to take this as a good objection.

They don't think I can do this, Jamie realized. *Is there some undercurrent here about being Gay?*

"Maybe we need to discuss this among ourselves," Prosecutor Brown suggested.

It **was** because Jamie was Gay. "Wait a goddamn minute, I'm not going anywhere. We're going to hash it out right here, right now. No one else got the death threat, I did. I'm a full participant here. I do want you to say whatever you have to say, we need to respect everyone's input; but I will be in the room or there won't be any operation."

He breathed to calm himself, and was calm. Slaughter sent him good vibes. Carson smiled.

Bulldog spoke next; stood up to do it, too. "Fellows, Officer Campbell, Ms. Anderson, I have known this individual for, what's it been, Jamie? Three years? Four?" Jamie nodded. "And in that time, he has always done exactly what he said he would do. He has worked these cases tirelessly, when nobody else in the media gave a rat's ass about 'em. He has been courageous, he has always kept his word; he's supplied us with very important information, always reliable. He's a very, very bright individual, and he's cooperated to the fullest extent with the officers involved. You can see that here today with these tapes. I don't know how he gets the information he does. I'm sitting here amazed.

"Now I don't agree with his lifestyle, and Jamie, you know that. But these murders aren't about anybody's lifestyle, and they're sure as hell not about whether Homer Sauer happens to agree with it. They're just murders. And sometimes when I've forgotten that, got caught up in the Gay aspects of 'em, Jamie's been the one to remind me. They're just murders. Forget the Gay thing." Bulldog looked around the room. Dr. Steve Helmreich nodded vigorous encouragement.

"Me, too," Kent spoke up.

"I learned it from him," Jamie said, pointing at Helmreich.

Blaney spoke. "And the fact is, Jamie's the one who got the threat in that phone call. He's the one the suspect wants. Now we know why Ferguson ended up where he did in that slough up north. To send a message to Jamie."

"I don't see how there's any other way to do it," Chief Watson said. "If you're willing," he said to Jamie. "Who else we got?"

"No one," Bulldog said. "Otherwise it's a picayune terroristic charge at best, from what the prosecutor here is saying, or a maybe-doable murder prosecution."

"We're getting ahead of ourselves," Slaughter said.

Carson of the FBI cleared his throat. "The Bureau doesn't like working with this type individual."

That was it! Instantly Jamie's voice was white hot. "The Bureau has non-discrimination orders from Janet Reno, you son of a bitch. I'll have the White House on your ass so fast you'll wake up on an iceberg outside Fairbanks. It's even bleaker than this godforsaken cowtown." He rose, took two steps toward Carson. "I haven't seen your office take any effective action in these cases in twelve years, because the Bureau is filled with homophobic bigots like you. Why are you here, anyway? Was your Klan camping trip rained out?"

"You little punk," Carson snarled.

"You're not from Behavioral Sciences. You have no expertise. Your office has done nothing but obstruct this investigation, foot-dragging all the way. Don't forget, Agent Carson, I've got tape recordings of your wasted promises and delaying tactics to prove it. They're in a safe place and you'll never guess where they are. You won't be able to steal them or subpoena them. There isn't even a paper trail."

"Jamie, watch it," Kent warned.

"I've already put in a Freedom of Information request for the file you've compiled on me. Yes, I know all about it. The waiting period to get the report expires in sixteen days. We're going to print every censored word of it, along with the obvious question of why you're spending taxpayers' dollars investigating a reporter who's clean, instead of going after some jerk who's killed a dozen people. And we fully intend to sue, you personally as well as the Bureau." Jamie's face was red. They were almost nose to nose. "Whether I'm dead or alive, you're gonna be living with me for a long, long time."

Carson looked ready to crush Jamie's face. Jamie didn't back down. Kent's breaths came in quick shallow gasps.

"That's enough!" Slaughter shouted, his bass voice bouncing off all objects.

Jamie ejaculated, "Suckah," punched Carson's shoulder and backed away.

"We've got an operation to run here, people," Slaughter demanded. "We've got a 13-man killer to nail, and I don't give a shit who fucks watermelons!"

Everyone but Carson laughed.

He stood slowly, claiming his dignity as a Federal agent, and said calmly, "My office signs off on this. We will not participate." He surveyed the room, didn't like what he saw. He did not look at Jamie, but kicked aside his own chair, grabbed his brown leather valise. "You're on your own, suckahs." He headed for the exit.

"Don't let the screen door hit ya," Bulldog cracked as Carson walked out.

Julie Campbell watched him go.

Jamie lost it. "Watermelons? How did you come up with watermelons?"

"Ten-minute break," Slaughter said, grinning at Jamie.

In the corridor, Jamie lit a menthol right under the No Smoking sign. "Thanks, Bulldog, I needed that."

"You're not supposed to smoke in this building," Kent said gently.

"I don't give a fuck what I'm supposed to do," Jamie snapped. "I may be dead in six hours. You want to write me up, do it."

"Sorry," Kent yelped. He ducked into the nearest office with a computer.

Damn. Dumped on my team leader again. Get with it, Jamie. Why can't you cut this dude some slack?

Knew why. Cursed the selection of Kessler all over again. Weaseled into a conversation with Chief Watson and Steve Helmreich to divert the thought.

* * *

"The FBI's got a file on him?" Blaney muttered as they filed back into the conference room.

"No criminal," Kent replied. "It's classified, when his background's impeccable."

"As you said, major, let's not get ahead of ourselves," Jamie said as he sat down. "Will you re-state the questions?"

"You said it succinctly this morning. With a case as complex as the Mafia, do we take them down one at a time or all at once?"

The others went back and forth: a bird in the hand or two in the bush? People came up with Jamie's earlier arguments, so he didn't participate. He let his mind wander, looked out the window. *Kelvin. Haney. Cardinal. Riley Jones. Barry Lynn Turner.*

Ricky. Mama. Danny, my only connection to family, to life itself. He worked to control his emotions. He took a deep breath, tuned back in to the discussion. Looked at Kent, who had an encyclopedia in his face.

Steve Helmreich was facilitating the discussion now. "So we've got roughly half of us saying if we can get a conviction now, do it. It's easier, it honors the victims, friends and families, and we'll get a very dangerous man off the streets and prevent him from killing anyone else, for awhile or maybe for life. Is that accurate?"

Several people nodded; the chiefs of staff, Col. Potts, Chief Watson.

George didn't nod. Neither did Julie Campbell. Jack Snyder didn't. Bulldog, Hickman and Blaney were stone-faced. The county prosecutor was silent.

Kent didn't nod.

"Okay. That's the bird-in-hand point of view. And it's a good one," Steve said. "Now then, the other officers, who happen to be the ones closest to the investigation, not that that makes them any better, will buy that, but they feel they're close to getting the possible other accomplices; and it's hard to walk away from taking down everyone, especially since the Schmidgall example turned out as it did. Right? Very hard to walk away." Everyone else nodded but Jamie.

"And the bottom line for the two-in-the-bush view is that going ahead with it all depends on Jamie; without him, they have little or no chance at the additional arrests. If there are any to be made, which we don't know. Is that correct?"

Another round of bobbing heads. All eyes went to Jamie as Helmreich sat down.

"If I do it, what's the plan?" Jamie said wearily. "We don't know what he has in mind."

Kent stood and said, "He's given you no incentive to do what he says. He can't just invite you to the bars, invite you to get into his car and get killed. He has to have a hammer over your head." Jamie nodded. "That suggests to me that he picks up someone else and then offers to trade him for you. That he plays on your desire to prevent further loss of life. In which case, we let him do that, and you show him by your presence that you're playing along. We've got you protected at the bar. Then at some point he has to offer to make the trade and you have to agree to it. Then you find out the location of the swap, relay it to us, you exit and we swoop in with overwhelming force."

Jamie said, "Kent, that's very logical." Kent smiled slightly.

IPD's Chief Watson asked, "But how does that get us to any accomplices?"

Kent exchanged looks with his closest task force members. "It's somewhat of a gamble, chief," Bulldog said. "But we have a gut feeling that since Jamie's been such a thorn in the side of these people, if they think they're going to get him, he'll pull in the other accomplices. Lt. Blaney, what did you call it?"

"Star power," Phil said. "Ford wouldn't be alone for this job, they'd have the accomplices there…"

Jamie shivered, "For a photo shoot."

"It's darn risky, Jamie," Kent said. "You're free to say no."

He sat. For some reason Jamie thought of all the losses he'd been through. *Rick is gone. My mother is gone. My fabulous career lands me working for Louie Mascaro. Working the Gay beat limits my chances. But I love the Gay beat.*

I'm no martyr. Jesus did that once already. Ain't nobody asking me to climb up on that cross. How to decide, then?

Then it hit him, and he became certain of what he should do.

Looked at Kent to make absolutely sure. *Tall, strong, the only one who ever got these cases off the ground? The only one who didn't try to catch a Gay killer by staying away from us? The one who got this powergroup together, the only one with a reasonable chance of nailing the dude?*

The one who came to me the night I needed him?

He thought of a song from "A Chorus Line"—"I Can Do That!" It wasn't even choreographed by Tommy Tune.

Jamie centered himself, stood. "Ladies and gentlemen, thank you for everyone's input, airing all the pros and cons; ultimately this task force must act, as one unit, under our Commander. We cannot break into factions; we're tracking killers. Before we settle on a plan we should ask, of whom is this task force made up?

"I look around this room. Some faces are new to me; others are familiar. Some of you are just meeting for the first time; others have worked together for years. Let me tell you who your fellow task force members are.

"Two of you, Bulldog and Hickman, are partners; when you found yourselves with four dead Gay men from Indianapolis, you made a decision that you would dedicate yourselves to solving those murders, to bringing those victims justice regardless of their sexual orientation. For over a decade, in every spare moment, you worked to solve the insoluble. Bulldog, Barry, I'm not only proud of you, I thank you.

"Three others of you are known to me. Jack, you've traveled many miles, worked scores of hours, interviewed, sifted evidence, all on behalf of a Red-Haired Boy you never knew. If he were here today he would say, Thank you, Jack. Thank you, Marie.

"Lt. Phil Blaney, you reopened these old, cold cases on your own initiative. You became the point man for Indianapolis P.D. when these crimes needed a central focus. That was pure leadership, Phil. These other officers needed someone in Indy they could turn to, and you volunteered.

"Dr. Steve Helmreich, you're a street cop with a Ph.D. When you found yourself, as these officers have, facing a serial killer up in Michigan, you not only solved the case, you committed your life to studying multiple murder for one reason: to bring these evil killers to justice faster, in order to save innocent lives.

"Major Slaughter, you never let these cases get cold. The minute you heard of Mr. Ferguson's murder, you went beyond bureaucratic boundaries to assign the toughest, smartest, most open-minded and skillful investigator in the state. Two weeks later he's got us within striking distance. He has earned the job of Commander of this elite force.

"You men are heroes to me.

"Now we come together, from many jurisdictions, to form one unit under our Commander. In the short time I've known him, he's shown incredible intelligence and dedication. He asks us now to follow him. His views are well-reasoned; his leadership is undisputed. He has inspired my confidence and yours as well. Let us follow him." He looked right at Kent. "I choose to follow my Commander."

He sat. Slaughter's chest rose and fell, his soul gently touching an ancient stone.

Kent spoke. "You don't have to do this, Jamie. You don't have to take this chance."

Jamie took a long, long time to reply. *It's what he wants; why not give your effort, your self to this fine young man, this officer for peace, and take your chances? If it doesn't work out, you get to play with the Rickster through eternity. Kewl.*

He was quite sure in every possible direction. Then he knew they were waiting on him, so he sat back, tossed his blond hair elaborately, "I assume we're going to have some wireless mics!"

* * *

A few minutes later, the chiefs of staff tried to excuse themselves, assuring the officers that their bosses would support the operation. Dr. Steve Helmreich asked for written documents instead, signed by the governor, mayor and U.S. attorney. Staff chiefs stared. "These folks will put their lives on the line, and they need not to be second-guessed by politicians after the fact."

Steve had an authority about him. It came from Green River and Ann Arbor, a toughness seldom seen in academics. He wasn't just an academic—he was a cop.

The staff chiefs agreed to request such documents. Captain Steve, Ph.D., asked for faxes "or we don't move." The pols couldn't scurry out fast enough.

When they were gone Bulldog laughed. "I been waitin' my whole life to see a politician's ass put to the fire. Steve, come to Quincy County any day. We got some county commissioners we'd love to sic you on." Hickman gave Bulldog five.

Slaughter suggested, "Let's divide up strategy and tactics, logistics and personnel. Commander, what's your preference?"

"Doc, help me out here, make sure I'm not leaving anything out. Great job, thank you. Committee heads are me, George and Bulldog. Phil, Julie and me on strategy and tactics. George, Chief Watson, Sheriff Grumwald and Sgt. Gillespie on personnel. Bulldog, Barry and Jack, you figure out what logistics and technology we need and report to me. Mr. Brown, coordinate with Bulldog on logistics if you want to have prosecutors there. Harvey, brief the media spokesperson. Doc, you're my floating observer to make sure our committees mesh. Jamie, do you have input?"

"My concerns are technology and backup. I want to make sure that the personnel are capable of being Gay-friendly in the bars." There was a pause here, official discomfort edging up slightly, the Gay Issue. "Chief Watson, Sheriff, I'm sure your personnel are well-trained for the police operation, but there are people skills to consider too. You've got to have guys, not women, in the bars, except at The '69, and they have to be perfectly at ease. They can't, uh…"

"Come strutting in like Marshall Dillon," Kent finished. Jamie flashed him a grin.

"Right," Watson said. "George, Sheriff Grumwald, Eamon and I will consult. This has to be a City-County-State Police team. There's no guarantee where this scene will take place. Inside the old city we're the leaders, if that's acceptable; in the county the sheriff takes his territory. But all departments report to Cmdr. Kessler." Indianapolis has an unusual political system; the city and county governments merged, in everything but police, fire and schools. Uni-Gov was designed to make sure White, Republican suburbanites could always outvote Black, urban Democrats, and schools stayed segregated. So a Federal judge ordered school busing.

"Right," Kent ordered. "We're going to follow normal jurisdictional lines as much as possible." He liked commanding. He was good at it.

"Can I put that in writing too?" Steve asked. "Clarify the lines of authority and responsibility, that each jurisdiction has pledged to cooperate with the others? Very simple, a two-page document, but colleagues pledging to back each other up in this one operation?"

"You drive a pretty hard bargain, doctor," Chief Watson frowned.

Helmreich stepped down for a second. "I don't want to push it harder than I should, but you all need to know where everyone's coming from, and it sounds to me like you're heading that way anyway. All departments might work together better with a teamwork statement that clarifies everyone's responsibilities. State police are the leaders, so only they will speak with the press?"

It was a new idea, one nobody had ever heard of before, this notion of putting things in writing. Chief Watson was right, it felt a little dangerous. But they were there to work together, and they were hungry for success. When no one spoke, Kent ordered, "If we get arrests, every department here will get full credit. Put that in writing, too, Doc."

Jamie winked at Steve. Kent he couldn't even look at.

They spent several minutes on police procedure. As an inside look, Jamie found it fascinating. He also wished he weren't quite such an insider. Then it was time for committee meetings. "Jamie, you're with me," Kent said. He glanced at his watch. "Report back here at 1500 hours. Let's move."

Jamie grabbed his camera case, asked for a favor.

They let him take a few shots, which Casey could use if he wanted. Then Kent insisted on one more, asked Harvey to point and shoot at the Task Force, Jamie standing in the middle, Kent's and Bulldog's arms on his shoulders, Jamie holding up his cassette; his other hand shyly around Kent's waist, because he had no idea where else to put it.

* * *

After the meetings and the reconvening, Kent pulled Jamie aside and said, "The reason we want you at the bar is so we can protect you. We can't have him confronting you alone a week from now at your Mom's house, or back home in Columbus. For us to protect you we have to be there without him knowing it. It's easier for us to protect you at a bar, where we can blend in and control the situation."

"How do I set it up? What actions do I take?"

"With you being in a public place, it's much harder for him to snatch you. I'll have my eyes on you at all times. If he tries to get you direct, I'll be there to apprehend him. He won't get past me. Instead, he'll have to grab somebody else, then offer to trade. All you have to do is see him, Jamie, let him see you."

"How will he and I make contact afterwards?"

"Your Mom's probably. Same way he contacted you before."

"Then what?"

"Get us directions to the rendezvous. We get that, you split immediately."

"How do I cover the story if I split?"

Kent stared, exasperated. "Forget the damn story, I'm trying to save your life!"

Jamie blazed back, "Why can't I join you when you apprehend him?"

"You shouldn't be anywhere near there."

"If I'm with you I'll be safe. Why can't I be there?"

"I want you well back from the scene. You're not allowed on the front lines."

"I'm allowed to risk my life, but not be on the front lines? I want pictures of the arrest! I want to report the story without getting in danger, but without your holding me back from the action, either. Kent, I deserve that. You're using me to try to arrest a serial killer. What do I get out of it, some merit badge six months from now?"

Kent frowned, looked away. "I'll get you as close as I can, but you do what I say, damn you. I'm your Commander. You follow my orders."

"I can take the next flight to San Diego. Without me you don't write a traffic ticket."

Kent made a fist. "I'd love to pop you, boy."

Jamie stuck his chin out. "Not as much as you'd love to arrest a killer. Go ahead and pop."

"How'd you get to be so tough?"

"You think Gay guys aren't tough? Watch!"

"Here we go. Gay rights again."

"Ain't Gay rights," Jamie sneered. "Gay survival."

33

Thoroughbred

After dinner—Straight and in the far suburbs—Kent drove an unmarked, dented-in Chevy to the hotel. “We’ve got a search warrant when we need it, but he still hasn’t come home. The surveillance has electronics to intercept any conversation inside the home; his trailer will call us if and when he goes out and tell us where he’s headed. If he goes to a bar you’re not at, we’ll get you there. Also, the prosecutor is going to the grand jury tomorrow, even if he has to ask for a sealed indictment.”

“For threats or murder?”

“Murder. We all know he killed that guy, Jamie. Took you to rub our noses in it.” Kent parked, got the gym bag with their equipment out of the trunk. “You ready?”

“I’m Freddy.” By the eyes, by the strut, Kent knew Jamie was hyped.

*　　　*　　　*

Jamie sent him away, took a pre-bar nap, then showered and toweled his hair. He told the mirror, “Tonight you dominate.”

He shaved, flossed and brushed his teeth, treated his skin, snipped any oddball hairs, made himself perfect; if he was going to die, he might as well look good doing it.

He took his time, mentally focused, preparing for this performance as he would any other, making himself outstandingly handsome; there was power in that. He finished his routine; Kent knocked on the door. "Come in." Jamie walked away, wearing jeans, boots and no shirt. He'd discarded an undershirt after grave deliberation. He didn't want Kent to see his body, but he didn't want to roast all night. He kept his back to the door.

Kent came in, stopped, loudly whistled, "Whee-oo! The lats. The waist! Turn around." Jamie's waist was tiny, which made his V-shape so dramatic. He turned, faced him, got looked at. Kent surveyed him for fifteen silent seconds. "That is the body of a thoroughbred."

Jamie's ears burned. Why else but to breed blond children had Thelma married the worthless Ronald, whose only redeeming features were his hair and his dick? Kent said, "Do you shave your chest? That's part of it. Man, you're beautiful."

"No, I've got fuzz if you look in the right light." Jamie tried to find some.

"Straight, ideal abs, amazingly deep cuts. Striations in square pecs. Big arms, great triceps. Wonderful delts. But man, look at that little bitty waist. What's your sport?"

"I love my hoops, but I'm no athlete."

"Jamie, get real, that's an athlete's body if I ever saw one. You're too smart not to play to your strengths. How did you use it?"

"Show business. Briefly, only during college." Jamie turned away, embarrassed.

Casually Kent said, "I guess being in show business, you got photographed at times."

Don't ever lie to a cop. "Many thousands of times. That's how I paid for my education."

"Man, you're handsomer than Brad Pitt. You should be a movie star."

"I don't want to portray illusion, I want to describe reality. All my life I've wanted to be a reporter."

"It's a professional body, man, why not use it?"

"It's a professional mind. Can I never get paid for my ideas?"

That hit hard, and Gay-Straight confusion fell on them; they had a job to do. "You have the tiniest waist, though. How'd it get so small? You ain't normal."

"By not eating greaseburgers, you moron. By working out six days a week. And before you can say anything, I'm 5'10" and taller than both my parents… were. Can we please get on with it now?"

"Yeah, let's get this thing secured." Guiltily, Kent took out an oversize, red Indiana University sweatshirt, turned it inside out and clipped a mic to the chest, then turned it rightside out. "Here you go, slugger." He held it up.

Jamie raised his hands, got it on; it was commitment. He looked in the mirror. "No, not an Other School sweatshirt! I can't wear this, my mother would shoot me. I asked for Purdue. You know I did."

"They didn't have any in your size. This was the best I could do."

"What a betrayal. My whole family would shoot me." *Except that stupid Stone.*

"Let me see." Kent turned him this way and that. "You look good in red. The extra size helps conceal the mic. Besides, baggy's in style. How does it feel? Does it scratch?"

"No, and I look better in gold!" Jamie turned away for his smokes. "Bought a fucking Chair-Thrower sweatshirt. The minute we're done I'm burning this thing."

Kent sat on the bed. Maybe this wasn't about sweatshirts. "Are you all right?"

Jamie quieted. "I'm not going to back out, if that's what you're asking."

"You can, you know. No one will blame you if you do, Jamie. Nobody in the world has the right to tell you to do this. Back out at the last minute if you want to."

Jamie drew in a lungful of smoke, sat on the other bed. "I feel confident, a bit pumped; otherwise calm. At some point I may need to tap into my anger. I'll know if the time comes to turn it on."

Kent thought of Cy Young winner Tim Virdon; same attitude on game day. Kent nodded, then snickered.

"What?" Jamie said. *Are my wrists too small?*

"I was just thinking how you had your anger going with Carson. Whee-oo! Remind me not to cross you. You were ready to take on the entire FBI. And wouldn't nobody in that room have bet against you, neither."

Jamie smiled ruefully. "What a jerk."

"Why does the FBI have a file on you?"

"I don't know, but somehow it's related to this case. There's something very strange going on. Everything changed when FBI jurisdiction was transferred from Cincinnati to Indy. You saw it today with Carson. Cooperation turned into complete opposition. I don't trust his office, Kent. Something's not right."

"Do you really know the attorney general?"

Kent's face was so serious-doubtful-wondering that Jamie smiled. "The attorney general's never heard of me—but the White House has. If it comes to it, I'll contact their political people, and they'll contact DOJ. I've tried to avoid it up to now, I don't want to exert political influence in a criminal investigation. If I get an uncensored Freedom of Information report, I won't need the attorney general. The FBI will hang itself."

"Shee-it," Kent chuckled, falling back on the bed. "I kind of thought you were bluffing."

"But you bought it anyway."

Kent grabbed a pillow and threw it at him, caught him full in the face. "No way I wasn't gonna buy it. You even had me scared, you little fucker. Blaney and me both."

Perfect tension breaker. Jamie stood, faced a wall, stepped back three paces and did ten pushoffs, a full-body stretch.

Then Kent maxed out the tension; reached into his pocket and took out a handgun. "Jamie, I wouldn't feel right without asking you to protect yourself."

Jamie turned, recoiled at the thing in pure fear. "Kent, this is all going to go just fine. I'm not getting near these people. All I have to do is get the address."

"Take the gun, Jamie. You may need it."

"I wouldn't know what to do with it. I've never fired a gun in my life."

"Never?"

"Is there a rule that says I'm supposed to have? Take that thing out of my sight."

"Well, no, but gee. I've never met a guy who hasn't fired a gun."

"Go to Gay bars more often."

"Jamie, this could be dangerous. What if something goes wrong?"

"It goes wrong. I'll have to use my other weapon."

"What's that?"

"The one between my ears."

Kent's voice rose, "Jamie, I'm your Commander. I order you to take the damn gun."

"You're my Commander, all right—and I'm a civilian. San Diego's nice this time of year. There's a limit to the orders you can give."

"I know, man. But please take the gun."

"Kent, I have an aversion to guns I can't begin to tell you about. I won't touch it; I'm terrified to be in the same room with it. Take that awful thing out of here. Let's catch a killer using my Commander's good plan."

"Jamie, no plan is foolproof."

"Buddy, if your plan is flawed, theirs is a recipe for disaster. Commander's going to arrest them without a shot being fired."

Reluctantly Kent put the gun in a drawer, told his monitor to call the room if he could pick up their conversation. Five seconds later the phone rang.

"Taxi's on its way," he said, tossing the Chevy keys to Jamie, who attached them to a key ring on his left hip. Kent would hold the cab, which was really a police car, until Jamie and the Chevy were away, then Kent, as his bodyguard, would follow to Chez Nous. George Slaughter would be stationed at Six of One, with a mic and a monitor car. Mic'd officers were deployed inside all other Gay bars and restaurants, and everyone had unmarked backup outside. Slaughter's assistant Harvey coordinated communications at headquarters.

It amused Jamie to imagine Slaughter at Six of One, but Kent hadn't questioned the decision. "It feels good to be back in the saddle again," Slaughter had said. "I get claustrophobic in this office box sometimes."

Privately Jamie teased him, "It's really just an excuse to wear your leather."

"That too," Slaughter grinned, daintily batting his eyelashes.

Plain cars were assigned to the library, Washington Street and the bathhouses on Capitol and North Keystone. A patrol car was at Monument Circle because that was normal behavior, with another floating among the monuments north of Washington Street and a third making a circuit past each bar in turn. Col. Potts, Chief Watson, the sheriff and the prosecutor had command cars on the perimeter. Post 52 was on alert, every trooper available.

The whole thing even acquired a nickname. "Operation Pride," Kent told Jamie over dinner. "I picked it for you. God knows, officers have a lot of pride staked on this thing."

Jamie was deeply pleased. Now he said, "It's ten o'clock, Commander. Ready to go to the dance?" He swung his camera bag over his shoulder.

"Let's boogie," Kent said, following him out the door.

Jamie sang, “We Will, We Will Rock You!” By the second line Kent was supplying foot-stomps and handclaps, Jamie the fist-thrust choreography. If the thoroughbred was going to die, he might as well do it to a song by Queen.

Kent couldn’t help but watch that tiny little butt stomp away.

34

Spotlight

Jamie didn't like his parking place. His monitor car was supposed to save him a spot in the small lot west of the bar, but it was full, all of the cars there unoccupied. He squeezed the clunky old Impala back onto the street, dodging theater traffic. "Where's my monitor?" he yelled into the microphone. "He's not here and I don't like it. Tell Kent to let me know once we're inside that everyone's where they're supposed to be."

He found a spot around the corner, managed to parallel-park the old boat and describe his location. He checked in the mirror; he looked okay, not edgy; shut off the ignition, breathed twice and stepped out of the car. He strode toward Chez Nous. Fifteen feet from the door he muttered to himself, "Made me wear a goddamn IU sweatshirt. One size too big." He tossed his head. "But tonight I dominate."

A cab with a single black-haired passenger pulled up to the entrance as Jamie went inside the bar. He paid a $3 cover, proceeds going to Hoosiers Care About AIDS, declined the change from his ten-spot, got his hand stamped.

Semi-crowded, surprisingly so. *It must be because of the fundraiser.*

Two shirtless leathermen stood in the dim left corner. Pool tables were active. This music had the beat he needed tonight, unlike the sappy Straight crap on the hotel radio. He walked to the bar. "Bud Light." Realized that was a mistake; *no booze tonight.*

"Coming up," the bartender replied. A glass was set before him. Jamie paid for his Diet Coke and left a tip for Lt. Phil Blaney. "Thank you much," the bartender smiled.

Jamie leaned forward; Blaney cocked his head. "Does this mean I can expect good service tonight, barkeep?"

Phil guffawed, "In a Gay bar? Takes more than a buck. But it rhymes with buck."

"Ain't that it." Jamie headed off for the terrace. *Phil, I wondered but didn't know. Thank you for reopening those cases.* A wave of pride and respect washed over him.

Ten minutes later Kent passed, wearing a Colts sweatshirt. Kent gave him a nod without looking. The music was heating up, Jamie's right foot was working.

First john break. Soon Kent was at the next urinal, unzipping his fly. Jamie made a fist, kept staring ahead. Kent said, "Message received, sorry, we're clear, your monitor's in place. This joint is busy for a weeknight."

Jamie finished. Made another fist. Outside, he looked for any hot man to divert his attention. Saw one. Followed. No killers visible.

The bar was filling up, and Jamie checked his watch, 10:40. The DJ was spinning "I Will Survive." Jamie Gaynor sang along, hoped it was true, watched the dance floor and the rest of the place.

Second john break, same urinal. Spot next to him quickly filled up. Jamie glanced over, troll alert! "Well, hello hello hello," a voice chirped.

Jamie buttoned up, flushed. "Goodbye," he winked. Kent was frowning in line.

Boredom kept Jamie moving, but the music was still decent. He went up to the front bartender, who served him promptly. "Bud Light," he growled.

"Yes sir."

Left Lt. Blaney money for Diet Coke and tip.

The bar was big for Indianapolis, but it wasn't that big a place. Waiting was hard. Jamie wanted to talk to anyone about anything. Presently a voice filled his ear, "I'm sorry for staring. Don't tell me you're here alone." Jamie turned to find a brown-haired young man, a couple inches shorter, maybe three years older, very White Hoosier corn; Jamie's idea of pleasant looking. "'Cause I won't believe you." The guy had a nice smile.

"I've been stood up," Jamie smiled back. His eyes danced and he didn't even know it.

"Right. Now who's going to stand you up?"

"Just a guy, a friend of a friend. We were supposed to have a drink together."

Mr. Pleasant grinned, looked toward the pool table. "I hate it when you lie to me."

"My name's Joe," Jamie lied, his hand outstretched.

Hands and eyes met. "Your name's Gorgeous. My name's Joe."

"Hey, Joe."

He was very gentle. They talked sports. Real Joe was excited about baseball's home run derby, and was working up to asking Jamie to go to a Triple-A game when the Indians were in town. Jamie saw it coming, felt the need to remind him of the friend of a friend.

"I knew it," Joe sighed. "My one chance at a tall, handsome, butch, blond muscleman. Would it help if I knelt, signed over my mutual funds and kissed your boots?"

"No, but it would be highly entertaining. Tall, huh?"

"Especially when I'm on my knees." Jamie kissed him, thanked him, affirmed his soul and their mutual attraction; then moved on, spying Kent in a corner and realizing he'd just watched him kiss Joe.

Third john break. His only neighbors were there to piss. Jamie fought exasperation.

* * *

Four beats came, then the sound of a midget saying, "Twenty seconds and counting."

Jamie screamed, *homosexual anthem!* Dancetime. He headed for the floor, killer or no. Lightning cracked. It was a sin not to dance to the Pet Shop Boys, and he was a very good dancer. Jamie grabbed the arm of the closest man. The fellow was at least sixty. "You lovely boy, why me?"

"Gray's cute too. You've honed your technique."

"Mercy me, where is my Viagra?"

A small brown bottle was passed to Jamie on the dance floor by an athletic, shirtless Black guy with dreadlocks. *Shouldn't, working. Serial killer!*

Did anyway, *fuck this shit.* Inhale. Passed the vial back to the brown hand. Kissed air in the guy's direction. "Hey," Dreadlocks mouthed back. Blood engorged in two brains. Kent climbed three steps to a little balcony above the dance floor.

Lt. Phil Blaney got a call, but with the loud music he had to take it in the office.

Jamie felt his heartbeat. A small circle of space formed around him and his partners, though the floor rapidly got crowded with this song and these boys. "The blond! How in the world. A face like that?" someone shouted on the perimeter.

His neighbor shrugged, "Maybe he likes spankings over daddy's knee."

It's not a sin. The beat segued into the cynical Boys' most positive sound. The older guy begged off. Jamie swatted daddy's butt goodbye. Then before him was Dreadlocks, with pretty eyes. They started off slow, minimal motion, just a basic up, down and around; saying hello physically, then deliberately ignoring each other until a word of lyric brought them together. Then spins with the light show going into the chorus, where they danced together, face to face, lean-in, lean-out, to "One in a Million Men."

Another hit of poppers during the second verse; the same separation as before, but more animated now. Jamie's toot hit him as the second verse built up. A bright spotlight found him, stayed on him.

Kent didn't want him that visible, but nobody'd warned the DJ. Across the room the same thing occurred to Thomas Alan Ford, newly arrived and delighted.

Jamie and Dreadlocks made full eye contact now. Touching each other for micro-seconds, touching themselves, showing the sex they could have, projecting it to the room and getting it back again as smoke billowed, floorboards trampolined, walls swayed—two in a roomful of tribesmen, dancing and singing and grooving together.

At the musical bridge, Pop Cliché #1—who but the Pet Shop Boys could get away with it?—a simultaneous notion to pose in contrast four times, and one last vial-pass; then whirling into the payoff, knees floorward, hips thrusting, hand on neck, on thigh, mouths ready, asses too, for all the world to see.

Jamie pivoted and thrust his crotch—ten feet in front of Kent's face.

Jamie replaced his frustration with freedom; the DJ miraculously played the original, grandiose ending intact, mood changes made for image-making, tympani helping Jamie and Dread strike last sexpositions; then an embrace which welded them, Dread's leg around Jamie's waist, Jamie's hands supporting his back, arms up and graceful, black locks cascading to the floor, an ecstatic finale, as Jamie possessed the man's body.

The whole room waited to breathe or come. Kent exploded.

Lights changed; the room breathed. Next was a dance-rap, and Jamie and his friend headed off the floor arm in arm to applause. Their lone white spotlight turned into nine spinning reds. They passed unseeing by Kent, who stared furiously ahead, working his jaw. *Good Christ, in a gaybar.* He shoved past a fat woman and hurried off the platform, desperate for the nearest john.

35

The Hunt & The Chase

Blaney learned that Ford had left home, destination unknown. Left his post behind the bar to find Kent.

Another john break. Jamie headed to the far one by the pool table. It was getting late. The adjoining space was quickly filled.

As he exited, a laughing young man hurried in, calling something over his shoulder to his friends. Wet spilled all over Jamie's chest. "Oh. Sorry!"

"No problem," Jamie said, wiping cocktail off his sweatshirt. He was soaked from his shoulder to his belly button. *Where's Kent? Find the bartender.*

No Blaney. An Asian guy in a leather and steel harness came at him from behind the bar. "What'll you have?"

"Nothing, sorry," Jamie said, turning back.

And he saw Tommy Ford wrap an arm around a small, diffident-looking young guy in a dirty tank top. Ford's and Jamie's eyes locked. Ford grinned, pointed to his Muscular Dystrophy T-shirt, pushed Diffident toward the door.

"I see him! Ford's here, exiting right now! Has a guy with him!" Too much crowd between. "I'm going to lose him!"

Jamie pushed. The bar was at full capacity. Some guy yelled, "Hey bitch, watch who you're pushing."

"Sorry." A space opened up, Jamie squiggled through it. A fat man he'd seen earlier, "Excuse me," he maneuvered another foot and a half. "Hi, thanks," to someone who let him through.

Where are they? They can't be gone!

Drag queen in the way. "'Scuse me, honey," and a firm shove. Nothing between him and the door but barrels. *Now!* Hugged a barrel and got outside. "He's leaving, but I don't see him. Blink your headlights so I know you're here." Looked both directions. Nothing. *Forget the lot.* No headlights blinked. Across the street? *No.* Just guys heading toward him. "What should I do?"

Ran to Alabama Street. Could that be an old Toyota pulling away? "He's driving south on Alabama. I'll try to follow." Ran up to his Chevy as the maybe Toyota hung a right. Shouted his location into his microphone. Jumped in and started the Impala. "He's heading west towards Meridian. Kent, where are you? Call my cell phone."

Rear-view mirror as he skidded around the corner. No cop cars stirring. No phone call. He flipped on his phone to call Harvey, but got no dial tone. Banged the phone against his chest, listened again; nothing.

He was on his own. *Bail out? Follow?*

He pictured Diffident's face; drove on. Acid guts again.

Kent hurried out of the bathroom to find Jamie. *I'd know that damn yellow swoop anywhere.* He looked and looked, shoving past people. Lt. Phil Blaney caught up with him. "We have to talk."

"Not now, I've lost my witness."

"Ford's in his vehicle. He left eleven minutes ago, could be here by now."

"Great. Just when I've lost my witness. Let's go to the pool room, he's not here."

They fought their way past people to the pool room. At 6'4", Kent could see over the heads of most customers, but still no Jamie. "I'll try the corner john."

"You want me to search with you, or post on the door in case Ford comes in?"

"Yeah, watch for Ford. I'll find Jamie."

He wasn't in the john, but two perverts were. Jamie wasn't in the pool room. He wasn't in the main room. Major Slaughter arrived. "I heard Ford's on his way."

"Yeah, but he should be here by now, and Blaney hasn't seen him. Jamie's missing."

"Shit."

"Look on the dance floor, Chief. I'll take the terrace."

The terrace was crowded, but no Jamie. Kent re-entered the dance area, hooked up with Slaughter. "You seen him?"

"No. I checked the dance floor john, too."

"I don't think he's here, then. I've looked everywhere. My God, what if he's slipped out? What if Ford's been here and they've already made contact?"

"Radio Ford's tail car."

"Yeah." Kent hurried up to Blaney, could tell he hadn't seen Ford. "Still no witness. Stay here on the door till further orders. We think maybe he and Ford have already made contact. We're going to check with Ford's trailer."

"Got it."

Kent sprinted out to his taxi/police car, called. What he heard sickened him. IPD said, "I had him, then he ducked into a parking garage. I followed and got stopped by some old broad in a 20-year-old Mercury blocking the lane, and somebody behind me too. I was pinned in. The garage has entrance and exit opposite each other, and this lady was trying to fit into a space too small, so I got out and parked the damn car for her, and by the time I got out he was gone. I called Harvey as soon as it happened."

"Ford's eluded his tail," Kent told Slaughter, who climbed in with him.

"No Jamie, no Ford."

"Tell all cars to rendezvous at HQ." Slaughter notified Harvey. Kent tore that taxi downtown. "We're falling apart, George. This is like looking for a needle in a haystack. Notify all state, IPD and sheriff's cars to be on the lookout for the Toyota and the Chevy. Give the plate numbers. Maybe we'll catch a break."

The major relayed the order. "The chopper maybe."

"They've got a head start on us. Why did this happen? What went wrong? Get Campbell on the horn."

"I haven't seen him," Julie said. "Isn't he still inside?"

"No. What do you hear from his mic?"

"I haven't had a report in five, ten minutes. Nothing. Not even the music."

"Shit, his mic's dead then," Kent muttered. "I should know, the man never shuts up."

"Did you see him exit the facility?" Slaughter barked at Campbell.

"No. I thought he was still inside."

Kent said, "Is his car in place? Are you in place? Where are you, Campbell?"

"In the parking lot at the side. Where I was assigned."

"Jesus Christ," Kent cried.

"Any Chevies in that lot, Campbell?" the major growled.

She looked at the other cars. "No, sir."

"What's he driving, Campbell?"

"Oh no."

"Search the area for that Chevrolet, if it's not too much bother, then rendezvous at HQ, Campbell," Kent ordered. He cut the call. "You'd think she'd know something was wrong when she stopped hearing the music. Otherwise there's no excuse. There's music on the terrace even. Human error, equipment error. Damn."

"Jamie's resourceful," George reminded him. "He's got good judgment."

"He doesn't have a fucking gun!"

*　　　*　　　*

If it was the Toyota, it was turning south at Meridian, heading for the interstate. Jamie ran stop signs and flashing red lights to catch up. Turned left on Meridian.

Cop car coming his way! Jamie pulled the signal on the steering column to flash his brights. Nothing happened.

GM car, not the Acura. His right foot gunned the gas, his left foot searched for the brights switch. *Where?* Patrol car passed him. Jamie honked. The cop car went the other direction. The Toyota, if that's what it was, ran a red at 10th and Meridian, straight up the ramp.

Speedometer at 50. Jamie radioed his location. *Is anyone listening?*

Little traffic, but a cab headed his way in the near lane. Jamie calculated space, speed, tromped the gas pedal, swung left in front of the cab but too far wide. Cabbie's angry horn, *miss this parked car on 10th!* Brakes and he was clear by two inches.

Ahead of him, maybe Toyota climbed the ramp and disappeared.

The choice was soon: I-65 South or I-70 West? *Where are you, econobox?*

Not here. Not there. Jamie chose 65 South. *Maybe that's why you're a stupid IU fan, you're from southern Indiana.* Going 70 now, *come on let's have 80,* he floored it.

Topped out at 74 and a half, and no econobox.

He drove searching and cursing all the way till he hit I-465. Drove west around the beltway, looking for a gas station, not finding one. Finally he did, pulled off and screamed a moment. He'd had one good look at Diffident's face, which was all it took. He called HQ on a pay phone and roared, "Where the fuck's my backup?"

"Where are you?" Harvey scolded.

"Um, 65 South, then 465 West. Southwest Truck Stop."

"Stay there. Kessler's ordered all cars to rendezvous here. Stay where you are. Give me your number."

Jamie waited, and he waited, and the phone never rang. It was the kind of pay phone that couldn't receive incoming calls.

36

CEO

"Where are we going?" the passenger asked. While Jamie turned south at the highway split, Ford turned east, to make a little nostalgia tour; Ohio is east, the previous victims were east. But at the beltway, as the bugman predicted, he turned south. "This car stinks."

"Roll down the window. There's a motel I like just out of Greenwood," Ford assured. "Real quiet, mom and pop kinda place, they don't ask any questions. We can get as wild as we want."

"Cool. Unh, that feels good." Davey patted the hand groping his thighs.

"You ready to smoke?" Ford took a joint out of the right inner pocket of his leather jacket. He held a skinny cigarette in front of Daveyboy's face.

"Cool," Davey said again.

"The whole joint's yours," Ford soothed, checking his mirrors. *Nothing. Why not?* He was sure Jamie saw him.

He fished another joint out of his left inner pocket, held it up for the dude's inspection. "I got another one here for me. All the reefer we want, man. Fire that badboy up." He flicked his lighter for Davey.

Davey sucked deep. Ford put the other joint back in his left pocket, lit a Marlboro. "That's right," he said. "Let's get high. What kind of music you listen to?" Davey named a country station. Ford dialed it up.

* * *

Davey woke up in the car outside a motel in, well, it might have been the outskirts of Greenwood, but it was more like the middle of nowhere. Tommy Ford was at his door, opening it, a hand on Davey's arm, "Right this way."

Davey followed the arm that pulled him. They got inside a room. But he felt so sleepy.

* * *

Ford surveyed his handiwork. Davey was naked, face down, handcuffed, feet tied with rope. He'd be able to walk, but only with small steps. "Piece of cake, Doc," Ford said out loud. "Six cents worth of horse tranq and he's out like a light."

He turned on the TV, shucked his shirt and loosened his jeans, waiting for the phone to ring.

The graphic under her face said Tonya Tilley. He hit the mute button, leaned against the cheap headboard, adjusted his pillow. Reached into his left jacket pocket, fired up the undoctored doobie and sat back to watch the show. The most mundane things in life—commercials, budget cuts, hailstorms, murders—became fascinating through reefer eyes.

Thirty minutes passed. He got into his outfit. The phone hadn't rung, and Tonya was ready for repeats. "Jesus, get a move on, willya?" Randy was always so slow. "Shit, he's an old man." When the same weather segment came on, he dialed Foster's number.

After four rings, the familiar voice gave the familiar message. After the beep, Ford rubbed his jock and said, "Jamie, my lad, I'm disappointed in ya. I thought you'd have a force the size of the Kosovo invasion around all the bars. But I'm sitting here by myself, rubbin' my big dick, waitin' for ya. You know you want it, cocksucker."

This made him laugh. "Oh, I forgot. Daveyboy's here." He glanced at the passed-out form. "He's taken all his clothes off and fallen asleep. Don't know what's gotten into that boy. I can't wake him up no matter how hard I try."

A kick of knee into kidney, and a nice sickening thud. "Hear that?" Laughter. "He just will not wake up.

"So tell you what, Mr. Gay Newspaper Man. I wanta make a deal with ya. I'm willing to go easy on you. I'm a nice guy. Haven't I always told ya I'm a nice guy?" His throat rumbled again.

"See, I'm willing to trade you for ole Daveyboy here. I don't wanna hurt the guy. He's just a dumb shit, and me, I couldn't hurt a flea. Not a flea, you hear that? Just like Roger. He'd always watch 'Rudolph, the Red Nosed Reindeer' every Christmas. He loved that show, he really did. No matter what we were doing, we all had to sit down when Rudolph came on."

He belched. "Oh, excuse me. Guess it's not polite to burp on the phone, huh, Mr. String Quartet? You fuckin' faggot, a goddamn string quartet at a fuckin' funeral. Might as well put a sign outside your mom's house, 'Faggot Lives Here.' Cocksuckers like you make me want to puke, you know that? Sissies like you give the rest of us a bad name."

He coughed. *Better get off the phone so Randy can call.* "Anyway, here's the deal." He squinted to consult his watch, 2:42. Randy was due to call in three minutes.

"You've got until 3:15 to meet me at the Family Court Motel, outside a town called Providence. You like that?

"It's south of Greenwood, take 37 south to state route 154. You gotta watch for the signs. Then you go five miles east to Providence Road. There's a sign for Providence, but ya gotta stay sharp. Got that, faggot? Oh, I'm sorry; Mr. Gay Activist Newspaper Man Reporter."

Daveyboy stirred, but only for half a second. Ford patted an inert asscheek.

A siren sounded outside. Or was that on the TV? Ford got instantly alert.

The siren grew fainter. "Oh, and Jamie? You come alone, you hear me? No cops, no nothin'. Nobody, you got that? Or else I blow your fuckin' head off and Davey's too. I've got friends, see, they're all down here with me. I've got every road between Indy and Providence covered." He giggled. "You know how I did that? There's only one road between Providence and dirt! We're talking country, man. So broadcast this. My people and I, we got snipers posted along this road. You and the cops want to come in here, they're gonna be takin' you out in body bags on Eyewitness News." It was too much fun. He had to laugh again.

Maybe he's alone. Maybe he doesn't have any cops. Who'd believe a Gay activist anyway? It was a sweet thought.

"And you know why, Jamie? I don't have to tell you this, but I'm gonna. I always was a generous person. And then I have to go. Get off this line.

"It's about this. I'm gonna make you a star. It's what you've always wanted, you think you're so good-looking. So you're gonna be the star attraction. Jerry and Randy's bringin' camcorders, and they're gonna tape you, see? But I have to warn you, it's gonna be R-rated for violence, or even X. They're gonna cut your heart out while it's still beatin', and you're gonna star from coast to coast. You always did wannabe a star, so here's your chance, faggot."

Anticipation filled him, and his dick ached. His breath came choppy and his chest heaved. *Go ahead, why not? Tell him, he might as well know.*

"Yeah," Ford said. "Yeah." His head got very clear now, and his dick burned even more. He didn't touch it; he wouldn't, until he had Jamie in his power.

The Whisperer demanded, "*Tell him!*"

"Here's where I'm going to dump you. Changed my mind, got a better place now. Since you always wanted to be a star, where's the best place for them to find your body? I'm driving to California. Nobody there will care about an unidentified fag. So I'm going to take a nice, leisurely drive to L.A., and come four o'clock in the mornin', I'll drive up to your spot, pop the trunk, show you to your final resting place and shove off.

"You'll be so proud," he chortled. "They'll find your body on the Hollywood Walk of Fame!"

He cackled for half a minute. Then he eyed Daveyboy's naked ass; not bad. Ford didn't want to spoil the main event with James R. Foster, Chief Correspondent; but a little foreplay wouldn't hurt. He found a large butt plug in his toykit, lubed it up; then realized he didn't need lube, Davey wasn't going anywhere.

He loosened the hole with his fingers, then shoved the big prong in. Davey didn't even move.

"Yeah, he likes it." It was fun. Tommy moved the dildo in and out. He loved taking advantage of Gay guys. It was so easy to do, and it made him feel big, powerful—like a man. His guys, his so-called victims, weren't masculine like he was. He spent his whole life learning how to be macho, and he was good at it. No one ever harassed him on the street.

Roger was good at it too; but Tommy didn't like to think about that. *I'm the man here.* "You like that, Davey? I know you do, you stupid sissy queer."

He held the phone down to pick up the sounds of fucking. "Hear that? Are you gettin' off on it, bitch? You know what I'm doin'. I can't wait to fuck you when you're dead."

He gathered speed. "You're a reporter, I know you'd like to hear the rest of the story. That FBI agent you talked to up in Canada, Jamie, remember him? He told me the whole conversation, dumbass. About how there's no such thing as snuff films?"

He waited as long as the clock allowed, timing it perfectly. “Take it, bitch. Take it up your ass like you love it. The guy at Quantico’s the fuckin’ Angel of Death, Jamie. The CEO of Killer Video!”

The hysterical laughter curdled even Slaughter’s cold blood.

37

Dominate

Jamie leapt a quantum. "E.T. Call home."

It wasn't a movie, not strategy and tactics, it was Thelma and her illuminated finger at Hoosier Hospital. He redialed HQ, got a patch to his Mom's house, punched in the code. Noted the directions to the motel. Wished for fast-forward. When he got to the beating heart, he dropped the phone, whomped the gas, back onto the highway.

"Jamie, don't go anywhere!" Kent yelled.

Jamie had 19 minutes before Davey met Providence.

* * *

His watch read 3:06. The smell of armpit reached his nose. He couldn't go fast enough; too many hills and curves. "Goddamn southern Indiana. Where's the prairie when I need it?" he said to the sweatshirt, as if it still contained a microphone. *No wonder I have lousy karma—what else could I have in an IU sweatshirt?*

He lowered his window. A tractor trailer rolled toward him. Left hand on the wheel, his right hand reached over his shoulder and yanked. The sweatshirt came over his head and his contacts readjusted. *Steer!*

The big truck barreled past, horn blaring. He switched hands, pulled again, flung the sweatshirt out the window.

Flashed briefly on the heart that was beating in his chest. His cell phone rang. He grabbed it, "Hello? Hello?"

It was nothing but static. He beat it against his chest. "Hello?" He listened to static, then the line went dead. A red light came on, Batt Low. Open-mouthed, he tossed the phone onto the back seat.

Close now. Very quiet. No evidence of snipers. Were there gunners in the trees?

His watch said 3:11. He hoped it was right.

There was the motel on the left; rundown, seedy, impoverished, the sign not lit up, only a neon NO for vacancy. There was one car in the lot, a brown econobox.

He pulled off the road opposite the place, turned off his lights, waited. Nothing happened.

When his watch hit 3:15 he eased into the gravel lot, parked close to the office. He cut the ignition, stepped out into the night. The nearest light bulb was six doors away.

The office looked abandoned, not even a soft drink machine to break the darkness. He looked back at the sign and noticed a name on top he hadn't seen before: Crum's FAMILY COURT MOTEL.

Everyone's been killed right here. To be eaten by Southern Indiana bugs.

Tonight, I dominate.

He dropped his voice-activated recorder in his pocket, then crept toward the room. Tried the knob. It moved. "Tommy. I'm here." No answer. "Alone." Crickets without long to live chirped in the still night air. He waited, praying for Davey. Slowly the door opened.

Jamie saw black boots, a bare White leg, jockstrap, hunting belt with Bowie knife; leather harness, mouth, teeth, and mocking, delighted eyes. "You," said Thomas Alan Ford, "are one beautiful specimen of manhood."

It was revolting to Jamie, but Ford meant it as a compliment. "Nice touch, coming with no shirt. Your picture doesn't do you justice. Look at those muscles. Man, you've got a great body. Too bad I have to kill you," he smiled. "So let's get to it."

He flipped on a 15-watt bulb and Jamie stepped inside. Naked Davey lay face down, butt-plugged and handcuffed on the bed, a rag around his eyes, a narrow leather tie wrapped loosely around his neck.

He snored. Jamie could only wait, extend time. John-Mark, Christopher, Glenn flashed before his eyes. "You weren't fooling. You'd have killed him."

"Damn right. Help me move him. You got here in the nick of time. I thought we were going to have to settle for him tonight and get you later."

"Where are we taking him?"

"The woods behind this place. Let him sleep it off."

"How do I know you'll trade?"

"You don't," Ford grinned. "Still, he's not who I want. You are. So I'll trade. I always told you we were nice. But you've never gotten it through your thick Ivy League skull. How someone so smart could be so stupid I never have understood."

Jamie thought about it, took his time. "If you don't trade you'll have no ability to claim, to yourself or anyone else, that you're a nice person." Ford glared. "You'll trade, all right." *Dominate.* "You have to. After you kill me you won't want to be anywhere near here."

"I can kill you both."

"I won't let you. You'll trade, you're a nice guy."

Ford's eyes got big. "Now you get it! I always told you we were nice guys."

You're human puke.

Ford stepped into moonlight, opened the Toyota's back door. Jamie spotted a handcuff key on the dresser, grabbed it, dropped it in his pocket. Ford re-entered and Jamie said, "Take his cuffs off. It'll be easier to carry him."

"Shit, I know that. Think I'm stupid, Mr. Phi Beta Kappa?" Ford looked for the key, "Where is that thing?" But when he couldn't find it he just used another on his key ring.

Jamie got the ankles, Ford the shoulders. Jamie feigned weakness. "Gee, he's heavy. We're carrying dead weight."

"One, two, three," Ford said. They swung Davey off the bed, snoring uninterrupted.

Walking backwards, Jamie felt the threshold, then cement, now gravel under his boots. He looked behind him, ducked, stepped into the car, hoping for slow motion.

They laid Davey on the back seat. The car stunk horribly. Jamie knew from what. *God bless Glenn and Gary.* He opened the other door, stepped out a split-second before he vomited.

Ford's knife caught the moonlight, glinted hugely. "Get in the car."

"No. We should get a blanket."

"What for?"

"For your nice-guy scenario. Since you're going to trade, why should he wake up and find himself naked? Give him something to cover himself with. Why should he suffer the indignity?"

"Oh, jeez," Ford complained. But he went to fetch a blanket. The keys weren't in the ignition or Jamie would have driven Davey away. Ford came back, threw the blanket in the back. "Get in." Jamie didn't. "Or else I'll stab him right now." Ford unbuckled his knife. "You decide. You don't get in, you're the one who killed him."

"I won't stab him. Don't blame me for your actions."

"Get in the car or I'll stab you both!"

Jamie finally got in, stuck his head out the window for air. "How can you stand this stench? I may faint."

"It doesn't smell good. But it reminds me what I'm here to do." Ford drove to a lane in back of the parking lot. Its ruts led into woods. After 500 yards he parked. "Last call for alcohol," he chirped.

They settled Davey under a willow tree as comfortably as they could. Ford didn't recuff him. "He'll sleep it off, won't remember a thing. Won't know how he got here, but that's his tough luck."

"Thank you for trading."

"Thank you for noticing. He won't even remember what I look like."

Jamie laid the blanket around Davey like he was tending a newborn. Slowly he removed the butt plug; the sphincter didn't want to give, then finally it did. What is more intimate than easing a stranger's ass? He tossed the dildo into the trees. Ford took the leather tie from Davey's neck, hung it around his own. "Are you still using animal tranq?"

"How'd you know about that?"

"I'm a reporter. It's my business to know."

"No, tell me, how'd you know that?"

"The victims showed no signs of a struggle. Why not? They were already unconscious when you killed them, that's why. What did you use? Something seldom traced. You got animal tranq from your D.V.M. sugar daddy. Tell me, was Crum always so creepy?"

"Yeah, but he makes a good living. We were young, who wouldn't want to live in a nice house, even if some old troll owns it? We had the run of the farm and we could fuck whenever we wanted. All we had to do was let him take pictures."

"Roger topped you, didn't he? That's how you got into this. You've been competing with him ever since."

Ford frowned, "We topped each other, damn you."

"Walking around in his boots and fatigues, like he didn't buy them from army surplus. I guess he felt like a real big man. Then he'd come home and fuck you."

"We fucked each other, goddamn you."

"While Crum took pictures? And sold them?"

"It was fun. We were in a bunch of magazines, got paid for it. I've still got everything we were ever in. Hey, enough of this talk, this ain't no interview." Ford's eyes shone. "This is your execution."

Jamie felt a knifepoint in the small of his back. Time suspended itself.

He breathed. He could barely see among the thick trees. "Harch one two three," Ford said, carrying his bag of tricks. Jamie found a path and slowly harched.

But he knew one thing: *Now I dominate.*

He owed it to Glenn, to a dozen other guys who never got the chance to defend themselves. He didn't know how he'd do it, he didn't expect it to save him; but he wouldn't be Tommy Ford's passive queer.

* * *

After some distance through forestland, there was a large, circular clearing, and the moon shone on it. Steel touched his neck. "You see that oak tree on your left? The one with the big branch running parallel to the ground? Perfect height, ain't it?"

The tree was just like the one Schmidgall and Crum tied Barlow to, before they hacked him to death. "There." Ford poked Jamie with the butt of his knife.

Jamie moved. First his right foot, then his left. "Come on, move it," Ford growled. "We ain't got all night."

"I can't see well in darkness," Jamie protested. "Terrible night vision."

Ford seemed to buy it. Jamie's boots found dry leaves.

Hail Mary, full of grace. Come on, Kent.

And you were right. I should have taken the gun.

"Right up there."

On his left, Dr. Randolph Scott Crum popped out from behind a tree, all jelly belly, white disheveled hair, grinning yellow teeth and camcorder. His fly was open, and Jamie looked away.

Then he turned and stared the man full in the face.

Here was evil. Here was a homosexual who used money and position to entice two young men into a life of pornographic murder.

Dozens of Gay men had paid for Randolph Scott Crum's bloodthirsty perversions. Jamie stared at him. Crum recognized him from the Barlow trial. He did now what he did then, looked away nervously, in the face of accusation and truth.

Jamie spat on him. There was a flash of light. When his sight came back he saw Jerry Lash behind a camera.

"Hands behind your back, Jamie," Ford said. His voice took on a wannabe-hypnotic quality. "Assume the position."

"What position is that?" Jamie, far from hypnotized, played stupid and bored.

"You know. The submissive position."

"I wouldn't know what that is."

"Like you're not a bottom," Ford muttered, grabbing Jamie's wrists and yanking them behind his back.

"I'm a top, ace. See these keys on my left? You like tops. You liked it when Roger fucked you." Cuffs clicked anyway.

His boots were kicked apart. He struggled to maintain his balance. Then camera lights were thrown on, phoosh! Phoosh! Phoosh! And they stayed on. The clearing became an outdoor set for a nighttime photo shoot.

Jamie smiled. *They made it easy on you, Kent. You'll be able to see where you're going.*

Lash's high-pitched voice: "Are you getting him, Randy?"

"Yeah, heh-heh. Every bit of him." Jamie started counting. He found seven people. *It's all about pictures.*

"String him up. Then cut off his jeans. Let's get that pretty little ass out there," Crum said, directing his movie, squinting into his camcorder.

There was a guy in front of Jamie now, dressed in camouflage, who had a smaller knife on his belt.

Jamie didn't much believe in Christianity anymore, but he had a need for God whether He exists or not. *Holy Mary mother of God pray for us sinners now and at the hour of our death, Amen.*

Ford led him to the tree, grasped his hand, unlocked the cuffs to tie him up. Jamie elbowed Ford's gut, leapt free, kneed Littleknife in the nuts, went for the weapon. It was locked by some kind of clasp and the guy was writhing, doubled over. Jamie turned, kicked Ford in the stomach, sent him flailing backwards. Crum shouted, "Get him, somebody!"

Lash came at Jamie, who swung, caught a shoulder, sent him flying back on his ass. Jamie kicked Littleknife's jaw, flipped him up and over on his back. But the damn clasp would't yield. Others ran at them. Ford grasped a wrist, yanked it. "I've got you now!"

Jamie punched his jaw, got his other hand free, unsnapped the little knife and started to run, *go go go!* Crum stormed at him, taping it all. Jamie karate-kicked Crum's fat gut, decked him. And Jamie ran, ran, ran.

But there were others in front of him, "There he is!" He veered right, behind a tree—then someone was six feet away. Jamie stabbed and took off again. But two others were converging. He juked, dodged away. "Get the son of a bitch!" Crum yelled, struggling back up. "Don't let him escape!"

Then someone flew at Jamie from behind, wrestled him down. Jamie's knife fell away, hidden in the darkness, while he pummeled the guy. Three others ran up, caught his arms.

With adrenaline-strength, he elbowed the guy on his right, got an arm free, did the same to the guy on his left even harder. He twisted his trunk and smashed the guy behind him with both fists. Jawbones crunched, the guy screamed in agony.

Jamie's legs kicked at inhuman beings. But he was down on the ground, someone on his shoulders, two on his left, someone on his legs, pinning him, punching his guts.

He shut his eyes and exploded in all their directions. He sent two reeling, but not all five. They fought, kicked, yelled. Jamie willed himself into a dynamo, punching every which way. Filled with vengeful hatred, he murdered homophobia.

Then finally they got him; subdued him, immobilized him. *This time, Dr. Webster, there are signs of a struggle.* They dragged him by the arms, face down over rocks and exposed hard roots, back to the killing tree. Crum taped it all.

Jamie knew then that he would die. But in his head his readers cheered; Mr. Ferguson gave him a standing O.

They turned Jamie over. Lash sat on his stomach, so Jamie clenched his abs. His arms pushed up against four of his opponents'. "Jesus, he's so strong!"

"Sit on his arms!" Crum ordered, gasping and taping. His other hand rubbed his sore, saggy gut.

They did. Jamie pushed and kicked and snarled. One opponent fell back, but two more grabbed that leg.

"Damn, what a fighter!" Ford said, stepping onto Jamie's hands with heavy boots. He unleashed his Bowie knife and pointed it down at Jamie's nose. "Top this."

Knife glinted; resistance ceased. Jamie looked up at Ford, wondered why it took Mr. Brain Surgeon so long to remember his knife. *Criminals are stupid.* The tip of the Bowie knife, however, was not.

Lash struggled his fat ass up and kicked Jamie's hard oblique.

"Got him? Wow, this is the most fun we've ever had," Crum shouted. "I can sell this one for an all-time record!"

Rope came from somewhere, tied Jamie's feet together, bound his hands. Ford hung his obscene knife back on his belt, then lifted him up. They stood there panting.

Ford rubbed leaves and dirt off Jamie's face and kissed him right on the lips. Jamie groaned and leaned away, but Ford grabbed him and pulled him to him. Ford stood there in cheap jock strap drag and ground their crotches together, hands all over Jamie's ass.

Jamie said, "You waited to fuck 'em till after they were passed out. You can't get it up otherwise. What's your day job, prepping bodies at the mortuary?"

Ford sneered, "You're the only one who's lived this long. But your clock's ticking."

"Yours will stop in five minutes."

Littleknife kept writhing on the ground and moaning, "He stole my good knife." Finally he staggered up, switched on a flashlight, limped around looking for it.

"Stop it, Tommy," Crum yelled. "Straight people buy these movies too, this ain't your private sex show."

Ford scowled, lifted Jamie's arms up and tied them to the branch overhead. He untied his feet. Then he kissed him, stuck his tongue in his mouth and sucker-punched him.

Jamie gasped for air. When he finally got his breath back he sang, "Rudolph the Red-Nosed Reindeer, died of AIDS up on Death Row!"

"I hate you, faggot." Ford slapped Jamie's face so hard he left a bruise.

Jamie whispered, "You love me, faggot. Can't keep your hands off me. Why hurt this hot body when you want me so bad?" Ford looked confusedly at Jamie's chest. Jamie flexed for him. "Admit it. It's the best body you've ever seen."

Ford fingered one of Jamie's big nipples. "It sure is."

"So let's do this right. Come on, stud, you're the only one with a weapon. Let's get out of here and go to Mexico, where we can be nice to each other and forget this stuff."

"How?" Ford whispered.

"Cut me down, brandish your sword at these wimps and let's escape. Run to the car and get out of here. Show me your nice side, the one I want to believe in."

"What's all this talk about?" Crum yelled, back at his tripod. "Get on with the action."

Ford eyed Crum. "I can't," he whispered to Jamie. "He's got records on me. If you think I'm bad, he's a cold-blooded killer."

Jamie was negotiating with one; so he led with his strengths. "I've got a big dick and I love to fuck. I'm also a virgin up the ass. I've always been a top, left side keys. My ass has never been touched." Jamie looked down at Tommy Ford's jock, then back at his eyes. "Maybe you can teach me how to like it. Maybe I can teach you."

"Wow," Ford gasped. "To be with somebody like you. You're the hottest man I've ever seen."

"Then come away with me. Right now."

"Randy'd never let me get away with it. He'd find me. He'd launch an international manhunt."

"He doesn't have the power. Stop letting him intimidate you. Tommy, I've got millions at Merrill Lynch. We can make it, come on! This is the best offer of your life. The cops are coming, they heard your message at the same time I did. I was just closer to your location, they've got a huge task force. If you stay, you'll die here. Every minute counts! Decide now. Take the best offer of your life. Do it right now!"

Randolph Scott Crum took out a petite handgun and aimed it at them. "Don't try anything, Foster. We're in this together, Tommy."

Jamie's heart sank. Ford looked at the gun, had to step away. "He was telling me his theory about animal tranquilizers, doc. He knows all about 'em. It's important. If he figured it out somebody else may too. What if he's already told the cops?"

"Kill him, so he doesn't tell anymore."

Jamie stood there alone.

More photos from different angles. Everyone had a camera and he had a face.

Another knifeblade was on his right asscheek. Then slice, no jeans there. Soon the same on the other side.

I love you, Rick. I love you, Mom. I love you, Danny, Stoney too.

I love you, Casey.

The blade was on his left hip, cutting a swath across his crotch. He held his breath, didn't want his sex cut off.

The jeans fell to his ankles, but he still had the waistband and his dick.

I love you, Jamie.

Then he thought of someone else, who crowded his mind.

He swallowed. It was his last living chance. There was no reason not to now. Electrical charges shot down his body. His sweat popped out.

He pictured him at the Slough, shaking Jamie's shoulders and demanding why. In the car, speeding him to the hospital; at the house, bringing groceries and a homemade pie.

At the Victory, making him laugh, vowing to wear a tiara if necessary, taking command, "you won't out-commitment me!"

And on a pallet, smelling of sweetness, gently snoring.

I love you, Kent. Thank you for these two weeks.

Now get these guys!

Camcorders whirred. "Heh-heh-heh."

High-pitched voice: "God, he's a pretty one, Randy!"

"Yeah, heh-heh. Like a fashion model, ain't he." Jamie winced.

"You guys, come around here and get his face. He's—it's quite a face."

"And his dick! He's hung, Jesus."

"Get him from all angles! He's gorgeous."

Jamie was almost pleased with that; shooting pictures takes time. *Get all you want, boys, I'm not going anywhere.* He posed and flexed and gave them a show.

There was movement behind him. A hand was on his left shoulder. He tightened up. "Easy," Ford whispered. His hand traveled down to grasp Jamie's naked ass. The touch was perverse, but Jamie didn't cry out.

Ford stepped around. "Act human, you fool. The Angel of Death will only raise his price the braver you are. Break down a little, it's your only chance. Please, Jamie."

Jamie stared at him. "The best offer you'll ever get."

Ford paled, looked down at Jamie's pumped body. "I know."

They abused him with their lascivious remarks, small minds and free gropes, as they took shot after shot. Jamie's mind's eye pictured a cauldron, red-orange lava boiling over the sides, scorching everything, consuming everything, the whole earth opening up in fury.

Ford's hated hand stroked his butt again. Jamie hardened his mind. Finally the others moved away. *Tonight I dominate.* "Hey," he called out, "if I'm going to die anyway, why not make this fun?"

Ford stared. "Are you insane?"

"Let's have fun. Let's get off," Jamie replied. Loudly he called, "Line up, cocksuckers. Down on your knees. Take advantage of the beautiful blond stud who's tied up to the tree. Show me what you can do, be a movie star."

"You're crazy," Ford muttered.

"Or maybe you'd rather get fucked. That's even better, just bend over and climb aboard. But take turns, no pushing, I'll do the shoving. Who wants to be first?"

They were totally confused. A victim enjoying himself? Jamie smiled. Ford told Crum, "He's crazy."

Jamie said, "Believe me, Tommy, it really is more fun with a guy who's alive. Get down on your knees and grab a mouthful. Taste that big young blond muscular cock."

It hit Jamie, the psychodynamics of these scumbags. They were all so self-hating they couldn't give a blowjob to the living.

But Jerry Lash appeared. "How about me?"

Jamie eyed the slob. "Sure, Jerry. Down on your knees, suck my cock. I'll give your mouth a workout you'll never forget."

Crum called, "We don't have time for this." He was upset, his movie wasn't going as planned. He was losing control.

Ford said, "I should fuck you instead."

Jamie said, "No, for that you'd better kill me first. So I don't mock you for how little your dick is."

"You'll pay for that, faggot."

Crum yelled, "Get on with the whip, Tommy. Jerry, get the hell out." But Jerry didn't, he knelt in front of Jamie instead.

Jamie knew it was the right thing to do, but he couldn't imagine tolerating it for one second. *Dominate!* "Hey Crum, come over here and get some closeups of my cock. Take a real good look at it. Come over and suck it. It'd turn me on. I'd love to get a blowjob from you."

"It would mess up my movie."

"Did you ever hear of editing? Come on! Let's have fun. Guys, now's the time for every gang-bang fantasy you've ever had. Come suck the hot blond muscleboy."

Crum said, "I'll shoot any cocksucker who tries it."

With that, Lash got up and left, and Ford said, "I have to use a bullwhip on you now. Randy will be taping as you pass out from the beating. Once you're unconscious, then, well, we bring out the knives. In honor of Roger. But you won't feel that, I promise."

"In honor of a man who murdered 21 people. You have the brain of pond slime, trying to convince yourself that killing me won't hurt. Victims hurt, Tommy! You're not just a psychopath, you're an idiot."

"You're a wise ass."

"Last chance, Tommy. Just circle around Crum, take your knife out and kill him. Get his gun and let's leave. No one will stop us. Kill him, Tommy, and be done with it. You know it's all his fault. Let's make a new life at our villa in Mexico."

"It's too late, Jamie, I'm in it too deep."

"No, you're not, you have 60 seconds to escape."

They looked in each other's eyes. "But I like killing."

That was the essential problem. "Then tonight you find out what dying feels like. Enjoy it! Kent kills you tonight."

They heard distant gunshots. Trees, snipers? Ford, in fury and fear, flipped his whip. "Then tonight we all die!"

On Jamie's back, a searing pain—but inside his head, a very bright flash, an organ chord at fortissimo. He saw Kent's face; his courageous, sensitive, avenging face.

Ford began a frenzy of whipping. Over and over he punished his worst enemy on earth, the one who wrote the truth about him.

Another strike, and blood trickled down Jamie's back.

More lashes, terrible pain; he dreamed of Kent holding him, comforting him. A voice, desert-dry and very old: *Let not your heart be troubled.*

Horror now on his ass, his sex; the Devil himself appeared in the thickest mist, smiling without a face, a red-dressed pope.

Sharp new pains in Jamie's back and side, reaching all the way inside him. "Take that, you motherfucker!"

Jamie didn't cry out. *Littleknife. And more pictures. God, look at that blood spurt.*

His vision began to blur. Waves of weakness washed over him. He retched with the pain; but he didn't cry out.

"Didja get me stabbing him?" Littleknife cried. People seemed to be running around, there was confusion.

Crum was pissed. "You weren't supposed to do that till I said so! You start hacking, I'll blow you away."

A leather tie was wrapped around Jamie's neck. He could not breathe. Life was spilling out his side. He watched it in a daze, somehow alert. *Oh God, I'm dying. My heart will not be troubled.*

His legs gave out. He separated from his body.

Distantly he knew a pair of hands picked up the tie. He heard something, smiled slightly. His body passed out.

A helicopter zoomed over the treetops. "Police, don't move! Put your hands up," Slaughter ordered. Kent wanted as many alive as possible.

"Oh, God, run!" Crum yelled. Kent, shoulder braced against the open door, aimed his weapon and squeezed. Tommy Ford screamed in agony, then experienced death first-hand.

Bulldog squeezed. Lash fell wounded.

Jack Snyder pivoted and fired. A photographer twitched and left.

More shots exploded. Barry Hickman got someone's leg. Lash's high-pitched voice screamed, "I surrender!" Others ran for the darkness.

"I surrender too!" Crum cried.

Eight feet before Slaughter landed the aircraft Kent jumped out, trained his sights on Crum. Other officers poured out of the chopper.

Someone else tried to flee and Phil Blaney dropped him, Gay on Gay, bang!

Gunsmoke singed Kent's nostrils, tears burned his eyes. The semi-automatic felt too small, he suddenly wanted an Ouzi, as many dead as possible. Then he saw Littleknife trying to escape and he squeezed. The stabber died.

"I'm on Crum, Kent," Helmreich yelled, weapon drawn, hand pushing Kent's arm down. His arm was trained, so it dropped, but his legs wouldn't run yet. He stared at Jamie. His naked body hung on the tree, but his spirit seemed to be airborne.

38

Blood

It only lasted a split second. Kent ran and the sensation was gone. "Victim!" he commanded, dashing to get Jamie free. Someone radioed HQ.

Armed officers—soon to be 50—brought survivors into the clearing. Helmreich, weapon drawn pointblank, snarled at Crum, "Who's missing?"

Crum looked around, petrified as his peter drooped. "Let's see, oh, don't shoot."

"How many total?"

"Thirteen."

"Count bodies!" Slaughter yelled as he ran to Jamie.

"Systematic sweep," Kent shouted. "Core group on the victim." *Stop the bleeding!*

"We're gettin' 'em," Hickman whooped. He came to snap cuffs on Crum, tried not to beat him to a pulp.

Jamie, on some unknown plane of existence, saw a bright red vision; his ears heard the roar of consuming fire. The famed TV preacher was done up like the Devil himself, blood-freezing; speaking in tongues of hatred, smiling on cue. Devil had no horns—he had satellites, advertisers, a studio audience and ten billion dollars.

His eyes were furied, ecstatic; his set was dressed with skulls stacked from here to Cambodia. His throne built of Bibles burned without ceasing, the heat flesh-melting. His angels rent bodies scabbed of lavender sarcoma. His fire stole oxygen from gasping lungs. He was a sadist. He enjoyed murder as much as Tommy Ford did.

Kent saw, heard, smelled it all too; shook it off, searching for arteries to squeeze shut.

Then Jamie saw a white pinpoint of light, far off, intense; getting bigger, welcoming and wise. *Rick.* He watched his rescue with reportorial detachment.

Kent felt hot blood spurt onto his chest. He pressed his hands on the wounds while Doc Helmreich sawed the rope. Kent felt open flesh, hot, soft and mooshy. He tried to find those arteries.

Jamie's arms dropped free from the branch overhead as Doc cursed.

Gently, quickly they laid the body face down on the ground. Hickman felt the neck for a pulse. It was there, but irregular, weakening fast. They had no blankets. "Cut off my sweatshirt, Doc," Kent cried. "Wrap it around him to prevent shock." Helmreich chopped at the fleece.

Kent found a blood vessel on Jamie's side, squeezed it; felt his guts try to vomit. The spurting there stopped, but continued from the back like a hydrant flushing. "Stay with me, Jamie!" he shouted. "Help's on the way. Stay with me, partner!" He kissed a swoop of blond hair.

Jamie stopped being able to see anything but the light.

Blaney finished checking Ford's body, hurried over. Campbell came running with a stretcher. Doc got the sweatshirt round Jamie's back, obscenely striped.

Where's that other artery? Kent couldn't find it.

They got the body onto the stretcher. Campbell and Hickman carried while Kent kept pressing down, down, watching the sweatshirt get soaked. With a stick Bulldog grabbed Crum's videocam, ran to load it on the aircraft. "What's the nearest hospital?" Kent cried. They ran, he held on. *There!* He squeezed, the bleeding stopped.

"Shawnee, and it's got a pad," Phil said.

Kent yelled, "Hang on, Jamie! Let's go, let's go!"

Slaughter jumped into the captain's seat and in seconds they were away.

* * *

They made Kent leave him once they got Jamie onto the table and clamped.

He stood aside to watch the doctors prep the body. Then a gloved nurse and a chaplain forced him into a scrub room to wash off. "Get in the shower. You've got it the worst. We'll give you a hospital gown," the nurse said.

"Forget it," Kent growled, "I ain't wearing no gown."

The blood on his jeans caked. He didn't let the nurse touch him. Someone threw him a towel. He wiped off his chest and arms. He caught himself in a mirror and froze.

The other officers were led to a room for those who wait. Kent stared at rusty blood on his lips.

Everyone looked up as he was brought into the room. He shook off his escorts politely, stood motionless a second. Slowly he walked over to the near wall, in front of a bank of windows with heavy drapes drawn. As a police officer he was trained to die. He was not trained to have Jamie do it for him.

Kent moved deliberately, almost in slo-mo. He reached up, yanked the curtain rod out of the cement blocks and screamed into the night.

There lay Jamie, pale and naked as death.

* * *

Someone was holding Kent down. Others patted his shoulder, held his hand. He was still wracking; his eyes ached. In a minute he would try to open them. He gasped for air.

He made out that it was Slaughter who was holding him down, holding him. The hand in his right was soft, so it had to be Julie's.

He didn't want his hand held, so he let go. Bulldog was above somewhere, murmuring comfort. Kent could feel wall on both his shoulders. They had taken him to a corner. He sat on cold tile with his knees to his chest. Someone had taped blankets over the windows.

He gained the ability to look at George. "They're doing all they can," Slaughter said.

Another round of sobbing overtook Kent. "Oh, man, no!"

At some point he convinced them to let him stand. Slaughter hung on his shoulder. Kent needed to walk, get the stiffness out of his knees. He was keening softly now. Slaughter patted Kent's chest as they walked together.

Campbell was frightened. She had never seen her partner lose it like this. She had never seen any officer lose it like this.

A chaplain spoke quietly at the table with Blaney and Bulldog. Doc Helmreich stood away from everyone, illegally smoking. Jack Snyder joined him. Hickman asked about coffee.

The nurse came back, or maybe hadn't left; he leaned against the back wall. Kent walked up to the guy, looked him in the eye, then down and away. "Sorry."

"You okay?"

Kent mumbled, "Getting there."

"Everybody has to get an AIDS test."

Kent turned slowly to confront this. "Why?"

"You came in contact with a lot of blood," the nurse replied, palms up like the answer was obvious. "Look at your britches."

The room was silent for a minute. Kent just shook his head; shook it and shook it.

Campbell spoke up. "Think about it, Kent. He was a homosexual. I sure as heck want that test."

He looked at her. She was standing only six feet away.

If she were a guy he'd have slugged her. It didn't matter that she'd been in on the rescue, he'd have slugged her.

"He **is** my partner! He is my **living** partner!" He slammed his fist into his other hand in lieu of her face.

Campbell stepped away, tried to make amends. He turned his back on her. She put her hand on his shoulder. Carefully, firmly and in control, without turning around, he removed the hand. He paused, felt the tightness of his grip, let loose.

It did not violate him again.

The nurse said something about making arrangements at the lab, and how everyone would have to be retested three and six months later. "I refuse," Kent told Slaughter. The chief looked at him, made no reply.

"Kent, maybe we should listen to what the nurse here is saying," Bulldog offered. "I'm pretty sure Jamie's negative, but a little needlestick won't hurt anybody. We'd know that way, have peace of mind."

"I refuse," Kent repeated to Slaughter.

"Okay, son. Okay. You're on the record. Relax now."

Kent tried to, couldn't. *Jamie's in there dying and they're worried about themselves? Puh-lease.*

In the corner, Campbell complained to anyone who would listen about how scared she was of getting AIDS. "I told you we should have worn our rubber gloves," she told Hickman. "These damn homosexuals scream bloody murder if you try to protect yourself from them. God, what a night. First it's a gaybar and then we get doused with a homosexual's blood."

As nearly as Kent could make out, the most she'd gotten was two drops on her right boot. *How selfish can you get? "Bloody murder," huh?*

"If I get it I'm going to sue," Campbell said.

"Who would you sue?" Hickman wondered.

"His estate maybe. The state of Indiana. I don't know."

"You're getting worked up over nothing."

"How would you know?"

"I've known him a lot longer than you have. Four years, right? Homicide, right? He was our witness long before you people came along."

"That doesn't prove anything to a virus."

"Listen," Barry Hickman said. "I'm not thrilled about homosexuals either. But one of them just saved my life. And 50 other officers, including you. So lay off! We could have gone flying down that road and gotten shot. But no, we got notified about snipers. I'd sure as hell rather take my chances with AIDS than a bullet."

Barry Hickman had never defended a homosexual in his life. But he wasn't going to stand there and listen to this. He knew the homosexual. He was a friend to the homosexual. He was proud of the homosexual.

Coffee arrived, "Thank God." He hurried to get some. Elsewhere discussion started, in dribs and drabs. It was about the suspects and the great evidence from all those cameras.

Not the victim. Either Kent was going very crazy, or there was something not right here.

Someone medical came in to report that surgery had started. Kent listened hard, but "it could be several hours" was all he really heard.

The others went off to get their blood drawn. Steve Helmreich patted Kent's shoulder on the way out, "I've known Jamie for years. I knew Rick, too."

"Really, Doc?"

"They were both negative, and Jamie still is, trust me. It was a weird disease that got Rick, vasculitis, a terrible killer. Don't worry about this testing shit. You did great out there. Textbook, though you may not be ready to hear it right now. Anyway, get the test if you want to, don't if you don't. Won't make a bit of difference. I'm just going through their little procedural motions, being the hired consultant. You know the damn bureaucracy, they're more concerned with their liability than your health."

Kent chuckled. It sounded rusty, but at least it was a laugh.

The others went from the lab to individual debriefings with chaplains and the crisis psychologist corps. Troopers came to inform Slaughter about a statement made by Lash. "Don't tell me, tell your Commander."

Kent took the report, issued an appropriate followup order; Slaughter praised him. TV crews began setting up outside; there was a rumor that CNN was going live. Kent said, "I can't deal with TV. There's a police operation to run, a man to protect."

So Slaughter talked to Col. Potts, who was far away from the action as usual; briefed the press spokesperson; woke up the governor, who congratulated him and asked to be kept abreast on Jamie's condition; spoke to the mayor, who resented being awakened; was told of more possible suspects out-of-state, and heard Kent issue new orders; conferred with an assistant Attorney General in Washington, and even a White House politico; finally satisfied himself that the good guys had effective control.

A message was relayed from Casey Jordan of The Ohio Gay Times. Slaughter went out to take that one himself. Casey and someone named Dyson claimed they had tele-photos from the scene. Casey had Jamie's mother's answering machine code. He wanted to see his reporter.

Slaughter explained Jamie's situation, demanded the film. "It's evidence. Don't make me detain you and get a court order, Casey. I can have one in two minutes flat."

Casey insisted that his newspaper control the photos, but offered to share prints as soon as they could be made in the morning. Slaughter agreed, assigned a trooper to secure them and bodyguard Jordan. Casey again pressed to see Jamie.

"He's in surgery, Casey, on the operating table as we speak. We're not keeping you from seeing your writer, Shawnee Hospital is." Slaughter put a hand on Casey's shoulder. "They're doing all they can, son. He's told me you're a great editor and his best friend."

Casey trembled, changed tactics, asked for Kessler. Slaughter suggested the ISP flack. Casey demanded Kessler. "Your incompetent department has my number one reporter in surgery because you couldn't protect him. I have a right to ask for Kessler. This is our case every bit as much as it is yours. Don't forget: I know you and Jamie are friends. I'll be happy to tell CNN all I know."

Then he backed off from blackmail. "Come on, chief. Five minutes?"

Slaughter weighed it, couldn't care less about blackmail. "Sgt. Kessler is traumatized," he said sharply.

"So's Jamie. So are we! He's my reporter and my best friend. Major, put yourself in my place. What else can I do for him now but get the goddamn story?" Casey wept one tear, shut his eyes furiously.

Slaughter agreed finally to ask Kessler. "If he says no, it's no deal. You have no idea what thin ice we're on." Casey didn't back down. "Just you. No photos, no tape, off the record. And only if he agrees to it, which I highly doubt."

"He killed my guy's killer, chief," Casey pleaded. "Just let me be with him. Thank him, condole with him, you know? Not a real interview. Dammit, he's the closest thing I've got to my buddy."

Despite Slaughter's stern advice, Kent readily agreed to it; Casey was the closest thing he had to his buddy.

*　　　*　　　*

The visit ended with a hug, Casey's body light in Kent's arms, which made Kent clutch a little tighter, then release and reject harder than he expected. "Sorry. I'm so whacked-out right now. Jamie's told me about you, and…"

Casey wiped at an eye. Asked Kent to recommend a hotel. Kent gave the address on Washington Street, the key to their room. "Take care of him, man," Casey begged.

"I will. I swear to God I will."

Slaughter made a brief appearance before the TV crowd. The media relations person had already given the official line, and the questions directed at Slaughter weren't ones he could answer without jeopardizing the case. The session was turning pointless, so he called a halt to it. A voice called out, "How's the Gay reporter?"

Slaughter's jaw set. He aimed for the CNN camera and said, "We have every hope for the swift and full recovery of Jamie Foster of The Ohio Gay Times, a courageous young journalist. He saved the life of every police officer on this task force and helped us nail a serial killer ring. Does that make him a Gay reporter? No.

"It makes him an American hero."

* * *

Finally only Slaughter, Kent and a chaplain were left in the room off the ER. Slaughter maintained light physical contact, a hand on Kent's arm. "Where there's life there's hope. He's alive, Kent."

Immediately Kent shook his head. "You know to Christ it should never have happened. I take full responsibility, chief. Bring me up on charges, I take full responsibility."

When he got over his shock, Slaughter was both pleased and horribly sad. "For what?" he croaked. "A disabled mic and bad timing? You saved the guy's life." He watched Kent reject the whole idea.

"Kent, Blaney got the phone call, but couldn't hear in that noisy bar; once he got the message, he went to notify you Ford was on his way. He had to leave his post, but only for a few minutes. It was exactly as you designed it. You got just the advance notice from surveillance you had ordered. No one could anticipate that that was when it all came down. Once the scene started you were on it immediately." Kent looked away.

Slaughter drove it home. "Ford stepped inside that bar and waved a joint in front of the first loser he found. He only wanted the guy as bait anyway. What'd it take, ten seconds? Jamie saw it and responded immediately—too fast, really; he didn't have the experience or training not to go chasing off by himself without backup—if he even knew his mic was knocked out. An officer would never have left the bar without confirming contact. Better to let the guy go than get killed himself. If there's a mistake it's that we didn't stress that enough with him. That's everyone's fault, not yours. He overcommitted himself. He trusted the plan too much."

"Don't blame the victim," Kent spat. "Chasing after Ford is what I set him up for."

"I don't blame the victim, and don't blame yourself, sergeant. We both know why he did it, because he cares so much about his community. We saw the measure of the man tonight, by what he's willing to die for."

Slowly Kent nodded. "God, what a hero. The courage of ten men."

"And thank God he's still here, and we do have hope. Even though the operation got a little ragged after that, you accomplished your mission, we hope without further loss of life."

A little ragged. My guy's in there dying and you're telling me it got a little ragged? Puh-lease. Kent remembered who taught him that pronunciation; who, where, when.

"Why didn't his cell phone work? I'd have ordered him off before he ever went to the motel. The location was all we needed. He didn't have to be there at all, we'd have taken care of it."

"But the surviving victim would have been dead."

"I know. God, Jamie. It takes a stud to catch a killer. Hi, stud."

"When Ford gave him a deadline of 3:15, Jamie didn't know where we were. So what could he do? He went ahead and traded for the trick. And succeeded, let's not forget that. He succeeded! The kidnap victim's alive and sleeping it off in this same hospital.

"You know how much Jamie wanted to nail those killers. And you got them, both of you did, and Jamie's still alive. He may recover. Think about that. There's still a chance for a happy ending here. Damn it, listen to me, man. Where there's life there's hope."

Kent took it in. He couldn't make sense of it. He tried; he must be insane. But when in doubt, he tried to trust his chief.

Gradually something else took over; it didn't matter about the case anymore, what's done is done. They got the killers. Maybe Jamie would die.

But if he lived? *Dear God, if he lives…*

Kent's gut took control. He stared at George Slaughter, eyes transfiguring horribly. *How will I ever explain to Jamie that I let him down?*

"Why did he keep going, chief? He knew all we needed was the address."

"No, we needed the address and more time."

"Thank God we had the chopper."

"I'm just realizing some things about him, Kent. He never walks away from a fight. He was very protective of his late lover, and he's the same way towards his people. If someone tries to harm them, Jamie stands in the way, a gunslinger with a keyboard. He never loses. He's taken on wealthy, powerful men. He never loses."

"If he's a gunslinger, why wouldn't he take the fucking gun?"

"His weapon is words."

"Don't I know it." But Kent had a duty to report his own negligence. *Tell him, before you die yourself.* It took a long time, though. "Chief, um, something else happened tonight."

Slaughter nodded slightly, "Tell me." Then, more forcefully, "Tell me, sergeant."

Kent couldn't look at him. But he did manage to say, "At the bar."

Slaughter's eyes crinkled. He exhaled, looked into mist, felt. "You want to go outside and talk?"

Kent nodded, weak. They left the chaplain behind and walked the corridor.

Finally Kent said, "He danced with some guy and... all of a sudden I had to... go to the bathroom. It was an emergency. I was in the wrong place at the wrong time. All I could think was I had to clean myself up. That's the very minute the scene came down! Chief, I let him out of my sight. That's why I should be up on charges. You have to. I beg you to. I take full responsibility. The most important person to this operation, and I let him out of my sight."

"You got sick? You peed your pants?"

"I creamed my jeans! Chief, I've been with two dozen women in my life. I never once had a sexual reaction to a guy. Then in walks Brad Pitt and I lose it. I can't believe this. It's totally at odds with everything I know. Swear to God, I've always been Straight."

"I know." *I should have seen this coming the minute you said Pitt's name.*

"I deserted him—at the moment he needed me! You heard him up there. 'I choose to follow my Commander.' Oh, Jamie. How could I be so fucking stupid!" Kent beat his head with his fists over and over.

Slaughter's strong arm stopped it. He had to reach deep inside. "You weren't the only one pushing him. I pushed him too, half a dozen of us, the whole group. We don't send a civilian into a situation like that unless he's the only one who can do it; and unless we have complete confidence in him. And we did, after he got in Carson's face. It was a team decision. And he took responsibility himself. Respect him for that choice. If we second-guess ourselves, we second-guess him. And that's not right. If you don't feel this victory, his victory and yours and your task force's, then his death, if it happens, is in vain. And damn you, sergeant, I'll never allow that in my unit."

Kent stared at the chief, then into space.

Slaughter looked at his handpicked man, handsome, tortured, and so young. Old experience, Vietnam, came unwillingly back. He fought it but it was right.

"Suppose this is war," he said quietly. "Nothing makes men closer than having to rely on each other for their lives. So the worst happens; you might lose your best buddy. What do you do, sergeant?

"You honor him; you hate like hell to lose him, you'd rather someone ripped your arm out of its socket and threw it away.

"And then, goddammit, you fight on. Armless even, you fight on. For what you both believe in. For the time when there's no more killing. That's what Jamie wanted more than anything, the time when no one dies." Kent watched the tough old face.

"He would hate to see you torture yourself. He knew what he was getting into. So let him be the soldier that he is! Jamie got the takedown on thirteen people on-site, maybe others. It's his takedown. We just mopped up."

Kent felt another sob explode in his chest. "And cut him down." His eyes hurt, their rain resumed.

Slaughter rubbed Kent's back, wordless.

"I know you're right, chief. It's just so hard to take in. Remember what he said about acting like Glenn Ferguson was our brother? Jamie and I've gotten close these last two weeks. His Mom and all, the Walkers, the insight he brought to this case—we've gotten close. Then I send my buddy to his execution? Augh!" Kent was right. There was no comforting that.

Like men they cried together, arm on arm. Slaughter tried not to think of a certain helicopter gunner, now just a granite name in D.C. But here and now was way too hard, and there was comfort in the old familiar ache.

* * *

A little after dawn, Julie Campbell found them. She had done all she could here, and maybe she should drive Sgt. Kessler home? "No way," Kent monotoned.

"Chief?" Julie appealed. "There's nothing we can do here but wait."

"Campbell, you're an idiot," Kent snapped. "The work just started."

Slaughter said, "Commander Kessler coordinates the ongoing investigation and the 24-hour armed guard. If there are surviving killers I wouldn't put it past them to try and get at Foster. IPD's got the facility; Kessler, you're on the CI, same as before."

He considered what to do with Campbell. She was not the highest priority at the moment. "Campbell, go home, get some rest," he growled.

"You okay, partner?" she asked Kent, not touching him.

"Yeah, go home," he forced himself to answer, and only because the chief was there. But he refused to look at her. "I'm sticking here. I've got orders."

"Okay, well, good luck," she said, moving reluctantly away.

Kent didn't watch her retreat. Slaughter patted his bare back twice. "We need to get you in clean clothes, son."

Kent looked down. His Levi's were stiff with dried blood, and they crinkled whenever he moved. Would he ever wear them again? He couldn't see washing them and acting like it never happened, just a pair of jeans.

"What size are you, Kent?"

"31/38 baggy, big shirt, XL." He remembered the tag he'd spied on Jamie's Levi's, 27/34, Student. *How could a grown man have a 27-inch waist?*

Jamie, in his head: "*By not eating greaseburgers, you moron.*"

It made Kent smile, which made his face hurt. He thought his prayers all the harder.

Slaughter ordered a third-shift rookie to go to an all-night store to buy clothes. "Underwear too, a complete outfit. Get stuff that looks good, the best they have."

Kent reached for his wallet. The hand-tooled brown leather was sticky; his money was soaked with blood.

He stared, disbelieving and grieving, as Slaughter handed the rookie three crisp hundreds, told him to put on his lights. "Yes, sir."

Then a surgeon, Asian-American, came up to them in greens, pulled off a scrubcap, shook out her hair. "How is he, doctor?"

Kent's heart pounded.

"He survived the surgery. That is very good news. We'll keep him in recovery for awhile, then he'll be taken to intensive care." She looked awfully young.

"And the prognosis?" Slaughter asked, steeling himself.

"It's extremely tough with this type pattern of multi-system failure."

Before she could describe the technicalities of the wounds, something in the young cop's face made her change course; the first dawning of a bedside manner. She'd seen distraught families before, they were a dime a dozen; this guy looked like he'd seen a real ghost.

"It's the amount of blood he lost, and the transport time that are the variables. You were in some remote location, huh?" Slaughter nodded. "People don't die of stab wounds usually, they die of loss of blood. If you hadn't squeezed him shut, or hadn't had the chopper, either one, he'd have been dead on arrival. So far he's extremely lucky. The stab wounds were direct hits on the arteries. He lost 3500 cc's of blood, over half his blood supply. That's more than I've ever seen anyone lose and still survive."

"God," Kent mourned.

"But he's made it this long. He's young and strong and in excellent health. That's a huge help. Right now, though, we have him on a ventilator, and we expect him to stay in coma for awhile." Kent stared at the floor, shaking his head. She said softly, "Maybe a long time."

"Maybe forever?" Kent tried to make his body not shake.

She glanced at the older officer, decided to ignore the question. "If he makes it through the next 24 hours, it increases his chance of survival. Then if and when the lungs begin to return to normal function and he starts to breathe for himself, that increases the chances of the other systems kicking in. If the central nervous system begins to recover, he wakes up from the coma, it's possible he'll be okay. Brain damage becomes the concern at that point, and it could be severe; but it's too early to worry about it. He would begin a lengthy rehab, several months. Meanwhile we're planning on procedures to perform these other functions for him. So focus on the next 24 hours, okay? One step at a time. He makes it that far, then we focus on the next 24."

Kent listened. *Good God, he could be a vegetable. The one thing worse than death.*

It was unbearable; he had to switch. He tried very hard to remember his optimism. He had trained it all his life, it had always helped him. Would it now? Could he even find it?

He asked tremulously, "Is full recovery possible at all?" Then he had to look the doctor full in the face.

"If we did our jobs right, a full recovery may be possible sometime in the distant future. That's what we're hoping for. But we have to take it step by step. I'm not going to lie to you, most people in this situation do not recover. Nothing in his body is working right now. It takes an extraordinary person and set of circumstances. Maybe he's that lucky one, I don't know. But he's young, that's a big plus. Is he an athlete?"

Says he's not, but… "You're goddamn right he's an athlete!"

Her eyes widened at his ferocity. "We thought so. Athletes are good at healing. So it's possible the damage is reversible. We'll have to wait and see. In the meantime, just because things look pretty bad, we don't stop hoping." Dr. Chen amazed herself, pulling for a patient so publicly.

Kent turned shuddering away.

The surgeon watched him get distance. She said to the senior officer, "When he's stable, we'll transfer him to IU, the rehab unit. They're excellent." Slaughter nodded. "I didn't hear what all happened tonight. But tell him he saved the guy's life, squeezing those arteries shut. Our whole staff is talking about it. Most people couldn't do it, even if they had guts enough to try; just the physical strength it takes to hold on for a long time would be too much. He's an athlete, too."

"He sure is." Slaughter hadn't been able to save T.J. Williams once they got him to base camp from the Huey. *God damn.*

"That's what saved him. Without that, a rocket couldn't have gotten him here fast enough."

Slaughter thanked her deeply, watched her walk away.

Kent he allowed to mourn by himself, hanging onto the bannister, staring out windows into nothingness in the early-morning gloom.

*   *   *

Kent's mother showed up. Campbell had called her, upset, but told her very little. Kent clung to his Mom, wept some, wouldn't let her go, much less out of his sight.

Then he switched, standing apart outside the recovery room, working his duty weapon in and out of his holster, in and out, in and out, making sure it didn't stick on the blood; almost hoping someone would try to get at Jamie again so he could fire and fire.

Slaughter didn't take his eyes off him, but spoke softly.

Whatever it was, her only son was unhurt; but Martha Kessler knew this was major, catastrophic.

He'd always had a mysterious hole in his personality, something inaccessible that she'd never been able to reach; though he loved her like a six-year-old, completely. Now somehow that hole was revealed; but not knowing what it was about, she couldn't say or do a thing to help him. She saw her son in abject misery, and heard herself mouthing clichés. What on earth was going on with him? How could she heal a hurt he didn't know or wouldn't show?

All she could do was watch as he worked his gun, in and out, in and out. All she could do was hold him, and love him, and pray.

39

Jeans

The rookie arrived with Kent's clothes. He changed in the bathroom, then handed the bag with his bloody jeans to his mother. Looked in her eyes and said, "Take these home for me. But don't wash them, don't touch them."

"Why not?"

"They could be evidence."

Neither of them was much experienced with his lying to her, but she said nothing.

The major came up. "Let me take you to breakfast. The rookie can stand guard."

"What about Mom?"

"Police business. I'll take her down when we're done."

They found the cafeteria. Coffee smelled good and bacon was frying somewhere, but otherwise the place was fluorescent as hell's waiting room. They got some food, sat. The major said, "You'll have to turn in your weapon."

Kent pulled it out of his holster again, made sure it didn't stick. "This one wasn't fired."

"A trooper who fires any weapon goes on immediate paid time off. You'll have to see the shrink, too. You've been through a critical incident. Have you ever fired your weapon before?"

"No, sir."

"How do you feel about it?"

Kent didn't answer for a long time. Finally he said, "I feel fucking great about it. I don't like killing people, but they were killing him, so I'm proud I fired. I'd do it again. I'd do it right now." If this wasn't the expected answer, it was pure honesty. "Please don't send me away, chief. You can have my weapon, but there's more investigating to do. Don't put me on paid time off, let me finish the job. Let me run my investigation."

Slaughter looked at him; still a police officer, even through this. There were regulations, but it was an enormous case, with 13 suspects and a task force led by a fine young trooper. The followup would take weeks. "I'll find a way to get you away from this; but till then, and on to the end, you're still my Commander."

"Thank you, chief. Help me figure out the next steps. There's a ton of work to do. The Justice Department, the FBI. Can you believe that fucking Carson, lurking in the trees?"

George sighed. "Not really."

They designed a command structure, since so many officers statewide would be assigned to follow up leads. Kent looked at George. "But no Campbell."

"Regs solve that one. She's on paid time off."

"She didn't fire her weapon. She carried the fucking stretcher."

"No Campbell. You'll need a command center."

Kent rubbed his face, suddenly very tired. "I'm not leaving him. We've got phones and modems. The hospital can find me an empty room."

"You need distance, Kent."

"Chief, of all the stupid things you've ever said, that takes the cake." Kent chuckled bitterly. "I haven't had distance since the day he walked in. And I ain't gonna start now. You tried to warn me. Call him Foster, you said. Chief, I never have. He's too smart, too much a leader, a little stud. You don't dehumanize somebody like that. This CI ain't no lowlife junkie you use and throw away. It's Jamie. I'm proud I called him that."

Having made his confession, he got more honest. "And I admit, he's too damn good-lookin'. Pressuring me about bikini butts I never even looked at."

Slaughter patted him. "It's okay, son."

"Once we got over being scared of each other, finally became friends, we've had so much fun. He ain't always easy to be with. But his heart… is as golden as his hair."

Slaughter sighed. "Will you get some sleep for me?"

"You wanna hear a crazy one? I'm almost afraid to sleep. Afraid I'll lose him while I'm sleeping. Afraid I'll never wake up." Tears came again. "Or he won't. God damn. Give me a pallet on the floor."

* * *

The other guys came down to the cafeteria, everyone but Campbell. George waved them over, Kent stood up for them. "Sorry, guys. Some Commander I am, huh? Let my CI get wounded critically, then I go crazy on you."

Bulldog sat. "You were just acting out what we all felt. I got in with the counselor and five minutes later I was crying. Don't beat yourself up, Kent, you're a great Commander. He's holding his own. We finally got these guys."

Dr. Steve said, "Till you brought us together as a task force, we had one thing in common before we even met."

"Jamie," Jack Snyder said. "He worked with everybody here." *Marie's going to be so upset about this.* He teared up, because he didn't want her upset. *Still, it's justice for the Red-Haired Boy.*

Hickman looked off. "I didn't realize how much I admired him until this. He's a hell of a man. I don't care if he is a homosexual—no wait, by God, I'm going to learn to say it right. I don't care if he is Gay, I'm glad we're on the same team."

Bulldog knew what growth that statement was. "I can't believe it's over, Barry. These victims can rest in peace."

Kent said, "I'm going to pull it together, guys. Sorry I let you down. I guess I just needed to go off."

Phil Blaney had a quiet instinct. "Better than keeping it all inside, Kent. Throughout this operation you've been cool as a cuke. Even when things fell apart, there you were, poised, calm, an ideal Commander. Issuing orders, going over all the possible things we'd find, making sure we knew our roles and the rules of engagement. Major, you made a great choice in this officer. Soon as I met him, when we talked on the phone even, I felt real comfortable. I'm proud to serve with you, Kent."

Bulldog said, "Thirty years I've been in this business, and I was scared to death."

Jack muttered, "We all were."

Kent said, "You guys gave me everything I asked for. Thank you, all of you." He looked at Doc, then said, "We signed a teamwork statement. So as your Commander, I'm deputizing each of you as Assistant Commanders for your jurisdictions; and ordering you to appear with me later on today in front of all the media. We're going to celebrate what you men did. And we're going to call the TV stations in Dayton, 'cause we've got two Ohio officers here. And the same with Chicago for Doc."

Bulldog and Hickman smiled a little.

They got ready to break up. Phil said, "One last thing?"

"Prayer," Bulldog mumbled. They stood, held hands, bowed their heads.

Phil said, "Each of you say the names of the victims in your jurisdiction. Major, you fill in any that aren't represented here. Kent, you get the last one."

So they prayed for them: Riley Jones. Kelvin Farmer. Barry Lynn Turner. Aaron Haney. Michael Cardinal. The Red-Haired Boy. Christopher Carnes. Buddy Trueblood. Brian Greene. Bobby Hanger. Wayne Allen Wilson. John-Mark Barnett.

"Glenn Archer Ferguson," Kent said. "Jamie Foster."

* * *

Back at Kessler Farms, Martha washed those Levi's immediately. The bloodstains came right out, but she hadn't noticed a spot on the crotch; it stayed discolored. She hung them on the line to dry. If they were evidence, he wouldn't have sent them home.

She knew not to hang onto a gut-wrench, but to turn them right back into jeans.

40

Dillinger's Mother

Kent oversaw Jamie's transfer from the recovery room to intensive care, and ordered the rookie to come back in a half hour. As nurses arranged their equipment Kent stood by the far wall, out of the way, where he could see the doorway and Jamie's face. Kent's emotions went numb.

Gradually, without thought, he decided that the one thing he could do for Jamie besides protect him was to finish the investigation, get to the bottom of the crimes; to bring him and all the others justice.

It felt so right that Kent gained a new reserve of energy. He would not sleep now, he would direct his investigation in these early, critical hours. There were search warrants to obtain on all the perpetrators; that meant awakening a judge. There were next of kin to be notified, a rookie job. There were mountains of evidence to obtain at the crime scene; he'd order Lt. Warnecke down from Lowell. The motel and the car would have to be gone over with a fine-tooth comb. Warnecke would need a battalion of assistants, therefore every crime scene specialist in the state would have to be called in. All these personnel would need special equipment in a volume seldom seen on a single case; the Quartermaster would have to coordinate that. Kent tapped Harvey, Slaughter's assistant, as deputy commander for communications.

Lab technicians would be inundated, so they and all other personnel had to be notified that this case was the department's highest priority. Potentially it could affect every post in the state, so the regional and post commanders would have to be briefed.

The rookie returned from break. Kent ordered him to bodyguard the witness. "If necessary, shoot to kill." The rookie saluted, went outside to wait.

Kent leaned over Jamie's inert body, whispered in his ear, "Gotta go, partner. Hang in there. I want to see your eyes open when I get back. I need you, partner. See you soon." Kissed what remained of his swoop.

He found Slaughter. "Where's the colonel?"

"I was afraid you'd ask," the major muttered. "When he found out we made the capture he went to bed."

"Sir, my task force just got bigger. I need Col. Potts's assistance and I can't wait until morning to get it. The entire command structure has to be briefed; that's his job."

"Do what you need to do, Commander."

Kent respectfully awoke the superintendent and asked him to report to Shawnee Hospital. Then he turned back to Major Slaughter. "What is your role now, sir? I report to you as my superior, and as deputy chief, you oversee me and all other investigations."

"Correct."

"Seems like a waste of resources for you to go back to an administrative role when you've been so involved."

"If you can use me in an active role, Commander, issue the order."

"Most important role, sir, interrogating the suspects. I lost my partner tonight. How'd you like to do a little good cop/bad cop on nine surviving murderers?"

"At times your partner could be a very bad cop."

"That's what I need, sir, a cop who's real bad."

George Slaughter got ready for a barroom brawl.

* * *

Eight hours and one celebratory news conference later, Kent knew a great deal about this crime and a dozen others. Ford's house was a treasure trove of evidence, thirteen sets of trophies, clothes, sextoys, driver's licenses, the works. Jerry Lash kept an address book and a large collection of European boy pornography. All but two of the suspects' homes contained evidence; but the two that didn't were the two Kent most needed. He drove Slaughter to the home of Mrs. Frank Carson.

"Not police again," she said bitterly. "You've already turned my house upside down. You're not coming in here without a warrant."

Slaughter said, "There's no warrant, ma'am, but don't think I can't get one. I've got judges on standby."

Kent said, "Ma'am, your husband was secretly involved in criminal activity. He shot at the state police helicopter. We returned fire."

"For all I know he was there on official business. You can't compel me to testify against him or to cooperate in any way, other than as ordered by a court of law."

"That's right, ma'am. I won't press you, I know you're in as much shock as anyone. All I want to do is talk, easy background questions, nothing a lawyer could object to. How long have you and Agent Carson been married?"

"Twenty-six years."

Kent looked down, not at her. "Good years, I hope?"

"For the most part. We have three children."

"And your youngest still at home. Having to face the kids at school. I'm sorry."

"I'm not sending her to school. She's staying here with me. Maybe I'll send her somewhere else."

"He dishonored you and his own daughter, ma'am. I'm so sorry."

Mrs. Carson cried dry tears. "Assuming he's guilty."

"He's unquestionably guilty, ma'am. Don't harbor the first doubt he's not going to prison for the rest of his life. Ma'am, let me respectfully suggest that you need to start thinking of the future, for your own sake and for your daughter's."

"What am I going to do?" she asked, half-panicked.

Kent looked at the surroundings. "Nice house; an Agent-in-Charge. Do you and he save at all, ma'am?"

"As much as we can, with children to put through college. He's very conservative with money."

"Will you be able to get by without him?"

"I don't know. He handles the money. I don't know what we have, or what I'm going to do. Get a job, I suppose; doing what? I have a B.A. in art history and twenty years' experience as a soccer mom. I'm sure Microsoft can't wait to meet me."

"No other tangible assets that you might sell if need be? A boat? A vacation home?"

"Why, yes, I hadn't thought of that. The house on Lake Monroe."

Slaughter all but sympathized with Dillinger's mother.

Kent said, "Is it a good location, ma'am? There are upscale homes on Lake Monroe."

"A very good location, 400 feet of lake frontage. I go there so seldom, it didn't occur to me. It's his place, a retreat from all his pressures as a Federal agent. He seldom invites me, only once a year."

Southern Indiana bugs. "Monroe County or Brown?"

"Brown County."

Kent smiled sympathetically. "Then ma'am, you'll have nothing to worry about money-wise. Brown County has very expensive properties. I'm so glad for you and your children."

"I suppose so. That would be a help, wouldn't it, if I need to sell?"

"It would give you time to sort out any other assets you might have. You wouldn't have to worry, with several hundred thousand in the bank."

"Thank you, sergeant. With all the horror of this day, you're the best news I've had."

"Good luck, ma'am, we'll go now. Best wishes to your family."

"Thank you, sergeant, thanks so much."

They left. Slaughter chuckled as he got into the squad car. "Get me to a doctor."

"Why's that?" Kent asked, driving smoothly away.

"I just developed sugar diabetes. Jeez, the broad even thanked you."

"Brown County has doctors," Kent grinned.

But so does Shawnee Hospital. His heart equatored. He phoned in for a report. Jamie was still unconscious, to be transferred tomorrow to IU Hospital's rehab unit, *Coma Central.*

* * *

Brown County recorder, judge, warrant, and bingo: snuff films. Mutilations. Castrations on CD-ROM. Dismemberments. Contact lists, financial records, Internet footprints. Pictures of Carson's own daughter being raped at three years old.

It wasn't news to Kent that people could be evil; only in how they went about it. But this was as bad as it could get, worse than he'd ever seen.

He wondered again what kind of man Jamie was, to have unearthed all this.

* * *

Finally the sadness and exhaustion hit. He had a listless supper back at the hospital with his Mom, who brought suits and casual clothes. He listened to her advice about laundry. "If you wouldn't let your dirty clothes build up so much, they'd be easier to handle, whether you wash them yourself or bring them to me. I don't mind doing it, son, but eight or ten loads is a lot for anyone."

He let her do her Mom thing, even took comfort in the mundanery of washday woes. "Thanks for bringing my stuff. Looks like I'm going to be down here for awhile. Could be weeks."

"Then I'll come down every night with food. You give me washing to take back, just don't let it build up."

"Mom, you don't have to do that."

"I want to. How's the victim?"

"Holding his own." Kent shrugged at the handy phrase that meant *not dead yet.*

"Let go and let God, son."

He figured he deserved a cliché back.

She too tried to comfort a hurt that wouldn't go away. Finally, thanking her, he told her he was tired. "I know, I can see it in your eyes. Get some sleep, son. I'll be back tomorrow night." He kissed her, thanked her, told her not to worry, he'd be all right. They hugged and he went upstairs to Jamie, to sit in a chair all night, to sleep with him on the world's worst camping trip.

* * *

He couldn't sleep, though. Partly it was the chair, no position that felt halfway right. Mostly it was the situation, sitting with the body of a spirit he ached for, with no way of knowing whether he'd ever know the guy again.

At something past five it happened. The famed TV preacher, eyes ecstatic and advertisers lined up, had Jamie strapped to an electric chair, finger on the button, some wacko-sermon about Armageddon, the fall of the Soviet Union, America's moral decline, the Year 2000, all prophesied in Revelation and all Jamie's fault; and Kent was present as a police witness to the execution, armed and in uniform ’cause his Mom ironed his shirts; and he had his duty weapon and wanted to fire at the preacher, keep him from doing it. But no matter how hard he tried, he couldn’t get his gun out of the holster, it was stuck, dried blood, and the preacher fingered the lever, and Kent wanted to shout, “No, never,” as the preacher smiled, “Two minutes to frytime.”

Kent woke up drenched in sweat, and there, in the little room in intensive care, lay Jamie and the ventilator, *wihh, hooh, wihh, hooh, wihh.*

41

Miss Davis's Nominations

At his office the next day, Major Slaughter said, "The pictures are ready. Can you handle it? It's okay if you can't, they're traumatic."

Kent steeled himself. "Of course I can handle it. I'm an Indiana state trooper."

They went to an evidence room. There were stacks of carefully-inventoried photographs, topped by printouts. In the corner was a big screen TV with state-of-the-art clarity. George popped in a videocassette. "The camera on Jamie's left, Crum's, has the best angle on the action."

Kent took a seat. "Pornographic pigs."

"Great evidence, though. Tape your crime, show us every detail."

"Let's put them all on Death Row."

"The only issue's going to be sentencing, so the prosecutor's focusing on that."

"Sir, have you heard what we're getting from the home searches? Gary Tompkins has positively identified Mr. Ferguson's clothes and wedding ring found at Ford's house. Gary wears an identical ring. Perfect match."

"It's everything but the smoking gun. And there's a new lead just in. Kent, Crum's got the smoking gun. We just never knew where he hid it. Jamie helped with the psychology of that years ago, and Schmidgall's lawyer in Chicago. We may be able to close out the entire shebang, not just Ford's 13, but Schmidgall's 21 and maybe others."

"Tell me Jamie and the psychology, chief."

"He was at Crum's trial years ago when Schmidgall accused him of participating in Barlow's murder. Jamie believed every bit of Schmidgall's testimony, found the Gay part completely credible. The words Schmidgall used on the stand, how they picked up the victim—Jamie said a Gay jury would have convicted Crum in ten minutes.

"Jamie observed him throughout, his body language, clothes, where his eyes went, what he smiled at and got nervous over, everything. He's a very nervous man."

"Jamie's a trained observer."

"The picture he put together we've now confirmed. We've got a real compulsive freak here. Crum took constant notes all through that trial. He's obsessive about keeping records—and now we may get proof. There may be computer documents on some or all of these cases. Financial records, diary entries, pictures."

"Jamie's cover story when Schmidgall died and his lawyer had that news conference—does that have anything to do with this?"

"Sure does. There's a line in there he emphasizes, coming from the lawyer."

"'I Know Who You Are.' He's looking for those records."

"She says, 'Even if it's after you're dead, we want those records. We have a right to them.' Jamie's account makes that front and center, when every other reporter emphasized the sensational admission."

"Jamie's speaking directly into Crum's ear. Imagine the responsibility of that."

"Pressuring him. Making the freak nervous."

"What was our break today, chief?"

"We found a store clerk in Eastwood, an all-night copy shop."

Kent looked at George. "He rented the computer! As many times as we've raided his house and office, he knew not to keep anything there."

"He goes in at the deadest time of night. Most of the computers are set up in carrels where anybody in the store can see what's on the monitor. But there's one little space off to the side where no one else can see. That's the one he used. If it was busy, he'd come back another time. He'd sit at his carrel, and the clerk said he'd laugh a lot. Except not really laughter, more like heh-heh-heh."

"Enjoying himself," Kent spat.

"Here's the good part. When he was done, he would always buy a diskette mailer. The store does shipping too. He'd address his package, pay his bill in cash, get his receipt and leave. He always got a receipt."

"What address?"

"Clerk could rattle it off from memory. It's Crum's parents in St. Pete."

A chill went down Kent's back. "Subpoena."

"On its way."

"Yes!" Kent pumped his fist. "That's fantastic."

George sang, "Over the river and through the woods, to Grandmother's house we go." They laughed together. "As soon as we get the paperwork from the judge, you're jumping a plane to Florida. Commander, you'll be the one who finds the smoking gun."

"Thank you, chief. Gosh, I don't know what to say."

George put his hand on Kent's shoulder. "I know you hate to leave Jamie. But he's not going anywhere. And this is important, Kent. I want you out of here for a couple of days. It will do your mind good, son. We just go in, load up all the evidence, and come back after you've spent two days on the beach on paid time off. The hospital will notify you of any change in Jamie's condition. We'll sort the evidence back here, and you supervise that. You can still spend all the time you want with Jamie. But life goes on, and where there's life, there's hope."

"Yes, sir. Thank you, sir."

They looked at the video. Slaughter used a pointer to describe the action. When Jamie broke free and started fighting, Kent stared. "Look at that! Man, he's fighting hard. Boom, down goes another one. Look at how strong he is!"

Minutes later Jamie was recaptured, and Kent soberly asked for Rewind. They watched the fighting again, then George moved them on to the stabbing. "We have an audio record of everything they said. See this bulge in his back pocket? Looks like a pack of cigarettes, but it's his voice recorder. By itself the tape's enough to convict."

"Jeez, little man. Always thinking." Kent recoiled as he watched Ford put his slimy body on Jamie's pristine one. "God, look at that. It's like rape!"

"But as soon as it starts, Jamie uses it to his advantage. He tries to turn Ford against Crum, get him to run away with him."

"Seduction, you mean? Divide and conquer?"

"He's extremely persuasive. He tries to turn them on so they're more interested in sex than murder."

"Man, how did he think of that? My skin would have been crawling."

"He offers to take Ford to Mexico with him, gives him some very good incentives."

"Look at that, it makes me want to puke. I guess getting stuck with one killer's better than facing thirteen, though. God, that's disgusting!"

"Right here, Crum puts a stop to it by drawing his gun. Otherwise Jamie would have had him."

"That little sissygun. Jeez, Jamie, you told me you had other weapons. Now I know what you meant."

"He used up an awful lot of time, Kent."

"Minutes that enabled us to get there."

George hit Pause, held his sergeant's shoulder again. "There's one other thing, son, we know it from his audio. Jamie knows you're coming."

Kent looked up sharply. "Really?"

A shiver crawled down Slaughter's spine. He hit Play. "He not only predicts the outcome, exactly as it happened; he calls you by name. These are his exact words. 'Kent's coming. You'll be dead.' Remember that, son."

"I will. Oh, Jamie." Kent straightened. "I will, sir. Thank you very much."

Then Kent got to watch the play-by-play of Jamie being whipped and finally stabbed. Kent rubbed his face, his voice went wooden. "He must never see this. Never."

"With guilty pleas we'll be able to seal it for life. Won't even have to show it in court. He'll never know."

"He'd be devastated. It's devastating to me." Kent covered his eyes.

George held him, "How are you sleeping?"

"Nightmares. They'll be worse now."

"How about eating?"

"Mom takes care of me. Chief, I can always eat. It's no fun but I do it, and it helps to have her food. We eat together. My Mom's the greatest."

"Are you working out?"

"Yes, sir, that's a help. Guess I'm working out for both of us now, since he can't do it. But I want you to know, as tough as this thing is, I'm all right. I'm not damaged goods, sir. I'm real emotional about it, but I'll get through it. Even if he dies, I got to know him for two weeks." Kent fought back tears. "I got to care about the man."

"I liked what you said earlier. 'Of course I can handle it, I'm a state trooper.' That's the right attitude, son. It's exactly what I expected of you. This is a terrible time, but I have nothing but confidence in you. Are you talking to the counselors?"

"Chaplain. It's in God's hands, ya know? I've seen the shrink once. But who helps the most is Doc Helmreich. He knows first-hand what officers go through. And it don't bother him about… Gay people. Doc knew Rick. And he really respects Jamie. I'm so glad Jamie got me to pull Doc into this. He's been important."

George knew. He'd been lobbied too.

When the shootout footage was over, Kent said, "They've all got reservations at the Hotel Death Row."

"Damn right. Now Kent, listen up: by befriending Jamie, getting in tight with your CI, you carried out my orders when we met here that night. I asked for the killer's head on a platter. That's exactly what you gave me. And that is why, sergeant, you face no disciplinary action by this department. I've reviewed it, like you asked. Instead of disciplinary action, I've nominated you for Trooper of the Year."

Kent's brown eyes looked at him, trying to take it in. "But I let him out of my sight."

"Shit happens," Slaughter muttered. "Reagan got shot. You think they fired the Secret Service? They didn't. Faced with a shooter, it was the Secret Service that saved Reagan's life. It's an exact parallel, Kent. You saved the man's life."

Kent let out a huge sigh. "Well, thanks, I guess."

"Don't be foolish. You solved a serial murder ring that's eluded us for fifteen years. It's not like you to think so negatively. The only reason you're beating yourself up is because you have feelings for your informant. You have to create a new mental file to analyze this correctly. If it were any other CI, sure, we'd all feel terrible, but we'd also recognize that he was a fully responsible team member who knowingly put himself at risk and paid a price. Suppose it was an officer who went down. There'd be five hundred police cars at the man's funeral, bagpipes, the works. But there hasn't been a funeral yet.

"Son, I'm not telling you not to feel. I'm telling you to have, in addition to your feelings, some professional detachment."

Kent had to think, but he knew the major was handing him a big puzzle piece. "You're right, sir. I've been lax, huh? I'm sorry."

"Your reaction is completely normal, son. Any officer in your situation would need that reminder. You haven't been lax, you've been torn apart. Who wouldn't be, for Chrissake?" *Hell, I fell for him too, years ago.*

"You're a tremendous man, major. I couldn't have done this without you."

"Kent, it's so good to work with you. One thing more. You've said you study every week for your lieutenant's exam. Saturday nights, isn't it? Saturday nights, when everyone else is out getting loaded and trying to get laid, there you are, studying to improve in your profession. Man, I want you to take that exam next spring; I want you to pass it. I want you promoted. I want you the youngest lieutenant in State Police history."

Kent suppressed his emotion; asked if he could see the footage where Jamie fought back one more time.

Slaughter rose, clapped him on the back and said, "Once. Then you're dismissed." He left, dimmed the lights, closed the door so his sergeant could be alone.

* * *

The most important thing on that video to Kent wasn't the evidence, it was Jamie's getting aggressive; how well he fought back.

It even almost turned Kent on. He didn't understand it, just felt it, with instant pangs of guilt; maybe the combination of sex and violence can stir Cro-Magnon feelings in anyone. He wouldn't watch the whipping; once was too much, he felt every blow. It was Jamie's fighting back that enthralled him.

Jamie's mind; Jamie's body. Kent allowed himself to feel turned on. *Pure, strong, masculine beauty.*

The beauty was overwhelming. That was what a man should look like. That was how a man should act.

Nothing is more attractive than physical courage.

Dominating them all, an alpha male. Fighting back, it's nature's way. Pow, bad guy! Bet that one hurt!

Against all odds, against thirteen ruthless killers, the gun-hating Gay guy fought back.

42

St. Pete

At 6 a.m. the next day, before schoolchildren stirred, Kent drew his duty weapon, pounded on the door, aimed. Lights were on; an old lady came. Kent let her see the weapon and said, "Mrs. Crum?"

She saw twenty other officers behind him, weapons drawn. She looked scared, surprised, but not quite.

"Sgt. Kent Kessler, Indiana State Police, with a warrant to search your house."

"A warrant? Herman? Herman, get in here."

"A warrant, valid in the state of Florida, which I now present you with. We've got your house surrounded. Does Herman have a weapon?"

Herman Crum appeared, yawning in his pajamas with no weapon. Kent said, "Ma'am, please admit us. It's the law. You must admit us. Please let us in."

She opened the door wider. "What do you want? Is my son all right?"

Kent stepped in. "Ma'am, you know exactly what we want. It's all detailed on the warrant. Computer diskettes, videotapes, CD-ROMs, photographs, paper records, checkbooks, anything belonging to or relating to your son. He's all right, we've got him on suicide watch.

Please sign here. By signing you are stating that you have been served with this warrant and you admit us to the premises."

"Oh, my poor Randy."

Kent snorted. *His poor victims.* "Ma'am, sign here."

She did. Kent noted the date and exact time, gave her a copy, pocketed the paperwork, motioned his team in. They holstered their weapons, hauled in boxes, garbage bags, equipment, fanned out to every room. St. Petersburg P.D. let George, Harvey and Bulldog in the patio door. Jack, Phil and Barry Hickman came in from the carport. "Now ma'am, you have a choice," Kent said. "We will search every inch of your home. We'll dig up your yard if we have to, we'll rip open your upholstery. It's your choice.

"If you'll take me to the diskettes and other records you've received from your son, we'll try not to trash the place, you're a senior citizen. But if you stay in denial of a lawful order, you can expect to do home repairs for the next year."

She led him right to the diskettes. Considerately, Dr. Randy had labeled and dated every one of them for Kent's perusal, even supplied a handsome carrying case. With gloved fingers, Kent popped open the plastic box, beheld scores of neatly stacked disks.

Then she showed him the videotapes, in the spare bedroom with its own TV and VCR: Barlow. Billy Gregory. Chuckie Pont. Crum had been in on several of Schmidgall's murders, but Schmidgall was right, he had nothing to do with murdering the Pont boy, that was all Crum's doing. *Freakazoid, I Know Who You Are.*

*　　　*　　　*

At Major Slaughter's suggestion, the other task force members used the St. Petersburg trip as paid time off too, so after the evidence was secured, they got to relax together. Jack brought his wife Marie and everyone got to meet her; she was a brunette beauty. Everyone went to the beach that afternoon; Kent was glad to strip down to swim trunks, soak up sun and think of nothing. Phil was his natural companion age-wise, little conversation, just occasional jokes and guytalk they could both do in their sleep. Bulldog and Hickman looked slightly ridiculous in their sunglasses, Hawaiian trunks and pale Ohio bellies, but they had the time of their lives ogling young, tanned Florida girls. Harvey sat under an umbrella with a sketchpad, while George sunned face-up, smoked stogies and took an occasional nip from his Glenlivet flask. Marie wore a one-piece bathing suit, had a very nice, fit, 40ish body with some serious cleavage. All the guys felt warmed by Jack's love for her; a little envious. Jack teased Kent, "It ain't just you young guys who get hot. Sweetest girl you ever met, Miss Jasper County, and she's been mine for 22 years."

"Life begins at 40, I've got 14 years to prepare. Who set your nose when it got broke, the town blacksmith?"

A couple of bikini'd women came up to Kent and Phil and invited them to play volleyball. Kent looked at Phil and said sure. They followed the ladies, while behind them Bulldog called, "Go for it, guys, ooh-la-la!"

Hickman told Bulldog, "Wouldn't violate my marriage vows to play a game or two."

"Why, Barry, what would the preacher say, you lusting in your heart?"

"Ain't my heart that's lustin'."

Later they ate seafood at a place the locals frequented. The major got a little tight. They weren't driving, so Kent did too.

The hospital didn't call.

*   *   *

The next day at the end of his workout, Kent knew he wanted to be alone, not with a big group; he had things to sort out in his mind. He didn't want to face them directly, but he knew they were there.

Bulldog and Hickman were eager to get back to bikini beach, while Jack and Marie talked about hitting the antique stores. Everyone suspected that really meant staying in the hotel with the shades drawn, but they grinned and went along. Slaughter said, "I know a beach near Sarasota, forty miles south of here. Very different."

Phil asked, "How so?"

"Families at one end, clothes-optional at the other."

"Cool," Phil said.

Harvey smiled, "Cooler still with no clothes on."

George said, "Kent, what do you need?"

Kent shrugged, "Alone time. To kinda brood, I guess." So the four single men drove to Sarasota. George and Harvey paired up, Phil headed straight for the nude beach and Kent sat, looking at the gulf, seeing universal waters, seeing nothing.

He slowly realized he was depressed. He had every right to be, but still.

In front of him little kids squealed, chasing waves out, then running back hollering when the waves rolled in. He looked at their little legs and chests, the delight on their faces. Wanted his own kid someday.

Might not have one, now that he was in love with Jamie Foster.

It was the first time he consciously had the thought. Then his mind went blank.

* * *

Half an hour later he stood and stretched; maybe he didn't want to be at the family beach anymore. Why confine himself to other people's kids when there were clothing-optional adults a mile or two away? He told himself he'd just look. Maybe he'd meet a girl there. Maybe he'd meet a guy.

Maybe he'd meet himself. He headed for the nude beach.

It took quite a bit of hiking; he began to doubt the place existed. Idly he watched the families, the couples having fun or yelling at each other. It seemed like a world he no longer quite belonged to.

He needed time off after a critical incident.

Would Jamie ever see this place? Would Kent ever take him there? Probably not.

He so wanted the hospital to call, to say Jamie was all right.

Either Kent's directions were wrong or there was no nude beach. He was about to turn back when he spotted a tall, topless brunette with a nice set of knockers.

He smiled, suddenly cheered up. He liked knockers, always had.

She wore a bikini bottom and held hands with a little boy naked as a flamingo. Then the boy took off, trying to capture a seagull, which lifted effortlessly away.

Few places in the world emphasize freedom of knockers; it ought to be a constitutional right. Kent grinned, wondered what Phil was up to by now.

Kent headed past teenage couples, naked families who surprised him; a couple of retired ladies didn't mind that their breasts no longer qualified for *Playboy.* People on this end of the beach chattered happily, they played, they didn't argue. They were utterly blasé about the nudity surrounding them. Men didn't have erections, they played catch with their kids. Eight teenagers played volleyball, guys and gals both, and though they had to be horny, they didn't say a single thing different from what clothed teenagers would say.

He began to want to take off his swim trunks.

Other people wore bathing suits, spectators, odd people out. Why would anyone wear clothes when the norm was nothing at all?

Clothes weren't nature's way. He slipped his trunks off his hips, wadded them up and walked on.

He felt the gulf breeze on his ass, between his legs. Wind on skin, was there a finer sensation? He liked his body, and he could tell from the looks he got that others did too, men and women both, boys and girls.

He passed a young man, longhaired, with a slim, tanned body. Kent openly looked at him. Why go naked if not to be looked at? Did Kent like that body?

Maybe, a little, but compared to the blond picture in his head it wasn't so great. What did he feel about the guy's body?

It had a certain beauty, like the brunette with the knockers, like the naked son who tried to capture seagulls. Like the older ladies worshipping the sun. What pleasure and surprise he felt to stumble into freedom, to feel the sensation of his quads and gastrocs and glutes propelling him ahead.

He had seen athletic men's bodies his entire life. They didn't all look the same. Pitchers and catchers carried some extra weight because of the pounding their bodies took. First basemen were taller than second basemen and shortstops. The hot corner required muscle and speed, a great throwing arm. Outfielders, himself among them, had the most proportional bodies, the most beautiful ones. For home run hitters like himself, add big, soft hands and an extra 10 or 20 pounds of muscle.

He missed playing and hitting home runs.

He'd always touched guys' bodies, teammates, coaches, and they touched him back, the game couldn't be played without it. Touching was so normal he never thought a thing. He enjoyed it, though, missed teammates' hands on him the last few years. The last time he got a therapeutic massage, he realized his skin hungered for touch, had grown unaccustomed to it. He jumped when the therapist started to work on him.

He liked touching Jamie, but Jamie never touched him back. Like it all meant something sexual, when it didn't. Or maybe did.

With Jamie, touching was definitely sexual. Pat his butt and he'd haul out an M-16.

That was why Jamie never touched him back, he'd never move on a Straight guy. Kent wanted to tell him it was okay sometimes. Then, screw the sometimes, it was okay.

Kent's eye was drawn to a blonde woman who sat with her back to him. He paused, studying her. He remembered the first time he'd ever seen yellow hair, on a mistreated little boy in a movie musical. Kent stared at Oliver's hair, trying to make sense of such a wonder. Why did it stir such feelings in him? Why did he almost envy it?

Natural blond hair is rare; that makes it special. Kent felt rare and special as an athlete, but he didn't have blond hair.

He frowned, shrugged and moved on. A few nights ago he'd creamed his jeans, blond hair was so special. Couldn't argue that wasn't sexual.

Without thinking enough to decide anything, Kent knew he'd love Jamie without becoming Gay. Jamie was an individual. Kent loved his personality; he didn't wear dresses and Kent wasn't Gay. Jamie was an aberration maybe, a phase.

If not he'd deal with it later. Kent had loved guys before; Tim Virdon came immediately to mind, sitting in a lounge off the locker room as Tim cried his eyes out for his horribly sick daughter, and Kent held him. He remembered the feeling of holding a man.

It was fine for guys to love each other, nothing wrong with that. Kent didn't have to throw over his whole self-image; he and Tim loved each other. Tim's daughter beat the cancer; oh, the joy of that.

Kent liked knockers and he liked Jamie. He could live with the news.

Then something hit him in the pit of his stomach; what Jamie was doing to Dreadlocks that made Kent cream his jeans. Jamie was putting it to the guy, acting like a man. That's what turned Kent on so much. He pictured the video of Jamie fighting back. Jamie was so manly, maybe he wasn't Gay at all. Maybe he'd just fallen in with the wrong crowd.

Kent started to feel aroused, which wasn't appropriate on a nude beach. He tried to think about building a garage for his new pickup.

He walked further, up a little dune where the vegetation changed. Something told him he might have crossed an imaginary line. He traveled on until he stopped in his tracks. Nothing but naked guys here, the air charged with sexheat. Turn around or walk on? Half-panicked, he let his body decide. He felt somewhat aroused again; he loved people looking at his major-league body. His feet walked deeper into the Gay section, until he finally came to a little swale so soft and private and inviting he had to lie down on it.

He soaked up sun.

* * *

At last Jamie came to him, naked too. Jamie touched his face, ran his fingers through his hair. They hugged and kissed, naked athletes together, making love on the beach.

Kent felt wet warmth on his dick. "Oh, Jamie, this is fantastic." He opened his eyes and saw the setting sun on bright blond hair, bobbing up and down between his legs, Jamie's back to him, sucking. "Man, come up here, let me love you."

He pulled him up and around to kiss him—but it wasn't Jamie at all, it was some unshaved beach bum with missing teeth.

Kent screamed, scrambled up, grabbed his trunks and ran.

* * *

He didn't want just sex; he wanted Jamie. If Kent was Gay, maybe he'd have let the beach bum blow him.

He wasn't Gay.

But it didn't seem likely that someone as smart as Jamie fell in with the wrong crowd. At any rate, the hospital didn't call.

43

Iota

When Kent got back with the smoking diskettes, nurses suggested that he try talking to Jamie, since Kent was on guard duty every night; some people believe the comatose can hear.

The coma dragged on three days, five days, longer. So Kent talked, said everything that came into his head, with no one else around. Did something else too; kissed little fingers, blessed them, begged God, before he left every morning. Found no response, just Jamie's body imperceptibly curling into a fetal position.

* * *

Operation Pride was successful, with nine arrested and four dead, Kent told him; Jamie was fantastic. Kent talked about the patch when Jamie called home like it was the most brilliant idea in history. "You could have called direct, but by working it through us, we knew what to do." He described the chain to the FBI, the ongoing investigation; he praised Jamie to the skies. He told all about Carson, the most evil of the bad guys, because he was a lawman. "We searched his vacation house and found child pornography, Jamie. Pictures of three-year-old girls with no clothes on. And adults doing things to their private parts. His own daughter! It makes you so mad to see them. I mean, little babies? Guys like that should be shot."

Kent was the one who shot him, lurking in the trees. One flesh wound and Carson tumbled right out of a maple.

Kent talked about the press coverage; he babbled and didn't care. "It's a media zoo. We've been invited onto Larry King, Barbara Walters, that show with Jane Pauley—I always liked Jane Pauley, she's a Hoosier girl. '60 Minutes,' let's see, who else? Letterman. I've talked to David Letterman's mom, Jamie, can you believe that? She's very nice, down to earth, like your aunt who always gives you a shirt for Christmas, the same shirt every year. Of course, I'm not going to do a show like that, even if he is from Indy. It wouldn't be right, it's an entertainment show and this ain't for laughs. He's off limits. But it's kinda nice to be asked.

"The tabloid shows have all begged and begged, but I vetoed all of 'em, don't want nobody talking to 'em. There's a show called 'Cops' that wants to do a re-enactment, and we might do that someday; the major kinda likes that show and other officers watch it. All the morning shows, what else? Oh, '48 Hours' with Dan Rather."

He thought he saw Jamie twitch at the last one—he couldn't be sure—so every night Kent watched Dan Rather and talked about him, but Jamie never woke up.

* * *

When he ran out of things to say, Kent confessed the other thing that happened that night. "I wasn't there for you." He cried; his tears were burning hot. "I let you down." He screeched, he'd never hurt so bad in his life.

But it led to the ultimate confession, of his feelings for him.

Jamie slept right through it.

* * *

Afterward Kent felt a little better to finally admit the truth. He prayed that if Jamie woke up, Kent would say one-fourth of what was on his mind, even if he had to force himself. "You deserve to hear the truth, man. Even if you hate me, you deserve to hear."

Major Slaughter brought him magazines to read during the slack time: Gay ones for Jamie called *Out Is In, The Clarion, Into the Streets;* plus *People, Sports Illustrated, Newsweek, Time.* The crime was on the cover of most of them. *U.S. News* got the whole team together. *People* trotted out an old shot from that time they named Kent the Sexiest Man in Baseball. *SI* had action photos from his playing days.

He read articles to Jamie, though he didn't understand what he was reading with the Gay stuff. He described the pictures; his commentaries were more amusing than the stories. "You should see this guy, he's got piercings and tattoos and I don't know what. Wild spiky hair, a whole row of things up his ear. A ring in his nose, with chains that go up to his earlobes and down to where? The picture's cut off below his waist. Good grief, you'd think he'd rust after awhile. Put him in a rainstorm and he couldn't move. The Tin Man. Maybe he carries 3-in-1 Oil in his backpack."

Over and over Kent spilled his guts to a silent snore. The situation was hopeless, though, every night the same.

But Jesse Jackson played in his head: "Keep hope alive." Kent cried some, and got tough; and cried a little more, and talked, in case it helped. "It can't hurt anything," his mother told him. Martha Kessler visited her son every evening, and Kent always told Jamie what she wore, the food she brought, how things were going on the farm.

He watched Jamie's body melt away for lack of food. Every day beautiful muscles atrophied as the body devoured itself. It was heartbreaking, grotesque, terrifying, and there was nothing Kent could do to stop it.

He brought his chair close, studied the bruises on Jamie's face, the backs of his hands where Ford stood on them. The wounds on Jamie's side had no way to heal. The body can't repair when it's fighting for survival. Yet Kent loved those bruises, like he loved the footage of Jamie getting aggressive.

"You portray yourself like you're not the fighting type. You'd rather talk about old movies. You have an aversion to guns you can't even tell me about.

"But there you were, fighting for your life. Thirteen against one and you attacked! It took 'em five minutes to get you back down, it took seven guys to do it. Man, your arm strength was awesome. If Ford hadn't had that knife you'd have beaten 'em!

"Jamie, I just wish I'd gotten there sooner. If it was you and me, I know we could have taken them. The guy with the little knife, the one who stabbed you, they did an autopsy. He's the one you kneed and kicked. You broke his jaw, Jamie. If he hadn't been killed on the scene, he'd have needed surgery after you got done with him.

"I'm sorry for the way it came down; but I'm proud of what you did. You were incredible! But you know what I'm proudest of? That after all that work for other people, you finally fought for yourself. Man oh man, that just fills my heart with pride. Sometimes in this world, it's kill or be killed, Jamie. I know you don't want to live that way, but sometimes that's how it is. And when they tried to get you—you went for the kill.

"You hated those killers as much as I do. You hated, man. Hate's not a great thing. But sometimes it is. Let loose! Hate them.

"And you did. You traded your life for some poor stupid guy you didn't even know.

"That's why you gotta stay alive now, Jamie. You gotta wake up. They're dead, some of 'em, and now's your time to live."

It was bottom-of-the-heartfelt. But it didn't help one iota.

*　　　*　　　*

Kent ran the whole gamut of emotions. "Jamie, I was so scared. Shakin' in my boots. How could you do this to me? Man, I was terrified. I still am, damn you. Wake up!"

*　　　*　　　*

A nurse came, late one night, leaned into the doorway, watched Kent trim Jamie's fingernails. His nails grew even as his body wasted away, and here was a state trooper giving personal care. She was pained by the intimacy of it.

Kent picked up a slice that went flying into the bed, lest Jamie roll onto it and feel discomfort. She said, "Care to talk?"

"I'm that bad, huh? Sure." Kent pulled out the other chair for her.

"It's so hard just to wait."

"What can I expect if he wakes up? You've seen this before, I haven't."

"Well, on coming to, he won't be able to function. It's such a big step, regaining consciousness, that you can't expect anything more than that. Everything is measured in steps. He won't be able to talk at first. He'll be in pain, extremely uncomfortable. You'll want to communicate with him, but you won't know whether he understands a word you say. Still, go ahead and try. Maybe all he'll be able to do in reply is blink. Maybe he'll be able to squeeze your hand. But realize, he won't know you from Adam."

"Why the heck not?"

"You met too recently. You're not family, a friend he's known for years. He'll have no short-term memory. He won't know what happened to him or why he's here. He won't be able to feed himself, he'll have no eye-hand coordination, he'll be like a baby who has to be taken care of."

"Gee. Poor guy." Kent trimmed Jamie's little finger.

"Waking up is no guarantee, either. We could still lose him even after he wakes up."

"Give me the good scenario. I already know the bad one."

"He wakes up, and day by day he gets a little stronger. We'll get him drinking full-nutrient liquids. His body starts to recognize that it's getting more nutritional support, so it gradually improves systemically, cell by cell, organ by organ. The central nervous system begins to respond. Slowly he'll regain the power of speech. We'll test his vocabulary, help him relearn words. We'll begin physical therapy, first in bed, later in a chair, simple things like pointing to body parts. All this improves his coordination. As his nutrition upgrades, so will his physical functioning and his mental alertness. We give him, while he's unconscious, the best nutrition we have, but it's so inadequate, all it really does is keep him alive. There's no substitute for real food. And the lack of that, as well as the physical trauma, works against his waking up. The longer this goes on, the worse it is. If he stays under for more than a month, he'll never completely recover."

"Oh, God." Kent wasn't sure he could cry anymore, but inside he cried, as he trimmed Jamie's thumb.

"Take heart, though. It's only been a week. So far this isn't too terrible."

"I heard this is within range for people who do wake up."

"So don't lose hope. But do think about the time when you don't stay here anymore."

Kent sighed. When he thought about going back to the cabin, he thought about taking Jamie home with him; caring for him, every day if need be, till he was well.

His mother would say he shouldn't. Taking care of a sick person for years? Only a madman would do such a thing.

But Jamie had done it for Rick; and caring for Jamie was exactly what Kent wanted to do. He worked on his guy's index finger.

The nurse said softly, "I'm not religious, half the time I'm an atheist. But I can't stop thinking about this Bible verse. Greater love hath no man than this..."

"...That a man lay down his life for his friends."

Kent flung aside his clippers. He and Jesus wept.

44

Citizen

Kent took a call from Phil Blaney. "Commander, I've got someone here at the City-County Building you might want to meet. A citizen claims someone paid him to throw a drink on a certain blond patron at Chez Nous."

"You think this citizen's credible?"

"Halfway. You might want to take a listen."

"Hold him." Kent called the crime lab and ordered an investigation into what caused Jamie's mic to go out. "Also the sweatshirt. Does it contain a foreign substance?"

"It reeks of beer," the lab director replied. "Big investigation."

"Then find out the make, model and serial number."

* * *

Phil brought in the citizen, a scared-acting 22-year-old male White. "Commander, this is one William Franklin Gowdy. Lives with his parents in Brownsburg, claims he works at a bank in Castleton. No priors."

Kent eyed him. "They let you wear all that jewelry at the bank, do they?"

"No," Gowdy mumbled. "I work Saturdays, this is my day off."

Phil said, "Tell the sergeant what you told me."

"Well, um, I was at Chez's last week, when the stabbing thing happened..."

Kent interrupted, "What were you doing there?", just to intimidate the guy. He wasn't in the mood for Good Cop today.

"Dancing. With my friends."

"Do Mom and Dad know you're hanging out at Gay bars on weeknights?"

"No. It's none of their business."

"Don't make me play 20 Questions, say what you've got to say."

"Well, we got to the bar late, Jimmy and me, and as we were going inside a security guard asked if I'd play a trick on a guy for twenty bucks." Phil moved his hand in circles to speed the guy up. There weren't any security guards at the bar that night. "To spill a drink on this blond guy in an IU sweatshirt."

"Blonds in a Gay bar," Phil said, "how original. Wearing an IU shirt. How would you recognize which one?"

"Bright blond hair, built, 5'10", a face that's pure Hollywood. I'd know him the minute I saw him, there wouldn't be anyone else like him. If I wasn't sure, it wasn't the right guy, keep looking."

Kent said, "What else?"

"To be sure to throw the drink on the chest area. Not the shoulder or the back, the middle of the chest."

"Did they say why?"

"He's this rabid IU fan, always going on about his precious Hoosiers. The sweatshirt was brand new and it'd screw with his head to have his shirt messed up. That way his Purdue friends could tease him all night."

"So, you're in the habit of taking $20 bribes to mess up someone's outfit. A stranger who never did anything to you; a fellow Gay guy."

"You must have been drunk already when you got there," Phil said.

"I didn't drive," Gowdy said.

Kent said, "No, but your drunk friend Jimmy did. I'll be sure to pick you out the next time you're wearing new clothes."

"I know it wasn't right. But I was doing the guard a favor. For twenty bucks, why not?"

"Maybe I can pay you fifty bucks to slash this officer's tires. Maybe for a hundred you'll knock over a liquor store."

Gowdy looked glum. "I said I'm sorry."

"No, you didn't. Why are you coming forward now?"

"I think it was the guy who got stabbed."

Kent and Phil exchanged looks. Kent said, "Pictures of him have been all over TV for a week. Newsweek, Time, the BBC. And you just now recognized him? Lieutenant, you got yourself a real citizen here. Yeah, this is the kind of solid citizen we know we can count on to help us catch criminals, to provide us with information we need to know. And to do it so timely, ya know? Making sure we've got all the facts we need to apprehend the bad guys. Lieutenant, I think you got a candidate for a special citation here."

"Citation?" Gowdy asked.

Phil snarled, "Accessory before the fact."

"Oh no! I didn't know what they were going to do to him."

"You little punk," Kent said. "You spill your drink on a perfect stranger, find out he's an incredible hero saving the lives of…"

Phil supplied, "Faggots like you…"

"…Then you wait a week to come forward with the news that Fact A is connected to Fact B!"

Kent turned away. Didn't want to browbeat the guy, just wanted to make sure he was properly scared and 100% honest. "What drink was it?"

"Huh?"

Phil demanded, "What did you spill on him?"

"Beer."

Kent sighed, "Bottle, can, draft? Miller, Budweiser, Pabst, Coors? What was it, Mr. Helpful Citizen?"

"Bud draft. In a plastic cup."

"Tell me about the guard. Did you ever see him before? What was he wearing? How did you know he was a guard?"

"Well, a uniform, patches, a nightstick, no gun, at least I didn't see one. A baseball cap, I remember that, Pioneer Hi-Bred. No one I'd ever seen before. But it wasn't a he, it was a she."

"How could you tell? It was dark outside."

"I may be Gay, but even I can tell she was a woman. She had tits, a high woman's voice."

"A woman guard at a Gay men's bar? Wearing a baseball cap? Gee, a guard like that'd intimidate me real quick."

Phil said, "Was she big? For want of a better word, dykey-like?"

"No, average size, petite almost. But she was a real guard, I could tell. We were going to ignore her and just go inside, but she made us stop."

"Would you recognize her if you saw her again?"

"I don't think so. She kept her cap real low, I couldn't really see her face. Plus it was dark, like you said."

"What else?"

"That's all."

"Why did you wait so long?"

"I was scared."

"Of what? We arrested 13 people. Someone's going to retaliate when they're behind bars?"

"I didn't want to get involved."

That really ticked Kent off. "Tell it to Davey Shuey, you son of a bitch. Tell it to Glenn Ferguson and a dozen previous victims. Tell it to Mr. Ferguson's lover, how you didn't want to get involved. Tell it to the Gay undercover informant who's lying in a hospital bed right now thanks to you!"

Phil said, "When you find yourself the victim of crime, maybe I won't want to get involved either."

Kent told Phil, "Get his information, his employer and his next of kin, then get him out of my sight."

"Was what I did so wrong? Are you going to charge me?"

Kent walked out, left him to Phil to deal with. Phil said, "I don't have to tell you this, but I will. For twenty bucks you destroyed the communication system of an undercover informant investigating the murders of 13 Gay men. Under his sweatshirt was a microphone, which is why the chest area was so damn important. Because our informant lost his backup, he got stabbed. He's now in a coma. You tell me how wrong it was, you slime-sucking dickhead."

A tear ran down Mr. Gowdy's face. Phil wasn't impressed.

Five minutes later, after the paperwork, he mumbled thanks for coming forward, better late than never.

* * *

He made calls; the Chez Nous did employ two female security guards, but they weren't on duty on a weeknight. Both denied being present and had solid alibis; one was a sheriff's deputy and mother of two small kids, the other was an IPD reserve officer who spent half the night with a Gay guy and four women friends, trying to get her lover pregnant with a turkey baster. Both willingly let their closets, laundry baskets and vehicles be searched for baseball caps; no Hi-Bred, no seed corn of any kind.

The lab reported finding beer in the sweatshirt fibers, with a 99.7% likelihood it was regular Budweiser draft.

As advertised, Mr. Citizen was halfway credible, but his story didn't add up. Phil shrugged and forgot about it.

45

Commander

Kent didn't give up.

He read Jamie the newspapers; not coverage of the case, but the sports section—Purdue football, keeping him up on the Big Ten—Yugoslavia occasionally, but it was depressing; advice columnists, editorials, business news he couldn't make heads nor tails of; he read the comics and described the drawings. Every day he read Jamie his horoscope; he'd known from day one that Jamie was a Gemini on the cusp of bullheaded Taurus. "Today is a good day for traveling. A chance encounter with Sagittarius may lead to passionate romance. (Hey, that might be fun. Guess who's a Sagittarius, Jamie?) A close friend needs your encouragement."

Kent babbled and liked it. He never felt freer or worse.

But mostly he sat quietly with the blond, bruised face, bland and unvarying, both of them numb and half dead.

* * *

Kent finally gave up. He'd cried five million tears. He'd said fifty thousand words. He'd prayed five thousand begging prayers. None of them mattered. God cared about zilch. There was no God.

Kent learned to accept that his friend, his sweet, pure heart, was a vegetable.

"Augh!" And with that scream, one last rebellion struck in fury. "Here's the bottom line," he cried, pacing around the tiny room. "You faced a choice! You or Daveyboy. Who would it be? Jamie, you stupid, ignorant fool, you have all the talent in the world. And you traded it for that lowlife? What? I'm supposed to stand here and let you trade? Get fucking real!

"He ain't worth one-half what you are, one-fourth, one-tenth. When you gave us the patch we knew where to go, you asshole! Even if Davey had died we'd have caught 'em. Stand aside, you stupid civilian, and let me do my job!"

He exhaled deeply, over and over. The patch wasn't enough; he knew it, hated accepting it. There was no escaping the central fact: when they lost contact with Jamie, had to regroup at headquarters, Ford and Jamie got such a head start on them that not even a chopper could get there fast enough.

So Jamie traded his life for some Daveyboy's—some guy who, whatever his worth, didn't deserve to die. "Jamie, I can't deal with this. Not losing you! This is the most incredible act by a human being I've ever seen. Your life for a stranger's? Wake up, damn you!"

He sat in sorrow and fury. And from somewhere Jamie said, in Kent's mind, "Davey's as important to humanity as I am. To your humanity; to mine.

"In this life we can take or we can give. You've faced that choice, and look at yourself, a police officer, a giver. And I've faced it. Don't ask me to let the killers go, to let the poor man die. That would have destroyed me more than anything the killers could have done. I'm a Hoosier, a smalltown boy. Don't send casseroles if you can pull victims out of the car wreck instead."

As sentiment, as hope it was fine. Not a word of it actually got said. It was just Kent going berserk, trying to hang on.

He took a break. Minutes later he was back in the room doing a relaxation exercise.

* * *

On Day 9, a Thursday evening, particularly dull, Jamie's eyelids fluttered, opened; he tried to focus. He canvassed a wall near-sightedly. He felt extremely weird.

It took him three minutes to realize he was alive.

A hospital, I think. God, this place is ugly. Who designed this, Phyllis Schlafly?

He glimpsed a tall, dark-haired man. The man was looking down, maybe reading. Even near-sighted, Jamie could see the man was handsome.

Jamie closed his eyes, so overwhelmed by all the pains in his body he couldn't think. He wanted to cry out but he didn't have the energy for it. So he tried to switch off physical awareness entirely, feel only his emotion.

It was very difficult. But gradually he concentrated on the man; on the man's face.

Didn't know who he was or why he was here. But reading; waiting on him. Jamie had spent too much time waiting in hospitals not to know why the man was here. So they knew each other. Who was he?

Jamie opened his eyes again. Feelings came, intense, cascading. *Masculine. Intelligent. Sensitive.*

Is he my lover? But Jamie knew he didn't have a lover. Rick was gone, Jamie was alone.

Alone, yet somehow in love with this man.

That felt good for a minute, bizarre; what is so strange as being in love with someone you don't even know?

But he was quickly overpowered by a dark, menacing shroud that made him want to hide under the covers. He didn't have the energy to cry, no way to express his terror but to let it wrack his body, already wracking.

He wasn't **supposed** to be in love with this man. That meant the man was Straight.

His spirit plummeted, the heartache of falling in love uselessly. He wanted to die. But he couldn't even manage that, it took too much energy.

Minutes later, he tried to figure out, to sense really, who the man could be. The man waited; that counted for something. *A friend, maybe.*

He sank into his body, let it feel whatever it felt, *no words, let go of words.*

From somewhere deep inside an image slowly formed; *Kentland.*

He knew the man wasn't from Kentland, but there it was; *the Nu-Joy.*

A car. Riding together. We didn't stop, we talked about it. Headed where? White Sox.

Ice cream. Morocco to Kentland.

Why Morocco? What's there anymore?

The Slough?

Oh no. His body shivered, ice cold for minutes.

Some poor guy; God no, those poor guys. Every cell of his body filled with pain.

Policeman. A trooper? He shook my shoulders. I was terrified.

And then, I wasn't. Nice man. Safe.

He saw another image, another highway. *South. Toward Mom's? Blue lights. Oh no!*

Oh God no. He wept, tearless into eternity.

Finally, another image, same car, to Indianapolis. *Woods. A clearing, bright as day.*

Devils? He could see them, horrible fright. Anger too; fury.

And I told God I loved this man.

He opened his eyes, and this time the man saw him. His eyes got big, he put down his report, his tanned face turned white. He hurried over.

You look like you've seen a ghost. Let not your heart be troubled.

Kent stood motionless, watched green eyes move. He wanted to shout, but he was scared beyond belief. He finally whispered, "Hi."

Beautiful brown eyes, so worried. The man was in as much pain as Jamie was. Jamie wanted to reassure him. How, though?

Jamie blinked. Breathing was a horrible chore. He looked down at his body. There were plastic tubes everywhere, he could feel them—including places they ought not to be. His dick ached. A catheter? *Get this goddamn thing offa me.*

And this handsome man, looking like death warmed over and life overjoyed.

Prettyboy, relax now, you're making me nervous.

Jamie tried to smile, tried to remember the man's name; but his skin felt like sandpaper, all taut and wrinkled too and nasty.

He thought of his mother for a long time. His feelings wanted to cry, but his eyes were so dry, even blinking hurt.

His side ached. His stomach felt folded in on itself. His back was on fire. He tried to shift but couldn't manage it.

He had a tube down his throat, a plastic lung machine. His throat was raw and dry, had been invaded. His throat wanted to scream from the pain.

He remembered the forest. *Lots of people. Bad people.*

You came. I knew you would. You came.

The murders somehow. A wave of horror passed over him. He didn't know what happened. *Something terrible. I prayed, though. I love you.*

We slept on a pallet and I fell in love with you.

His head clicked. He knew exactly who the man was.

Then he knew what to say, what would help him. But it took minutes to work up to a single word. He got his lips apart; he couldn't get any breath to go out. He had to breathe more deeply, and that hurt.

Like this man hurt. "Com-mand-er."

Kent stared, eyes like saucers.

Jamie's voice was strange, weak, raspy, slow, disembodied. But it was his somehow, he knew it was, so he visualized pushing words and breath out of his mouth, like Sisyphus up the mountain, past the ventilator tube. "How man-y, did we, get?"

Kent's heart burst. "Oh, Jamie! Thirteen on the scene, four higher-ups. And maybe more, it's not done yet. My God, you're alive! Oh Jamie, you're alive! We did it, man. You did it! Welcome back!"

Jamie sighed, felt incredibly tired, knew he'd conk out soon. That scared him; what if he never woke up again? Commander wouldn't like that. Jamie concentrated like Sisyphus near the summit. "Fan-tas-tic," he said, in his wispy, grating voice. He pointed his finger shakily at the trooper. "You, big, s-tud."

He gasped and fell into a stone cold sleep.

Kent dashed for the nurse. "He woke up! He's alive, he woke up, he talked to me!"

Nurses ran, gathered, celebrated, stared at the TV monitor on Room 9 while two hurried in to check. "What did he say, what did he say?" Kent told them, glorying in every word.

"A complete sentence? Two of them? Ten whole words?" Nurses stared at each other; no coma patient starts out in sentences. Most take days for words.

It was lost on Kent. "Yes! He's out of the coma! He talked! Two whole sentences!" He laughed, wanted to run, clap, sing, turn handsprings the length of the corridor. "He's out of the coma. Thank you Jesus. Thank you Jesus. Oh God, thank you Jesus!"

Major Slaughter happened to arrive then, carrying flowers for the nurses, a sandwich for Kent; he saw the commotion, set down his bags.

There in the hallway, Sergeant Kessler told him all about it; then clung to a macho shoulder and, without warning, cried his goddamn guts out.

46

Flashcards

They tried removing the ventilator; Jamie breathed okay. His brainwaves were always very active; indeed, Kent could set his Timex by Jamie's REM-sleep erections. His urine output was moderate, his blood pressure was good, his pupils reacted to light, and he didn't like it when they stuck a pin in his arm to test his spinal cord. He was never decorticate or decerebrate, and easily tolerated nurses' repositioning him flat on his back—an improvement over his withdrawal into the fetal position. These were all crucial readings. His stab wounds, though severe, were relatively easy to sew up; but when he lost so much blood, his brain started to die for lack of oxygen.

There was talk of removing the tiny tube inserted into his right front brain to relieve swelling. But still he slept, didn't wake again.

The next day the neurologist removed the tube and briefed Kent, the major and the nurses. Without being rude, the doctor basically called Kent a liar. If Jamie had in fact awakened, much less recognized him and spoken ten whole words, he was highly conscious. All tests were favorable. So why couldn't they wake him up today? "We can't get any response."

"I didn't imagine it," Kent said hotly. "He talked, he was lucid. Please remember, sir, I'm a state trooper. I deal in facts."

The doctor apologized. "But he's off the charts. I don't know whether to worry or be optimistic. I've got calls in to Harvard."

Slaughter said, "Maybe his brain's wired differently. He does have an abnormal brain, doctor. This is a very intelligent individual."

"You're telling me," Kent muttered.

Slaughter said, "He was tested in junior high, shipped off to Purdue and tested again. One of our crisis psychologists ran the tests. Jamie's got an IQ in the 99th percentile."

Kent asked, "Would that make a difference in your charts, doc?"

"This isn't a question of intelligence, it's brain physiology."

A nurse suggested, "Maybe he's got so many brain cells that when some are knocked out, the others take over."

"Come on, little guy," Kent prayed.

Slaughter looked into space. A feeling started up in his gut. He let it grow, closed his eyes, emptied himself, tried to tune into what Jamie needed.

For some reason Slaughter's testicles moved. He tried to puzzle out a sexual motive. Finally he smiled. He opened his eyes, which rested on his young sergeant. "Kent, you try this time."

The doctor and nurses gathered around the monitor while George stood outside Jamie's door. "Go ahead, son."

Kent swallowed, went to the side of the bed, looked down at the pasty-white, bruised face. He crouched, picked up a hand, held it. "Jamie? Can you wake up, man? I need you, partner. Will you wake up for me, Jamie? I need you."

Kent breathed. Nothing happened.

Then Jamie's green eyes blinked open. There, at eye level, were Kent's beautiful browns.

A peaceful feeling settled over Jamie. Maybe it was wrong, he wasn't supposed to feel what he felt; but he felt it anyway. He loved those eyes and that face. "Com-mand-er."

Kent burst into a grin. "Oh, Jamie! Wake up, partner. Wake up!"

Jamie tried to clear his throat, couldn't. "Uhh. Wa-ter."

Kent straightened, poured, tried to be calm about it, kept hold of that hand. He brought the tumbler; Jamie stared at his cold little hand in Kent's big warm one. Kent got the straw to Jamie's lips. "Don't gulp, just sip."

Jamie sucked in slowly, and tasted water. *"That's the best stuff."*

He nodded slightly, and Kent withdrew the water, crouched again. "The doctors want you to stay awake as long as you can."

Jamie groaned, tried to shift. "I, hurt." An unseen nurse charted his every word; those two qualified as a complete sentence. The doctor frowned at the TV screen.

"I know, man. But you're alive, Jamie. Thank God, you're alive."

Jamie looked into brown eyes. *My body feels like it's dead.*

Oh, look at you. I want to live.

He felt again his hand in Kent's, and tried with a mighty effort to squeeze. Kent must have felt something, because he squeezed right back. "Do it again," he said excitedly. "Squeeze my hand."

Jamie did it again. "Cool," Kent cried. "Another rep. Let's work out!"

Jamie squeezed. This was fun. *What a wonderful guy.*

"Danny's coming, he's on his way."

"Dan-ny. My big, Bro."

"Jamie, I'm so overwhelmed I don't know what to say."

Jamie squeezed. "Just… hold my, hand?"

Kent squeezed back. "I will, partner. I will. Now stay awake for me."

A woman came in, introduced herself, asked what she could do to make Jamie more comfortable. "Ack," he coughed, trying to tell her. Coughing was excruciating. She didn't understand. He pointed at his catheter, forced out more words. "Take… this out."

She smiled, turned into a nurse. "Do you know this man's name?"

"Com-mand-er." Jamie's brow furled. "Makes Dil-lin-ger's mo-ther, sing like, cana-ry."

Kent chuckled proudly. "You're very close," the nurse encouraged, "Commander is his title. His name is Kent."

Jamie smiled for the first time, at big brown eyes. "Ser-geant Kent Kess-ler. Indi-ana State, Police. You, take down, bad guys."

"Man oh man!" Kent yelled, so excited he made a fist in front of his chest. "You know my name!"

Jamie stayed awake for twenty whole minutes, and Kent held his hand. They squeezed back and forth the entire time.

* * *

Jamie was tested for balance, coordination, motor control, his mother's maiden name. He was told that functionally, his condition was similar to a light stroke. What one half of his body could do, the other half might not for awhile. "But we're amazed at your verbal skills."

He smiled, "The mouth, al-ways did, work, pretty well."

He read first-grade flashcards and did a thousand stupid tasks, pointing at his ear, his nose, his chest, and finally caught on to a mean nurse's game. It was the same one he'd gone through years ago in school; nobody ever believed he was smart. He pointed between his legs, "My dick!"

She stopped playing, went away in a huff. Kent high-fived George. Jamie told the major, "The Times."

George went to the lobby, bought The New York Times, laid it before him on the pull-table. Jamie read, haltingly but aloud, "Pro-gress On AIDS, Brings Move-ment, For Less Sec-recy. More Re-porting Urged. The Med-ical Benefits, of Early Detec-tion, May Outweigh, Some Priv-acy Concerns."

He was proud of himself, but frowned at the headline. "No, they don't. Wait till, Casey and I, get hold of, this. Start with, Ry-an White's, moth-er. Doc-tors can be fasc-ists. I want, this cath-eter, removed!"

Slaughter tossed the paper at the doctor and walked out.

The fascists waited a day, but finally Jamie sat in a chair, shakily fed himself Jell-O, even demonstrated his remarkable ability to pee without plastic jammed up his urethra; so he made another request.

That gave Kent an idea. "Tell me what to bring you, just name it. Something to comfort you or entertain you, something that tastes good, anything you want."

What would comfort him? "A toy, basket-ball? Or lit-tle weights?"

Kent got excited. "I know exactly where to get 'em." That night he presented Jamie with two one-pound dumbbells covered in plastic.

"Pink," Jamie frowned, "for la-dies. Sor-ry. But use-ful. Th-ank you." He did a curl or two.

And then the crown jewel, a six-inch foam rubber basketball marked PURDUE BOILERMAKERS, with Boilermaker Pete waving his sledgehammer. "You can squeeze it, see? It'll help your hand strength."

Jamie, eyes shining, rubbed it against his cheek and squeezed. "Wonder-ful."

"Man oh man, you're gonna come back!"

* * *

A different doctor sat quietly with Jamie, asked a bunch of questions. "I can't believe you remember Officer Kessler. You only met him a month ago. The same part of the brain that goes into coma knocks out short-term memory. It always happens that way, the parts of the brain are directly connected. But not with you. Do you have any idea why you remember him?"

I'm in love with him, that's why. But this doctor wore a wedding ring and bragged about his baby daughter. "He has, a great deal, of emo-tional, signif-icance, to me. Per-haps I, stored his f-ile, in my longterm, mem-ory." The doctor looked doubtful. "He is not, just some, off-icer. He is an, im-portant, friend."

"And it was an intense case." The doctor showed him the photo of Glenn and Gary that Glenn kept on his desk. "Do you know these people?"

Jamie studied them. "No."

A picture of Trooper Julie Campbell elicited a shrug. Mr. and Mrs. Walker with son LeRoy were just a nice-looking Black family. Jamie couldn't identify Lt. Jack Snyder. The only person Jamie'd met recently and remembered was Kent. The doctor seemed encouraged. "What do you remember of the night it happened?"

Jamie described the image in his head: bright sunlight, several people, lots of trees. That was all. Nothing happened.

"How does it make you feel?"

Jamie frowned, "Not good."

"Do you feel frightened? Angry? Are you worried or anxious or happy?"

"Scared, may-be. Ang-ry. Yes. But also, some-how, in control? They were, bad guys, weren't they?"

The doctor didn't say. "What can you tell me about Sgt. Kessler?"

"He played, Ma-jor, League Base-ball. Tall, mus-cled. A skilled, investi-gator, cert-ified, in some-thing. He thinks I'm, shorter, than I am." Kent, listening in at the nurses' station, laughed delightedly. "He's from, farm country, up north. But not, Kentland. He drives, a big, pickup truck. Shiny wheels. A… studmobile." George elbowed Kent. "He's, very, thoughtful. Kind. Funny. Smart. Eats a lot of, fat, though." Jamie pointed his finger. "But no one, will ever, out-commit him!"

Kent suppressed some emotion over that.

"That's a lot to remember about somebody you just met."

"He sat with, Arn-ie. He brought us, food. And a, pie."

"Anything else you remember about him?"

Jamie scowled. "He, ad-justs himself, in front of, women."

"How do you feel about that?"

"Hate it. But he said I, should have," Jamie grinned big, "insur-ance, on my, hair."

"Anything else?"

Jamie thought of the pallets, but shook his head no.

"Okay, good job, get some rest for me." The doctor left, went to the nurses' station. "Well, was he accurate?"

"Accurate, very detailed, in everything but the sunshine," Kent said. "It was nighttime, those were camera lights he saw."

The doctor propped his butt on the desk. "You drive a studmobile and adjust yourself in front of women?"

Kent laughed. "He just… never mind. It's a pickup, not a studmobile."

Alone in his room, Jamie thought, *When you fall in love, you don't put him in your short-term file. You pray he stays in your long-term life.*

Lord, a Straight man. What have I done?

47

Hospital Tree

When next he woke up, Jamie got his wish. He wanted desperately to go outside. Kent pushed the wheelchair into sunshine, a warm day.

Jamie's skin felt every ray. He sank into the warmth, pulled on the sleeve of his gown, trying to get it to stay up so more of his arm could drink. The sleeve wouldn't cooperate, so he absorbed sunshine through the cloth.

The whiteness was so bright it hurt his eyes. But he didn't want anything getting between him and his sun. He wanted to be naked in it.

He asked Kent, "Would you, untie, my gown? Help me, get it, off?" Kent got the gown off his shoulders, down to his waist. It made Kent think of Sarasota.

For the the first time Jamie got warm. How his body craved heat. He remembered sun baths, grateful for every one of them. He exhaled, soaked.

He shut his eyes, dreamed, imagined, smelled, listened—to birds sing, and traffic buzz, and grass grow; he could hear that too because growth has sound, it's active. Grass's sound is mostly water rushing through tiny living pipes, and cells expanding.

Far from him, small children squealed at play, human animals communicating uncensored. He loved those children, tried to figure out what their game was. He decided they were little girls, Black girls, jumping rope, having a wonderful time at play.

A machine bap-bap-bapped at building something or destroying it, the two necessities of life. He heard a basketball dribbled on a concrete driveway, and a motorcycle rev—Japanese, he thought, a Honda or a Kaw.

He imagined a fountain, he wanted to hear water run loud and fast; then he heard the seashore. Hip-hop snapped loudly out of a passing car, rhythm-perfect.

His fingers wanted texture—the sun was working on them, healing them—so he opened his eyes, slowly pointed. "Could we, go to, that tree?"

It wasn't a plastic tree, a concrete one; it wasn't a video of a tree or a memory of one. "Sure."

Kent pushed as near as he could get on sidewalk, then slowly eased the chair onto the earth. It was bumpy, because it was earth and hadn't been smashed by a machine lately. It had a smell, it was earth. Jamie slumped but held on, didn't fall out, but if he had, the earth would have caught him, held him up.

And they were there, and he looked up at a magnificent centenarian ahead, a hundred feet tall, a wise old maple.

They looked at each other silently, respectfully, for quite some time. Jamie's neck strained from looking so high, but even the hurt felt good.

The tree gazed down at him and prepared itself.

A tree's wisdom, its strength is in its rootedness; while every other foul thing locomotes. Sometimes life should be looked at from just one spot.

Of rooted species, a tree is the highest form; the human its equivalent, though not its equal. Trees know they are superior; their expirations are pure oxygen, keeping every body and thing alive.

Vulgar adolescent trees poke each other in the branches and claim, "My poop is better than vanilla ice cream." But tree superiority comes with age, and with age comes silence.

Trees do not speak, but they communicate. How else would a bird know which of all possible trees was the right one for her nest? The tree has to find the right bird, invite the right bird.

But in the daytime trees are open for business, completely democratic, the more the merrier, no fee ever, come and perch a spell; tell everyone what you've seen and where the good bugs are.

Trees are quite proud that birds fly away from humans and to them. Every creature of the forest uses the tree, though chipmunks are particular, pesky favorites.

Jamie raised both his hands, showing them, and silently asked if he might touch. A breeze stirred only the treetop, a lovely shh, for quietness and yes.

He tried to stand, forgot the brakes; brakes were Rick's job mostly. The chair lurched, Jamie sat back down in a hurry. "What are you doing?" Kent cried. "Jamie, wait!"

"Bark," said Jamie. "It's okay." *The tree said I could.*

Trees don't much like to be touched. They prefer the open air, and they've seen all the places our fingers have been. Still, this one knew it was a hospital tree, so it took a quiet pride in being a symbol of hope, of life itself. It was a survivor, too—though it was a lonely life for a tree, having to live at a hospital, always on duty, away from its family and its forest from the time it was a sapling.

Hospital trees, the good ones, always have time to give human survivors a treat. Time is something trees know everything about, though humans are mostly stupid and seldom ask them about it. Or about much of anything.

"What do you expect of humans?" snob trees sniffed. "They locomote."

It was said of humans that few of them could hear trees converse, people were insanely busy scurrying about for nothing. So most trees don't bother to speak with them; but only ill-bred trees discriminate.

Politically trees are divided; radicals tell horror stories about humans cutting down trees by the millions with all manner of torture devices; in some places it's a real holocaust, and clear-cutting humans are like Nazis. California Sequoias even offered to throw themselves in front of bulldozers to protect the last of the Amazon ("we'll crush them," one cried, filled with self-sacrifice and religious fervor); but alas, the redwoods were rooted like everyone else and couldn't make the trip.

Which was just as well; they were precious, a tree dynasty. It was a fine sentiment, though; forest senators agreed about that.

Millions of other trees, mostly low-level pines living in rows, were planted by humans, and said that humans are their friends. The silent majority of trees, however, simply stood their ground, heedless of tree talkradio.

Trees prefer movement to talk; their movement is much more subtle than legged creatures'. Trees' dance is a sway, and the wind can play a mean marimba.

Kent leaned down, "You want me to get closer?"

Jamie nodded. Kent maneuvered but it was clumsy going, avoiding old roots. He got as close as he could.

Jamie leaned, reached out his hand, and felt the roughness of fine old maple bark, rubbed it slowly, up and down, fingers in the ridges and cracks. Tree skin, unlike the inferior human kind, only gets handsomer with age.

Jamie wanted to feel bark on his face, but couldn't get close enough. So his fingers worked, loving the bark, memorizing it, so they could tell his face what bark felt like today.

Kent watched, humble and filled and silent. Jamie had beautiful hands, like a pianist's almost, with long, straight, slender fingers; sensitive hands feeling maple bark.

Kent patted a shoulder and stepped away from the chair; his hand felt the bark too. His right and then his left, both hands, moving slowly.

Kent rested his face on the bark; then he turned around and leaned against it, felt the bark on his back. The tree supported him; it was quite good at standing there, supporting life-forms. It had stood, supported and nourished, exhaled oxygen and sheltered all comers better than anyone else for a century.

Kent gazed at Jamie, who met his eyes. The three of them exchanged, carbon dioxide for oxygen, life itself; two partners and a kind old maple.

Kent covered Jamie's cold, small hand with his big warm one. Kent squeezed.

Jamie stared at him wide-eyed, then he squeezed. Kent squeezed back.

Jamie began to weep. His body felt so miserable and his heart felt so full. And this time he could not mistake it, argue it down, will it away. He tried; it was impossible.

He fell completely in love with Kent Kessler.

When people care for each other during illness, give their tenderness and their souls, it's the deepest, closest love they'll ever know.

If only Jamie'd realized what Rick received, what Jamie gave to him. If only he knew what lotion on cheekbones felt like to his Mom.

All he knew was that Kent meant everything.

Bewildered by tears, by his own strong emotion, Kent tried to make things better; he acted, it was all he knew to do. "Crook your arm around me." Gently he lifted Jamie from the chair, carried him the extra step he needed.

Kent stood there, so strong, a half-naked blondboy in his arms; Jamie's wet face resting on maple bark, communing eternally.

Kent held him there a long time; till finally Jamie's head lolled. Kent carried him back toward the hospital.

He liked how much his muscles strained; he was proud he had the strength to perform for his buddy.

Kent's entire body came alive. His arousal grew, too, and he enjoyed its side-to-side motion with every step.

That's when he learned, his ardor for Jamie Foster was nature's way.

48

Top Ten List

Jamie was conscious for up to an hour now, and Kent started to look optimistic again, like something he'd hoped for was possible and he could personally make it happen.

Jamie began to be curious about why he was in the hospital. Kent hit what he thought were the safest highlights, but Jamie was thoroughly confused. *A patch, what does he mean? What's so brilliant about a patch? The Internet. Snuff pictures. At least we got that part right.*

Grand juries, Congressional hearings, testifying. That means it's over. After all these years, now people testify. Wow. Whatever happened, Kent, you're fantastic.

Jamie tried to congratulate him, but Kent put a finger on his lips, told him not to talk, to save his strength. Jamie tried, but his head crashed and he fell asleep again.

* * *

The next day George explained it very differently. "Tommy Ford contacted you, threatened to kill you. To get at you he took someone else hostage and would have killed him if you didn't trade."

"Oh, no. Poor guy."

"He's all right, he's fine. We set you up with a microphone and lots of backup. We thought we had everything covered. But things went wrong. We had some unanticipated lapses and a mistake. You ended up in Ford's custody. You traded for the hostage. He was drugged, animal tranq, just like you said."

"Poor guy. He could have, been killed." Jamie's face twisted with concern.

"He's okay, thanks to you."

"They tell me I, got stabbed. Not strang-led?"

George stroked Jamie's hair. "They tried to do both, but we arrived in time to prevent the strangulation."

"Thank you. Sorry if I, screwed it up, chief."

"You didn't. You were great."

"Hos-tage is, okay?"

"The hostage is fine."

"Tell him, I'm so glad. Poor guy. Scared. Hurt-ing."

"He's fully recovered, his mother's taking care of him."

"A favor? Will you, take care of, my Command-er?" Jamie's eyes filled with pain. "I can't do it. He hurts, over this. He hides it, but he thinks, it's his fault some-how. He's not, Tommy Ford! Or that Crum. He caught them! At last. Thank God."

"I'm on it. You get well and I guarantee, Commander's going to be just fine."

"Thank you, bud-dy. Help him. Tell him, you guys, saved my life. Don't ever, ever, let my Hero hurt."

* * *

Two days later Kent brought Jamie a videotape of the TV coverage. Turned out to be a huge mistake.

The Indy stations had Casey's photo of Jamie's butt hanging out—the only photo cut off more or less at the waist—with Slaughter saying, "Tremendous physical and mental courage, that any Hoosier would admire."

Jamie frowned at Kent.

The networks varied; ABC was most comfortable with the Gay angle, NBC gave equal time to "Gay" and the derogatory "homosexual." To CNN the story could as easily have been a plane crash in Sri Lanka, they only cared about breaking news. CBS ran a longer piece, intense about the crimes and more accurate about their serial nature. CBS interviewed Casey and Dr. Steve Helmreich.

The national focus turned away from the victims and onto FBI involvement. Jamie resented it, but tried to follow the import.

Kent said, "We released a few seconds of video of the crime, but that's not included on this tape." His remark went over Jamie's head.

Then his worst nightmare happened. Tabloid TV showed photos of Foster, the former model. Did they show Foster in evening clothes, in designer fashions, the splash he made by coping with that mini-disaster on the runway in Milan? No. Thousands of such pictures had been taken, but no. They showed him 98% naked, leaning on a rock in a sensational string bikini.

The next day the networks caught up with Foster the Calvin boy, so the tabloids showed the rear nude European campaign for Garimondi. It was never seen in America—till now. "Oh no. Oh no. They've destroyed, my career. I'll nev-er, work again."

"It ain't that way, Jamie. You're a real celebrity now."

"That's the last thing, on earth, I want to be!"

"Gee." Kent liked all those pictures on TV.

"I'll never, be hired, again. I'll have to, work for Lou-ie, the rest of my life. Dear God, what did I do wrong?"

He turned away and cried. No matter how much Kent tried to help, Foster ruined Jamie's life.

Foster'd only gotten into the business to earn Jamie's tuition money, a freshman at the University of Chicago with a lifelong dream of being a reporter. But Foster turned out to be great at modeling, a little Attitude Boy, son of a Junior Miss. He made a lot of tuition, then quit the minute Jamie got his master's in journalism. Jamie always thought of them as two people.

Jamie kept modeling in the closet so he'd be taken seriously. For awhile Foster still worked Fashion Week in New York and Europe, but no one back home knew that; Jamie was on vacation. He had a real career now, and wrote features from glamorous places; he got to take Rick to Europe. Then Rick got sick and Foster retired for good.

And now the whole entire world had seen Jamie Foster's ass. The coverage went on for days, NUDE MODEL STABBED BY SNUFF FILM QUEERS!!!

He sank into total despair. "Please, just leave me, alone. Can't you see I, want to be, alone?"

Kent slunk out, and Jamie screamed and wailed for two solid hours. Everyone on the ward heard him.

* * *

Later he coped a little; the coverage wasn't Kent's fault. Maybe Jamie should see the rest of the tape so he'd know how bad it got. He asked for Kent, who came to the door looking terribly sad. "I didn't mean to upset you, Jamie."

"You didn't. The tape did, but you did not. You are, my friend. Come, sit with me?"

"I'd like to."

"You did, nothing wrong. I need my, bud-dy, to help me, get through this." Jamie threw him the toy basketball.

"I'm your buddy?" They played catch for a minute. Jamie loved his basketball.

"You're my, bud-dy." Jamie made a big hoop with his arms. Kent banked the ball off Jamie's chest, and it landed right in his crotch.

Kent hit Play. Cox's Dayton station quoted Josephine Hansen of the Tribune. "An unbelievable story of courage and dedication and self-sacrifice," she said in her lovely mid-South lilt, "between a Straight cop and a Gay reporter." The Dayton ABC station had Darla Collins twirling her tush in front of a courthouse again. Channel 7 in Columbus had video of their anchor walking along the abandoned railroad bed where Aaron Haney was found. "But one reporter stuck with the story," she said, "and made his hometown proud."

That felt great, until Jamie hit Cincinnati, where the homophobic ex-mayor, who wasn't even a reporter but was an anchor now, called Jamie "a soft-porn employee of a homosexual newsletter."

He'd worked nonstop for a dozen years to become a good reporter. Now he was nothing more than tabloid TV, victimized by his own profession.

Everyone showed his naked butt. Larry King had his butt. Barbara Walters had an artist's rendering of his butt. No doubt Letterman had his butt in a Top Ten list. And every last report highlighted the partnership between a Straight cop and a Gay reporter.

The final segment was Mike Wallace's jailhouse interview with Agent-in-Charge Frank Carson. Jamie mashed the volume up; this he wanted to see.

They weren't allowed to talk about the current charges because of lawyers, Wallace said. "But there is plenty more we wanted to ask Agent Carson about."

Carson said, "Homosexuals are unreliable informants, untruthful witnesses, not the kind of people that the Bureau is willing to stake its reputation on."

"Does that include former Director J. Edgar Hoover, a known homosexual?"

Color simultaneously drained from Carson's face, and intensified. He glanced down, then back at his interrogator. His jaws worked, but no words came. Finally he said, "Director Hoover was not a homosexual. He hated homosexuals, Communists, criminals and security risks, because they're so easily blackmailed."

Wallace: "All of them? Agent Carson, here is a photograph of J. Edgar Hoover wearing a dress at a party in Georgetown in 1952. Are you really going to tell me that J. Edgar Hoover, the foremost lawman of the 20th Century, was a security risk, and therefore Jamie Foster, this openly-Gay, unblackmailable reporter for The Ohio Gay Times, was the proper target of an FBI investigation; while you never went after the serial killer of 13 men that he almost gave his life to catch?"

"We had good reasons for identifying him as a threat."

"What did he threaten? To sing show tunes at a piano bar? People in Columbus admire this man. There isn't any dirt on him to be found—we've checked."

"I'm not at liberty to discuss that investigation."

"The Ohio Gay Times has requested a copy of your file on Mr. Foster. Are you prepared to justify its contents when it's released soon?"

"We performed a necessary assignment thoroughly and professionally."

"For what did you investigate him?"

"It's still an open investigation, so I can't comment."

Jamie hit the Stop button. He felt caught. "I don't, know what to say. I'm over-whelmed. Call Casey. I want to see, how we covered it."

"Sure, his articles are hardhitting, an inside look, and those photos are unbelievably good evidence. He focused on the killers, not just you."

That's my Casey. "Do you know, what I saw, on that video? Three things. The graph-ics keep, reminding me, of the scars on my back, and I'm not ready, to deal with that yet. They tried to, hand me, a mirror today, but I told them, I'd break the damn mirror, over their heads."

"Oh gee, I'm sorry, I…"

"Two, this was, the best story, I've ever had, prob-ably the best story I'll ever get, and every hack in the country, has already written, it up. That pisses me off real bad."

Kent didn't know what to say. "Maybe you can write something after you get out of the hospital." Then his awareness changed. "You're feeling competitive again!"

"And three—everyone, has now seen, my butt." Jamie fumed, hard as titanium.

"You're kidding, aren't you?" Kent searched his face.

"I could have done, without every-one in America, seeing my butt. There are some people, that I would be very happy, if they never saw, my butt. It is my butt; it's not Brokaw's butt; it's not Baba Wawa's butt. It's my butt, and I like to be, the one who decides, who sees my butt."

They burst out laughing. Laughter felt sweet, but it hurt Jamie's back, so he laughed about that, then threw his ball at Kent's head.

They both knew his butt was stop-traffic gorgeous. But not if it ruined his career.

49

Rule #1

"Hey, buddy, what's wrong?" Kent asked the next afternoon after Jamie woke up crossly from his nap. Connie, Thelma's longtime hairdresser, had driven down from Battle Ground and cut Jamie's hair; he looked better than he had since the incident, even had his swoop back. But the air was clearly negative.

"Don't get me started," he warned. *I look like shit, for one thing. Connie had me look at my hair in the mirror. Half my face is melted away. I knew the rest was skin and bones, but God, I look like a corpse.*

Kent couldn't stop himself, he was so eager to help. "You'd think that a guy who's on the front page of every paper in America would…"

"Be supremely, royally and permanently pissed to have all these fucking Straight hacks scoop me on the best story of my career." Jamie was feeling better, all right.

"Everybody in the country knows about you now."

"They know that I fucking got stabbed! Four years I work this fucking story—no one cares. ABC called me two years ago, two calls and out, Dennis Rodman's in drag or some bullshit, so they chased that instead. We even Fed-Exed my reportage to The New York Times. All they saw was that it was coming from a Gay newspaper, so it must have an axe to grind, there's no serial killer worth their vaunted, self-righteous, bigoted attention. Five years ago they offered me a job!" Kent, wide-eyed, sank into a chair.

"Now every fucking hack in the country's got my story while I fucking sleep through the fucking thing. I'm supposed to be fucking happy about it? Give me a fucking goddamn motherfucking sonofabitching fucking break!"

Kent's face twisted. It was an awful lot of fucking.

"In other words, I've been r-r-reading," Jamie said, rolling the R, head high. "Straight reporters can't get the story right. Didn't you see that homophobic crap in the Sun? The AP's no better, it's homosexual this and homosexual that. The story isn't sex, it's murder! When a man kills a dozen women is he the new heterosexual killer? No-o-o. I don't know who's worse, these motherfucking homicidal losers or the goddamn asshole-sucking media."

A nurse walked in, unannounced of course—the same nurse Jamie had tangled with over flashcards, and again yesterday over keeping his room door closed, like there was an actual person inside with privacy rights. "What's this disturbance here?" she sneered.

"Out, you bitch!" Jamie reached for something to throw at her. "Learn to knock!" He cocked his arm and threw the little tissue box. He missed.

Kent was on his feet in a shot. He motioned Jamie to calm down and signaled the nurse sympathetically. "He's upset right now, nurse, nothing personal, nothing I can't handle. Delayed reaction to all the trauma he's been through. Let me talk him down."

She stared daggers at Jamie, stamped her foot—and beat it, but not before finding something nursey to adjust in the room. "If you think you can handle it, off-i-cer!"

Kent watched the door close behind her, then turned to face the man in the bed. "Please, James, just one shootout a week, okay?"

Laughter erupted in Jamie's chest. "Oh! Oh, don't say funny things. Laughing hurts." But he laughed anyway.

He faced his buddy. "Sorry. I'd like to be back at the office having a fight with Louie. Not that the old hag didn't have it coming. At a time when I don't even have control over my own body, it would be nice to control this jail cell of a living space. They freak out when I demand that they knock." His nose started running again, some kind of medication reaction. "Um, do you think I could have one of those tissues?"

"If you promise to get a permit before you fire again."

Jamie chuckled, blew his nose. And that was when he formed the plan.

"Get me a pencil," he ordered. "Where's my laptop? How am I supposed to get anything done without my Macintosh? Find me some paper, if you would."

"Maybe the nurse's station. If you promise not to use the pencil to stab someone."

"Apologize to the nice nursey for me," Jamie grinned evilly. "Just roll your eyes and say something vague about queers."

Kent got writing supplies. Jamie wrote furiously. "What are you going to do?"

"Hand me the phone. How do I get an outside line in this joint?"

"Who are you calling?"

"Manhattan," Jamie told the phone. "CBS News, '48 Hours.'" He wrote a number down. "Thank you." He pressed a button, dialed again. "There's only one way for a working reporter to get back in the game." To the receiver he said, "This is Jamie Foster of The Ohio Gay Times, calling from Indianapolis for Dan Rather. No, I won't talk to his assistant. Give me the man himself or I'm going to Jane Pauley. Of the Indiana Pauleys."

Kent gasped, wondered if some of his conversation had gotten through; decided he needed some air. When he came back, the deal was done.

In the space of fifteen minutes, Jamie reached the manager of Chez Nous, lauded him for his cooperation, got a referral to the best makeup artist in town, manipulated that guy into giving him an outcall just before the live TV show, sweet-talked a dietary aide into disobeying doctor's orders so Jamie could smuggle in chateaubriand, coquilles saint jacques and a bottle of wine, ordered in French from the best restaurant in town—all by variations on Diva Rule #1: Expect it, demand it, make the bastards give it to you.

Kent worried about hyperactivity, but Jamie felt the power of adrenaline pump. Kent shook his head. "Is there anybody you can't talk into doing what you want?"

"My mother, used to be. But then, I learned it from her." He hung up, kept his finger on the button, but couldn't think of anyone else to call.

Soon he was exhausted. Kent woke him when the maitre d' arrived with hot boxes. Jamie could only be mellow and pick at his coquilles, watching Kent stuff his face with tenderloin, raving about sauces.

Slowed down, medicated, glad to be working again, Jamie was deeply pleased to have his partner enjoying good food. *It's the first time it feels like normal life.*

He wished he had more dishes he could serve the big guy; he visualized rows of plates, removing lids with a flourish. "*Try some of this. And some of this. And this!*"

But maybe it was a dream. He woke up the next morning to find dried scallop sauce in his hair. Shuddered to think of the ignominy in front of Kent—who gleefully presented him with a photograph of seafood in his swoop.

50

Showdown

"Three minutes to air," intoned a mousy young producer in red-framed glasses and a brown maxi-skirt. A sound man adjusted a microphone on Kent's suit jacket. "This is live, people, I want it mistake-free."

Jamie shifted uncomfortably in his chair. "Ow."

Kent, beside him, got concerned. "What's wrong?"

"It just hurts a little. Let's get this over with." It had taken Jamie two minutes to step into the 501's Kent bought him. They were the right size, 27s, but big as a house. Kent had to fasten the buttons because the holes weren't broken in yet, and Jamie's fingers didn't work very well. He looked away in maximum embarassment.

He'd wanted his most elegant suit, but it was back in Ohio, so Kent substituted a gold sweater with Purdue University on the chest. "It sets off your hair," he said. "And it's an improvement over the last thing I bought you. You chucked that IU sweatshirt out the car window, remember? We found it on the side of the road with the dead mic still on it."

Jamie didn't remember, but he said, "Ha! I wouldn't wear that thing to a dogfight."

A monitor was set up next to the bathroom. The segment with Davey at home ended, and Dan Rather stood in front of the nurses' station, promoting the next segment. Music. The producer said, "And we're away. Clear the room!"

Kent searched Jamie's face. "You all right, partner?"

Jamie saw hope and warmth and worry in dark eyes. His back started to ache. Hoped to make it through this; had to, it was his career. "We beat a killer, Commander. We can sure as shit beat this."

"Five. Four. Three," two fingers, one. Dramatic music, logo, segment title ("Stud Reporter") on the monitor; Dan in the hallway, speaking without script.

"Homicide experts like Dr. Steve Helmreich agree: despite sophisticated computer technology, DNA testing and the latest gadgets, tracking serial killers still comes down to people—police and other investigators: their commitment, contacts, street smarts and ability to work together as a team. Let's meet the men who nailed these vicious killers, one of whom almost gave his life in the effort." And he came through the door. "James R. Foster, chief correspondent for The Ohio Gay Times, in his first interview since the stabbing; and Sgt. Kent Kessler, task force commander for the Indiana State Police." Handshakes, macho with Kent, then much softer with Jamie. "Mr. Foster, thank you for getting out of your hospital bed tonight to be with us."

Jamie nodded, conserving strength.

* * *

Watching at home in Golden, Colorado, Danny Foster found it gripping, and not just because his little Bro was the subject. Danny had followed Jamie's reportage for years, then gobbled up every factoid he could get about the stabbing. What made the live interview edge-of-your-seat was Jamie's rising out of bed, amazingly articulate, a week after the coma. He was every bit a match for the toughest reporter in television.

Still, Danny had to turn away at first. Jamie had lost 35 pounds. His handsomeness was still obvious, but he looked horribly gaunt, like Rock Hudson a few months before death. It took courage for a supermodel to look like that on TV, when two weeks ago the world stared at the Hot Face with the Hot Bod.

Here was Jamie salvaging his career, giving the performance of his life. In the same circumstances Danny would have crawled under a rock till the world forgot him. But not Jamie; Jamie competed always.

He praised Casey, Louie and a stringer named Kenny Dyson, the Task Force agencies, personnel and especially the Commander in the superlatives they deserved; then he demolished every homophobic myth about the crimes. He denied that Gay men disproportionately become serial killers and proved the perception was a media-created distortion. He had choice words for the wild, hysterical coverage of the murder of Gianni Versace.

He made the case for Gay and Lesbian cops and got Kent to endorse them. Jamie lay the blame right where it belonged, on Ford and Crum first, then Gay-ignorant media, Gay-intolerant police and Gay-hating politicians—on Gay men too, who compromise their own safety "and jump in any stranger's car for a quickie"—and finally on the public for turning a deaf ear to Gay-bashing, when polls showed Americans opposed discrimination as long as they didn't have to do anything about it.

He was hard-hitting, intense; no different from what he did every week in print, but this went out live, electronic and national. Rather never mentioned the modeling work, because James R., as part of the deal, refused to address it; but still, this was a very handsome guy, and Jamie used his battered good looks to run his eloquent mouth.

The victims needed a Gay spokesman and he excelled at it; a cop critic, a media critic, above all a reporter of facts. "No one looks at Agent

Carson and wonders why so many Straight men are serial killers. No one looks at Ted Bundy and wonders."

Equally striking was the rapport between the Gay reporter and the Straight cop; their deep mutual respect, their teasing each other, their celebratory fist-pounding. Danny thought back to the funeral, wondered if there could be more between them than friendship.

For the first time he got an emotional feel for Jamie's sexuality; a butch little number who liked a big butch number. A close-up on Kent's face made Lynn notice masculinity, intelligence, sensitivity.

"Man," she said, "that Kent's a cutie. I wouldn't mind seeing him in some underwear ads."

"He isn't blond," Danny replied. "Besides, I'm starting my diet on Monday."

"You better, or I might have an affair with a man in uniform. Gosh, look at those eyes."

Still, the inescapable point was Jamie's courage; discovering the story, following it for years, going on to the motel to try to prevent further loss of life—living to tell the tale, to defend his Untouchables and to demand their fair treatment. He was an angry young man, but too intelligent, analytical, balanced and fair to dismiss as a mere hothead. What did he think of Gay guys who murder their own kind? "Don't stare at the stink, just flush the toilet."

"His career's going national," Danny predicted. "Gosh, I wish Mom had lived to see this interview."

He covered his eyes. Lynn held her husband, who didn't deserve to lose his little Bro so soon after their Mom.

Then Rather said, "Before we go, there is someone who wants to meet you, Jamie."

The producer nudged Davey Shuey inside the hospital room. He was a poor, mop-haired youth who tried to dress up for the occasion. Jamie blinked at him, then realized he should stand. Kent assisted him.

Davey walked up. "Thank you for saving my life."

Jamie just looked at him. Kent punched Jamie's shoulder, "Now you understand what you did, partner. Don't ever deny your heroism again."

Jamie shook Davey's hand. "You are well? Please be."

"Yeah, I'm fine."

"I'm glad. But it's not I you must thank. It is he."

Davey reached out to Kent. "Thank you, officer."

"Man, we're glad you're okay."

Then there seemed little more to say, so Jamie hugged Davey, a Gay guy too. "Jamie, you saved this man's life."

"Kent, you did."

Dan Rather settled it, "You both did, as America witnesses the results." He shifted position to camera three and the TelePrompter. "Another serial killer caught at last, through the efforts of brave men like these, one Gay, one Straight. Devastating charges of FBI misconduct, police and media neglect, prejudice—and evidence of stunning police professionalism. Americans trapped by fear for their safety. And somewhere on our nation's streets tonight, another fifteen confirmed serial killers, maybe as many as one hundred, lie in wait to lure the innocent, the powerless, the too-trusting.

"And the FBI, thought to be in charge of apprehending serial killers? Tonight one senior official and three agents sit in jail, charged with masterminding a snuff film conspiracy, a story we'll track like Texas bird dogs.

"That's '48 Hours: Circle City Showdown.' Now stay tuned for your late local news. We'll be back next week with another edition of '48 Hours.' Till then, Dan Rather, CBS News, live from Indianapolis." A suddenly earnest pause. "Good night."

Theme music. "And we're away," the producer cried. People whooped or applauded. Jamie sat and slumped.

"Thank you, sergeant. Excellent work. We meet heroes every day in this business, but you are outstanding." Rather pumped Kent's hand, and Kent grinned. Jamie opened his eyes and watched.

"And you, Jamie Foster," Rather said, deciding against a handshake, "make dynamic television. Call me the next time you're in New York."

"I will. Don't say it if you don't mean it."

Rather smiled. "I mean it, Jamie. Give me a call."

Credits flashed by, with stills from the show: Glenn and Gary; Davey Shuey; Major Slaughter; Bulldog and Hickman; Schmidgall's lawyer; Casey writing; Doc, Phil, Jack; the Red-Haired Boy's pauper plaque; LeRoy Walker, his parents and a very important paper; Crum in handcuffs; Carson in jail; Tommy Ford strangling—Kent holding up a fist and Jamie pounding it.

Kent watched circles form under Jamie's eyes. The TV people, eager for beer or bed or a latenight phone call, scurried to clear the room. Major Slaughter strode in, dodging cables and technicians. "Kent, Jamie! Excellent." He grasped Kent for a big bear hug, and slapped his back so hard Jamie cowered for fear he'd do it to him.

Instead George took Jamie's hand in both of his and held it tenderly. "You looked good, son."

"That was the make-up man."

"You spoke well too. As always. I'm glad you're back."

Casey entered, snapping photos, as Louie hung by the door. They waved. Chief Melvin Watson barreled in, clapping Kent on the shoulder and congratulating him. Someone said the governor was coming. Jamie hoped he'd make it snappy. Still, it was the governor; Jamie wondered where his equipment was. *How am I supposed to get any work done around here?*

Oh, Casey's got it covered. Thanks, bud.

Someone at the door asked to see Jamie. It was Gary Tompkins, Mr. Ferguson's lover. The earth stopped spinning for a beat.

Jamie stretched out a hand to him. Kent introduced him to the room. Gary solemnly shook Kent's hand, thanked him "for killing my lover's killer."

Kent frowned, spoke a few lame words of comfort.

Gary shook hands with Major Slaughter and the police chief. The governor leaned against the doorway, watching.

Gary came to Jamie last, stood for a moment looking unsure. His eyes filled with tears; he looked away. Jamie murmured, "Come, let me touch you." Gary crouched. They held each other as Gary cried.

Even Slaughter had a hard time. His voice shook as he said, "Well, guys, that's what it's all about. Right there." He shook Kent's hand. "It's been a privilege to work with you, son. You're one hell of a man."

Kent didn't know what to say and wouldn't even try.

"Governor," Slaughter called.

The governor started working the room, "Hi Melvin. Great work! George, you old dog, congratulations. You know who I want to meet, though. Sergeant, I'm Brad Pendleton." Jamie savored the moment; Casey got it. "I want to thank you on behalf of the people of Indiana. You and all the task force members make us very, very proud."

"Thanks, governor," Kent gulped.

Jamie whispered, "Do you want to meet the governor, Gary? He'd very much like to offer his condolences." Gary sniffled, said yes. Jamie gathered his last strength. To Casey he said, "Switch to tape." Casey found his recorder, pressed On. When it was Jamie's turn, he blew past Pendleton's congratulations to ask, "When are you going to issue an executive order banning anti-Gay discrimination in state employment? Indiana's the only state in the Midwest without one."

The governor sputtered, "Well, that's an interesting question. I'm not sure this is the time or place to…"

"I'm a reporter, governor, this is the time and the place. Are you going to tell me that Gary Tompkins here, or his late lover who was a marketing whiz for an NBA team, is unfit to work for the state of Indiana?"

"Well, I… No. I'm not going to tell you that."

"Then ban discrimination, governor. Just in state employment. We're talking about people's jobs here, hiring the most qualified employees. Gay ones don't need you, they can move to Illinois."

Pendleton frowned. "Now I know what Dan Rather just went through. I'll think about it, okay?"

"Your father would have done it. Why don't you?" *Zing!* The governor's father was governor before him.

Pendleton eyed him. "I agree, he would have. And I'd like to. I'd also still like to have my scalp the next day."

"If you work it right you will. Talk to Dick Celeste in Ohio. He did it a dozen years ago with no political consequences at all. Will you talk to him?"

"Will it get you off my back?"

Jamie smiled. "For now. Not for long."

"Bastard," Pendleton grinned. "I'll talk to him."

"Thanks, governor." Jamie looked at Casey, who held up his tape recorder and his thumb.

Then someone strode into the crowd, all 400 pounds of him, smiling, white-haired, vital—attractive, regardless of weight. Didn't care about TV people or governors or other shoo-flies. Jamie cried, "Kenny!"

"Don't you look gorgeous," Kenny Dyson exclaimed, bending and hugging. "Caused any traffic accidents lately?"

Jamie chuckled. "It's your story. Always will be."

"You're so full of bullshit I'm thinking of selling you for steaks. Don't have enough fat on you to make hamburgers." Kenny winked, pointed, "Do not retort!"

Then there was a photo op. Casey put Gary in Kent's chair next to Jamie, with the bigwigs, Kenny and Kent arrayed behind them. In the photo, Jamie holds Gary's hand; Kent's are on Jamie's shoulders.

Finally everyone left; Major Slaughter pulled the door shut behind him. Jamie pushed up wearily; Kent watched him with brown liquid eyes. Everyone else hugged, but the last time, Jamie rejected him.

Jamie looked up at Kent, wanting to hug him, afraid to; they both were. Then fear was nothing but fear. Jamie took three small steps toward his Commander.

Kent opened his arms, clasped Jamie's shoulders, avoiding wounds he knew so well. They stood together in the hospital room, a tall, dark trooper, ramrod-straight; a small blond bag of bones. Jamie whispered, "Thank you. For everything you've done, everything you are. You're my Hero, Kent, my forever Hero."

Kent was quiet, absorbing, memorizing. Their bodies touched. Then something about a shoulder made Jamie rest his head there.

Kent gazed down at blond hair, with a swoop around the sides. "Jamie, thank you. This feels so good, you can't imagine. Man, you were awesome tonight, and… I don't know how you do this stuff. I'm so proud of you. I'm no good with words the way you are, but I have to tell you some things. They're real important, okay? Jamie, I…"

Jamie fell asleep.

It like to killed Kent. "Standing up, even. Poor little guy." His shoulder sang a wistful lullaby as he cradled that blond head.

A minute later, he picked him up and put him to bed. It was the sweetest pain, getting shoes and socks off him, Levi's, the gold Purdue sweater, seeing his wasted thighs, his ribs, a body which had nearly starved to death; but was alive, gloriously alive, never more than on this night, their night together on national TV; their night in each other's arms.

Kent pulled the blanket up, glanced toward the door. "Good night, partner. I'm sleeping here with you. See you tomorrow." He stroked a swoop of blond hair.

That opened Jamie's eyes. "Good night, Commander." He dropped off again, exhausted.

Kent savored that hug for the rest of his life.

51

Dangerous

Casey hit the nation with a bombshell.

"I've got your exclusive," Kent told Jamie, early on the paper's street day. "Will you give me permission to search your mother's house? Also your place in Ohio?"

"Sure. Why do you want to do that?"

"Casey sent me your FBI file. Read 'em and weep."

Jamie read; the first page stunned him. The FBI called him "the most dangerous homosexual in America."

This was alleged because he was young, highly intelligent, an aggressive journalist from an Ivy League school who wrote stories critical of the President and the Pentagon; because he had "no responsible editorial supervision" and "wealthy friends accumulated during his six years as a fashion model," because of "his considerable self-discipline," and because "his perceived physical beauty, as seen by other homosexuals in countless semi-nude photographs, makes him a prime candidate to unite them in ways that may undermine the military, the Constitution and the rule of law."

But what really pissed off the Feds was that he was the founder and principal shareholder of infashion.com.

The company was a very smart collaboration between Jamie and Foster; they were lucky they thought of it first. At the height of his career Foster complained bitterly about being paid 20% of what women supermodels made; he even walked off a set and filed a groundbreaking discrimination complaint. Jamie's lawyer successfully argued that while women's fashion is much bigger than men's, Foster was hired for the women's market and should not be paid 80% less for the same amount of work. Haute couture drooped like a failed soufflé.

So Jamie came up with a win-win settlement. The way to make money in fashion was to own all the designers, all the models, all the clothes and accessories and workout videos and signed posters and home furnishings and upscale retailers, and sell them all on the Internet through one memorable name. He wasn't Calvin's lover, but his business partner—and everyone else's. The IPO made Foster obscenely rich; while Jamie lived in Dublin, Ohio off his newspaper money.

There was no allegation in the FBI report that he'd committed a crime or was about to. Congress banned domestic surveillance 25 years ago, which didn't stop Agent Carson. "They don't even mention that for a terrorist, I'm well-hung."

Kent laughed. Jamie thumbed through other pages. The FBI took a prurient interest in sexy pictures of him, page after page of Foster's swimwear, his workout trunks, his jock. The Bureau tracked Jamie's movements, reported on who he saw, what he wrote about; there were photocopies of his reporting on Gays in the military. A memo complained that "for a homosexual, he appears unassailable in terms of sexual misconduct. A five-month study by the Columbus office since the death of his male lover reveals no known sexual liaisons. This is such a bright and cunning predator that he carefully avoids such activity. In short he keeps it in his pants, so other points of attack will need to be identified."

"They're attacking my pants."

"Have you ever seen a stupider thing?" Kent chuckled. "Still, it's real important. They were following you, Jamie; they may have bugged your house. That's why I need to enter your domiciles, to check for eavesdropping devices."

Kent was so cute, using jargon words like domiciles. "Suppose they'd put this effort into catching Tommy Ford? These people have corrupted the rule of law without my help."

"There's one detail I'm real curious about. I'm sorry to bring it up, but your mother's funeral, the string quartet. Ford wasn't there, none of them were. How'd he know about that? Maybe Carson bugged your Mom's house."

"Did we ever discuss the case there?"

"No, we started to but we never did. Read the last page."

Jamie did. His face turned purple. For years, the Bureau sent HIV-positive informants to try to infect him. When that didn't work, they tried the same thing with Rick. It was finally halted by a section chief in Washington as "not cost effective."

Jamie flung the pages at the wall. "Get 'em, Commander! Check my car, my office, everything I own." He got out of bed, started grabbing for his clothes. "They're about to meet the most dangerous homosexual in America."

"Between that file and those bugs, I may get attempted murder on every FBI agent between here and Columbus."

Jamie pulled on a shirt. "Then how far up does it stretch? Agent Carson didn't go to Ohio, the local office did it for him."

"It ain't over yet, buddy. Get well."

"Kent, you're an incredible officer. I'd never have focused on criminal charges, to me it's a Constitutional issue. But you immediately attack it as a crime."

"I need you, partner. Can't have my best investigator lying around here vacationing."

Jamie turned to him, near tears, picturing his beloved Ricky, targeted in an FBI attack. "Take me home. Please, to my mother's. Kent, take me home."

Kent backpedaled, "You ain't even half-rehabbed yet."

"They're not doing anything medical for me; it's all nutrition, physical therapy. There's PT at home; we have food at home."

"Man, we should talk to the doctor."

"I can't help you here. I want to go home."

"Jamie, you're tremendous. Let's talk to the doc." Kent teared up slightly too. "So I can take you home."

* * *

At 4 p.m., with the issue on the streets, Casey held a news conference. His copyrighted Exclusive, "FBI Tried to Infect Jamie," led every newscast in the nation.

Leaving the hospital was gruesome. TV cameras lined up to watch Jamie being wheeled out. Kent deployed decoy vehicles at the front, and they escaped by the receiving dock instead.

His patrol car, lights flashing, preceded the ambulance up I-65. Kent tooted his horn at Kessler Boulevard, and later as they crossed into "TIPPECANOE COUNTY, HOME OF PURDUE UNIVERSITY." Even the ambulance driver honked. Still, the ride wearied Jamie. When they finally stopped at the house on Tad Lincoln Drive, Kent insisted on carrying him inside. "You don't want that bumpy gurney with the steps and all. I know where to hold you so it won't hurt." The wheelchair-to-ambulance transfer had jostled like hell, not to mention every pothole.

Kent patted him once he had him settled into Thelma's bed. "You okay, buddy?"

"Fine, Kent," Jamie said, turning away, pulling Florence Henderson on top of him.

Kent called the nursing service. Friends from Ohio were scheduled to arrive in an hour. Then he scoured the house for electronic devices. It took awhile, but finally there it was, under the rim of an occasional table—right between the twin La-Z-Boys.

As Jamie slept, rioters with AIDS trashed the Federal Building in San Francisco.

52

F.O.I.

Jamie was up and about every day, sleeping a regular schedule, gaining a few ounces. Danny and Lynn, Casey and other friends took turns staying with him. Casey brought winter clothes, some of Jamie's stylish attention-grabbers. Jamie had no place to wear them, but he was glad to get his look back. He liked Hoosier basics, but he loved fancy. He sat in a La-Z-Boy wearing a cobalt, banded-collar silk shirt, matching double-pleated pants, a stunning gold belt and patent leather shoes as Casey interviewed him. They cheerfully made up stuff. Then Casey deleted the lies and made a column out of it.

Kent visited every other day, met all Jamie's friends. LeRoy Walker sent a bouquet, "Depositions today, propositions tomorrow?"

Martha Kessler enjoyed hearing Kent talk about his visits; everything was getting back to normal. She baked another pie, her killer meat loaf and scalloped potatoes to send. Kent drove the food over in the studtruck F-250, saw a minivan in the driveway. He rang the bell. Stone appeared, took the food, said, "Gee, thanks," and started to shut the door. Kent, jaw agape and hand out, blocked it.

Stone glared. Kent got ready for a fight.

Stone wouldn't back down exactly, but he yielded half a step. "He's sleeping. Which is what he needs. We're glad you brought this. But I can't deal with you yet, okay?"

"What did I do, besides save the man's life?"

Stone looked away, then got in the trooper's face. "When your brother goes on national TV to tell the world he's a cocksucker, then you can tell me how to act!"

"You stupid bigot, he's more macho than you are. They suck him." Kent curled his lip, "You can suck me."

He turned his back and walked away.

* * *

He got Jamie a day later. "How you doing, partner?"

"Better, now that I threw Stone out. I can stay by myself okay."

"Good. He gave me the creeps."

"Moaning around here like he's doing me a big favor, when what he really came up for was to chew me out. The '48 Hours' gig bothered him more than my ass hanging out all over the world. Get this: he actually said, 'Everybody in the country knows you're a faggot. Thank God Mom's dead so she didn't have to see this shit.'"

"What a thing to say about his mother."

"Isn't it!? Plus he drinks vodka every waking minute."

"How did you get rid of him?"

"The instant he made that crack I told him that as Mom's trustee, I control this property and he was trespassing. I claimed to have friends at the state police."

Kent chuckled. "I wouldn't want to cross you, boy. But the great news is you're well enough to be by yourself."

"Thanks. What's with you?"

"Hey, I got two tickets for basketball. You want to go to the Miami game in a month? It's an afternoon game on national TV. Do you think you'll feel up to it?"

"Purdue home opener against Miami University and the legendary Bingo Peters? I would love it, man." It was just a friendship thing; but hoops at Mackey Arena! Kent wanted to socialize with him after he got well. "That would be fabulous. I hope to be able to drive soon, short trips. Can I pick you up?"

Kent insisted on the other way around so hard Jamie gave in, quicker than he usually would; there was no stopping Kent when he took a notion. Besides, in all the excitement, Jamie was getting tired again. "Thank you, Kent. It's something I'll look forward to every single day."

They rang off. Jamie rummaged in his suitcase, found the T-shirt, put it on. Went back to the family room, sat in a La-Z-Boy, put his feet up. Fell asleep knowing that "Purdue Basketball Is Life. The Rest Is Just Details."

* * *

Marion County Assistant Prosecutor Rob Willingham came to West Lafayette to depose him on the FBI file for the grand jury. It was videotaped in the living room, lasted most of two days. Kent and Phil sat in.

Before they got started, Jamie gave Rob a present with a bow on top. Inside a box of red velvet lay the photo of his sister Cassie, with small diamond earrings for her. "You kept your promise, Rob. You treated Mr. Ferguson like your sister." They shook hands, went to work.

Rob got through the preliminaries, then asked, "How did you learn about the FBI file on you, Mr. Foster?"

"It was only a reporter's hunch. I had interviewed the public information officer at the Cincinnati FBI office, which has jurisdiction over Quincy County, several times. This was to establish what assistance the FBI could provide to the local investigators. The spokesman was very helpful, and he made several promises about FBI assistance, yet the help was never forthcoming. We printed this information each time, as dates of conferences kept being delayed. Then the Cincinnati spokesman informed me that jurisdiction had been transferred to Indianapolis, where we got zero cooperation. The spokesman there was quite rude. He denied the legitimacy of my newspaper; he denied everything I already had, on the record, from Cincinnati, including jurisdiction over these murder cases or even knowledge that they had been committed.

"Yet I knew that police officers in Quincy County had filed very lengthy and detailed reports with the FBI Behavioral Sciences Unit. I had confirmation from Quantico that these reports had been received. I knew that attempts were made, through the VICAP program, to search national crime databases to see if there were similar unsolved homicides elsewhere in the country.

"So I simply began asking myself why the Indianapolis office was dragging its feet; why the spokesman there was so rude and even lied to me. I asked the Cincinnati spokesman about it. He could not comment for the record, but he told me off the record that the Indianapolis office saw me in very disparaging terms. Why? Because I tried to get Federal assistance for a small, rural sheriff's office?

"I was doing the right thing, but to Indianapolis I was the enemy. That made me suspicious. So I filed a Freedom of Information request and was informed that the FBI file on me would be available in six weeks."

"What about its contents surprised you the most?"

"It's an admission of attempted murder, directed at innocent people, my lover and dearest friend." Jamie got emotional for a second, then continued, "It was the Indianapolis office which had to forward the material to Washington, so I had no expectation I'd receive such a complete, unedited document. There is a notation that the final version is completely unlike the original one first forwarded by Indianapolis prior to the stabbing. But the FBI's under a lot of scrutiny now, I take it Washington wants to show the Indianapolis office was a renegade operation—so they released the whole file."

"I will introduce both versions to the grand jury and let them draw their own conclusions from the disparity. Meanwhile, are you involved in any criminal activity? Do you belong to any organization which advocates the overthrow of the United States Government?"

"No, sir. As a reporter I can't join organizations, in case I later have to report on their activities. I belong to my church, to my college alumni associations and the Society of Professional Reporters; but no Gay or Lesbian groups, it's a conflict of interest."

"Do you support the Constitution of the United States?"

"Of course. My late lover was a decorated veteran of the United States Marines."

"Is it possible, as a journalist, to support the overall mission of the Armed Forces, while publishing articles critical of the military from time to time?"

"It's not only possible, sir. If a reporter discovers information which might cause reasonable people to question the military, it's his duty to publish it."

They took a break. Kent said, "Gee, you're so good at this you even wrap yourself in the flag."

"Buddy, it's our flag too."

"Eliminating somebody by infecting them with AIDS is a slow boat to China, though."

"The Bureau still thinks HIV's an immediate death sentence. And their role would go undetected. My infection would be the result of my own actions."

"That's why they were so pissed you never had sex after Rick. Attacking your pants don't work."

Jamie smiled. *Depends on the attacker.*

*   *   *

The second day Rob asked, "Did you have reason to suspect these men who systematically tried to involve you sexually were FBI informants?"

"No, sir."

"Your late roommate, Rick Lawson, was also approached several times. Did he ever mention a suspicion that FBI informants were involved?"

"No, sir, but he certainly commented about the approaches. May I ask you not to call him my roommate? I loved him, we lived together. The proper term is lover."

Rob nodded. "What did Mr. Lawson say about these approaches?"

"We discussed how odd it was that men were making passes first at me, then at him, after he was sick and in a wheelchair and had had multiple amputations, when they never made passes at him when he was healthy."

"These men tried to take advantage of a man in a wheelchair. Where did they approach him?"

"In his bookstore, after he was able to return to work. They were never regular customers, just people he'd seen once or twice. He turned them down and never saw them again. It happened three times that way. Something wasn't right. The man was on chemotherapy, he lost his hair and was bloated by steroids. He was hardly interested in having sex outside marriage." *Or inside it, either.*

Rob clarified what Jamie meant by marriage, then asked, "Were these approaches primarily verbal, or did they involve physical contact?"

"In my case they were all verbal. I don't allow people I don't know to touch me. In Mr. Lawson's case, he was in a wheelchair, and they tried to take advantage. One guy started touching Rick's arm and shoulder a lot, like they were close friends. Rick grabbed his cane and threatened to hit him. Another man rubbed himself suggestively. Rick all but ran him over with his chair."

"The second person with AIDS rubbed his penis suggestively?"

"Right. That one really made us angry."

"Who were these men?"

"I don't recall their names, but I found out who they were and kept a list. I can have Mr. Jordan obtain it from my computer for you."

The videotape ran out, and Kent said, "Jeez, Jamie, even if it hadn't come to the head it did, you'd have gotten D.C. to nail Carson. You had the guts to go after the most powerful police force on earth."

Phil said, "Told ya he was sharp, Commander. Told ya he was someone you should talk to."

A week later four more FBI agents were indicted for conspiracy.

53

Horse

Kent saw his chance and took it.

With the friends gone and Jamie alone, Kent came by every night, always with food and asking if he was making a pest of himself. "Yeah, a bad penny always comes back. It's just the opposite, man," Jamie admitted. "As soon as one visit's done, I look forward to the next."

So Kent took over. He brought bathroom scales and insisted on a weigh-in every night. He made a chart listing dates and Jamie's weight, posted on the refrigerator. The day he woke up, he weighed 140, a 35-pound loss after nine days of coma. When he got home, he weighed 147.3. "Almost an eight-pound gain," Kent exulted.

"Do you know how hard it is for me to gain weight?"

"Milk shakes with protein supplements," the athlete ordered. He brought powdered stuff. "It tastes like malt."

"I hate malt."

The next night Kent cut up bananas in it. "Banana malt," Jamie griped. Even strawberries didn't go over big. So Kent brought fixings for a beet malt; Jamie drank his shakes cheerfully and never complained again.

They played cards and board games, things Jamie hadn't done since he was ten. They went for rides in the country. Jamie could climb into the pickup, though the big wheels made him stretch awkwardly; he really liked it when Kent drove the Acura. From then on Kent drove Jamie's car, and he removed Rick's hand controls so Jamie wouldn't wrack his knee getting in and out.

One evening as they watched college football on TV, Jamie got up to take a leak. Half a minute later Kent heard a groan and a wall-shaking crash. He jumped up, found Jamie slumped over in the hallway. Kent's worst fear returned in a nanosecond. "Man, are you all right?"

No answer. He found a pulse. Slowly Jamie opened his eyes. "What happened?" Kent cried. "Are you hurt?"

Jamie surveyed his splayed-out arms and legs. "I felt fine and then the walls closed in on me."

"Get into a more comfortable sitting position." Jamie untwisted his arms and legs, and Kent urged him to put his head between his knees; but Jamie wasn't about to look like **that**, so he said he'd be okay.

It turned out the next day to be within normal range, the doctor said. "Periodic blackouts, which we hope will diminish in time. This isn't the first one. That's why you can't drive."

Later they got to where they could joke about it. Kent took Jamie shopping and pushed the wheelchair grocery cart. Jamie's disability scared the customers, so they got rowdier, Jamie lolling his head, flailing his legs and drooling on the canned asparagus.

"I start to worry when he wets his pants," Kent confided to an alarmed shopper. "Once he had a seizure in the cereal aisle, and just like that, we were knee deep in piss and Post Toasties."

She hurried off. They turned into another aisle and Kent said, "What's your favorite cereal?"

Jamie froze. He stared at boxes up and down the aisle, grew increasingly agitated. "What's cereal have to do with anything? Go back that way. Why can't I remember?"

"Easy, man, it's okay, no crisis."

"I know I eat cereal." Jamie scanned boxes on top shelves and low ones. "I ate Frosted Flakes as a kid." Kent picked it up. "But it has sugar in it. No way I'd eat that."

Kent tossed it into the cart anyway. "If you liked it then, you still do. No perfect nutrition now, a little sugar won't kill you. It's how much you eat that matters."

"Cheerios?" Jamie said, panicky. "That was Rick's favorite. I think I quit eating Cheerios, sick of them, the only cereal he'd eat. Kix? Why can't I remember?"

Kent spied something, "Here you go." He lifted down a variety pack. "This'll work." It was sugary stuff for kids, not right at all. Kent pushed the chair with one hand, patted Jamie's shoulder with the other, and got him away from the cereal aisle before he pulled a seizure for real.

* * *

Having nothing better to do, Jamie experimented with his hair all the time. *So you're a tease, Kent, I'll take what I can get. When you touched me in the store I felt so safe.*

Jamie, you stupid jerk! Falling for a Straight man, how pathetic.

Then he realized that the pain of his desire lay in his hope that he could actually be with Kent. Since he knew he couldn't, that made Kent a fabulous fantasy. Jamie had lived on fantasies ever since Rick got sick, so he knew to bring them out, not lock them up. Lust blew through that house like a hurricane.

But learning to masturbate again took some doing; his right hand didn't have the coordination for it, and he couldn't get off with his left. He laughed hysterically at himself, the world's most incompetent faggot—but where there's a hardon, there's a way.

* * *

A few days after his grocery panic he called Kent at the post. "I know what my favorite cereal is. Special K!"

"I'm here," Kent Kessler said brightly. "What's your favorite cereal?"

Jamie rolled his eyes, "You're a complete egotist."

"Special K's real tasty, it's your favorite."

Jamie cut the call immediately; but when Kent showed up right away on his doorstep, he let him in, glad to see him and too far gone. *How tasty is it?*

"Hey, buddy, have you weighed yourself today?"

"One fifty three, I've had my best day yet. Can I make you dinner, Mr. K?"

"Sure. You can also call me Mr. Special."

"Why should I, when you'll do it yourself?"

Kent grinned, "Need any help?"

"I love to cook with friends, but not this time. It will be my first try, and I want to see if I can do it."

So Jamie carefully chopped onions as Kent snoozed in the recliner. When the food was in the oven, Jamie sat at the kitchen table, sipping tea, listening to the little snore; taking deep, quiet pleasure, just watching Kent sleep.

Food; a quiet, safe place to rest; this was Jamie's aspiration, to provide for one man's needs.

*   *   *

When Kent awoke the house smelled great, so he followed his nose to the dining room, where Jamie was lighting candles. The table was decked out with porcelain birds, fine china, salads, baking powder biscuits and a serving dish. "What's for supper?"

"Grandma's Goulash. I wanted to make a casserole for my boy scout."

Kent grabbed him and hugged him tight.

Then they sat and ate. "Jamie, Grandma wins a merit badge. And man, your biscuits are great."

"Thanks, casseroles are easy."

"How's physical therapy going?" Jamie rehabbed two hours a day, five days a week. Kent missed being part of it.

"That's the other good thing today. He had me do squats at a machine on the wall, tiny little increments. I asked when I could start lifting weights again and he said now. I'm cleared to work out!"

"Fantastic."

"I've lost so much strength it's scary. No free weights, though, it has to be dumbbells or a pulley machine. He's worried I could lose my balance with barbells. So as soon as I got home I called the sporting goods store. I found a pulley machine for $300 and a used, very good stationary bike for a hundred. They'll deliver in a week."

"I've got a pickup, I can go get them."

"Kent, thanks, but no, I'm just impatient as usual. I want to feel normal again. I want to work out."

"I'll get 'em here tomorrow." Kent was more than eager to help Jamie rebuild his body.

The gym consisted of a long box and two cartons of weights. They worked at assembling it, trying to decipher the Korean translation, identifying the parts and laughing. Jamie drove bolts until his back hurt.

Kent made him take a nap. When he woke later, the machine was largely put together and Kent was gone. There was a note on the kitchen table, next to a box of Special K, to which Kent had affixed a picture of himself.

"Hey Big Guy Who Ain't Even 5'10",

"I got as far as I could with this, but it's not ready so **don't use it yet.** The last step has to be a 2-man job. I'll come over tom'w night and we'll finish it up. It's going to be a good machine for ya, help you build your strength back up. See you tom'w. Meanwhile Eat!

"Mr. Lightly Toasted Rice."

Jamie ate his cereal, studied the penmanship, read the note over and over, put it in his suitcase.

The next night they finished the assembly. Kent watched Jamie through stretches and aerobics, then it was time for the big test. Jamie checked the setting—not quite the least possible weight—and sat on the bench. He eyed the bars, slowly gripped them. He breathed a time or two to get his rhythm; inhaled, then let his breath out as he lifted weights for the first time in his new life.

He managed four and a half presses of 20 pounds before he couldn't budge the bars another inch. Kent eased them back into place, "Great, you're getting back into it."

"Get real. I bounced the entire time." Jamie closed his eyes. Before the incident he could bench 300.

"Sure, you bounced. You think you're going to have perfect form after all this? Think positive."

"Oh, suck a rock."

Kent lowered the setting. "Try again. Finish your set."

Jamie bounced, but he finished his set. His method was to do a full-body workout three times a week. As he moved through his routine Kent varied the weight for him, depending on how tough the exercise was and what he thought Jamie could handle. "Not enough," Jamie would say. Or "way too much."

He bounced throughout the negative side of quad extensions. When he got to preacher curls at the lowest weight, he could barely move the bar an inch. He raised his fists, looked at his biceps. His left arm had a little leftover muscle, but his right had none, zero, it was skin and bones. He swore, got teary, fought off emotion. Kent said, "Count as a rep any movement at all." Jamie was furious, ashamed. He tried desperately to get that inch twelve times. Finally he did.

Kent designed the workout to assure success; some exercises, especially involving Jamie's back, were fairly easy. He finished a second set, then came preacher curls again and he still could barely move the bar. He forced himself to keep going, benches, lats, abs, triceps, bouncy quads, heel kicks for his butt—his glutes got stronger as the workout went on—and reverse butterflies until it was time for biceps again.

The first few reps he got a quarter inch, maybe a half; but on the fourth, somehow the bar finally moved up like it was supposed to. He curled his arms all the way to his shoulders and sat there, wanting to kiss the bar, glad he'd finally made a fucking ten-pound curl.

He made five more reps, then he didn't have it anymore. The workout was nothing, he didn't even break a sweat, but he got through three sets; afterward he bounced just to raise a water bottle to his lips. Kent heard him groan the rest of the night every time he moved.

But that little bit of weight training improved Jamie immediately. He knew it the next morning, unmistakable. He woke up aching, but with real energy for the first time—with a positive attitude and a desire for food.

Workouts gave him his vitality back. He loved focusing on his body, his total self, not just his mind. He loved the Pump; he loved how he felt and used to look, and maybe one day would again.

That night Kent read the instruction book more carefully. "Hey, look, the pulleys add resistance. That wasn't a 10-pound preacher curl, it was 24. It wasn't a 20-pound bench press, it was 45. Those are decent numbers, Jamie, for a beginner. You won't be one for long. I bet you gain real fast, if you keep drinking those shakes."

"Would you really have made a beet one?"

"Be glad it wasn't brussels sprouts." Jamie threw his toy basketball at him, and Kent head-shot it into the kitchen.

Kent noticed a change after the second workout; Jamie stood taller, walked more fluidly. He was kinesthetic again, living in his body, like an athlete.

Every morning Jamie stretched, rode his bike and did crunches on the floor. His abs came back nicely; he gained some weight. He got in his training while Kent was at work, until one night Kent's face fell. "Jamie, will you work out while I'm here? It's a safe machine, but..."

"What's more boring than watching someone work out?"

Kent looked away. "I like to see you do it. I was there the first time you tied your shoes again." He had a way of bringing Jamie to a screeching halt. "Most people like having a workout buddy, for the extra motivation."

"Okay. But I feel so embarrassed."

"Don't. You're not competing with me, you're competing with a coma. So go out and beat him."

"Will you be my workout buddy?"

"If you'll call me Special K." Jamie popped him.

So Jamie changed his schedule, humiliation or no. Except for one glorious season, he was too limited athletically his whole life, too young, too short, too this, too that—too competitive to like losing, much less to Mr. All-Star Bodybuilder Trooperdude.

But then, Mr. Dude wasn't the competition.

* * *

"Lord, it's always hot in here," Kent complained, unbuttoning his dress shirt and discarding it. He strode into the hallway in his undershirt, checked the thermostat. "Good grief, you have it set on 78."

That's where Jamie and his mother always kept it. Kent came back into the family room. The shape of his upper body stole Jamie's breath. He sputtered, "I can put on a sweater if you want to turn it down."

"That's okay. Long as you don't mind me sweating."

How tasty is it? "Would you show me your tattoo?"

"Sure." Kent held his left upper arm out. Jamie didn't focus on the big muscles, but on the design; it beautifully reproduced the back of Kent's baseball jersey, his name a blue semi-circle above his number, red numerals outlined in navy and etched in the segmented way baseball prefers, KESSLER 22.

"May I touch it? I've never touched tattooed skin."

"Of course."

With a finger Jamie traced the name and the shape of the two 2's. It felt slightly scarred, almost but not quite like normal skin. "I don't usually like tattoos. I suppose I'm disloyal to my generation. But yours makes perfect sense. If I'd played ball it's the very thing I might have done."

"I got it two months after I was called up. We won the division, I made the playoff roster."

"Did it hurt?"

"Heck yes. You try having needles and dyes in your arm."

"That's the appeal, I guess. Suffering. Very macho."

"Shoot, Tim had to strap me down or I'd have never gone through with it. He laughed at me the whole time. When it comes to pain I'm a sissy."

"Tim Virdon? The Cy Young winner?"

"My best friend, Jamie. I'm thrilled he's your favorite player."

The next day Kent said, "I got you something. You know I'm egotistical." He tossed it onto a recliner. It was an Atlanta Braves home jersey, KESSLER 22.

"Oh, my. I'll treasure it forever."

"Nah, put it on. I'd enjoy seeing my name on your back." Jamie changed in the bedroom.

He didn't realize it, but Kent was marking him. *Here's who you belong to, boy.* Kent had to adjust himself.

Jamie came back, turned a 360. "I feel a little silly, since I'm not you, but also very proud to wear your jersey."

"Looks good on you. What does Michael Jordan feel when he sees people wearing his name and number?"

Jamie faced him. "Will you autograph it?"

"Get a marker." Jamie found a black one. Kent held his waist, stretched the cloth tight and signed clear across those bumpy abs. *You're mine now. You're mine.*

But he couldn't bring himself to kiss those sexy abs; while Jamie had the whole world telling him, "Straight cop, Gay reporter."

More than that, he was shamed by the myth of the Gay predator; too young to grasp the politics of shaming.

* * *

It turned out Kent never watched baseball. The Braves won the division again, Tim won a playoff game; but they were tossed early, all pitching, no hitting, like they'd been ever since they lost their once-a-generation centerfielder.

Jamie finally wrote his cover story. His fingers knew where all the keys were, not even a coma could obliterate QWERTY; but his fingers didn't always type in the right order. But there were Bulldog, Hickman and Phil in print, "Cops Knew All Along, But Couldn't Prove It" by James R. Foster. The issue sold out.

* * *

After their next workout, Kent brought out a tape measure, but Jamie absolutely refused it. They argued. Feeling better was one thing; Jamie wasn't about to reveal himself to Kent. Jamie covered his mortification with fleece and dance music and a great many words. Finally Kent said, "Please don't be shy; not with me. At 140, I combed your hair, Jamie, I brushed your teeth. You're 15 pounds stronger now."

Jamie turned away. "Thank you for taking care of me."

"How about if I don't show you the numbers? I won't bring them out till you've built yourself back up. Then you'll see how far you've come, and you'll feel good about it." Jamie wavered. "Athletes measure their progress so they can achieve their goals."

"I'm no athlete."

"You always say that, and I'm sick of it. Off with the sweats, let's get this over with. Now do it, Commander's orders."

Under his sweats Jamie's trunks packed a pouch, and suddenly he saw them as faggoty, like a European bikini. What else would a Gay guy wear? Of course his shorts were all crotch. But if he got excited, being so near to each other, Kent would notice, the truth would drip out. Jamie couldn't let that happen. He went clinical, and flipped on "Wall Street Week" for the sole purpose of watching ugly guys talk economics.

"Come on, Modelboy, you've done this before."

Jamie yanked off his sweatshirt, "Measure away." But his fingers had trouble with the drawstring on his pants. Kent finally reached out and pulled the knot loose. Pants fell to ankles, and the erotic possibility dawned on Kent.

He was the one who got aroused. He got to touch Jamie's neck, his shoulders and arms, his big nipples; trailing the tape around his waist, across his crotch, around his butt. He did the job slowly, savoring Jamie's skin.

He knelt and measured the calf, then softly said, "Widen your stance." Then he measured Jamie's thigh, which is biggest at the center of a man.

He looked up at Jamie, who casually handed him up.

Kent put the paper in his wallet, Jamie put his sweats back on. Kent sat, filled with a thousand different feelings of pleasure and pain. The waist was down to twenty-five and a half. He pictured muscles eaten alive, wanted to throw the paper away after all. If Jamie saw himself as a puny, pathetic, 97-pound weakling, Kent saw a bodymind that never gave up, a fierce and deadly competitor.

An athlete, by God. Stop letting this Gay thing work on your mind, Jamie, enough already.

Jeez, how will I ever break through?

* * *

It changed things a little; Jamie got freer with his body, stopped wearing sweats to work out. Then there were days when his body was okay, but his mind went on holiday. He'd forget between the family room and the kitchen why he went to the kitchen. Kent would have to say, "You wanted ice water."

There was an episode about cardinals on the power line, where Jamie ordered a hundred pounds of bird seed C.O.D., no cash and no feeders in the yard. Even with feeders, he'd forget to fill them.

Caregiving hurts. Kent couldn't stand to see Jamie reduced to such lunacy. Kent's mother had to step in and help her son relax, "He's making good progress. You're pressing, let the game come to you."

That ushered in some golden days when Jamie was as sharp as his old self. Sarcastic, witty, intelligent, intense; the boy wasn't easy to live with, but he was fun to be around. Kent never stopped believing Jamie'd come back.

On the last hot day of summer, Kent drove his pickup to Tad Lincoln Drive and beheld a wondrous sight: Jamie rollerblading up the street towards him, wearing nothing but those tight yellow workout trunks, blond hair flying. They waved to each other, then Kent slammed the brakes and yanked the wheel.

Jamie skated up, surveyed the damage. "Mom needed a new one anyway." He skated inside as the state trooper backed up and tried again. Kent's cowcatcher toppled Thelma's mailbox.

*　　　*　　　*

They watched some TV but their tastes clashed, one voting for Bravo, one for the Nashville Network; one for C-SPAN, one for the Comedy Channel; one for "Keeping Up Appearances," one for "Taxi"; one for "Now, Voyager," one for "Shootout in Little Tokyo," hi-yah, chop chop chop, kablooie!

Jamie tried to turn Kent on to the university's classical radio station. When a talky program finally came on, Kent tuned in Kick-Ass 98 and his buddy gritted his teeth shut. When Kent went to the bathroom, Jamie mashed the minus button.

On his way back Kent noticed, in the sewing room, photos on the wall: Thelma, Indiana's Junior Miss; Danny and colleagues on the set of "NFL Today," Stone giving a speech to a big crowd of businessmen—Jamie a few years ago, blond and shimmering, muscled and tanned, in a suit with no shirt underneath, "L'Uomo Vogue." *The most dangerous homosexual in America.*

* * *

In mid-October, a sunny day when Jamie could travel longer, they drove north to Jasper-Pulaski State Wildlife Area to see the migration of the sandhill cranes. Jamie had never heard of them, though their staging area was only 30 miles from Willow Slough. "Are they big birds?"

"Huge, a yard tall, with wingspans over seven feet and bright red foreheads. Northwest Indiana is their most important stopover. They spend winters in Georgia and Florida, then fly in big flocks every spring to their nesting grounds in the upper Midwest and Canada. You should see them during mating season, they do this hilarious dance, bob their heads and jump up, then they land and bob again and throw twigs over their shoulders, males and females both. They're so eager to get started they're practicing building their nests. They always stop here, ten, fifteen thousand of them—if we maintain their habitat."

They could hear the birds before they could see them. Kent drove to a handicapped parking spot next to the crane viewing shelter. Jamie climbed the steps slowly; he wasn't very good with stairs yet. He got to the top and there before him was a meadow filled with a thousand light-gray sandhill cranes.

A stiff breeze blew right in his face and he quickly got cold, but they enjoyed the majestic birds through Kent's telescope. Kent told how important the cranes were in the mythology of the native Miami Indians. "They called them *twaa twaas,* after their call. An old Miami legend says the cranes led them to victory against some marauding Cherokees. The cranes showed the Miamis the enemy's whereabouts. A decisive battle was fought, with all but one enemy killed."

"*Twaa, twaa, twaa,*" called the cranes overhead. And one or two of them did their little mating dance, even out of season, bob, hop, bob, toss—then check to make sure the mate was watching. If not, do it again!

Kent said the cranes all but disappeared from northern Indiana for decades because the Whites drained the wetlands; and bringing them back home, setting aside state preserves for them, was a huge triumph, paid for by outdoorsmen like himself. "We can't undo what we did to the Miamis; but we can give them back their cranes."

Between the birds and the words, Jamie was utterly moved. Plus there were cattails and prairie grasses in the park, and the state trooper even poached a little cutting of them so Jamie would always have a keepsake from home.

Kent loved breaking the law for his buddy.

He noticed Jamie's fancy black leather jacket with braided accents and lace-up sides. Jamie looked like a little lawbreaker too. With that mind, that face and that body, the boy was dangerous, all right, a blond Hell's Angel. Kent knew all about the angel; it was the hell part that turned him on.

On the way back, he asked if Jamie wanted to listen to some country music. "Okay, but there are some mispronunciations my ear can't tolerate." He thought country singers twanged it up to boost sales in Redneckville. "Let's hope we don't hear any." So Kent kept it low and drove them down the highway.

Then a song came on and Jamie turned it up, "I know this one. Is it country?" Kent started singing along. He had an excellent voice, baritone to tenor, and this record was right up his range. Jamie'd sung this song alone in the car a hundred times too. He listened to Kent sing the melody, and suddenly Jamie started harmonizing with him. They drove down the road singing together.

Jamie was inventive, didn't stick with the recorded version, added to it. Their bodies loosened and they sang, full-voiced and free, four minutes of unalloyed happiness.

Followed by a screaming commercial for someone's carpet hut. Jamie yanked the radio off. "That was fun!" Kent said. "How'd you pick out the harmony like that?"

"That's just how I hear pop songs. I want to sing with the professional, not against him; I want to hear his or her performance too. But man, you've got a voice."

"I love singing. It's like sports to me, something you do with your body."

"And your emotions, vocal dancing. I love to dance. Which I haven't done in ages."

Kent frowned, *Yes, you have, Jamie.*

He turned the radio back on, hoping for another song in common, but none came.

* * *

One night was a total disaster. Kent rang the bell, Jamie let him in, Hi, Hi. Extremely subdued. They sat and Jamie stared into space, didn't say a word for five minutes. "I'm sorry, Kent, I'm out of it."

"What's wrong, man?"

It took a long time for Jamie to say, "I'm in shock. In mourning."

"I'm sorry. Something reminded you of your Mom?"

"No. I'm in mourning for Matthew Shepard."

"Oh."

Jamie stared at the black TV. Kent felt increasingly uncomfortable. He wasn't sure what to say, how to help. Who was Matthew Shepard, and why the heck wouldn't Jamie say anything? It seemed passive-aggressive almost. But Jamie was in mourning, he said so right out. "I'll go. Let you grieve in peace."

"No, Kent, don't, you don't have to go! Please stay." Jamie didn't know how to talk to a Straight cop about what happened.

"No, I should. It's the right thing to do." Kent stood, Jamie saw him to the door. "I'll say a prayer." And he left. Jamie felt even more bereft.

The next morning Kent found out exactly who Matt Shepard was; the Wyoming student horrifically brutalized a few nights ago, all of 5'3", strung up, beaten savagely, left for dead. He never woke up from his coma. The whole country knew about it, Kent too; but it was "University of Wyoming" to the country, not the guy's name; "hate crime," not another of our sweet, smart, gentle boys. Kent kicked his own ass, *All I had to do was ask.*

Jamie answered the door again; Kent, giant mums, a card, "In memory of Matthew; in mourning with you."

Tears. Gratitude. Quick departure. Suitcase.

That night when Kent came back, the mums weren't just displayed on the dining room table, they were spotlit like the Empire State Building. Kent and Jamie didn't talk about it, but for the first time Kent realized the punitive power, and therefore the deterrent effect, of a great, crimefighting Gay newspaper.

The next day he stood at attention and solemnly asked Major Slaughter for training in investigating hate crimes.

*　　　*　　　*

Jamie frowned, "You're wearing trooper gear again. Bring your laundry, we'll do it here."

"But you don't like doing laundry."

"No, but maybe I'd feel useful for once."

"My shirts have to be ironed, Jamie, it's regulations."

"Kent, ironing is a level of productivity I aspire to."

Kent brought six huge duffel bags, as "we" turned into "you." He wouldn't be caught dead ironing, but he swore that Jamie was under no pressure whatsoever.

Slowly, Jamie found he liked doing laundry, when it was Kent's. Every night Kent took home a few shirts, pressed jeans, bundled-up socks; jocks and underwear always found their way to the top of the pile. Every night Jamie slept in nothing but his KESSLER 22.

*　　　*　　　*

He listened to his mother's Broadway CDs and could tell all the plots by heart; Kent turned out to be a sucker for musicals too. "At last, something in common," Jamie exclaimed. They showed favorite movies to each other; for Jamie, "The Sound of Music," for Kent, "Oliver."

He took a risk, exposing himself like that. He'd never told anyone but his parents how much he loved that show from his toddler days. Jamie talked about everyone in the cast but the little blond star. Harry Secombe had a show on some Episcopal Channel they had back in Columbus, touring English churches and singing hymns. Kent had seen "Oliver" 46 times and never once noticed the man. But now he had to, and the fat old dude was pretty good. His big song was "Boy For Sale," which had only broken Kent's heart 46 times.

The bookmobile came by and Jamie found Dickens, Miss Austen and Ms. Brown, the later Jimmy Baldwin, Larry Duplechan, *A Smile in His Lifetime.* He sent *Oliver Twist* home with Kent, who tried to get into it, but it was "pretty thick. And it's really, really old, Jamie. I mean, dusty. All those old-timey words? I know the story, but I still couldn't figure out what he was saying half the time."

You can lead a horse to water but you can't make him literate. Jamie shrugged and polished off the Twist boy again in a day and a half, loving every installment. Whit Miller, though, he savored like fine chocolates, no more than two chapters a night, at bedtime.

* * *

Under Kent's supervision, Jamie learned to drive again, around the subdivision at 10 miles an hour. Honda's Gay employee group in Marysville, Ohio once wrote him, "We all read you, you're terrific. Our new Acura's fabu, we'd love to build you one." So he test-drove, and fell in love, and the car arrived with gifts, a vanity plate with his name, a rainbow decal, a copy of The Times signed by all the members. He wrote a story about them, "Out on the Assembly Line." He cherished that car.

He turned on the radio, sped all the way up to 15. But the classical station played atonal dissonance; he hit Seek until something made him stop, sounding good, kicking ass. It was a love song, with intelligent lyrics, "Something That We Do."

He started actively to listen to Kent's music. If he ever found out in New York, poor Foster would die. But it was a fine song, by real talent, Jamie loved it; so did his buddy.

* * *

Jamie asked, "Thanksgiving's coming; what do you typically do?" He loved to cook for the holidays.

"I work," Kent shrugged. "Thanksgiving's a washout for troopers. Wednesday I work a double, eight to midnight, then on the day itself I'm on noon to eight."

"A detective pulls traffic?"

"The whole post does, busiest travel days of the year. Speeders on Wednesday, drunk wife-beaters on Thursday, mall patrol Friday and Saturday, then speeders again."

So Jamie volunteered at a turkey dinner program for the poor and elderly, and got to be the captain of mashed potatoes. He helped serve 287 meals and gave thanks for all his blessings—especially a trooper on Ronald patrol.

*   *   *

They played video games to work on Jamie's eye-hand coordination; Kent always won and Jamie always accused him of cheating. Kent bragged, "I can't help it if you're slow." Competing was the finest thing they did together; they were both fierce about it, just one of them a little slow. They got into a habit of hitting each other like brothers do. Chattered like magpies and ate nonstop.

Kent was superior to Jamie in every game but one. Like all Hoosier homeowners, Thelma had a basketball hoop atop her garage; on the driveway her youngest son had painted a free throw line at 15 feet and a 3-point arc at 19'6". Kent realized what he was up against when he saw two dozen Rawlings NCAA balls racked up in the garage. Every night they played Horse. Every night Jamie won, 5-4; but he cursed his misses, terrified he'd lost his shot.

He hadn't, but he was uncoordinated rust. His shot slowly came back—with hours of practice while Kent was on duty. Then turnarounds, reverses, trick shots, Kent tried everything. He stood thirty feet away in the middle of Tad Lincoln Drive and miraculously sank a jumper; so did Jamie, eyes closed, trying not to smirk. Not once could Kent beat him. Scores dropped to 5-3, 5-2, even 5-1.

Kent hadn't played basketball since high school, hated him—and played him hard every night, knowing how much Jamie loved it. Jamie could barely keep from screaming his delight. Yet he only said one insult per night, a competitor but nice about it.

Kent might not have liked him as well if he didn't rub it in at least once. But the ego part of Kent was glad it was only once. He muttered, "You ain't even five-ten."

"I am too!" Jamie marched him right into the garage, stood in his stocking feet next to the wall, daring him to measure. "Be sure to mash down my hair!"

Kent made a mark. Measured. "Whaddayaknow, 5'10" and a quarter." Jamie jumped up and down like a madman over that longlost half-inch.

The next night Kent was getting skunked, the horse about to be saddled; Jamie grew nervous, but he made his shots. When 4-0 came, everything on the line, he dribbled from eight feet in the right side of the lane for a full minute. Kent knew something was up, so he had to use his final weapon. "You ain't got the guts to try it and fail."

"Ooh, fightin' words. You can't psych me, flatfoot. Prepare to meet your dee-struction." Jamie gathered his confidence, visualized; then all at once he bounced the ball hard on the left side with a killer spin. The ball caromed off the concrete, back high above the board—as he leapt with all his might and jammed it home.

Kent stared, flabbergasted and screeching at a five-foot ten-inch comatose slam dunk.

Jamie got his own rebound, looked away. Kent came to him, grasped his shoulders; Jamie clutched the ball, looked up at him, a little scared. Softly Kent said, "Horse."

Jamie smiled proudly, led him wordlessly inside.

* * *

Another opportunity lost; and Kent didn't even realize it till two days later. *You shoulda just kissed him, you retard!*

Kissing, the thing Kent most wanted; the last thing he could make himself do.

54

Pillow

At the cabin, Kent got his sleep pattern back to normal. All those nights at the hospital had messed up his rhythm. Throughout the coma he'd fought off the image of Jamie hanging from the tree—naked, beautiful, spurting red. When Kent did nod off, he dreamt the same horrific nightmare. He could never run fast enough to get there on time, his legs were weighted down. He'd scream out, wake up.

Then Jamie woke up and took the nightmares away. It was over now, it was the past. Kent was good at consigning losses to the past. He came up with a new sleeping strategy.

He reached for the second pillow, got it in the position he liked these days. Before, the other pillow had always been for show, to make the bedspread look right. Now he put it vertical and touching his left shoulder.

It was the second time he'd changed. When he was little he slept on his side, fetal position, pillow as big as he was between his legs, holding onto the blondest Oliver; protecting him, loving him and his cute English accent when no one else would; two boys together, best friends, an orphan and an only child on a great big Indiana farm.

They sang songs, and rode their ponies, and went exploring, and had adventures, and held hands, Kenty helping him climb over fences, or the big rocks behind the barn, or up trees in the hickory grove. Oliver was never as good a climber as Kent was, even then the big little man; English boys weren't Americans so Kenty always had to help him and arranged it that way, so Oliver needed him, loved him. And no one ever knew, not Mommy or Daddy, it was a secret.

Kent remembered little of this, only the feelings, and how he slept on his side until he outgrew the pillow. He was a back sleeper now, had been since third grade, the year he announced he should be called Kent.

But he still had every Oliver toy and lunchbox and game they'd ever bought him, the easiest child to please. Most of it was still back at the farm; in the attic, he thought, snorting at himself in the dark.

He got out of bed, went to his closet, found the little plastic statue, knew right where it was. Put it on his dresser without turning on a light. Went to his desk, took out the business card with the color mug shot on it. Propped the blond card on the little blond statue; then had to turn on the light, had to look. Framed on the wall was the $20 download, Jamie naked for Calvin Klein.

Got back in bed, wondering how he'd ever tell now; hoping lightning would strike, a magic wand, a happy ending with dancing and a wonderful song.

But no. He'd have to do it, and he had no earthly idea how.

He had trapped himself, afraid to speak the most basic truth to the one person in the world who would understand. *Don't ever lie to a reporter.*

Jamie might not love him; but he'd understand. And that was a form of love too.

Maybe Kent should just come out and say, "I'm Gay" and be done with it. But he honestly didn't believe that. He didn't know what he was anymore. Maybe there was another category that no one had thought of yet, for normal, masculine guys who love each other.

But he knew what Jamie would say; "That category exists, all right. It's called Gay." The boy had too much mouth on him.

But there was a much deeper problem; Kent's integrity. He had no right to ask Jamie to love him, when he hadn't told him that he let him down.

Kent wanted to tell him; he didn't look forward to it, but it had to be done. But when? As he recovered from a coma in the hospital? As he fell asleep standing up after the Dan Rather show? Or now that Jamie was home and they had so much fun together? How do you tell someone, "I'm the reason you got stabbed, but I love you, will you love me?"

If they were two separate issues, they fused in his mind. He wanted to kiss Jamie and make love to him. He had no right to entertain any such thought.

But he thought it constantly. He hoped it every night as he went to bed alone.

He pulled the extra pillow to his chest, closed his eyes, held it, loved it; not a boy anymore, but a man. He replayed the dream he had about Jamie that first night; the dream he'd gone to Slaughter in a panic over. Now it was his favorite bedtime companion.

Soon he slept, naked, and he'd never done that before either.

55

Sanctum Sanctorum

They spent Friday apart, so they could spend Saturday together.

The Day came: Purdue basketball. Jamie swooped his hair within a millimeter of its life. He wore Kent's gold Purdue sweater over black stretch jeans, the smallest pants he had. The school colors were old gold and black, but those jeans also hugged his little butt.

The bell rang. Kent wore tight Levi's, a red flannel shirt, fancy silver cowboy boots, a black satin baseball jacket from the Louisville Redbirds, an energetic look on his handsome face. He exclaimed, "You got your swoop back." Jamie hadn't expected him to notice. "You even wore my sweater. How much do you weigh today?"

Jamie was so proud he almost couldn't say it. "One seventy-five point two."

"Jamie, man, you're all the way back!" Kent hugged him. "Thank God. I can see it in your face. You're back, man, you're back! You look great. How do you feel?"

Jamie pumped his fist, "Go Purdue!" He left to get his jacket. Kent looked around the room till he happened on an oval mirror. His pressed jeans had a discolored spot on the crotch. He stared, eyes widening, till

Jamie returned. They went outside. The big red F-250 gleamed in the driveway. "Wow, your truck positively sparkles."

Kent swaggered, wordless and proud. They drove Boilermaker Avenue to Mackey Arena, listening to pre-game hype and farm commercials on the radio. Jamie stared out the window, trying to control his excitement.

Kent parked. Even the lots were buzzing. They could hear the crowd cheering inside, thirty minutes before gametime. Happy people headed for their gates, past TV trucks with satellite uplinks. Inside, the atmosphere was charged up. Gold-clad people were everywhere. Kent and Jamie passed displays for famous athletes, All-Americans, championship teams, national coaches-of-the-year, academic all-stars. Jamie made Kent stop at the last one, the greatest shrine of all, for kids with a Purdue University education, like Thelma had.

Then they went under the dome, saw the polished gold floor and scores of championship banners from the oldest, biggest, best conference in the nation, for the Big Ten's winningest university.

Jamie ran down to courtside, bolted over the fence, knelt and touched his lips to the floor. Anyone else might have been arrested, but a state trooper yanked him back up, "Only do that at IU!" Jamie punched Kent's shoulder, pretended to vomit. The band was jumping, so Jamie jumped with it.

They got their seats—great ones on the lower level, behind the scorer's table. "How did you rate these? People bequeath these seats to each other in their wills."

"Connections," Kent winked. He was an assistant baseball coach at the Right School, not that he let on. He liked keeping little advantages over Mr. Brainhead.

Cheerleaders turned somersaults, a locomotive let out clouds of steam. The visiting RedHawks entered, Jamie and Kent applauded them. Then The Team took the floor and the place went nuts. Students with giant P flags ran around as the band played "Hail, Purdue," 14,123 people jumping to their feet, the 104th straight sellout crowd clapping in rhythm during the verse. Jamie's abs worked rapidly in and out, suppressing a sob over that All-American band. For the first chorus it went into sing-along mode, only the woodwinds carrying the melody, and everyone sang and clapped, "Hail, Hail to Old Purdue, all hail to our Old Gold and Black!" Kent beat his hands together for Jamie's school song. Then the full band blasted a repeat—drum work was new and more intense this year—cheerleaders flipped each other senseless and Jamie sang his heart out, "All hail, our old Purdue!" Trumpets went into a fanfare to close on a high note, with low-pitched brass belting the final ta-dah, ta-daaaa!

And then the roar…of shared ecstasy, the season opener in Basketball Land.

The band went into its followup jingle and Jamie danced along, Bump, bah, bum, bah-da—bump, bah, bum, bah-da—bump, bah, bum, bah-da—dot-dah-da, doot-de-deedle-oo, pow pow pow! "Go Purdue!"

Shivers raced down his back. He'd been to Broadway, London, Paris, Milan, Tokyo, Rio, Hollywood; but Mackey Arena in Basketball Land was the most glamourous place on his earth. Dot-dah-da, doot-de-deedle-oo, pow pow pow! "Go Purdue!"

It was because of the students. Players, certainly, but the kids in the band, on the sidelines, in the stands, they all had it. They were Indiana kids, farm and city kids, kids from around the nation and worldwide, studying to be astronauts, engineers, pharmacists, physicists, dancers, poets, businesspeople—fresh-faced, innocent, ready to go. They brought tears to his eyes, but here as nowhere else, he fought tears off. Tears in this arena he reserved for the National Championship, nothing less. Tears in this arena he converted into defense, into points, into wins.

But it wasn't just the students; above all, it was his mother. Purdue University made her, and therefore made him. Sports provided the occasion to publicly declare his loyalty. "Go Purdue!"

Kent studied him, highly amused, then poked him, "I should have known you'd be this rabid."

Below them famous TV hypemeisters did their intros: "We're in one of the greatest environments in all of college basketball, baby!"

And that was an understatement. A buzzer blared. Coaches and players were introduced. The crowd quieted as ROTC students presented the flag. Jamie tried not to think about military discrimination. The band played "The Star-Spangled Banner."

In Basketball Land everyone sang the National Anthem with their hands over their hearts; no whooping it up till after the very last note. It was a point of honor. The Big Ten did the same. Hate each other cheerfully, they loved each other dearly, as neighbors, as rivals, as friends.

Then a reprise of "Hail, Purdue!" Men cheerleaders tossed women cheerleaders to the rafters and caught them. Even the cheerleaders were athletes.

Finally what everyone came for, jump ball. The Boilers raced to an early lead, but missed coverages led to some easy Miami points, and Purdue's Coach Reed jumped to his feet and flung his jacket off after four minutes. Bingo Peters substituted carefully, matching up his boys to grab whatever advantage they could. Miami took its first lead with 8:02 in the half. The crowd was loud but anxious.

At the next time out, Reed drowned out the band, screaming to the top row, flapping his arms, stomping up and down the sidelines. He was a wonderful guy, but he sure looked mean on TV. His boys stared at the floor, assistant coaches gave furious lectures; order was restored two seconds before the camera's red light went back on.

It was Purdue 41, Miami 38 at the half. Jamie and Kent stood, stretched, moved with the crowd toward restrooms and concession stands. Half the mob wore Purdue sweats, T-shirts for the football team, women's basketball, Final Four teams, track and field, golf, swimming, baseball, crew; anything athletic, everything Purdue. There were older couples, families with kids, undergraduates on dates, foreign engineering students grinning and yabbling, long-limbed Black guys jiving and joking in groups of eight or a dozen. The whole international town was there.

Kent and Jamie headed outdoors. They discussed the game for a few minutes, then Jamie mentioned that his mother's house sold yesterday.

He might as well have shoved an anvil into Kent's gut. "That's awful quick, ain't it? You just listed it two days ago. Did you get what you wanted out of it?"

"Five thousand more than the asking price. It's a custom home in a modest neighborhood; market it as a starter and demand is strong. It's a good area for children. I never could believe, really, that she bought on the outskirts instead of in the city of West Lafayette. West Side is the best school system in the state."

"So I've heard. Remind me to send my kids to the county schools." *Jeez, how stupid, Kent.*

"She liked to live inexpensively, cutting costs was her thing. Two bidders competed over price."

"Nice work if you can get it." Kent knew he'd never get anywhere this way, but he couldn't think.

"It moves along settling the estate, which is the important thing. With the trust and all that legal mumbo-jumbo, the lawyer says it could be settled by March."

"What are your plans?"

"I'm going home tomorrow. There's nothing to keep me here and Casey needs me back. It will be good for me to start working again. Give me something new to think about." *What a rip it will be to lose you, Kent. But it has to be done, so the sooner the better.*

"You can't go yet. You're not cleared by the doctors."

"I'm tired of having doctors run my life. I'd like to run it myself for a change. Besides, I have a fine osteopath in Columbus."

What Jamie was doing with the world's handsomest Straight guy who constantly threw temptation at him, he did not know. But this trip to watch hoops made it clear; they were good, even permanent friends, though they'd never have the intimacy he craved.

He looked at the arena. *This is the first time I've been to Mackey since I hauled ass through the sleet for the Rickster.*

I love you, Rick. He was answered with a slow, quiet, unmistakable current down his spine, that both told him Rick loved him, and told him he was gone.

Jamie sighed, picked up the conversation again. "I called Casey yesterday after I got back from signing the real estate papers. He's been doing my job and his both. After this, I could use some nice, wholesome greed, graft and corruption. Maybe the treasurer of an AIDS foundation's socking away a few thousand to keep up the payments on her BMW. Something nice and clean like that. No blood, no dead people."

Kent stared off across the street.

"I've been busy packing Mom's personal effects. Kenny Dyson's arranged to sell the good furniture for me, then there's the AIDS thrift shop to call."

"Is it hard to pack up her stuff?"

"Excruciating. All these little things to remember her by? But it's also sweet. She was a good old girl, even if she could be a terror when she had to have her way. We're all getting family photographs, mortars and pestles, kitchen gadgets that say 'her.' Things none of us needs and none of us can live without. It's a real job, dividing the stuff up. I want to be perfect at it, to see that Danny and Stone get their full measure of things with sentimental value. But there is no perfect. She loved mashed potatoes and gravy; her 59¢ potato masher is our most beloved icon, with three sons to give it to. I'm making it a traveling trophy. Every year on her birthday, it goes to the next son."

"You're packing up for Ohio just like that?"

"Kent, it's time. Your work on the case was fantastic. It's over now. You've been my number one booster to try and recover, and now I have. I wanted you to see me at full strength; you've given me my health back.

Kent, you have my undying gratitude for all you've done for me…" Jamie hesitated, their eyes locked, "…and for my people."

Kent frowned, didn't feel he deserved such praise. "What are you going to do, though? Just go back to your job?"

"Either that or I'm moving to New York for CBS News." Jamie glanced at his watch. "Hey, Jocko, think we ought to go back in?"

"Guess so. Darn." They headed inside. Jamie'd never called him Jocko before.

"Stop." Kent stopped. "I get to enjoy the most normal, exciting thing, a basketball game at Mackey Arena, because I'm alive. Kent, I thank you most profoundly."

Kent watched the banty rooster push in ahead of him.

The game stayed tight the entire second half. Jamie was totally absorbed, commented throughout, yelled a lot, cheered every good Purdue play and a few good Miami ones. Kent asked, "Did you play in high school?"

Jamie hesitated, then proudly said, "I played the point for one glorious season at Chicago. That's where I went to high school."

Kent didn't catch the subtle preposition. "Way to go, thoroughbred." Jamie smiled. "Did Danny play?"

"Stone's our athlete, Danny's our coach. I can't tell you how many hours I spent as a kid while Danny drilled me on the fundamentals; or just watching sports on TV, listening to him. I love that man. Every day I read The Rocky Mountain News online to see what he's writing. He taught me everything I know about sports." He glanced at Kent. "He knew exactly who you were, which made me so proud."

"I was surprised. I'm four years behind him, why should he know who the local athletes were? But he did."

"You earned his attention. Your career was brief but brilliant. You sacrificed your body for your teammates."

Kent grew silent, thinking about someone else who did that.

"Great pass, D'Shawn! Oh, Gary, don't put it on the floor, whip it around!" Purdue was using its size now, working the ball in underneath to a tall, cute freshman. The fans could see it, the network could see it, the blind could see it—and the pass went off the freshman's fingers, out of bounds, Miami.

Jamie smiled in frustration and forgave the clumsy guy; he was cute. Jamie found the clock, 6:16 to go. Kent stared ahead, making fists and relaxing, making fists, on and on. Jamie said, "We're the better team, but we always lose confidence if we're not in control."

"Unh." Kent looked all focused concentration.

Bingo Peters put his star back in and Miami elevated its game. The RedHawks worked the ball inside, trying to take advantage of the cute freshman. Purdue's point guard left his man to help out and instantly the ball flew back out beyond the arc, a three-point shot, good. Miami by one. Time out. Jamie exhaled, leaned back. Kent was still working those fists, staring ahead.

Jamie cast about for something to say. He decided not to talk so much, maybe he was ruining it for Kent.

They were silent for several minutes, till Kent said softly, "Don't go."

"I want to. Why would I not go? I just sold my mother's house. I have to go."

"Don't. Stay here." A beat. Some cheers. The fans. The band. "Don't go."

"Man, what are you talking about? I'm tired of being disabled. I want to work. Why are you saying this?"

Purdue tied, Miami went ahead, Purdue regained the lead, slowly built it. There wasn't much time left. Then Purdue broke the game wide open—a sensational steal by the star forward, who charged down the floor for the basket. Jamie, Kent, the fans leapt to their feet, the forward ran closer, one more step and a no-look flip back to the tall, cute freshman, who jammed it home.

And was fouled! Jamie cheered his lungs out, glad to be alive. Kent put his hands on Jamie's shoulders as he jumped up and down; then Jamie faced him, Kent's arms slipped around him—and the moment turned electric.

They stared at each other; their bodies went physical. Jamie broke out in a sweat.

Kent breathed in shallow gasps. He felt danger all around, but he didn't care anymore, he couldn't lose Jamie, not after all this. But still, Kent was paralyzed.

He wanted Jamie with a pure raw hunger.

And this time, Jamie knew it.

With two fingers he traced from Kent's cheekbone, down slowly to lips. Then he raised up on tiptoes and kissed him.

Kent's jaw dropped. That scared Jamie, but he knew what he'd just seen. He stood tall and unapologetic and terrified.

"Man, don't leave me."

"I love you, Kent. If that's wrong for you, just say the word, I'll never trouble you again. But I love you."

Jamie turned back to the court, trembling at what he'd just done; he'd moved on a Straight man. Kent's hands fell away; he stammered, "How do two guys do this?"

"Is it only attraction you feel?" Jamie stood like a statue till Kent pulled him down. "If it's only physical, tell me this instant."

"It's completely physical. But Jamie, I love you so much it hurts."

Jamie's mind shattered. "Can this be happening?"

"I've been so scared, Jamie. Intimidated."

"It's only that we're two men."

"I'm masculine, you know I am."

Kent's logic was so nonsensical that Jamie punched him. "You're a stud. Two men, don't you get it?"

Kent liked getting punched, something familiar in this unknown territory. Still, he knew his words would never be more important than they were right now. "If you'll let me, I'll show you love every day."

"This is magic, it's impossible. How does a Straight guy love me?"

Kent looked around, then said under his breath, "Jamie, I feel normal, same as always, but… I might be Gay. I ain't sure no more. I didn't know I could have these feelings till I met you." Saying it changed him. "Man, I'm burning up for you. And you feel the same for me?"

Jamie searched for articulation. It was time for complete honesty, his strongest suit. "When my mother died and I went crazy all alone, who came and slept on a pallet for me?"

"I had that big air mattress built for two, and there you were down on the floor. I wanted to pull you up with me so I could hold you. But I was scared, I couldn't do it."

Finally Jamie realized that Kent needed him to make the first move—the one thing he'd never do with a Straight man. Until now! "When I woke up from the coma, before I found words, I knew I loved you. Since then it's grown a thousand times deeper, I cherish every minute we have. But I thought there was no future. Then you come again and I fall for you every time."

"Just tell me two guys can make it in this feeble, stupid world."

"We can, I promise. I'll show you how." Jamie put his hand on Kent's shoulder, calmed and centered him. "Kent, I want you in my life forever. You are the kindest, most thoughtful man I've ever met."

"Jamie, I ain't perfect. Just let me be in your life forever."

"Can we sleep together? Tonight?"

"Naked? Please?"

"Skin to skin, warmth to warmth. Oh, man."

Kent jumped up, fist raised to the dome, "All right! All right!" The rest of the arena stood too and cheered as Kent pulled Jamie back up, hugged and danced him around, jumping for joy. Everyone else danced too, shouted, hollered and generally went nuts, as they often do in

Basketball Land. "Man oh man, I just won the lottery! I am gonna get laid by the most gorgeous man alive. Brad Pitt, eat your heart out!"

Jamie burst into laughter.

Kent pulled his little guy down to the bleachers again, just an excuse to touch him. "Naked, man," Kent said huskily. "We gon' make us some naked love tonight."

Jamie found out why naked love got them a standing ovation. The announcer intoned, "Personal foul on Wilson of Miami, that's his fifth; plus a technical foul on the Miami bench, the team's twelfth." Jamie searched his memory banks at warp speed, found a file marked Basketball Land. "Oh." He looked at Kent, smiled like a doofus.

"Oh," Kent agreed delightedly, squeezing Jamie's knee.

Jamie glanced at his knee, then at the scoreboard: Purdue 84, Miami 76, 2:04 to play, Purdue at the line, two freebies and the ball, the season opener on national TV—and he'd just kissed Kent Kessler in the Holy of Holies!

Plunk, Jamie keeled over dead, 'cause this had to be heaven.

Kent set him back upright and winked, "Yeah, man, it's in the bag."

"It's in the sack!"

"That too. Man, I can't wait."

Jamie spied their thighs. Two lumps were forming. He hitched his eyebrows at Kent—and ostentatiously adjusted himself like a cocky centerfielder. He yelled at the cute freshman waiting at the foul line, "Go, Boilers, let's put it in the hole!"

56

Vincero

Kent pulled Jamie's arm, "Let's go." Jamie never left games early, but Kent Was Life, Everything Else Just Details. They ran the corridor, then Kent grabbed him and spun him around by the forearms, Jamie squealing, his feet orbiting in front of the All-Academic Best-Evers. They laughed their way to the exit—where Jamie opened the door for Kent, stood aside, staring him right in the eye.

Kent smiled and strolled outside. Jamie broke into a run, "Beatcha!"

"Oh no, you won't," Kent vowed, turning on his sprint. Jamie pounded the pavement. He slammed into the pickup first, but just barely. In a fair race he'd be no match for Kent's long legs. "Cheater," Kent smilingly accused. They climbed into the cab.

"How, Kent, why? When, for heaven's sake?"

"Let's go to supper, man, and talk about it there." Jamie had to eat so he'd keep that weight on. "Lord, we're in my truck and you love me back. Hot dawg!"

Kent draped his arm around his boyfriend, pulled him close and honked the horn all the way up Boilermaker Avenue, celebrating the biggest win of his life.

He spun into the parking lot at Costanza's, found a spot by the pizza parlor in the rear; but he headed them to the fine dining room in front with a hand on Jamie's neck. They got to the doors, Kent held one open; Jamie shrugged and wandered back where he came from. Kent ran, grabbed him and shoved his butt inside.

Jamie got decorous and asked for a quiet booth. Costanza's was the best restaurant in town. "Thank you for bringing me here."

"I know enough not to take you for pizza on our first date. I'd never live it down."

"Is this our first date?"

"Why did I make that truck sparkle? I had a date."

"Man, I love you." Kent's chest swelled. Jamie didn't want food, he wanted manhood. So he looked around in self-defense; slowly other scenes came to him. "I brought my mother here often. This is the first time I've been here in awhile, though."

"I've never been here before. It's a nice place."

"Nice places are the kind I go to, ace."

"Can't feed you Cat Chow when you're expecting Fancy Feast." Jamie tried to box his ears, but Kent blocked him with big open hands. They read their menus to keep from grabbing each other. "What was that steak you got me in the hospital, with the vegetables and sauces? It was great."

"Chateaubriand. I couldn't go wrong getting you a slab of beef tenderloin."

"I'm a meat and potatoes man," Kent agreed. But Costanza's was expensive. He studied, announced for ten-dollar lasagna. "Is that okay?"

"You're asking my permission?"

"Don't I have to?"

Jamie plunked his elbow on the table, bent his arm backwards. "Ooh, copboy do bite back."

"That night was such a turning point. Serious as you are, I got to see your fun side for a change. And man, I loved that guy. Thank God I finally told you." Kent got quiet. "Thank you for introducing me to your Mom. It's terrible that she died, Jamie, but at least I got to meet her. I'm awful glad. I never got to introduce you to my Dad."

He missed his father every single day. "She said of you, 'Nice eyes.' Right to the heart of the matter."

"I've never heard you talk about her. If you feel like it, I want to hear everything."

"It would be a sacrilege not to talk about her here. This was one of our places." Jamie looked into the past. "I picture her in a classic red dress from Talbot's, with a silk scarf and a gold pin I got her at Saks; whenever she was with one of her sons, she wore jewelry he gave her. She was a good dresser, put together impeccably.

"But her professionalism far outweighed concern for her looks. She worked with seriously ill patients, even saved lives by preventing drug interactions. She knew her patients personally, their baselines, their histories; she went to see them in the hospital. She was very diplomatic, but at times she fought with doctors. She questioned orders; on rare occasions she refused to fill a prescription. Doctors were outraged at first, but she was right; they learned to rely on her, twelve scripts turned into four and the patients got better. She was amazingly good."

"You're so proud of her."

"I sure am. She was an utter professional. She was also Indiana's Junior Miss, first runner-up in the national scholarships for high school seniors; academics are a major part of the scoring, it's not just a beauty pageant. It's brains, talent, fitness and poise under pressure."

"The same qualities I've seen in you."

"She was born dirt-poor. When she didn't win it all, she didn't get to go to college. When she finally did go, she did it on her own. Pharmacy's tough, man. Mom graduated early, but a bachelor's degree takes six years. Engineers graduate in five."

"You're not just a Purdue fan. You're a Mom fan."

"Always. It takes genius to overcome poverty. Purdue is where she overcame it. We owe everything to this university."

"I'm proud I went to IU; but all of a sudden I'm sorry I went to the Wrong School."

"So am I. But I'm glad you went to the next best place."

"What was she like when you'd bring her here?"

"We dressed up. She knew good clothes and she'd pay for them; but she hated to pay for good food. Even after she made professional money, the price of food was unreasonably important to her. What a meal costs is often proportional to its taste. If you can't cook—and she couldn't—pay the person who can. But no, food was a place to cut costs. That was the poverty talking. She was crazed. So I brought her here every chance I got. So did Stone, it turns out, for the same reason, with the same results."

"Reminds me of my Dad. He'd blow a wad anytime he felt like it, but for years he bitched about 100-watt light bulbs when I could still do my homework with a 75. Mom finally marched him to the store and made him compare. There's no big difference in price based on wattage. The protective box costs more than the light bulbs do."

These were like the stories the Foster boys told each other after the funeral; intimate, family-building. "Mom and Arnie lived off early-bird specials at cafeterias, Senior Night at some VFW hall; 99¢ all-you-can-eat catfish, my idea of dreadful. So I'd take her out and she'd let me order for her, sometimes we'd nosh on appetizers all night. You get variety that way, and you learn what a restaurant is capable of." Kent could picture Jamie with his Mom.

"Then the bill would come, and of course I was paying, but she'd always ask how much it was, 'Now son, don't spend so much money, grump grump.' Then she'd leave a good tip. It was all a ritual, though, she was thrilled I spent the money on her—she loved the food and the fact that we did something special together. She was terrific to take out. We had the finest, freest conversations."

"You two had fun."

"It's the great thing about dining out. You turn normal life into an occasion with no effort at all. People cater to you, all you have to do is give them money. What's a better bargain than that? And here we are, on this life-changing night. Our first date!" An idea popped into Jamie's head. "You're not having lasagna, boy. We're doing this up right."

Kent grinned, "See, I knew I had to ask first."

Someone came to take their drink order; Jamie asked for a modest champagne. When the cork was popped, Jamie lifted his glass. Kent's brown eyes shone in the dim light. The sound system began Franz Schubert's Unfinished Symphony; romantic, Gay music Jamie first heard live at Purdue University. "To Beauty. To Hero. To Commander."

They clinked. Kent shivered, *He likes how I look! Little blond stud with the movie-star face, and he wants to be with me?* He let himself enjoy what he felt. It wasn't hard, but then again it was. He adjusted himself.

"Don't do that, man," Jamie warned. "I can't take it. I'm going to eat you alive."

Kent panted, came out a little more. "I want you to."

"I'll cover you with sauce and feast on your tender loins."

If Kent thought Jamie was intense before, he picked up a clue about what their future love life might be like.

Kent said, "I can't believe this is happening. This is the most beautiful day of my life, and it's just now dawning on me how stupid I've been."

A waiter hovered in the vicinity, straightened silver. Jamie motioned, asked Kent, "Do you like paté?" Kent shrugged. "Chicken livers?"

"Heck yes, one of my all-time favorite things."

"If you'd rather have chateaubriand, they do it well here. Or try something new?"

Kent smiled, "You pick."

"Beef Wellington, baked potato and steamed vegetables for this gentleman; linguine speziale for me. Romaine salads, no iceberg; low-fat dressing, but not until ten minutes from now. If your tomatoes are good, I want a ton of them; if they're pink tennis balls from a Florida crate, forget it. A glass of top claret and one of chardonnay with the entrées; and will you ask the chef to take his or her time? One of us likes to wolf down his food, while I like a leisurely dinner." Kent poked him. "And since we're here to talk…"

"I'll get the drapes, sir." The waiter untied them at the front of the table. Kent thought they were there for show.

Jamie said, "Thank you, you're quite good. We're glad to be here." When they were closed into the booth he chuckled, "We're like Perry Mason and Della Street, hiding out from Lieutenant Tragg."

Kent had never been in a booth with drapes to shut out the world before. Jamie said, "Man, you're the complete package—brains, heart, health, looks. I can't believe I'm so lucky. Tell me your story. I love you, Kent, but I know so little of your past. Maybe now's the time to say all the things we've hidden from each other."

Kent rolled up his sleeves, exposing huge, hairy, muscled forearms. Jamie thought about devouring them. *And for my appetizer, a nice big order of brachioradials.*

"Well, ever since I've been on my own, all my energy has gone into either work or play. None of it's gone into… me, the way I am now, with you. Jamie, I've loved you for months, and I kept my mouth shut. I was stupid—scared is what it was. Me, the one who ain't afraid of nothin', except 175-pound blondboys. Then when I do finally show you my feelings, you're here with me, just like that. I'm trying to take it all in. You told me from day one you'd never put a move on me. If I'd opened up to you sooner, we could have been together this whole time, when you were recovering. I could have helped you more, maybe."

Jamie struggled to absorb such tenderness, sweetness, honesty. "You couldn't have helped me more, unless you slept with me. Man, I wish I knew what you were feeling."

"Know what I was going through till I met you? I was lonely, Jamie. This gradual creeping loneliness was killing off my insides."

"You needed a friend to be intimate with."

"A buddy to kick back with, who didn't expect me to be a big bad trooper all the time. I've got a softer side, Jamie."

"Kent, that's the part I love the most."

"You bring it out in me. 'Cause you're so loving yourself."

"When have I shown you lovingness? When have I had the courage?"

"Ask Davey when you've shown it. Ask the Gay-bashers, ask Glenn Ferguson, ask your Mom!"

Jamie covered his eyes. "But I want to do loving things for you."

"You have, by letting me in your life. Know what amazes me most? I'm not just a dumb jock or a robo-cop anymore; with you I'm a whole human being. I need you, Jamie. For the first time in my life I know who Kent is."

"Hard and soft both."

"Poached egg, huh?"

"No, Commander, you're squiggly sperm."

"Wanna be. You sure are. Now my loneliness is gone, Jamie. I met you, and all of a sudden life got exciting. Different every day. A little too exciting, as a matter of fact. That coma scared the poop out of me. Don't you ever pull that stunt again."

"I won't." The idea of coma as a stunt made Jamie smile. "Were you mad at me?"

"At times. Then you woke up and I was overjoyed. These last two months I've had so much fun, I can't wait to get to your house every night. All day long I wonder, What's Jamie doing now? Is he eating, working out, is he pissed off at the news again?"

Kent loved to tease him about this, because Jamie was very free with his views about the news. "Kent, you said you might be Gay. You're not sure?"

"No. Can I be Straight, tonight at least, and want your body? Love your heart?"

"You sure can. When did this start?"

"The day we met. It took me a long time to sort out, but every time I saw you, my body was just… drawn to you. Like a magnet, I didn't have a choice about it. I'm sure you could tell."

Jamie studied his champagne. "Indeed I could not. Only at the arena did you indicate your attraction."

"But every time I saw you I had my hands on you. Then I'd decide I wasn't going to touch you anymore; then I'd see you and there I was, on you again. That time I tried to hug you and you pushed away from me? Man, that scared me off. Then after the TV show you actually came to me. Jamie, I was ecstatic. But I still didn't say nothing. I should have kissed you right then. A Gay guy, what would you have said but stop? I was so intimidated."

"Homophobia intimidates. So does outness, I guess."

"Talk about mixed feelings—I want you, I'm scared of you, I don't want you, yes I do! Man, I had a wet dream the night we met. Scared me to death. Had to go see the major—not that I told him or anything."

"What were we doing in your dream?"

"Just touching. Shirtless, in jeans, both of us. Gosh, you looked so good. I was in the woods, setting up camp, mountains and a lake and no one else around. Then you came along the trail, we got to talking, I reached for your hair and… you touched me back. You touched my face."

With two fingers Jamie traced from Kent's cheekbone to his lips.

"I think you kissed me. And all of a sudden I was falling, or we were pulling each other down, and I knew we were going to make love somehow. I woke up before anything happened, I just knew you were going to… love me. Man, I soaked those BVDs."

Jamie melted.

"The feelings were so different from how I've always felt. Ever since then I couldn't keep my hands off you."

"You are the sweetest, strongest, most caring man I've ever met. Tell me how you got here. Start with school."

"I was never any good in class, I had to study real hard. My coaches helped me out all the time. Dad used to get after me something fierce. Not like you. You had to be the teacher's pet I just hated, and was so jealous of." They smiled; Jamie didn't deny it. "I drifted in high school, playing ball and having fun; we were worried I'd flunk out of college maybe. But once I got there something finally clicked. I learned how to learn, and then I just wanted to keep on doing it." Kent opened himself. "Learning's fun. There's a joy in it, you know? New worlds open up you never saw before."

"Those new worlds are important to country kids."

"I lucked out and got this great sociology prof my freshman year, a master teacher. At midterms I got my first A ever. You think Dad and me didn't get excited about that? An A, in college, when we were scared they were going to toss me out? I got an A!"

Kent pictured his father's enthusiasm. "Him and Mom drove down to Bloomington and bought me a steak dinner, so he could show me how proud he was. My Dad didn't get to go to college, Jamie. He was smart, though. He bought me a beer—even though we're Methodists and I was underage. He pounded the table and said, 'Give this man a beer, he's an A student!' Gosh, what a fun night.

"That whole business with school, before then? I was lazy, Jamie. I had a bad attitude I learned from a bunch of dumb jocks—peer pressure I didn't even recognize. I looked down on smart kids and used sports to coast my way through. Then once I got to IU and I saw how much better the players were, I had to buckle down. And I did, by gosh. Then soch led into criminal justice, and soon I was hot to be the best darn cop on the force someday, like Columbo or something, but smart, educated."

"You pack those jeans much better than Columbo."

"Glad you noticed." Jamie threw bread at him. "College was all baseball and hitting the books. As a sophomore I won Big Ten Player of the Year, at the same time rooks finally got bigger contracts; Dad said I should think of turning pro, so I did. Then a year in the bus leagues, living on burgers and TV, waiting to get called up."

Jamie's jaw sagged. His lover played Major League Baseball. Not just some guy he knew; his lover.

His thighs got very impressed. *It's not just the athletics; it's the work it takes to get that high. Awesome discipline. Total commitment to become the best.*

No one out-commits you!

He finally allowed himself to embrace it, and rattled off stats better than Danny could have. "In two years, 77 home runs, 259 RBIs, 352 hits, 72 steals, a .287 batting average your first year, .318 the second. An All-Star, you played the Braves into the World Series!" Jamie's eyes flashed. Foreplay was now. "You, big, s-tud."

Kent was amazed at Jamie's knowledge, his eyes, his mind. "You make me feel like one."

Jamie adjusted himself. "You make me act like a centerfielder."

"I want you to." They were desperate for each other, and in a public place. "Is sex going to be like this?"

"You're an athlete, I'm a professional sex symbol. Let's find out."

"Man, those pictures are hot. I want your body." But if he didn't chill out, Kent knew he would pop. "After I got hurt I went to the state police academy, got assigned to Bloomington, finished my bachelor's degree." Jamie praised him for that. "I got promoted to corporal the first year I was eligible, then the sergeant's job here; we sold a couple acres Dad willed to me, and I bought me a cabin on the Tippecanoe River."

"Will you tell me about the injury sometime? And your father?"

"Someday soon." Jamie rubbed Kent's hand, a small attempt at healing the pain. Kent brought Jamie's hand to his lips. Its bruises were gone; he kissed where they had been. "You're what I needed all along to get past it. I didn't know that until the last two months. Jamie, I saw you working so hard to recover, and it reminded me of someone I knew.

When you have a big chunk ripped out of your life, you gotta fill it up with something."

"I know. What has heterosexuality been like for you?"

"Half-dismal. I've wanted love in my life a long, long time. But I never met the right girl, and it ain't like I didn't try. I've had experiences. They were fun, I guess, but not all that great, and I realized I don't want just sex. I want love. Sure, I like to poke it, but ain't it supposed to mean something?"

"It means something to me."

"I almost got engaged once, but she hurt me bad. And there was never much spark there with other women, so I pretty much gave it up. Then Glenn Ferguson's killed and before I can even get started, in walks the famous CI, who just happens to be the cutest guy on the planet. And zoom, I'm off the hormone chart."

"But there are other cute guys out there. Why me?"

"You're my little Oliver."

Jamie was slowly astonished. Kent said softly, "My beautiful little blondboy, with the heart of gold. The one I've been in love with my whole life."

Jamie couldn't speak.

"You're openly Gay, don't hide nothing, put it out there front and center. Which made you available maybe. I've never met anyone who did that, Jamie. Man, the courage you have, when Gay people are so hated.

"I love your personality most of all, you have this strong character, I respect you completely. Gosh, you're so tough. My Oliver grows up and he's my crimefighting partner! That's beyond perfect, Jamie, I couldn't have dreamed you any better."

Jamie kept listening, wholly in love with this man.

"Your stance challenged me to know where I stand. He likes guys and he don't care who knows it. It's right there on his business card, Ohio Gay Times, wanna make something of it?" Kent chuckled, "So

I'm thinking about this and talking about hyoid bones at the same time. Branh, mental overload. System error, bombs away. Hit Restart, lose all data."

They laughed. "You're so witty, Kent. I enjoy you every minute."

"Do you know how hard it was for me to keep from touching your hair that first day? If you hadn't been such a pro the way you handled yourself, I'd never have gotten through it. That whole interview it's all I thought about. Like tonight. Your hair is so beautiful."

Kent eyed the curtains, realized what they were for; moved over to sit next to his guy. Their thighs touched; Sergeant Kent Kessler of the Indiana State Police reached out, and for the first time, stroked his man's hair.

Over and over he traced the pattern across Jamie's forehead, to the side, the back. The hair was thick and incredibly soft. His touch was so light Jamie floated. Kent's face filled with wonder. The electricity in Jamie's body flowed nonstop.

When the big dark hand came near his face again, he kissed it, long and slow, then held it to his cheek. The smallest of touches contained all the excitement and sexuality and tenderness they felt.

Kent nuzzled Jamie's ear. Jamie snuggled, patted Kent's belly, rubbed great abs. Jamie was queer for abs. "Stud didn't consider being Gay. I knew when I was 13."

"How did that happen?"

"One day I noticed Logan Gregory's ass. Then I noticed Chuck O'Hara's. Then it was Mike Phillips's crotch. Two's a coincidence, three's a pattern. So I read up on the Gay thing; turns out I'm a beneficiary of my elders' love and self-sacrifice. What American can't understand a civil rights movement? Is my mother allowed to vote? At 14 I was arrested at my first AIDS protest."

"How like you, Jamie." Kent grinned, "Did you fall for the cop that time too?"

"She was a nice Black lady who said I should have shouted louder. Man, I'm so proud of you, an enforcer of people's rights. Kent, there's no higher calling."

"What different paths we've taken to meet up. Me doing baseball, a traditional mindless jock. You arrested as a kid, standing up for your beliefs. Take me to a protest sometime? Away from home?"

"I'd love to. Now talk sex to me, Jocko, so you can get promoted to Double-A. It's about two men. Neither one plays the woman's role. We're two cowboys. You're Butch Cassidy and I..." Jamie shook out his yellow hair, "am the Sundance Kid."

Kent touched himself. "You like that, Sundance?"

"I like that, Butch, and I've got one too."

"Guess what I'm wearing, Jocko."

"Don't wanna guess, Jocko. Wanna see. Wanna show you."

"You show me yours, Sundance, I'll show you mine."

"Butch, crawl under the table and commit a misdemeanor."

"I might arrest you for soliciting, Sunny Boy, an hour from now. Put you in handcuffs. Strip-search you."

"Jocko, I'll make sure you're not hiding contraband up Uranus."

Kent laughed, quit playing, a little threatened; he went back to his story. "I just knew I was different, Jamie. I figured I must not have strong sexual feelings the way other guys do. They talk about how great sex is, and me, I'm just backward, the complete opposite of a sex-crazed athlete. But the night I saw you dance, I had no doubt anymore. I had proof I could be Gay. Maybe I've been lying to myself the whole time. I have lots of sexual feelings when you do stuff like that." Kent patted his abs.

Then he knew this was the opening he'd been searching for.

"We're taught to lie to ourselves." Jamie sipped champagne. "When did I dance? How does a guy get proof he might be Gay?"

"It started at the hotel, the first time I saw your body. Supposed to catch a killer and—man, I wanted to slam you down and love you. That's what you're built for, Jamie. That's what you need."

Jamie began to glimpse his future sex life too.

His masculine feelings came from deep inside him. But Kent's hand on his neck, his opening doors, were masculine too; that's what made him overpoweringly sexy. Jamie's strengths were considerable, but this year he'd earned a Ph.D. in vulnerability. He cared for Ricky for five long years. Then when Thelma died, when he got stabbed, he couldn't pretend anymore that he was invincible. He needed a strong man—and Kent was there for him, every night, fully there. For a man like that Jamie'd happily loosen up; it might be fun to get slammed.

Then he remembered Kent's softer side. "It's what you're built for, too."

"Probably." Kent didn't blink. "Let's find out."

"Man, I worship you."

That word excited and scared Kent; he went with the excitement. "I didn't want to catch a killer, I wanted to get naked with you. I wanted to sleep in each other's arms."

"And I ended up with Tommy Ford and Dr. Crumbo instead? Fuck this stabbing crap, someone shoot me!"

Every laugh put the trauma further behind them; and that called up Kent's long-delayed confession. "Jamie, things happened that night that I'm never going to discuss with you. It's a blessing you don't remember. Please trust me. I'm not filling in any blanks except on a need-to-know basis."

"I trust you, Commander."

"This you need to know. You danced with a guy at the bar that night, a stranger. I got super-jealous and super-aroused. I creamed my jeans over you, in a public place, when I was on duty to catch a killer.

"When the scene came down I was in the wrong john trying to clean myself up. I made Lt. Blaney go from place to place to place. I was locked in this stall next to the dance floor, trying to get out of my underwear, and meanwhile you're out the door. It wasn't just technology that failed, Jamie. I failed too. Completely derelict of duty. Then to have everything turn out the way it did…" Kent looked away bitterly. "Maybe I'm not such a hero now, huh? Maybe you'll change your mind about me. I wouldn't blame you if you did."

He felt total terror. He prayed to Jesus Christ to make Jamie stay.

"It wasn't you," Jamie said, his brow creasing, only glancing at him, then back to the scene, working hard mentally, his breath becoming a little ragged. "I'm sure of that." His voice came slowly, almost like when he first woke up. "I, was upset, wasn't I, when we first got there? What, wasn't right, at the beginning?"

"Oh, I remember."

Jamie's face contorted. He started panting, nodded. "That's it, I know it is. This may sound crazy, but my body tells me that's it. Outside, the little parking lot."

"No tail car."

"My backup wasn't there when we arrived! It was never there. That's why I was on my own, not that you were in the bathroom. Your operation didn't hang on just one man, you had backup systems built in. But someone was missing. That's why I was alone! It had nothing to do with your taking a minute in the bathroom. You've spent this entire time feeling guilty, but it doesn't take thirty seconds to get rid of your underwear."

Kent stared at an eerie picture.

"Who was assigned to that spot?"

Kent raked his fingers through his hair. "Trooper Julie Campbell. My ex-partner."

The waiter stirred the drapes to signal them, then brought their salads, half-hoping to find them under the table committing misdemeanors. Jamie dove his nose into red ripe tomatoes.

"I'm going to have to report this to the major immediately," Kent said. "I don't know whether that element was ever debriefed. Maybe nobody knows where she was but her."

"You can't rely on my flashback, it would never stand up in court. I've got brain damage."

It just popped out, shocked them both, the fact they would never admit to each other. His brain was damaged. Jamie was even a little proud of himself for coming out.

With his IQ, the worst thing in the world was to have brain damage. The back and the side of his perfect body were nothing compared to that. Scars began to heal. He had a little brain damage, and was recovering.

"We'll need more evidence, but she's going to have some mighty big explaining to do. Why wasn't she there? Jamie, that was one of the most important jobs in the whole operation, that's why Campbell was on it. I wanted somebody I knew and trusted to protect you. This man I love? I'm watching you myself on the inside, who else am I going to put on that duty outside? Someone I believed in. She and I used to be close. Not no more. Never again."

Kent never forgot the "dead homosexual" remark, never would.

"Close? How close?"

"Well, um, we dated a few times, double dates with another trooper. Then his kid got sick and he couldn't afford a babysitter, so we stopped going."

"Let me know what the major thinks of all this."

"Am I still your Jocko, then?"

"Try to keep me off you! You don't come this close, only to run out now. I bond like Superglue and I'm great in bed. One fuck, Jocko, your ass'll be begging for more."

Branh, system error! Kent chuckled, knew it was true, tried to pick up a logical thread. There had to be one somewhere; it wasn't between his straining legs. "Jamie, I've been so scared. I never focused on that car, we were just chasing you in the chopper and—I've been worried sick that I failed you; that I ought to be up on charges, ought to have you hate me; and gosh. You're saving my butt again right now. She should have been there."

"You know, copboys in love sometimes give each other any extra tomatoes they might not want." Jamie sounded twelve years old, begging in some junior high cafeteria for a carton of choco-milk.

Kent picked up his plate, swiped his fork, deposited his whole salad on top of Jamie's. They howled and hugged. Then Jamie threw Trooper What's-her-face and Killer Whoever-he-was out of the booth; there was love to be made, no others allowed.

But it wasn't that easy. They had been through a critical incident in very separate ways. Each needed to tell his closest friend, his newfound love, what it was like.

Jamie said, "There's one other thing I remember. I prayed, going through all the people I'm close to, telling them I love them. I remember very clearly thinking, 'I love you, Kent.' Trying to send you vibes so you'd know."

"Maybe I got your vibes. I kissed you that night." Kent flashed onto the mirror at the hospital, blood on his lips; had to close his eyes. "This stuff's so hard. We've really been through a lot. I wanted you to hang on until I could get you to a doctor."

"I watched you do it," Jamie said, dumbfounded. He shut his eyes tight. "Thanks for kissing me and saving my life. Being there for me this entire time." He turned away. "I don't want to think about it. I'm going to concentrate on the fact that you kissed me. That you love me."

But Kent was too worried. "What if her not being there was deliberate?" He weighed an impulse to call the major immediately.

"She's not allowed to steal this night! I've had enough of these people invading my life. This night is ours, man, our first date. We worked for it, we earned it. No more dead people. Just two guys in love. Please, Kent. Please."

"Jamie, you're the capital of my world." They ate their salad, two forks, one plate.

To make themselves feel better, Jamie wondered what the sandhill cranes were up to tonight. Kent's eyes shone as Jamie spun a tale about two male cranes in a little love nest. "The smaller one was named Ethan. His buddy was named Zack. They both thought they were loners, flying on the fringes. Ethan was very good at the mating dance, he bobbed deeper and leapt higher than anyone else. But for some reason no one wanted him; which was okay, he didn't want them either. But he was lonely all the time.

"Then one day he met Zack, and it turned out the same thing happened to him, though Zack said it was because he didn't dance as well as the others. So they flew together, two guys having fun, amazed at how well they knew each other's feelings; knew when it was time to stop and rest, knew when the other guy was hungry. Ethan was good at finding the best feeding places, the corn and wheat and bugs. Zack knew all the good shelters when the weather got bad. And somehow, without deciding or even knowing, they became a pair. The other cranes knew it when it happened; and after that, they always flew together, and no one could remember a time it hadn't been that way."

Kent listened to the softness in Jamie's voice, the imagination of his mind; Jamie loved being Gay. To be with a guy like Jamie, Kent might learn to love it too.

"One night they ran into terrible bad weather, windy, horrible, freezing rain. The flock scattered, trying to survive. Zack found his buddy a protected ledge, but he couldn't keep all the ice from pelting them, or the wind from howling; and Ethan started to shiver, couldn't stop. So Zack stepped closer, one step, then two, till they touched each other. Ethan had wanted to touch all along, but he was afraid Zack wouldn't allow it. But now Zack was touching him, a dream come true. So Ethan got as close as he could. They absorbed each other's warmth. But still Ethan shivered. He was young, he couldn't help it; he knew he was supposed to be brave, but he was freezing to death. If their bills iced up they would suffocate."

"Oh, no. That can happen to pheasants, too."

"At the height of the storm, Ethan suddenly flew off the ledge, searching the frozen earth for twigs to prop Zack's bill open so he wouldn't freeze. The ice rained down, made his wings so heavy he could barely fly. Zack shouted, 'Ethan, come back here, you could die out there!'

"But Ethan knew his buddy could die back there; which gave him the strength to go on. But there were no sticks anywhere that weren't frozen to the ground. So he flew up into a maple tree and tried snapping a twig off. With all the ice, it broke off finally. He propped his own bill open, then snapped another twig off, and with his last strength he flew back to the ledge and got the twig into Zack's bill so he could breathe."

"Ethan risked his life for his buddy. Oh, Jamie."

"Zack was so glad to have Ethan safe that he jumped up on his back, stretched out his wings and pulled Ethan under him. He covered his little guy, even though Zack was cold and scared too. Ethan crouched, got very small, he knew that Zack's wing muscles would hurt, stretched out like that. Ethan tried to fit their bodies together, so Zack wouldn't hurt.

"But Ethan loved being covered; loved that Zack would do that for him. And even though his wings hurt, Zack took pride that his brave little Ethan snuggled under him, giving warmth back, relying on him. To Zack it was the most masculine feeling he'd ever had, taking care of his mate; the masculine mate who saved his life.

"Finally Ethan stopped shivering. Their bills didn't freeze. They got some rest. The next day was sunny, much warmer, they flew fast and free. They didn't talk about what happened, but it changed everything. That noontime Ethan dove for food, over and over, down and down. He wouldn't let Zack forage, fought him when he tried to gather food. So Zack sat back as Ethan piled food at his feet, made a feast for him.

"For the rest of their lives, in good weather and bad, they flew together, and slept together, Zack the strong, warm one as Ethan the feastmaker snuggled with him."

Kent pulled his Ethan to him, the most beautiful soul he'd ever met.

"Jamie, don't go, stay here with me. I'll cover you always, keep you safe and warm. I know there's your career, you just solved thirteen homicides, the Gay community needs you. But don't leave me. And please don't go to New York. I mean, I want you to for your job, if you want it. I won't hold you back. But jeez, don't go to New York. Stay here with me. This is home. Stay here with me."

Kent's feelings were so tender and disclosive and fair that Jamie ached. But it didn't occur to Kent to move to Columbus, much less New York. It occurred to Jamie.

Kent got excited. "Come and live with me at the cabin. It ain't fancy, but I'll make you happy. I'll do anything to make you happy. I'll tear it down and build you a new one to make you happy."

Jamie looked at Kent's face, all naive sincerity. But life was complicated. Thelma's estate might be settled soon; there was Casey to consider, the career. Jamie was just learning how to write. Was Rather serious? *Suppose I get assigned to Topeka. Kent's the Hoosier Columbo, he loves his job with a passion. This is crazy.*

Whose career's more important, yours or mine? He felt it as a sudden turning point, a crucial, scary decision.

He was extremely ambitious. He had been to the summit once before and he could do it again. He fully expected to be a White House correspondent someday, shouting tough questions, making Presidents cower.

But he looked at the man he loved and quickly made the frightening choice. There was precedent, a guy named Rick, to whom he'd made a commitment and kept it, the highest achievement of his life—a lot more important than leaning half-naked on a rock.

Jamie could write anywhere; Kent could be a cop anywhere. But they had to be together. "It takes much more talking than just tonight. But I'd love to live in your cabin that's not fancy. I don't need fancy. I need you."

He shuddered from the risk, the possible abandonment of his expectations. Was his stock up in Columbus as a result of this story? How was his stock in New York? But no amount of writing or recognition outweighed his ability, his need to love. That, more than looks, brains or courage, was his biggest gift.

"You'd give up your home for me? Your job, even?"

"It scares me, it's so new. But yes, maybe." Jamie didn't want stardom, he wanted Kent. "Yes. I love you. But I need to know, would you do the same for me?"

Kent blanched; then slowly he smiled, wiggled his hips, "I could be the next bun shot on 'NYPD Blue.'"

"I bet your buns are photogenic."

"If New York don't work out, Jamie, come and live with me?"

"I have to go to Columbus at some point."

"To get your furniture."

"More than that; to thank Casey, to help him; to say goodbye to my readers. You have no idea how wonderful they've been to me."

"Okay, Casey and your readers then. Then get your butt back here."

"I'll go back home for awhile and return when the estate is settled. We can see each other on weekends. There's no way we're ready to live together yet. Is there?"

Kent's face hardened. "What have we been doing but living together? No way to this weekend stuff. What if you don't come back in March? What if you meet someone else? With your looks, I'll have to fight off guys with a stick. And man, I'm just a cop. The money don't go that far. Jamie, I make… all of 26 grand a year." This was a very significant, risky statement. He checked Jamie's reaction.

But Jamie knew about the paycheck. "It's a crime Indiana doesn't pay its police more. Arrest the governor!"

"Honey, do you need any help with your bills?"

Jamie stared. *You called me honey.* "My what?"

"I've been real worried, Jamie, you haven't worked in months. Is your boss okay, what benefits do you get? Do you need any help with your bills?"

Jamie was stupefied. He was filthy rich, and here was a cop offering to pay his bills. Jamie nearly cried. "Don't worry, my bills are paid, it's all electronic, I've got good benefits, sick leave at full pay. Thank you, Kent, how generous and kind. Just to have thought of it fills me with grateful amazement."

"If we live simply, you'd never have to work again. I'll support you, I'd love to."

It rapidly became the worst heterosexist claptrap Jamie had ever heard; but then, it was coming from a Straight Hoosier cop who didn't know any better. Jamie was a standout, and here was DiMaggio asking Marilyn to be a housewife.

But of the legions of rich men who had offered to keep Jamie, none of them was a heroic police officer who only wanted to take care of him, and had already done it magnificently.

Kent added, "I know you want to work, and that's fine, I want you to have your own goals too. But see, I've got money in reserve if we need it." He was so proud of his baseball money; so proud to finally tell about it. He could support his lover and set him up for life. He'd looked forward to it since the day he signed; and here, at long last, was the man that money was meant for.

Jamie reached for him. "Simply or grandly, we'll live together soon."

"But what if you go home and some millionaire sweeps you off your feet?"

"Buddy, millionaires have tried." At 18 some Brit on the Staten Island ferry offered Jamie an apartment at the Hotel Pierre. He chose graduate student housing instead. "I don't seem to marry for money."

"It don't matter to you I don't make anything?"

"No. I like enough money to live on, but my needs are few. I grew up on boiled potatoes and hamburger gravy. What I need carries no price tag. I don't even marry for looks; Rick was rather plain. Know what I marry for?"

Kent thought. "Goulash when people hurt?"

"Love you. Cherish you. Worship you!"

They hugged. How good it felt to have a man in their arms.

"Jamie, I probably won't say this right, but I have to say it. When you were getting well, and I came every two days at first? I wanted to throw your friends out and come every day. I never wanted to leave you. I wanted to move in and take care of you, not have your friends doing my job. That's what it is, my job!—to take care of you. So don't talk about leaving. It took you telling me today you were going back to Columbus to get me to stop being such an idiot and finally admit the truth, that I love you. God, to get you and lose you, all in the same day? I won't do it again. I did it before. Never again. If you love me, you're staying with me!"

Jamie shook his head at Kent's machismo; was also deeply pleased with him. "You took perfect care of me, Kent. I want more of that. I'll come back to get it."

"There's something else," Kent blurted. "Why did you have to say I was Straight all the time? I started to worry you wouldn't like me as much if I wasn't Straight."

"I never said you were Straight. Who told Dan Rather you were Straight?"

It landed like an uppercut. "No one, I, he… heck, it just started getting said. And I didn't do nothing to stop it. Should I have? I could barely figure it out myself, and I'm supposed to tell Dan Rather I'm

Gay? Get real. It ain't nobody's business. If I was gonna tell anyone, it better be you. But I was such a wimp I couldn't even manage that."

"It was all coming at maximum-stress time, you did the right thing. But why on earth would I like a Straight man better than a Gay man?"

"Straight guys ain't superior? They think they are."

"Superior to you? Puh-lease. Man, let's move you up to Triple-A."

Kent got the same instruction-ready look as always; a crisp little nod, eyes and ears wide open. "Go, Coach."

"No one on earth is superior to you. I may turn on to your toughness; but I love your softer side. Mother Nature created Gay men to combine softness with hardness, because both qualities are necessary for survival. Straight people need the opposite sex to become whole; Gay people already are. Kent, are you Straight?"

He took awhile to answer. "Maybe not. But how can I know, when I've never been attracted to another guy?"

"Then who's this Brad Pitt person?"

Kent guffawed, busted red-handed with bank dye exploding all over his cash. "I'm a normal all-American guy; of course I'm Straight. I just happen to be in love with a beautiful, all-American guy who ain't normal at all, who's challenging and sexy and brilliant and dangerous and my God, let's get naked and fuck."

"Hail Purdue!" They laughed and hugged. "Do you look at women?"

"Not no more."

"Why not? Women are beautiful."

"I feel some attraction for women, but I ain't that fond of their... inside parts." That was all Jamie needed to hear. "I like their breasts, though, and their open personalities. Unless they get too giggly. I hate helpless women, Jamie, they're so phony, like it gratifies a guy that she can't change a tire. If you can drive, you better know how to fix a Goodyear. I do best when I'm just friends with a woman. I got a lot of women friends. Not many guys can say that."

Only Gay guys. "Do you look at men?"

"Only you."

"What do you look at?"

"Your hair, your face, your abs, your stick-out nipples, your crotch, your attitude—and especially your little bitty ass." It was definitely going to be a knockdown-dragout for who was the alpha male.

Kent said, "Two can ask these questions. What do you see in me?"

"Kindness, strength; principle, intelligence."

"You think I'm smart?"

"Thomas Ford eluded the cops for 14 years. You apprehended him in 14 days."

"Gee. Not my body?"

"You're the sexiest man I've ever seen. But it starts with the windows to your soul. Kent, in mind and body, you are overpoweringly beautiful to me."

Kent's eyebrows danced. "Wanna crawl between my legs and commit a misdemeanor?"

Jamie disappeared beneath the table.

Kent laughed, yanked him back up, "You criminal, you'd ruin my career. Come to think of it, I got money, go ahead!" He tried to push Jamie back down, but he wouldn't go.

When they returned to the leaving issue, Jamie said, "You must trust the one you love."

"It ain't that I don't trust you. It's that I can't stand to lose you. I've waited 27 years for you, man. And now I've got you, you ain't leavin'. I want you with me every day of my life. I want to hold you every night. I want—I want so much, Jamie. I ain't completely sure what two guys do together, but I want it all, with you."

Jamie ate lobster, ready to show him on Broadway what two men do.

"You know what I visualize when I think of us together? Just lying in bed, holding you. I want that so bad, Jamie. I want to get naked and hold you."

"Kent, my favorite thing in all the world is to sleep together." Jamie was tempted. He uncrossed his legs and spread them apart. It wasn't at all better.

He also knew it wasn't right for either of them that he stay. They needed to date, get to know each other romantically, sexually, not just move in together. "We have to wait awhile. Let's not start out by making mistakes. We need to find out what we really, really want. We need to go slow."

"Aw, Jamie, I wanna go fast. Let's just get in my truck and go real fast!"

James R. would have given a cornea to write that line. "But we barely know each other. An hour ago I didn't even know you were Questioning."

"I've only told one other person, kinda."

"Major Slaughter?"

Kent was stunned. "How'd you know that?"

"I didn't; reporters guess a lot. The major didn't tell me. He would never break a confidence. I know that for a fact."

Kent sat back. "How do you know that for a fact? You held things back from me, too. All right, out with it."

"It's no big thing, I've known George since he was a regional commander. It's simply logical that if you've only told one person, it might be him; he's your boss. He's a trustworthy guy." Then Jamie wanted to change the subject. "How's your beef?"

Kent tried to think it through. "Let me get this right. You've known George before this. You knew he was high up in the ranks. So you were pulling strings on him, then he pulled strings on me; and you were pulling strings on this case the whole time?!"

"I don't have strings to pull. Once you got the case, you didn't co-opt me, you turned me into your marionette."

Kent shifted to look at the picture on the wall, the candle, anything but Jamie.

"Does anyone pull George Slaughter's strings? Come on. Man, I'm just a reporter. I don't have the power to do all that."

A light bulb fired up. "Is Major Slaughter Gay? He ain't married. That's how you got your blond, devious hooks in him." Kent stared. "There wasn't anything you wouldn't do on this case. You infiltrated the Indiana State Police!"

Jamie couldn't help a little head-toss, "About time someone noticed."

"Man oh man. You conniving little bastard."

"I got lucky. George picked you out, the toughest, smartest investigator he has. I didn't know you existed."

"But you worked him on those old cases. I've read that old stuff you wrote, pushing for a task force. Pushing all the time, like you always do. And since you knew him—man, this is deep. You masterminded this whole thing."

"Not at all. You took command and kept it. First time in a Gay bar but no one out-commits you. Kent, that's what the cases needed. I damn near swooned."

"Go on, then. Tell me the whole story, you little schemer."

"It didn't ultimately take a Gay cop; it took an open-minded, committed one. It took you. I could only help for a day, from my knowledge of the cases and the Gay community; a cop had to command. And here was one who didn't shirk from leadership. Finally, after 14 long years, a cop who refused to make excuses." Jamie's voice intensified. "Seeing you in action, I knew you wouldn't stop. I admired you for it. How could I not, as manly and decisive as you are? We finally had someone who would solve these cases, even if it took dressing up like the Queen of England. You decided, you acted, you ordered, you solved. Kent, I loved you for making that commitment. This hot stud would go after the killers of Gay men and never stop.

"Bulldog couldn't do that; he wouldn't enter into the victims' experience. And he's better than Hickman. How can you solve a murder if you won't even get to know the victim? They didn't solve it, either, did they?

You did. As I knew from that moment you would. Kent, think of this, it's the ultimate level for what you've achieved—a dozen future victims will never know you saved their lives."

Kent blinked. "Jamie, you make me feel so much."

"I'd like to go back to Chez Nous someday and just look at people. Pick out a dozen guys and think, 'Enjoy that dance, that conversation, that beer. You're alive right now because of what Kent did.' And not say a word to them. I'd get a lot of satisfaction out of that. You saved those people's lives."

"I loved you for putting me in that bar, pushing me to grow and learn. Jamie, I respect people who challenge me. You helped me get to know the victim, by your reporting, your visits with Gary. You reconstructed Glenn's habits, what went wrong the night of the murder. You came up with the psychology of this whole case. But I can't get over you manipulating it for years to get it done. Man! You're an even bigger stud than I thought. And you were ten feet tall before. Sure, I tease you, Shortstop—know why? 'Cause you're tall as the stars to me."

"I want to be. I like my size, I'm proud to be this tall."

"You ain't short, buddy. It's just that with you, I feel big and macho, a dumb jock with a smart, beautiful little guy to protect. A retro-caveman thing." Kent ate, a little pissed, kinda pleased. He wondered if the major knew he was Gay before he did. "I want to be masculine with you."

"You are, Hero. I'll be Sundance if you'll be Butch."

"I will be." But Kent knew he had a softer side; which Jamie loved. "Man, you were so sick, I cried my eyes out. The Wabash was at flood stage."

"It's over, don't hurt. I hate that my buddy hurt."

"Know my favorite word in the English language? Buddy."

It contained all their pain, all their happiness, their punches, their cranes, their basketball, their singing together, their hopes. "Don't make me more important than I am. I'm just a mouth. I talk, and I write, and that's all. I talk; you act. There's a world of difference. You got my ass out of a sling."

"Seems to me you acted. Traded your life for Daveyboy's. That wasn't talk, that was action."

"Kent, you got the takedown or I'd have bled to death."

The whole situation was more than Kent could put together. He was ashamed and proud, a tangle of emotions; stunned, ticked off, turned on.

But what he focused on, couldn't help but think about since it was explicit, was Jamie's bleeding to death. He reached for his lover, held him. "I had a little nervous breakdown, Jamie. They had to restrain me and everything. Man, that coma ripped me apart. Then it dragged on and on, and meanwhile I'm supposed to act like an investigator. Oh honey, thank God you made it. Now I get to hold you and love on you like I dreamed of."

It is always hardest on the caregiver.

Kent didn't do it out of altruism, but because it fulfilled him, enabled him to become himself. What looked like noble self-sacrifice was a selfish experience of intimacy.

The softer side excels at caregiving; that's why Gay men are here. Jamie took care of his mother, took care of Rick. To Jamie, wiping his lover's ass wasn't a whole lot different from kissing it.

Then Kent took care of Jamie; it's nature's way.

"At times I wanted you to crawl in bed with me."

"I almost did, the day of the hospital tree. But you were too sick. It was all so innocent, which made it beautiful; but that's the moment we first made love."

"I fell for you so hard. When I got back to my mother's, I gave myself permission to fantasize. As long as this stud wants to come by, I want him. My body's healing, I jack off over you three times a day now. Special K's real tasty, it's my favorite."

"You eat Special K three times a day? What a great way to get all your vitamins."

"And protein! There's so much come on my workout machine it's been tested for VD."

They laughed, then Jamie said softly, "And now we're together, and I know the man you are; and this impossible dream comes true. Hear me: I worship the ground you walk on." His words were tender; his look was hard as a rock. "I'll get aggressive at times. But always, with my body, I thee worship."

Kent knew it would take months to figure all this out. Meanwhile his little guy said magical words. Kent's scrotum tingled like never before. It was sacreligous, an issue he'd never sorted out. But he wanted it in the worst way; deserved it almost, needed it. He closed his eyes and saw The Picture.

Of his athletic body being worshipped, by a naked blond Oliver on his knees.

The Picture's gonna come true! His spine tingled, wave after wave of mammoth excitement. "I know you'll get aggressive. You always are. So am I."

"How do cowboys do it? We take turns."

"Jamie, I worship you too." Kent held him close. "Don't leave me tomorrow. Give us a week to be together as a couple. Then when you have to go, okay, as long as you come back. Or I can come to you."

Time as a couple made perfect sense. "Then I won't go tomorrow. I do need time alone in my own home. After that we'll weigh our options and live together. Kent, I'll never leave you."

Happiness radiated from Kent's face. "You are so beautiful. Not just your looks, Jamie—the inside of you."

Kent finished his Beef Wellington and wiped his mouth with satisfaction. He ate in great gulps, but he knew which fork was which and cut down the wolf factor. "That was excellent. You really know your food."

Jamie, with some linguine before him but no lobster, was getting full. Kent decided not to hammer him over leaving a little pasta on his plate. With the bread and salad, Jamie had eaten well. "I'm glad you enjoyed it. Would you like dessert?"

Brown eyes crinkled at the corners. "I sure would, but it's nothing they sell at Costanza's."

Jamie purred. Kent put his arm around him and pulled him in for a kiss. With their lips only inches apart Kent's beeper went off, Deet, Deet, Deet!

He pulled it off his belt, glanced at the number. Jamie snatched the pager, swore a blue streak and smashed the goddamn thing into the mahogany.

Kent grinned down at the little pieces, "Pager killed in the line of duty."

Then he blinked in shock. He didn't remember the citizen's name, just the anomalous evidence they'd overlooked. "There was a woman security guard there—a member of the State Police! Come on."

He commandeered the manager's office, put the call on the speaker-phone and dialed headquarters. He got the chief, outlined his suspicions and Jamie's memory. The major had news, too, phone records—"Someone in Lafayette Post 9 made repeated calls to Ford's house, and later from the task force room here at headquarters. Starting a few days after the Walkers, every time you made a move there was a warning. The last call was placed an hour after the bigwigs' meeting. Brazen about it, figuring no one would look there." As if George Slaughter, human bulldozer, ever failed to turn over the smallest stone. "Records show she was on the premises every time."

"She betrayed her oath; she betrayed everyone on the task force. Suppose we'd all gotten shot. Dammit, she almost got my boyfriend killed!"

So George's two favorites were finally together; he blessed his gods. "This is all circumstantial. But there's no justification for calls to a murder suspect."

"Subpoena her phone records. Lash is eager for a deal, he'd have to know they had a mole on the task force. Crum too, but I don't want this dependent on him. That man's going to the electric company."

"She had opportunity, sure, but what motive? Greed?"

Jamie asked, "Are there calls to or from Carson?"

Slaughter checked. "His house to hers. The timing is perfect. What do you make of that?"

Jamie grabbed the phone and shouted, "Jealousy, you idiot! She and Kent used to date. Carson recruited her when Kent was spending too much time with me. He's only the sexiest dude on the planet, who wouldn't kill for him? So the ex-girlfriend gets herself assigned to the new boyfriend. I couldn't die fast enough for her. But if you ever beep him again when he's kissing me, so help me God, I'll…"

Kent snatched the phone. "A bit of advice when he gets like this," George said calmly. "Cuff him and stuff a sock in his mouth. Or something that rhymes with sock."

Kent considered the possibilities. "I'm on it!"

* * *

Several things were memorable about the arrest, two days later, of Trooper Campbell; she was wearing a Pioneer Hi-Bred cap when Kent arrived. She was delighted to see him and invited him to hit the pizza joint like a cheap date. Instead he pointed his Glock and told her to "Start screaming bloody murder."

The dead homosexual scooped the mainstream hacks once and for all, reporting it exclusively for the CBS Evening News; after she was loaded into the squad car, Kent kissed his crimefighting Oliver right in front of her face.

* * *

But that was two days later; she wasn't allowed to steal this night. They returned to their table, the waiter came, Jamie asked for "Two Grand Marniers and our check, please. The wait staff can have the rest of the champagne."

Kent said, "Then no more booze for me, I'm driving."

Soon the waiter was back with generous brandies and a small styrofoam box. This he placed near Jamie, the bill he centered between them. Jamie took the bill, pulled out his wallet. "No!" yelped Kent. "Let me pay for it." He snatched the check.

"But Kent, I always pay in fine restaurants, it's a privilege for me to buy your food."

"I said no!" Kent produced a green plastic card. "Not on our first date, I want to remember this forever. Next time, sure. But not this time. Please."

"You're not the only man here, Butch."

Kent's face softened. "I know I'm not. But Jamie, today's my birthday. Every year I give my parents a present, and myself one too. Know what I wanted this year? A date with Jamie. I wanted to take you to Mackey Arena in my shiny red truck; and watch your face light up like my own private fireworks when the Right School won. Then to gain your heart with one little kiss, this is the greatest birthday I'll ever have."

"Then I'll feed you that dessert. A little whipped cream, some chocolate sauce, a birthday spanking…"

"That's nice, but can I also get a free autographed nude poster?"

Jamie pummeled him, after which Kent sought advice on the tip. Jamie calculated twenty-five percent for a great waiter and offered to cover it in honor of his mother. Kent, oblivious and proud, fished in his wallet, laid twenty more dollars on the table and tried not to think about the hundred bucks he'd just shelled out for one dinner with Jamie Foster, consisting of three-quarters of a plate of pasta and seafood. "'Dining out is wonderful. All I have to do is give them money!' We better live at the cabin or I'll go broke. Gosh, you're the cutest thing alive."

They stood and Jamie snatched up his leather jacket before Kent could get it. Then Pavarotti began to sing "Nessun Dorma" and Jamie felt it like a blow to the head. *Why now?*

He hadn't heard it since Rick died. Rick and Thelma both loved opera. The first Christmas he and Jamie were together, Rick gave Thelma the "Three Tenors" video and she gave him the CD. They sat on Jamie's couch and watched the video together with the volume cranked. The last Christmas they were together, with a new performance out, they sat in La-Z-Boys and a Quickie wheelchair in West Lafayette. Transfixed, Jamie left the take-home box where it lay.

He headed toward the back door and a waterfall. Kent, ready to lead them out the front, turned to follow. Jamie reached into his jeans, found some coins. "I need to linger a minute." He watched the water circulate noisily, an endless cycle; then he knew why now.

I love you, Mom. I'm glad we came here all those times. How beautiful you always looked. I tried to bring elegance to your life. You deserved the best.

He felt her answer, "*We always had such good times here. I love you, James.*"

Goodbye, Mom. I love you!

He dropped a coin and gasped as it died.

Another image came. *Rick, I love you. I wish you hadn't gone, man. But I'm glad you're not in pain anymore. I hated losing you. You're not coming back.*

I love Kent now. He's incredible. I worship him.

"Do it, pops. Make him as happy as you made me."

Goodbye, sweetness. I love you, Ricky! Goodbye.

Jamie heard the little plink, watched his dime sink.

Then he flipped a quarter into the tank, made a big splash. *And God bless Kent.* He strode to his lover, smiled crookedly and motioned for him to lead them out.

Kent knew that something had gone on; he gestured at the music overhead, "What's he saying?"

"He's a secret lover. He will reveal his identity and win the one he loves with a kiss."

"Like you just did at the arena, Jamie."

"Man, you've got a nice, spankable birthday ass."

Kent was all athletic grace and Hoosier style, massive shoulders, a body completely in tune with itself. Kent in tight jeans was a sight Jamie could now openly savor. Kent held the door for him. The aria wished stars away. Jamie wandered into the dusk, leaving things behind.

In the western sky, crimson rays from a dying sun mixed with low storm clouds. A brisk breeze stirred up off the prairie. Brown leaves rattled in a willow tree.

He reached up to raise the collar of his leather jacket. A winter of cold was coming. Mental picture: the ice storm; but now tonight, a heart to burst, a baseball star—a civil rights enforcer to cherish. He closed his eyes, overcome with pride.

Kent fumbled for keys, quickened his pace, headed for the big truck in the darkening lot. "Please," he called over his shoulder. "Let me do this. Just once."

The waiter, doggy box in hand, pushed open the back door, ready to—then watching, not imposing. Puccini drifted out.

Kent unlocked the passenger door, held it open. Jamie came and stood next to it, barely breathing. Then he looked up finally, into the eyes of one who knew him; another one who knew him.

Curly black hair; high cheekbones, brown eyes that were the first to greet him when he woke up; a litany of Kent's virtues tumbled into

Jamie's mind. Old-fashioned words, Midwestern ones; they all came down to Hero.

Strong, sure arms wrapped around him in the night. A gentle hand pulled him to a shoulder, a head cradled next to his.

Jamie stood on tiptoes and let himself be held. His arms stretched around Kent's back, and finally he was home. This place, these arms were home. He nestled, surrendered to everything.

Jamie's touch, his strong, small hands, awakened every part of Kent. He pressed his thighs into his lover's, ardent and gentle, bodylong.

They were sexual at last, two men in love. Kent lowered his hand, as he'd wanted to do for months, and grasped Jamie's tiny bottom; took a lover's possession of him.

Jamie's nostrils filled with Kent's sweet, distinctive smell, almost like baby powder—and clang! Jamie heard an organ chord at fortissimo.

Suddenly he could see Kent reach inside him, searching flesh for tubes of spurting blood. He saw the desperation in Kent's face, heard him shout commands. Jamie felt stabs of pain when fingers found arteries at last.

He watched Kent squeeze him shut for sixteen grueling minutes; till clamps replaced his numb, stiff hands.

This man exposed himself to homosexual blood. He didn't ask if it was tainted, he had no time for gloves.

He entered Jamie's body as a lover. They had been one body ever since.

What intimacy could Jamie ever return to him? Nothing could equal their first intercourse. But he guided Kent's hands to the little scars.

Kent touched gingerly, afraid of causing pain, but Jamie said, "There, touch me there." So Kent went ahead and pressed a little harder, then harder, more confidently, all around the wounds.

Jamie's scars made love to him. Kent's fingers finally healed; his mind, his heart.

It was never his fault. It was Campbell's.

He held in his arms the body of his partner, his **living** partner; hard, muscular, all man. He lifted his lover's chin. Jamie whispered, "Commander," as Kent kissed him full and tenderly.

They let go of all but man. It was over; they had won, and won each other. Pavarotti soared, "Vincero!"++

Murder at Willow Slough

or, The Caregiver

by Josh Thomas

About the Author

Josh Thomas is an award-winning investigative reporter and a native of Basketball Land. The former editor of *Gaybeat,* Ohio's Gay Newspaper, he has frequently appeared on radio and television. His writing has also been featured in *Nuvo Newsweekly* (Indianapolis) and non-fiction books on travel, religion and multiple homicide.

Visit his website at www.joshtom.com.

0-595-15686-X

Printed in the United States
1382900003B/19-24

9 780595 156863